THE

J-Word

ANDREW SANGER

Proudly Published by Snowbooks in 2009

This book is a work of fiction. Any resemblance to any individual,
living or dead, is unintentional. References to the editors of real
newspapers are to fictional characters, not to the real editors.

Snowbooks Ltd.
120 Pentonville Road
London
N1 9JN
Tel: 0207 837 6482
Fax: 0207 837 6348
email: info@snowbooks.com
www.snowbooks.com

British Library Cataloguing in Publication Data
A catalogue record for this book is available from the British Library.

ISBN 13 978-1905005-95-6

Printed and bound by J. H. Haynes & Co. Ltd., Sparkford

For Gerry and Josh

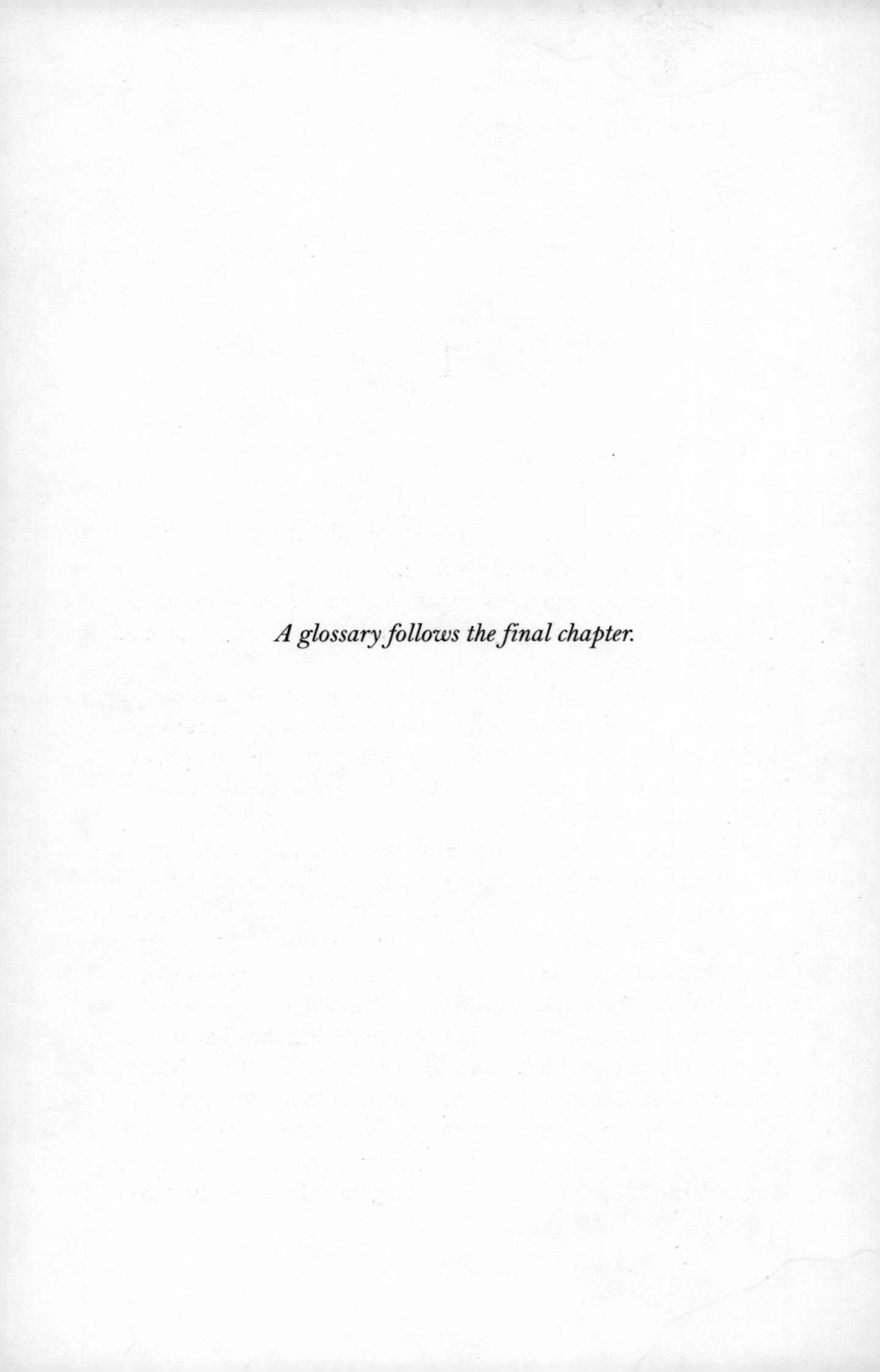

A glossary follows the final chapter.

1

'And just look at this, Miri!' he said aloud. Colours! Was it his eyes, the light, or a trick of the memory?

Dr Silver, gripping his small leather suitcase as if for reassurance, stepped out of the station and gazed around quizzically, astonished.

Golders Green had been – like everywhere he remembered in London – a place without any colour at all except an unnoticed drab redbrick, pale grey paving and pale grey skies. Black, too, of course: black coats, black dresses, polished black shoes, black umbrellas, black hats.

It seemed to have become a modern painting, vivid stripes and shapes, rectangular red bus shelters, bright blue railings, yellow lines, pink shop signs. Even the sky was unnaturally blue. And the clothes! He tried to tell himself Golders Green was not simply a place in his past, but a real place in this world. And this world, he knew too well, had changed.

Or was it himself that had changed? Maybe that was it. Perhaps he hadn't been able to see colours before. Maybe colour was invented at the same time as colour television?

For a long moment he stood perfectly still, a dapper little old man, broad and strong in build, with an expression almost pugnaciously inquisitive, squinting against the July afternoon.

The last time he stood here, he had felt repelled by the sedate, suffocating air of well-fed respectability. Now Golders Green was up to its neck in uncouthness and vulgarity, and certainly he did not prefer it. Women and girls wore strappy, indecent little tops and summer dresses, the sun glancing through the thin fabrics. Huge, roaring coaches turned into the bus station, accelerating to scare away pedestrians. There was litter everywhere… cans, drinks cartons, cigarette packets, fast-food boxes. These, too, were brightly coloured, like decorations. Spat-out chewing gum spotted the pavement everywhere. It didn't remind him of anything at all.

Where on earth was the big crossroads, right outside the station, with its neat rectangle of zebra crossings and belisha beacons? Yes, now he did remember a splash of colour – the flashing yellow globes on their black-and-white poles! There must have been half a dozen of them. You'd step outside the station, as if on holiday, and just here… and they flashed, on and off forever, as he threw back his thoughts. Not only the belisha beacons had gone, it seemed, but so too had the crossroads itself.

But there's a landmark. The old war memorial is still here. In the middle of a busy roundabout, the ugly square stump of clock-tower has a faintly embarrassed air. Once beside a quiet junction, it stands now with pained dignity on a traffic island encircled by modern cars and modern people, the air around it as thick as soup with pollution and noise.

He glanced at the station. He'd like to go back inside and get on the train that would take him to the Golders Green he once knew.

Jack Silver rarely felt warm. Even on this perfect summer's day, he wore his corduroy cap, a tweed jacket, shirt and tie, a thin V-neck sweater, smartly pressed grey trousers and leather shoes. Everything he wore looked new. A pair of reading glasses, clipped to a cord around his neck, rested on his chest.

Now, though, he did feel a flush of warmth and a wave of disconcerting emotion: something like excitement, something like sorrow, or something like being a visitor from another world, with no language, and all the wrong senses. His own world had been long ago abandoned and destroyed, but it too had occupied this space.

A sense of loss, always slumbering deep in his heart, stirred silently. Golders Green! The name gave him a poignant, thrilling, painful nostalgia for his life – his real life – back when he was a man, not just a bundle of dreams and recollections, but a man with a wife, and friends, a career and a family.

He tried to push that out of mind. Jack Silver was not fond of the past in any case. But among the crowd he seemed to see the very people of forty years ago, better dressed than everyone today, mingling silently with their modern counterparts. He even strained to recognise their ghostly faces. His mother and father might be among them.

And he turned his head as if to look down at another memory, of his own son Simon, the two of them holding hands as they came out of the same entrance forty years ago. As he looked down, Jack happened to notice lettering scrawled in the concrete – Yaron, Eyal, Ehud. Such names didn't even exist in those days.

Perhaps someone could advise him about buses. Was there a map? Dr Jack Silver stepped back into the station, but there were no staff in the hall. Inquisitive, bright, eyes sparklingly alert, he looked around for assistance. A young man stood talking into a mobile phone while staring at himself in the mirror of a photo booth. Inside the booth an older man simply spoke to himself, without need of a phone. A young black woman pushed past, a small gold crucifix bouncing on the words "fcuk fashion" printed above breasts as round as two cantaloupes inside her white tee-shirt. Three unsavoury, perverse-looking men, all with silver studs hanging from their lips, ears and nostrils, talked loudly in Italian. One had a two-inch metal spike thrust through the flesh below his lower lip. An oriental family made a heap of suitcases, and sat down on them like refugees in mid-journey. But they were no refugees; these were tourists.

And so came again that sharp sense of himself as an alien creature whose stride spanned decades and generations, who saw in one glance the rise and fall of great ideas and ideologies. His wife, all his ten brothers and sisters and most of his old friends were dead, while he had inadvertently lived to see into the world to come.

Dr Silver had told Penny he would arrive at about four. He looked up at a clock on the station wall. Twenty to four. He turned his wrist and stared at his watch; it showed the same time. He smiled with tight-lipped satisfaction, as if he had personally ordered the two timepieces to be synchronised.

Suddenly a crowd of Jewish children, not quite teens, burst into the station, all the boys in crew-cuts and kippot, all wearing baggy khaki trousers and black tee-shirts, with excited yells and shrieks of laughter and conversations shouted into mobile phones. Their exuberance rose to the ceiling and seemed to fill the whole space. The metal-pierced Italians, the oriental family, even the madmen at the phone booth were drowned out and silenced. Jack watched uncertainly.

Anxiety gripped him. These, then, were children. He had little recollection of them.

'How can I do it, Miri?' he asked aloud. 'How can I look after Daniel? A kid like this?'

* * *

Walking very upright, in quick, brisk little strides, Jack soon discovered that Golders Green was, after all, still a Jewish neighbourhood. Orthodox men dashed about in the street, almost running, or drove by in battered estate cars. Some were repellently shabby, with loose, stained suit jackets and down-at-heel black leather shoes, others with the shine of prosperity, plump in spotless waistcoats. Young women with flat shoes and modest dresses wearily pushed double buggies, or drove huge people-carriers full of young children. These, though, were frummers. He looked at them curiously, as if he were a goy himself. What had happened to the real Golders Green Jews, the unobservant, well-to-do showy business people, the pompous, besuited gents and coiffed, bejewelled ladies? Dead, of course, or living their last days in second-rate luxury retirement homes.

Naïve notions about life and the human condition swept in and out of his mind, benign or damning according to his mood, which changed from one street corner to the next. His thoughts flicked frequently to the Holocaust. Golders Green had survived, Britain's Jews had survived, perhaps the only large Jewish community in Europe to have escaped the danger. Thank God for the English Channel, thank God for England's benign lack of concern, wanting to ignore difference rather than tolerate it. Jack Silver lived in a village, so perfectly English, where his Jewishness had never even been mentioned.

On the other hand, 'Hitler's right about one thing, though – the Jews,' his army mates and work colleagues had said. He still heard their voices loud and clear in his mind. Plenty of English people agreed with that to this day. 'In every generation,' a line in the Passover service suddenly appeared in his thoughts, 'they rise up against us.' Still, Jews had survived, while the civilisations that tried to destroy them all passed away like froth on the sea. Islam, too, although in the ascendant now, would pass away one day. But something else would follow it, and the struggle would go on.

What struggle? He couldn't complain about his life. He embraced England, Englishness and the English language with a mighty passion. He had wanted his family to breathe this temperate air and flourish, thrust its roots deep into this cool nourishing soil and become part of it, and they had done so.

As he walked along the street that Simon had moved to a few months ago, Jack scanned every single house. Undistinguished, perfectly decent, rather small, semi-detached redbrick. He guessed at their value. Simon was now forty-seven years old. He wouldn't climb much higher up the ladder. This might be the most he'd ever achieve. Here then, his son was making the very same difficult journey that he himself had made, across the years. And he remembered how irrelevant his own father had been to him, as he made that journey, when he was Simon's age.

Passing each door, Jack looked for a mezuzah. It worried him that Simon and Penny had chosen to move to a Jewish district, but no, all was well. There were no mezuzahs in this street. Jack felt a hint of naches, that frisson of pride, that his son was so very English, that he lived in a respectable non-Jewish street. This was his great dream come true. For Simon to be an Englishman, and succeed in an English world – that had been all his ambition for a bright, clever son. That a flair for the English language had become the principal tool of his trade was an unexpected bonus.

Neat, well-kept houses. Brick walls. Nice gardens. And the people inside, Irish, English, perhaps West Indian? Good people, no doubt. People his parents would have been scared of. Scared to death. At that, many more thoughts crowded into Jack's mind, ancient fears of his own. He glanced at his watch – two minutes to four o'clock. He would arrive on time.

And suddenly in vivid memory he sees her: Miri. In a light blue dress, looking terribly thin and tired from the illness, the dress hanging from her gaunt skeleton. She bends down, and, in a single movement that takes all her strength, sweeps their grandson, little Daniel, into her arms, hugging him closely. It was the week before she died. She knew there were only a few days left. Holding Daniel, she turns her face to Jack, looks into his eyes, and smiles weakly: 'Thank you, Aloo. It's been so good with you.'

* * *

The hotel at Kandersteg had been concerned about Mr Silver, and in the morning dialled the London number that he had called after checking in. Penny answered it, and – after confirming he was talking to Mrs Silver – the manager told her that for four days Mr Silver had not come out of his room, he did not eat, and – well, they could not be sure – but it appeared that some other guests thought he had been, ah, how to put it, making a noise quite loudly, in his room. And now, I'm afraid –

'What kind of noise?' she interrupted sharply.

'Well, ah, maybe like crying, or sobbing. Which is… all right, but…'

Penny tried to understand and imagine what was being said. Crying? That didn't sound like Simon at all. 'You are quite sure?' she asked. 'Maybe he has been going out late in the evening after reception is closed and, and…' No, she knew that didn't make sense either. 'Can I speak with him? Is he there?' she asked.

'No, Mrs Tsilver,' came the concerned Swiss voice, 'You see, what I try to tell you, Mr Tsilver went out yesterday, very untidy, without his bag and did not come back. Also, he did not take any coat. It is very strange. Especially with the, ah, noise and... and not eating any meal… for three days.'

She repeated slowly in her mind that yesterday Mr Silver had gone out, very untidy, without any bag or coat, and had not returned. No doubt he had his reasons, she told herself. Simon would do whatever he wanted. He was independent. He could take care of himself. Maybe he was eating, but in a café somewhere. But Simon *crying*? What about?

'I'm coming at once,' she replied.

'But Mrs Tsilver,' came the gentle reply, 'If you come here, you understand, we can't help you. Because we don't know where he is. Do we keep his room for him?'

'I am coming today – keep the room. I'll stay in his room.'

She called his mobile again and again, each time hearing 'The mobile phone you have called is switched off', while scrolling through a travel website and clicking impatiently on the times of flights to Bern. Pondering an on-line booking form, she looked at the choices presented to her and realised this was something Danny should not be involved with, should not even know about, and clicked 'one adult' only. Who would look after Danny? She clicked 'one way' – she'd get a ticket for the return journey when she knew what was happening. So yes, who, then, would look after Danny? Without even knowing how long for? She ran through the names of friends, neighbours, parents of Danny's friends. She didn't know them well enough. It was too open-ended. It was too short notice. It was too much to ask. Her own mother was no longer fully *compos mentis*, and her father had enough to cope with, caring for her. She was too distant from her sisters. With misgivings, she called Aloo. In the past, it would have been Miri, who could be trusted to do a good job. Aloo had no idea about children, and probably had forgotten the very existence of his grandchild. But Aloo had time on his hands, had masses of energy, and would do as well as he could. If Aloo said no, she'd try someone else.

'Aloo? There's something wrong with Simon. He's in Switzerland, and I must go to him. Are you busy – now? Today? And for the next few days? I mean, I'm wondering, could you take care of Danny for a few days? I'm sorry, but there's no one else I can ask.'

* * *

He hardly recognised her. Simon and Penny didn't visit Jack often, nor he them. Yet it wasn't that she had changed in any way. She simply looked different.

Penny stood at the door in jeans and tee-shirt – thin, much taller than him even in bare feet, her face without make-up showing her age, but with strong features, dark eyes, attractive and intelligent. That much was normal with her.

And, as always, the thick mass of hair, almost black, scored with grey, flicked appealingly against her shoulders. What made it so unlike her, so very different, was simply that she had not brushed it. She did not have her usual calm poise, such an essential part of her character. She had not made herself ready for his arrival, even though Jack knew he was exactly on time. That was not Penny.

'Aloo!' she cried. 'Come in!'

Her smile was amiable and welcoming. Her eyes and voice, though, suggested suppressed panic. Jack wondered what went on in Simon and Penny's life during the long periods that he did not see or hear from them. He felt suddenly that he did not really know whom his son had married, or even who his son had become. Simon always had the excuse that he was away or too busy to call. Jack certainly agreed that it was more important for a man to earn his living than waste time visiting his parents.

He remembered the wedding of Simon Silver and Penelope Eisenberg. How she had aged since then. They had not married under the huppah, of course, but at a Register Office beside a main road in north London. He had gradually come to know Penny a little – quiet, sceptical, clever, rather primly modest, well-read, middle class, most respectable, very English. Yet the feeling remained that Simon's wife was a complete stranger to him. Perhaps it is always so.

Danny ran to Penny's side and smiled sweetly. Jack was slightly shocked to see how much the boy had changed, too. Lives are passing, he thought fleetingly, this child will soon be a man with children of his own, and I shall be lying under an unvisited stone slab somewhere. The thought was not maudlin – Jack contemplated his own death with disinterest.

'Gosh, you're smart!' Danny exclaimed, as Jack stepped into the narrow hall.

'Smart? You think so? It's just a jacket and flannels!' retorted Jack. 'Flacket and jannels! Flacket and jannels! Ha ha!' And suddenly he had grabbed the boy's hands and they were dancing a jig to the words: 'Jacket and flannels, flacket and jannels…'

His voice was pitched low, gravelly, with an accent somewhere between Yiddish and Cockney, between Eastern Europe and London's East End, between slum terraces and self-made suburbia.

Penny thought that this absurd clowning, typical of Aloo when he was in a certain mood, did not bode at all well. Danny, she told herself, wouldn't fall for such things any more. Yet Danny was laughing and joining in.

Just as quickly, they stopped. Danny clapped his hands happily, then asked, most seriously, 'What team do you support?'

Jack's brow lowered in genuine, kindly bafflement. He looked at Penny for clues.

'He means, football team,' she said with tightened lips, shrugging one shoulder and turning up her palm, as if to say, don't ask me to explain it. For Jack, 'football' was just shorthand for social disorder. In every exuberant cheer of a crowd, whether a football crowd or any other, Jack – Penny too – heard a counterpoint of chanting mobs on the march. When, occasionally, on the news, or when flicking TV channels, he saw or heard a football crowd, Jack sometimes felt a shiver of terror.

'He's mad keen on it,' Penny added, 'they all are, nowadays.'

Jack considered that he must not blame the boy, who no doubt saw football only as a game. He took off his corduroy cap and hung it on the end of the banisters.

'And which one do *you* support, boychick?' he grinned.

'Arsenal,' said Danny.

'Arsenal? That sounds… well, funny. Is there really a football team called Arsenal?' asked Jack, glancing again at Penny for help, to Danny's great amusement. On being assured that there was indeed a team of that name, Jack announced firmly, 'I'm with you. You support someone – I support them too. We're the Arsenal boys.' Then he remembered – *of course* there was a football team named Arsenal.

'And you can play chess, can't you?' Danny went on. Now Jack was on firmer ground. He assured the boy that he could beat anyone at chess, anyone at all… well, anyone under ten years of age. He noticed, on the wall beside him in the hall, Simon's framed awards for writing, various valuable prizes presented for his books, television documentaries, and articles in newspapers and magazines.

With a puzzled frown, Jack asked, 'Now, I know you moved quite recently. Have I been here before?' For an instant, he could not remember. It all looked rather familiar.

Penny was used to this. The man was astoundingly absent-minded. It wasn't a result of age – Jack had been terribly uninterested in life's important little details all the time she had known him. He became worse after Miri died. In fact, Penny reminded him, he had never been to the house before. 'Welcome to our new home,' she said.

He saw a stack of pale blue business cards on the hall table and picked one up, reading aloud '"Simon Silver, writer and editor." Editor, noch! Very good, why not? And here is the new address, I see. And what's this? So that's his website? I must take a look at that.' Somehow the card pleased him. 'Is this my little boy? You have a baby, and the next thing you know, he has his own business card.'

Penny laughed lightly at his remarks.

It worried her that Jack would be in charge of her child and her home. She told herself that friends were on hand if needed. They were willing to step in for a few hours or even overnight now and again. She could rely on them to help Jack in an emergency. If he couldn't work the oven or turn on the hot water.

For a while, she and Jack chatted in the kitchen. Penny was eager to get this stage over with. Some biscuits and cakes were arranged on a plate in the sitting room while the kettle boiled.

Jack's eye glanced around and he was puzzled to see Jewish religious books on the shelves, even a prayerbook. 'What's this?' he asked her innocently, 'A siddur?'

Penny peered as if she had never noticed it before. 'Ah, yeah,' she nodded her head, replying guardedly.

'I mean, is this your siddur? Or Simon's?' he challenged her. Penny ignored the question. She asked him blandly about the drive, but he replied that driving in traffic sometimes made his knees hurt, so today he had preferred to travel by train rather than use the car. This she considered quite an eccentric and inconvenient decision. She had not planned that Jack would use their car while staying in the house. Still, she must remember what a favour he was doing her.

Jack wanted to ask more about the Jewish books. They made him nervous. No mezuzah adorned his son's doorpost; that was good. Its unJewish nakedness reminded him of that liberating bareheadedness, of a Friday night table uncluttered with silver and glass, with kiddush cup or candlesticks, and of a joyous Saturday without prayer shawl or all the prohibitions of Shabbat (no cooking! no music! no playing! no gardening!). A life without mumbled blessings and incantations! There was a freedom from ritual about his son, and an openness of mind, and a knife-edge of intellect, which satisfied Jack deeply. After all he had done to keep the kid clear of religion and nonsense, it was good to see the effort had not been wasted! So what then was this interest in Judaism?

'A siddur, though!' He shook his head.

Penny responded, 'Well, Simon is interested in lots of things, you know. So many things. You know what he's like. He's interested in everything. Look,' she pointed, 'he's got a Koran as well.' She brought in the tea. 'Could I just say, Aloo, my flight is at eight o'clock. I have to check in at six. I must get going. Let's make it just a quick cuppa, can we?'

Each sipped a little of the hot drink. After a decent moment of silence Jack looked into Penny's eyes. 'Nu?' A shrug, a shake of the head, a questioning raising of eyebrows. He stared with baffled concern.

'You mean Simon?' she said.

He moved his head and shoulder – as if to say, obviously.

She couldn't reply with Danny there. 'He's all right,' she said, glancing meaningfully at the child, hoping Jack would understand. He did not seem to.

'All right?' He was surprised. 'So what's this about? Why am I here?'

Penny paused awkwardly. What could she say while the boy was listening? 'Well, of course, he's not all right. He's ill. I'm really glad you can help us. I'll tell you more about it later,' she replied blandly.

'Why not now?' Jack insisted. 'You say you're in a hurry. So talk.'

She nodded quickly towards Danny. 'Later,' she said. Jack frowned and looked at her as if demanding an explanation. She did not respond.

Eventually Danny lost interest and wandered away. 'Can I play on the computer?' he called from upstairs. He had been told that he always had to ask.

'OK.'

It was a chance to talk in peace.

'You must tell me,' Jack mused, quite brightly, 'about all the details, you know, like when the dustmen come and where to buy groceries.' He considered it had been rather clever of him to think of that. It made him seem normal and in the swim of things.

'The dustmen come on Thursday. The recycling collection is on Friday,' Penny said distractedly. 'Danny knows everything like that.'

'And it'll be for a few days? A week at most, you said. Ach, a week will be OK. Take your time. It makes a nice change for me.'

She would have to admit that it could be longer. Penny held her breath for a second. She nodded uncertainly. 'Simon is having a problem.' She did mean to tell Aloo about Simon. When it came to it though, she could not admit the truth. 'I don't know if you knew he was in Switzerland. He went to do a piece for someone.'

'Who for?' It was idle curiosity, again tinged with pride.

'I don't know, a newspaper, just a travel piece,' Penny replied impatiently. 'I can't remember what exactly. But the point is, that's where he is, and it seems he's having some sort of… crisis.'

Jack nodded sympathetically and, at the same time, sceptically. He had never had 'a crisis' himself, and looked upon it as a very modern self-indulgence. He would be more concerned to hear of his son having any *genuine* problems – that is to say, money problems.

'Because if it's more than a week,' he declared, 'I will need a haircut.' He was perfectly clear about that. A haircut every week was important, to stay trim and smart.

The change of subject baffled her. Disconcerted, she studied his face, his silvery crew-cut hairstyle. It seemed the irrelevant, obsessive remark of a confused old man. Was it the onset of dementia? She glanced anxiously into his eyes. But he looked quite serious and aware, and after all, why not – he was indeed entitled to his whims.

'You can use Simon's hairdresser,' she said. 'He's Israeli – Yaakov. He's in the address book by the phone.'

'An Israeli barber? Why Israeli?'

Penny shrugged. 'Why not?' She did not want to get bogged down talking with Aloo about Israel and matters Jewish. She desperately wanted to get ready to leave. 'He just is. He's a good hairdresser. And Aloo, I must mention… Danny absolutely doesn't know what's wrong with Simon. Don't say anything that might worry him.'

Jack nodded. 'A week is OK,' he murmured doubtfully. Penny was not sure if he had heard her request. Then, in another mercurial change of mood, he shrugged: 'Ach!' – he seemed to dismiss the whole subject with a flick of the hand – 'So it's a couple of weeks. A fortnight's holiday in London – who's complaining? Maybe it's three weeks, a month. What difference does it make? If that's what Simon needs. To sort himself out.'

'Aloo, I've written the names and numbers of a few friends who can help if you want them to.' She handed him a piece of notepaper, which he put on the table without a glance. 'There, Aloo? This list,' – she tapped it with her finger, but he did not look – 'these are the phone numbers of some friends who can help,' she repeated. Still he did not respond and she did not know if he had heard.

Forgetting that she was in a hurry, he poured another tea for himself, topped-up Penny's cup, and asked, 'What actually has happened to him? I mean, what are the symptoms?'

It took her a moment to find the right, evasive words. 'Hard to say. He's… honestly, I don't know what it is. He seems to be having some sort of breakdown.'

'Working too hard, I should think,' Jack suggested breezily, unconcerned.

She allowed it to rest there, unable to explain, struggling to read his thoughts. For a man reputedly so intelligent, he seemed remarkably obtuse sometimes.

'That could be it.' And indeed, she believed, that must have played a part in the peculiar catastrophe that had apparently overtaken her husband.

2

Well, Mummy has gone. She went to look after Daddy. And Grandad Aloo has come to look after me. Maybe it would have been better if Aloo had gone to look after Daddy? Then I could have kept Mummy here.

Aloo is terribly old, and has watery old-peoples' eyes that look like the colour has been washed away, as well as crinkly skin, and a rough, old-man's voice. I like the reading glasses hanging round his neck.

Another thing is that everyone calls him Aloo. I don't know anyone else called Aloo. It's pronounced to rhyme with Hey You, like 'Eh' and 'Loo'.

Aloo is always giggling, and likes playing games, and sometimes he doesn't seem old at all, except of course, that lots of old people are like that. And he does play in a rather old-people sort of way, all of a sudden deciding that he's 'had enough', and never really playing – I mean he never truly turns into a space rocket or anything like that – he just thinks he is pretending. He is very, very strong – he can pick me up with one hand and throw me right in the air. Afterwards, though, he rubs his left knee and says 'Oof! I shouldn't have done that!' Then he'll pick me up and throw me in the air all over again. He really is so strong. But he is rubbish at computer games. And he won't play football for more than about five seconds. 'Ach! Stupid game!' he says. Either it's because he hates football or because of the bad knee. He can play chess like anything, though. And he's interested in numbers, like me. I think he's the only person in the world who understands why I love prime numbers so much.

But the most amazing thing of all about Aloo is that he stays smart all the time. He wears a proper shirt and tie and trousers with a crease nearly all the time, and never takes off his shoes – shiny shoes with thin laces. When he dresses in the morning, he puts on his shiny shoes, then keeps them on all day! He keeps them on even if he's crawling around on the floor to make me laugh, or sitting with his feet up reading the paper. He just lies back on the couch and puts his shoes on the cushions. He doesn't know that he must take them off.

Daddy and Mummy hardly ever wear shiny shoes. Daddy usually wears trainers to go out, and only wears smart shoes like Aloo's if he has to go to an important meeting. When Daddy wins awards, and when he met the Queen at Buckingham Palace, he wore shoes like Aloo's.

Another amazing thing about Aloo is the piano. Whenever Aloo has finished eating, he plays the piano. Actually it's after every meal, but often he doesn't eat breakfast or lunch. If he does eat breakfast or lunch, he plays piano afterwards. When Aloo plays the piano it's really like listening to the radio, or to a CD. He plays for quite a few minutes, lovely tunes I never heard before, and sometimes sings along with them in his gravel voice. He sings in foreign languages. He plays the sort of music they have in films – kind of classical, sort of pop music with violins. He sings really well, like someone in a show. When I tell him it's good, though, he just laughs and says it's 'nothing', and 'I wish I could play it properly,' and stuff like that. That's the sort of thing he says about everything.

Something I like about Aloo is that he hardly ever cooks anything. He only buys food that's ready to eat, or just needs heating up in the microwave. He said his favourite kind of cooking is 'Open the bag and sit down.'

One weird thing about Aloo is he's very jumpy about noise in the street. If he hears anything at all, like maybe people talking quietly as they walk past, he wants to know what it is. Sometimes when you can hear people's voices as they pass, Aloo runs upstairs so that he can look out of the front window to see, as he says, 'what's going on,' even though nothing at all is ever going on. He likes to have the windows shut even when it's warm, so that he can't hear anyone in the street.

When there's the tiniest sound outside, like maybe if someone is shutting a car door, he gets quite frightened. I asked him if he was frightened, and he said, 'What of?' But that's not an answer. It's another question.

When Aloo goes out, he always wears his hat, which he calls a cap, but it's nothing like a baseball cap. It's made of cloth, in lots of narrow straight lines, called corduroy. It really doesn't look right with his other clothes. Aloo and me, we have a lot of fun together, more fun than I ever have with Mummy and Daddy.

* * *

Boiled bygels! It's years since I had proper bygels! We get them from a baker's and just nosh 'em in the street. Oh yes, dear Miri, you should see us now! An ill-matched couple, obviously. What a pair of good-for-nothings! We play the fool, buck the system, throw spanners in the works. That's the idea. We are mischievous anti-moderns, a pair of street intellectuals walking on the sunny side. We talk and argue and laugh about the world. I can't tell you what a good time I'm having. You would tell me to grow up, but – at this age? – it's starting to look as if I never will.

I'm exaggerating, of course. Mischievous? Anti-moderns? Are you kidding? We are not even intellectuals. We spend most of our time in coffee shops talking nonsense. Our boundaries are marked by Jewish bakeries – what else matters in life? Especially to a 10-year-old.

They said Danny was clever, that you have to spend time with him to really see just how clever he is. It's such a shame you missed it all. It's not just that he's some kind of mathematical genius. There's something about the way he understands things – I can't keep up with his brain, he's always ahead of me. And vocabulary! Did he learn all this from Simon and Penny – it seems impossible, but who else could it be? And at the same time, he's just a kid who likes football and cream cakes.

So we go as far as Isaac's (delicious challah rolls) in Temple Fortune, or to Golani's (the best bygels) in the Israeli quarter, and back to the frummers' favourite, Regent Patisserie (delicious pastries), near the Underground station.

At Isaac's, there are always queues, especially on Friday of course, for the challah, served by pretty shiksas talking Russian or Polish and wearing crucifixes. Everyone's buying challah for Shabbes – but for most of them, there is no Shabbes, it's just 'Friday night dinner', nothing more.

Golani's is big and bright and you can push to the front just by yelling out what you want. I like a place like that, where I'm free to shove in. After all, I'm only pushing in front of all the people who would get in front of *me* if they could. You have to use everything in your armoury – a loud voice, sharp elbows if you've got 'em. Wearing a pair of reading glasses round your neck can be useful. Being a Very Old Man is the best weapon yet. Why didn't I think of that years ago?

Then it's a leisurely stroll back along Golders Green Road,

past Bloom's, and Solly's, and the video rentals, Lemberg's Lingerie, Steimatzky's Bookshop, and the fast food joints. It's by no means completely Jewish. There are Thai places, Chinese shops, Indian supermarkets, a Turkish grocery store and East European places, like the Lithuanian *parduotuvė* and the Polish *sklep*[1] which have an unparalleled display of the booze that fuelled our attackers of old – Ukrainian vodka, Russian vodka, Lithuanian vodka, Polish vodka, flavoured vodkas and many wonderfully named firewaters to set the antisemitic soul alight – Balsam Mnicha, Ziołowa Gorzka and Žlub. In Golders Green Road of all places!

Poles, Belorussians, Ukrainians, Lithuanians. They came here and discovered yids again. Still alive! It's only a matter of time before the anti-Jewish attacks start. There are probably Cossacks in London now, working as waiters or plumbers, preparing a pogrom.

The Regent Patisserie is at the other end of the street, beyond the war memorial. There's no pushing at Regent. It's pious and off-putting, so poky that if there are as many as two customers, one of them may have to wait outside, especially if the other one's wearing a big hat, which he usually is.

Sometimes we go on one of our 'Mobile Raids'. We see someone talking loudly on a mobile phone and try to interrupt their call. We ask them the time, we ask for directions, we keep 'em talking even when they try to brush us aside. Danny had such a good one today: I was waiting to take money out of a cash machine, and the fellow in front of me was talking loudly into his phone. As he bent down to use the machine, he happened to be saying 'But they don't have any tax in Saudi Arabia, do they?' Quick as a dart, Danny is yelling into the guy's phone, 'But they have horrible insects!' I absolutely roared with laughter. So did the chap behind me. The fellow on

1 parduotuvė = shop (Lithuanian); sklep = shop (Polish)

the phone simply glared at me furiously, so I just shrugged as if to say, Kids! What can I do?

And some time during the day we usually go up to the café in Golders Hill Park for an ice. Golly, by the time we've shlepped up to the café terrace, I need it. I haven't done so much walking in… well, I've never done so much walking in my entire life. Danny dashes off to climb a tree or join in a football game. I sit at my table, cappuccino in front of me, listening to the yiddishe nonsense all around.

And I'm wishing that chair beside me wouldn't be so empty, Miri. I wish it would be you sitting there, and we could talk some nonsense of our own. My life's too quiet without you. Can't you come back for a little while? Slip away for one more precious moment together? We could have a coffee, and a nice chat. Darling, I'm sure they wouldn't miss you in heaven, just for half an hour.

* * *

Simon lay on his back on the cool earth. Here he would lie forever, and relax, alone, and clear his mind. He kept very still, to be more at peace. Comfortable, the ground took him like a feather bed, or a padded coffin. To be buried, in tranquil darkness. His physical hunger for food had become like a sharp treasure; enduring it was the oasis of meaning on which he stood and proved himself. Indeed he felt no physical discomfort, only vague longings and indefinable anguish. He stretched himself on the grass and gazed up, up, his sight taking him far into the vast serene depths of the sky. Behind that veil of blue, the black cosmos howled silently, its immense empty darkness swallowing the brightness of the day.

Alone, to be left alone, to be untroubled, to be free from all these bonds, to cut loose from things, to throw it all away, to take it all in broad armfuls and throw everything – life, work, family

– into a garbage truck, into a skip, into a shredder, and leave nothing, nothing, not even oneself. The sky like a screen, he watched his thoughts, poured and mixed together, kaleidoscope dreams, memories and horror film fantasies. His neck, wrists and penis seemed in danger, blood so close beneath the skin. No, he would clear his mind, here on the tranquil mountain, far above the stabbing hassles of the world. Clear such horrors from his mind. He tried to banish the colourful visions of blood, emerging from imagined openings in his flesh. The sunlight seemed like a sort of darkness, a dark mist. He felt a sensation on his skin, and wondered if it was blood seeping out of him. Afraid, he looked at his legs: were these part of him? His body seemed far away, unconnected, just clay, seeping. But when he looked again at his skin, there was no blood. His skin was intact. Was his penis bleeding? He reached into his trousers and felt no moisture. Then came a doubt. Perhaps there was moisture, even though he couldn't feel any. He unzipped his fly and looked at his penis. It was intact. He put it away.

Surprised and relieved, he lay back down. But there was no peace, even here. Luminous, dazzling feelings of anger sparked in the darkness, flares of resentment, flashes of self-pity. The longing to 'show' people, teach them a lesson. But all was hopeless, impossible, futile. Again came a desire to slash himself, to vent his rage, and be torn to shreds, to tiny shreds like a confetti, and become nothing at all, a shredded document. And the darkness of the sunlight became red. They cannot see me, they do not know what I feel, and care nothing about it. Invisible man, unphysical, I am nothing, not anything, I am not connected to anything, not part of anything, I neither exist nor don't exist.

Rolling over to press his face to the earth, he murmured aloud with his lips on the grass and soil – take me, digest me. He stared at the soil, dark as the sky. He lay still and felt a sort of frozen, immobile peace. The thoughts of blood ceased. Time passed, and Simon realised that he was still there, still alive, still separate from the earth. The light had changed, evening had crept over the mountain, and he knew he must not miss the last cablecar, and that it was an hour's walk away. And he felt weak from hunger, too weak to walk, and knew he must eat. His stomach begged him to return to the crass everyday world. In a mood of defiance he determined he would not. He would not descend to the hotel; he would not eat. At once a feeling of self-assuredness seeped into his mood: he would defy all hunger – and cold – and assert himself, and be something, something like a diamond. He rolled over again to look up. In the growing darkness, a star became visible; he knew the last cablecar back down had already left, and that he was doomed to hunger, and to sleeping out here among night insects and animals, for whom now he had become the food.

It reminded him of night walks, in many parts of the globe. Again his thoughts returned to walking, as they had for much of the day. In beautiful starlit, balmy places beside the sea. On beaches, quaysides and promenades. He walked in silver moonlight on a lonely beach below cliffs, he walked on a dark dockside next to black water. He walked along a wide Californian beach washed over by towers of silver spray, and stood alone on white Caribbean sands, in dazzling Greek island bays sprinkled with shingle, and in the awesome vastness of Pacific beaches on Australia's ocean shore. He strolled among the crowds, beside the sea in pretty resorts, all alike, and along Riviera waterfronts, the Croisette and the Promenade des Anglais, and turned to look beyond the beach at offshore yachts and cruise ships dazzling like floating pyramids of light. On such ships he had walked on the wooden decks at night, alone, lost in thought. The wooden boards under his feet, the starry darkness raised above the sea's restless blackness. He leaned on the side and could make out the lights of some shining city in the Mediterranean night – it was Tel Aviv. At last, Tel Aviv. And he felt again his feet on the swirling patterns of the wide Tel Aviv promenade. Walking, walking, past the hotels, the hawkers and the sauntering crowds, past the waterfront disco where Russian kids were blown to mincemeat by Arabs, past the park where big Arab families sat picnicking around fires in the evening, and along the walkway to Jaffa in the dark. And back again. And in the crowd he heard voices, the voices of his family – Hebrew, English, Russian, Yiddish – in all the languages that might be his, that were and were not his, talking all at once on the beachside at night. For in language there is history, but no history was his history. He stood and looked across the sand, where lovers walked, at the darkness of the sea, stretching away, away, away.

* * *

After dinner, when Aloo got up from the piano, I said, 'Can you make up a story about that music?'

'What sort of story, Danny?'

'About Daddy.'

And he gave me a funny look. He walked from the piano stool to an armchair and said, 'Are you worried about Daddy?'

'A little bit,' I said. 'I think I heard you say breakdown. Is it like part of him is broken, like the car when it has a breakdown?'

Aloo grinned at me, the way grown-ups do, to reassure you when they themselves are worried and they want to avoid telling you something. 'Nothing is broken, but he has too many problems.'

'What problems? Is it about money?'

'No, I don't think so. Mummy has gone to be with him and

help him sort it out.'

'If you have a breakdown, you need a… what's it called... a psychotheratist?'

Aloo smiled a great big smile and I knew I'd got it wrong. 'Pissed,' he said.

'Pissed!' I dared to say. 'Isn't that…' but Aloo was laughing loudly and shaking his head.

'What will Penny think of me, teaching you rude words! No, Danny, what I mean is that it's a psychothera*pist*. Anyway, you don't always need one. Daddy probably doesn't.'

I didn't want to talk any more about that. 'Are you going to tell me a story about it?'

Aloo screwed up his face and said 'Once upon a time…' Then, for a moment, he leaned back and held his chin in one hand. 'I suppose it must have been a long time ago and in a far-off land, because stories usually are, aren't they?'

'I s'pose so. Not always. Some good stories are now, and here.'

'Well, wherever and whenever it was, there was a charming king and a lovely queen …'

'What were their names?'

'The King and Queen of Otherland.'

That was a pretty good name, so I waited for him to carry on.

He said, 'They lived in a …' but I interrupted. I wanted to know who else was in the story.

'Well,' he began, 'There's Lord Sir Gentleman. And Miss Ladywoman.'

'If she's a miss, they aren't married,' I said.

'No, no,' Aloo agreed, 'Lord Sir Gentleman is a crusty old gent, who smokes cigars and drinks port, puts his feet up on a polished mahogany desk, and doesn't do any work. He's the King's treasurer, banker, and High Chancellor of the King's

Exchequebook. A *sterling* fellow, in other words – if you see what I mean.'

By the tone of voice I knew that was supposed to be some kind of small joke, but I didn't quite get it. 'And Miss Ladywoman?' I asked.

'She's the Queen's right hand woman.'

I didn't know about people being a right hand man, so I didn't get that joke either until Aloo explained. 'Is there anyone else?' I asked.

Aloo gave me a twinkly glance. 'Oh yes,' he said, 'I nearly forgot. There's Princess Prettybows. And Prince Scrapeknees.'

'Tell me about them.'

I smiled when he said, 'Princess Prettybows is a tomboy. She likes climbing trees, and football, and she often has scraped knees. She supports Arsenal, by the way.'

'And Prince Scrapeknees?'

Aloo grinned mischievously. 'Prince Scrapeknees is the dancing and singing type, and sometimes seen in pretty bows.'

'But… why are they called...' I began to ask.

'A classic case of a misnomer,' Aloo said. 'People's names don't give anything away.'

'Miss Nomer?' I asked. 'Is that another person in the story?'

Aloo chuckled to himself and said he meant that people sometimes didn't have their right names, and that's what had happened to Prince Scrapeknees and Princess Prettybows.

'Shouldn't there be a wizard, or magician, if this is a fairy story?' I admit the idea came to me because I had just been reading Harry Potter.

He agreed. 'Yes, that's a good idea. Maybe the wizard can save the day. And his name is… not Merlin, that's been done before… let's think, magic, mystery, marvel… yes, Marvelstein.'

'Why "stein"?' I wondered.

'A Jewish wizard, obviously.'

'And you were going to say the King and Queen of Otherland lived in a… what, castle?'

'No, no,' Aloo replied, 'Impossible nowadays, a castle. So many problems. Impossible to clean. And the expense! No, of course, they lived in a spacious detached residence with mature gardens in Hampstead Garden Suburb.'

'Did it have a moat?'

'Couldn't get planning permission for it,' Aloo said.

'Can we have a fairy in the story?' I asked.

'OK, Mrs Jolly-Jolly the Fairy can be in it. Perhaps she's the cleaner.'

'Jewish?'

'A Jewish cleaner? Are you kidding?'

I wanted him to go on, because he hadn't really begun the story at all, but at that moment Aloo said, 'That's enough. It's bedtime now. I'll continue the story tomorrow.'

'But which one is Daddy?'

'Daddy is the King of Otherland, of course.'

3

A quiet life? I should be so lucky. You think I've got enough tsores already, looking after Danny? Of course not. Every time I step outside Simon and Penny's house, I get some new grief. Maybe it's my own fault... maybe I should go around with blinkers on. Maybe I just shouldn't go out at all. I do my level best to keep myself to myself, just quietly minding my own business and looking after Danny, and what happens? I'll tell you.

The day started nicely enough, Miri. I had a bad night, though, waking up at every sound outside. I had that old dream of mine – or call it a nightmare – this time, I was in some smart neighbourhood of London – Kensington or somewhere – but I'm lost, and as I try to find my way back, the streets get narrower and narrower, and rougher and more strange looking, until the pavements are all broken up, and the roadway becomes muddy and full of potholes. The buildings get smaller and darker and now are made of wood. I'm thinking, what part of London is this? There's mud everywhere, and the smell of wood burning, and some of the buildings have wooden balconies. Suddenly ahead of me in the lane there's a gang of toughs with shaved heads. They have huge bare arms. They're staring at me with white-hot anger and hatred, and start towards me, walking with clenched fists. As the first one raises his fist for the first punch, I woke up sweating with fear.

But I did get some sleep at last. Eventually it was morning. I listened to a dawn chorus of car alarms, turned on a little transistor that's by the bed, and lay listening peacefully to all the latest about the intifada, the jihad, the suicide bombers, and atrocities being committed around the world. Danny sleeps late and I try not to disturb him. It's the school holidays; he probably needs the rest.

I sleep in the spare room. It's not especially comfortable, I must say. Nothing matches. Compared to our beautiful house, Miri, theirs is a complete hegdish. A home should be, as our home is and always was – when you were in it with me – a mechaye. How could it be a delight now that you're not there any more? But in those days, when we were together and you were still well, I'd open the front door and step inside, and – Ah! Comfortable, attractive, elegant, welcoming.

Simon and Penny's home is the opposite. It's a mechaye just to get out of the place. No wonder they're never in. It's a pleasure just to shut the door behind you and get away from all their clutter and ill-assorted second-hand junk. They don't know anything about quality of life, these two.

Unpretentious can be nice. After all, our home is simple and unpretentious. But this isn't unpretentious, it's just chaos. Maybe it's because they haven't settled in yet. But what a mish-mash in Simon and Penny's own bedroom: two old veneered wardrobes, much too small for them, a solid oak chest of drawers, a good-quality bookcase with rubbish on it, ugly bedside cabinets, not matching, a battered old armchair that we would throw out if it was ours. The total effect is like an auction room. I kid you not. These are the lots nobody wanted. And the curtains, and the bedding – shmattes. I suppose this is what they like.

You, Miri, would have had the whole lot taken to the dump and a completely new set made up in matching fabrics, in a pretty design.

Danny's room is the same. The squalor in there is unbelievable. I didn't find out until this evening, at the very end of this dreadful day, when I was putting him to bed. Danny's carpet – I thought 'This looks familiar', then I remembered – it's the old threadbare carpet we gave them years ago. Even now they are still using it! I remember when we went out to buy it, after the War, how very expensive it was, how happy we were to get something good for our life together in peace at last, and how lovely it looked. Yes, I do remember that. Now it's all worn out, but they've kept it. Ah well – everything has changed since then! Never mind the carpet, the whole of society is worn out and threadbare. Everyone and everything needs refurbishing. All our good work is being undone.

What a wonderful generation ours was, Miri. The 1920s kids. We transformed the world beyond all recognition. The 20th century was ours, Miri. And it was like the Hundred Years War – not just warring nations, mass-production death, but warring ideologies, Titans fighting to rule the world. Our century created 'the masses' – and turned them first into soldiers, then citizens, then customers. Our generation triumphed at every stage. We defeated Nazism, created the Welfare Sate, gave every child a decent education, nationalised all the necessities of life. We created laws to protect the ordinary man and women from tyranny and exploitation, laws against discrimination, laws to protect consumers. Those were our little contributions to European civilisation. We also had time to dance the jitterbug.

Tell me, what do our kids do to carry on the good work? Have they made the world an even better place? Next stop, Utopia? Don't tell me, I know already. All the good things we created have been spoiled. All of them. Everything.

I come down for breakfast. No instant coffee. Only real! Ach! Filter papers, ground coffee, a five minute wait… what a palaver for a cup of coffee! From the back of the coffee packet, Danny reads 'For Best Before Date See Top of Pack.' He's always reading things aloud, making them absurd.

'Why not print the date on the back and, on the top, have For Best Before Date See Back of Pack, instead?' he giggled. 'Or put it on all six sides? For Best Before Date, see other side of pack. For top, see bottom.'

He flipped the packet over and looked at the date. He read out, 'One hundred and thirty thousand, three hundred and seven. One-three-oh, three-oh-seven. I suppose it means 13th of March, 2007. Wow! Coffee lasts a long time!'

'Talk about coffee futures!'

'How old will I be? I'm ten now, but next year I'll be twelve. Do you know why?'

'For the same reason that I am eighty now, but will be eighty-two next year. Because I haven't had this year's birthday yet.'

'That's a nice number, isn't it Grandad?'

'What, eighty-two? Or twelve?'

'No, silly. 1-3-0-3-0-7. One hundred and thirty, three hundred and seven. I like the way there's a seven, and the rest of it adds up to a seven. So it all adds up to fourteen, which is how old I'll be by then. Twelve is a nice number, too. Twelve is like a lot of little boxes that fit into each other, and all fit neatly into a bigger box, which is still quite little and… you know what I mean? Twelve is a number you can hold in your hand, and share out with friends. But one hundred and thirty thousand, three hundred and seven is the opposite of that – it's too big to think about, and its neatness is all – like a long poem. And anyway, it's a prime number. So it can't be shared out. It's unbreakable. It's a mountain. A prime number is like a brick, only harder than a brick, in fact a prime number is the hardest thing in the universe. Much harder than a diamond. And this one is huge – except of course, that "huge" doesn't mean anything when you're talking about numbers.'

'How do you know it's a prime number?' I asked, trying to remember any of the tests.

'What, 130-307? Well it must be,' he said. 'It *feels* like a prime number. Try and divide something into it.'

I'm sure most children of ten haven't even heard of prime numbers. Jokingly, we divided our birthdays – individually and then together – into the Lavazza sell-by date. Sure enough, they didn't go. So we tried dividing it by the Shredded Wheat sell-by date, and doing all sorts of other crazy arithmetic until we collapsed in laughter.

I couldn't help wondering what my own sell-by date will be. Will I outlast this pack of coffee? Not birthdays, but death days interest me now. Strange that I will probably die naturally, instead of, like most Jews of my generation, being murdered. It was a glorious summer morning, perfect blue sky. While I had toast and coffee, Danny ate cereal. Over breakfast we decided to go to Kenwood, on Hampstead Heath.

Now it's the side of the milk carton he's reading, 'Use By See Top of Carton.' Glancing up with his sweet, open, bright face, he says, 'What I wonder, you see, Grandad Aloo, is why they don't all just print the expiry date somewhere on the pack and leave it at that. Why do they have to print on the *side* telling you to look at the *top*? Why do they? Is it against the law, or something – to print the sell-by date on the side of a packet?'

I don't know the answer. Maybe there is some kind of damn-fool law. Is there some sort of European Union edict? Some Health and Safety meshugass?

'Anyway, why have a use-by date at all?' he insists. 'What about Don't Use If Mouldy? Or what about Please Use Your Sense?'

'Because, my dear fellow,' I say, 'people in the shop might not have much sense, so they would get food poisoning and sue someone, and besides, they can't possibly know if it's mouldy till they get home and open the packet.'

'I said "Use By" not "Sell By",' he shoots back.

'You mean it won't matter if they *sell* it when it's mouldy? That's a bit daft, isn't it?'

'OK, OK,' he pouted. 'It was only an idea. But it's you that's daft – something can still be mouldy even with a use-by date, can't it? You think we should eat something mouldy just because it hasn't passed its use-by date?'

He's right, of course. Always is.

Danny has a meshuggeneh game – reading out signs and notices and labels. He likes to find the most nonsensical pieces of writing possible. When we're out walking and he sees a stop sign in the road in the distance, he grabs my arm and says, 'Stop! Look there, Grandad, you see that,' and he'll point down to the far end of the street. 'The sign down there! It says we should stop!'

'That doesn't apply to us,' I said the first time.

'Oh *really*,' he said. 'How do people know which rules they are supposed to obey and which rules don't apply to them? It's risky, isn't it, for rule-makers, to make rules that don't apply to people?'

'Can we walk on yet?' I asked the little lobbus.

'But it still says Stop!'

But I played him at his own game: 'It doesn't say stop *walking* – how do you know it means stop walking? I notice you didn't stop *talking* when you saw the sign. Why not, eh? Or maybe it means stop breathing? So why didn't you? Or *maybe* – just maybe – it means stop *driving* when you reach this sign? Yes, on reflection, I think that's the most likely – so let's carry on walking. What say you?'

And when we stood in a crowded lift in the multi-storey car park at Brent Cross shopping centre, with a sign that read Thank You For Not Smoking, he announced in his lovely, loud, clear voice 'What a pity you don't smoke, Grandad! Because it would be so funny to have them thank you for *not* smoking while you *were* smoking!' This raised a smile all round, and Danny went on, 'After all, they're not actually saying No Smoking. I s'pose they think that wouldn't be polite.'

As the lift went up, an electronic voice announced each floor. First floor, second floor.... Suddenly Danny pretended to be outraged by this. 'Hey, what about people who don't speak English!' he declared in theatrical tones. 'Well? That voice is basically saying, "If you don't understand this message we don't care if you miss your floor." We should protest about that, Grandad!'

While this was sinking in, and I was wondering how the immigrants in the crowded lift were taking Danny's humour, he went on with exaggerated sweet innocence, 'Of course, I s'pose it's better than the *old* days when everyone had to *guess* which floor they were on just by looking at the lit-up numbers above the doors, and get out at the right stop, *without any help from anyone.* Did lots and lots of people miss their floor, in the old days, Grandad? When they only had the lit-up numbers?'

'Suppose it was a blind person?' I suggested.

'What,' says he, 'going to the car park? Like, going back to their car, you mean?'

Oy!

Today at the breakfast table, he reads to me from the cereal packet. 'Oh *look*! That's nice! Shredded Wheat Bitesize are really *worried* about people's *hearts* and want to *help*.'

I wonder what's coming – I'm getting used to Danny now.

'"Join the Healthy Heart Campaign",' he reads. '"Shredded Wheat, committed to the healthy heart campaign." Grandad, would you like to help everyone to have less heart trouble?

Then you really ought to join in these Four Campaign Steps. "One: Cut down on fat. Shredded Wheat is 95% fat free. Two: Cut down on salt. Shredded Wheat has no added salt. Three: Eat more fibre. Shredded Wheat is a great source of bran fibre. Four: Take more exercise." Funny, that last one isn't about Shredded Wheat. And it's probably the only one that will really help people's hearts.'

The fluency of his reading impresses me – or maybe I've just forgotten what a ten-year-old can do. 'Wiseguy, huh?' I say. 'You think people should eat *more* fat and salt, maybe?'

'No, but Grandad, it would be awful if people follow their Four Campaign Steps, and end up eating less and less and less fat, less and less and less salt, and more and more and more fibre. They aren't saying what's the right amount – just *less* and *more*. Just imagine! It would be *scary*! Everyone just eating *massive* bowls of Shredded Wheat – with no milk, 'cos that's fat – and *enormous* heaps of steamed vegetables, with no fat or salt. And even that won't be enough, because this packet would still be telling them to Eat Less Fat, Eat Less Salt, Eat More Fibre.'

I had to laugh. 'Don't worry so much. No one takes the slightest notice of any of these things.'

'Oh, I know that,' he reassured me, with his funny little smile. 'I'm not really worried.'

And we set off to visit Kenwood in Penny's car. Straight away, would you believe it, there's something wrong with the car! I turned the key and it went uh-uh-uh then started with a huge roar. Smoke billowing out the back. As we drove along, it kept stalling. Simon and Penny will blame me, naturally! Even Danny had the cheek to ask if I had done something to the car, or if it was just the way I drive.

I had got no further than Golders Green station in this

ridiculous manner, when Danny pointed out a man staggering and yelling on the other side of the road. He seemed to be drunk, wandering into the road and shouting angrily at people. Even as we watched, he collapsed onto the pavement. I braked to look. Well, you might think, who wouldn't help a man who's passed out in the street? The answer is – no one would help him. Not one person stopped – not even the pedestrians.

The car had stalled again, so I left it where it was and ran across the road. People were walking right past him as if they hadn't noticed anything unusual. The English of course, from them you expect nothing better – they are ashamed to be alive. But some of these people were yidden – frummers, noch! Is *that* a mitzvah – to walk past someone who's lying on the pavement? Shouldn't you forfeit your share in the world to come, or something? No, they can beat their breast on Yom Kippur and it all will be OK.

The man was quite unconscious. In fact, his lips were blue, and his breathing was very faint and shallow. He had a little cut on his head – maybe from when he fell. When I spoke or touched him there wasn't the slightest response.

And there were tiny bloodstains on his shirt, which scared me, but then I saw that they were caused by a pair of broken sunglasses in his breast pocket. I struggled with him; he was far too heavy for me, and I didn't know the right thing to do. I pulled at his shirt collar, thinking to loosen it.

The buttons were too fiddly and slow, and I tried to tear the shirt open. On his collarbone I noticed a small tattoo of a butterfly, neatly cut right across by one of the pieces of glass. So strange it looked – a butterfly bleeding.

I leaped up and grabbed the arm of a man who was walking by, talking into a mobile. 'Quick, call an ambulance. This man needs help urgently,' I said.

He brushed me off and offered this piece of insight: 'He's just drunk.'

'Oh, he's *drunk*,' I said. 'So we'll just let him die then, shall we? This man is ill.'

And the fellow looked at me as if *I* was the nut, and carried on walking. Actually, the chap on the pavement had not a whiff of alcohol about him. He looked a fit young man. Very fit – maybe a weight-lifter or, like me, a boxer.

I tried someone else, who also kept walking without a reply, and then I ran into the Halifax Building Society – well, of course it's not a building society any more, what with everyone being so greedy, but that's another story – and went up to the desk and called out to the clerks there.

'Quick, can one of you call an ambulance? A man outside needs help very urgently.' I said. 'I think it's something serious.'

The customer at the counter, a scrawny little chap, grumbled in sharp, whining tones. 'Why don't you take your turn?' Luckily the counter clerk wasn't quite so stupid. I told her to call 999 and ask for a fully equipped emergency ambulance, and I dashed back outside.

Everyone has seen how mouth-to-mouth resuscitation is done, so for the first time I had a go at it, pressing his chest with my hands and blowing air into his mouth. Would you believe it? People carried on walking past. What do they think? We're in a movie or something? That nothing is for real any more?

All this time, Danny is sitting in the car watching. Between gasps I looked across to see if he was OK, and – just my luck – there's a traffic warden leaning on the car and speaking with Danny.

I called out to the warden: 'I'm helping a fellow here!'

He looks over at me suspiciously. 'Are you a doctor?'

'No, I'm waiting for the ambulance.'

'Well, I'm sorry. If you were a doctor, I might …'

'Look, don't give me a ticket, be a good chap, I'm helping a very sick man here.' But I had to shout over the noise of the traffic, and what with the mouth-to-mouth having made me a bit breathless, I don't think he heard me.

But I had already wasted too much time. While I'd been calling out to the traffic warden, the poor fellow's pulse had actually stopped, and as far I could see he wasn't breathing at all. For some reason I felt desperate that he shouldn't die. I became almost panicky at the thought of something as big, as immeasurably vast, as a human life, suddenly slipping away like some scrap of wastepaper blowing in the breeze. I started again very vigorously, pushing and blowing, and seemed to get a response – he literally started to breath again. I was shoving at his chest so hard I thought I might break his ribs. I figured he'd rather be alive with broken ribs, than dead. At last the ambulance came.

On an impulse I looked in his pockets. I just wondered who he was, if there was maybe something to identify him. I didn't get as far as taking out his wallet – that would have looked bad – but there was a set of keys with "Gavin" on a nametag.

The ambulance stopped half in the bus lane, half on a pedestrian crossing, just where traffic was turning into the roundabout. A huge boxy thing, like a small lorry, with bright stripes and a check pattern on the side, dazzling blue lights flashing – it brought everything to a stop immediately and caused utter chaos. Two ambulance men got out, looking comfortable and relaxed in short sleeved green uniforms like people on holiday, idly chatting and putting on white rubber gloves. At first, they were very casual, but as soon as they saw me struggling they moved quickly. The back was open in a flash and in no time they were giving him some electric shocks. He seemed almost to jerk into life. It was all done in seconds. That, I've never seen before.

So you see, Miri: life is not the great big world of experience and emotion that it seems to be to each of us. And life is not some magical mystery that binds us to something wonderful, as the rabbis and the clerics would tell us. In fact life is just electricity, just raw, soulless physics and chemistry, and here was the proof. They kick-started a life that had all but stopped. They didn't bother about soul or spirit. They made the physical, chemical body work, and the mysterious thing called life returned.

If spirit and soul depart from the body when it dies, Miri, as the religious think, how can they return when it's given an electric shock? Now, I know it's not fair to talk like this to someone who has already died, but you'd have to agree with me that spirit and soul – if those words mean anything at all – are like mind, like emotion, or for that matter, like hunger. They are part of the physical body. After death, what is there? Obviously nothing. How could there be anything? Except in your case, darling, obviously.

Not giving up, quick as a flash the ambulance men were shifting him onto a stretcher.

'Where are you taking him?' I asked.

'Royal Free Hospital.' I had half expected them to say the mortuary.

'Will he die?' I asked.

'No, if he's lucky, he won't. He probably had a stroke, maybe a heart attack. How long has he been lying here like this? If only someone had called us straight away …' There was something in his voice as if to say *I* was to blame. They lifted him into the ambulance.

I asked, 'How can I find out what happens to him?' but they just shrugged. One of them asked if he was a relative, and I admitted I didn't even know the fellow. They shut the door and screeched off with wailing siren.

You know, Miri, some people die between clean sheets, with their family all around them. They have a quiet bed for their last sleep, flowers on a bedside cabinet and everyone who loves them is there to say goodbye. That's how it was with you. And other people die in dirt, lying on the pavement like litter, with traffic driving past and people stepping over. But maybe this fellow won't die just yet. That strange butterfly, bleeding, keeps coming into my mind.

* * *

As Aloo walked back to the car he looked kind of small and old. Actually he is small, and of course, very old. He stopped to take the parking ticket off the windscreen. By the time he got back into the driver's seat, he was tiny. He turned the key, but of course the car wouldn't start. He seemed sad and annoyed. He took off his hat and put it on the seat. He sat almost shaking, and rested the bald part of his head on his two hands. All this was really worrying, because basically, I need Aloo to be OK so he can look after me. I wondered if Mummy had thought about what would happen to me if Aloo died of old age while he was looking after me. Had she forgotten to think about that? If Aloo died at that moment, what would I do about the car?

It was so worrying, that I actually started crying. I didn't want to, but I was just so unhappy and frightened about everything.

Aloo put an arm round me for a second, and patted my cheek. 'What's to cry for?' he asked.

I didn't want to say I was worried about him dying. 'Your trousers are dirty,' I said, 'Look at the knees.' He hadn't noticed, but kneeling on the pavement had made a mess of his trousers. His shoes were scuffed, too. I didn't like to see that, because Aloo is usually so smart.

He looked down at his knees very unhappily. He pulled a face. 'God, my knees *hurt*,' he said quietly, rubbing his left knee firmly. 'This is my bad knee – you don't want to worry about that. It's been bad for years. You're not crying about that, are you?' he asked. 'What else is wrong?'

'Nothing,' I said. 'Hey, did you know that man? That guy on the pavement?'

He said no.

'So why did you give him a kiss?' I asked.

He told me it was a way of saving someone's life.

I didn't know kissing was so important. Maybe that's why men and women kiss each other? To sort of, give more life? I wonder if people can die from not getting enough kisses.

'So did that man die, then?' I asked.

'Well, he's certainly very ill,' Aloo said, 'but I think we've probably saved his life. We did what we could to help, didn't we? What more can anyone do?'

I told him I wasn't sure about saving the life of someone you don't know. After all, suppose it is a horrible person. Aloo said you should save them anyway.

I just hope I never have to kiss a horrible person. I think Aloo was pretty upset about it himself, and when he gave me a big hug, it was to comfort himself as much as me. All this time he kept turning the car key, and suddenly it started. We set off again to Kenwood, the car roaring and nearly stopping every few minutes. Or maybe that's the way Aloo drives.

'What did that traffic warden say?' he asked.

I put on the warden's stupid voice: '"You can't leave the car here, I'm afraid."' I laughed. 'Bit of a stupid thing to say to a ten-year-old child, isn't it, Grandad?'

'And then he wrote out the ticket?'

'After he spoke to you. Yes.' Aloo tutted angrily and stayed quiet.

After a while I said, 'Funny to think you saved his life but he doesn't know. One day in the future, you might see him again, and maybe he'll push in front of you in a queue. Maybe he'll be yelling into a mobile phone and annoying you. Maybe you'll wish he was dead. What was wrong with him?'

'Probably his heart,' Aloo said.

'You see!' I said. 'He should have eaten more Shredded Wheat.'

* * *

As soon as the phone rang, Penny grabbed it, knowing that it must be Danny. Her 'Hello' was purposefully bright and good-humoured. Instead, though, she heard Jack's deep voice, greeting her with a cough and a few mumbled growly sounds before starting, unusually, by asking how she was and if everyone was all right.

'I'm OK,' she answered cautiously. 'Simon's not too good. I had to go and look for him. It was mad, terrible. He was sitting by the ski lift. I've got him back to the hotel. He needs a doctor; he needs help.'

'Oh dear!' Jack tried to show some concern and sound sympathetic. 'I hope he'll be all right.' But he did not want to talk about that just now. 'Penny, there seems to be something wrong with your car.' She noticed the note of blame towards herself. 'It just kind of judders along, and keeps cutting out.'

Annoyed because she suspected this must be Jack's fault, Penny gave him the phone number of their car mechanic, an Israeli called Yoav. 'Another headache is all I need,' she said bitterly.

'Why an Israeli?' Jack asked. His diffidence was all gone. 'Israeli hairdresser, Israeli car mechanic…'

'He just happens to be Israeli,' she replied defensively.

'Simon liked the idea of an Israeli, that's all.'

'Why?'

'Aloo, please, not now. Yoav's a first rate mechanic, hard-working, and he won't try to rob you. He's a mensh. You can have an interesting conversation with him, and he's nothing like the car mechanics we've used in the past. And he'll come and fix your car wherever it is. Besides, Simon likes to practise his Hebrew with him. Is all of that a good enough reason? I'm sorry Aloo, I'm worried about Simon and now I'm worried about the car. Do I really need to give a reason for preferring a particular car mechanic? Is Danny there?'

'Practise his Hebrew? Simon's learning Hebrew now? Why? What's the special interest in Hebrew?'

'Simon is a journalist, he's a guy with a flair for languages, and he wants to learn Ivrit, that's all. He's a travel writer. He knows Greek, too. He can read Russian. Why not?'

'Ivrit!' Jack balked at the Hebrew name of the language. 'You sound like you're planning to make aliyah!'

Penny laughed sharply. 'No. Don't worry, we're not about to do that. How would Simon earn a living in Israel?' – she lowered her voice – 'Not that he'll be able to earn a living anywhere, in this state. No aliyah, no nothing. We're not making anything at all right now. Is Danny there?'

Jack decided not to mention the parking ticket. He put Danny on the line.

After a spell of repeating the word Kiss again and again, interspersed with giggles, Danny suddenly asked Penny, 'Can I speak to Daddy?'

Sitting on the edge of the bed in a Swiss hotel room, Penny had known he would ask eventually, but still had no idea what her response would be. Three paces away from her, Simon sat expressionless, eyes not focused anywhere, apparently not listening to the conversation.

She found herself saying, 'Not right now, darling. He's asleep.'

'No I'm not,' Simon said. Penny's heart sank.

'Daddy's not actually asleep,' Penny corrected herself, 'but he's not well. Can I get him to call you soon?'

'Is that Danny?' Simon asked.

Penny covered the receiver. 'It is Danny,' she agreed, 'but I'd rather you didn't speak to him right now. I don't want you to get stressed out, and remember, Simon, that Danny is just a little boy. I don't want him to get upset or frightened by the way you are right now.'

'Why, how am I?' Simon said belligerently.

'Not now, Simon. I'm on the phone. You and I will talk in a minute.'

'Let me talk to him,' Simon insisted, getting out of the chair and coming slowly to the phone.

As soon as he held the phone, Simon understood that it was a mistake. Penny was right. The side of his face began to tighten, his jaw became stiff and immobile, his tongue seemed to grow.

Through clenched teeth, he said, 'Hello Danny.' His voice made him think of a heavy woollen blanket. To Penny he merely sounded hoarse. To Danny, unwell.

'Hello Daddy,' Danny said uncertainly. 'Are you all right?'

'Not too bad.' Simon realised that he must not, above all else, he must not, whatever happened, he must not, he must not, upset his wonderful, clever, innocent, bright little boy, so harmless and good, trusting and full of devotion, and – he felt suddenly – so much *not* the cause of his troubles.

What then, were his troubles? And what was their cause? In a single instant, Simon tried to grasp three thoughts: that he had troubles, that he must try to understand his troubles, and that if he could control his mood and behaviour for Danny's sake then he could control it for Penny's sake and for his own sake. A fourth idea rushed in, that someone or something had caused his problems, then a fifth idea, and a sixth, until he wasn't sure if he knew what he was thinking at all.

He noticed then that Danny was in the middle of speaking to him, but he had not heard anything. 'Sorry, Dan, I missed that. What did you say?'

'I said, we saw a man die today. Or nearly die.'

Simon felt that he must have imagined these words, that Danny had not really said them. Alarmed, he said, 'Danny, I'm gonna give the phone back to Mummy. She'll talk to you. I don't feel very well right now.' As he handed the phone to Penny, a vice that had been clamped onto his jaw seemed to be released. With relief, he rubbed the side of his face and the muscles began to loosen. He wanted to leave the room, get away from the phone, and made for the bathroom, thinking perhaps to shut himself in there.

It reminded him that even before he came on this trip and fell into this strange, deep hole, while he was busily working at home and abroad, increasingly he hated talking on the phone. It started about a year ago, the pains in his face. It wasn't just the phone – meeting people at press events, travel industry events, had started to cause pain in his cheeks, his jaw and even his neck. He hated the people he was talking to, hated trying to be ebullient and upbeat, politely listening to PRs talking up new initiatives, and selling story ideas to reluctant editors. Sometimes the boredom he felt made him nauseous or made him come out in a sweat. Increasingly, he was leaving events early, on the pretext of having so much work to do, because he just couldn't stand another minute. He was desperate for peace and time to think on his own.

He turned to look into the big bathroom mirror, and could not recognise the face he saw there. It was not even a face, or was, rather, a face painted by Braque or Picasso, unconnected features that would not come together into a single image. As he struggled to find himself in the mirror, he half-recognised other people instead, his father and his son, more than himself. And the eyes! So staring, and one different from the other. 'Who are you looking at?' he challenged the reflection in a whisper, as it challenged him. 'And that chin… it needs a shave.'

He returned to the bedroom chair and looked through the windows at dark trees clustered together, forming pointy patterns, ragged green cut-out shapes stuck on the steep grey mountainsides. Images of Danny lying dead, his fine little body mangled, kept flickering in Simon's mind. And up above, the peaceful silent clouds. How he longed to be up there, part of that unearthly silence. Not quite lost in thought, he wondered if Danny was to blame for anything.

'Saw a man *nearly die*!' Penny was aghast. 'What, really and truly? That must have been horrible for you! What happened? Where was this?' She felt, anxiously, angrily, that Aloo wasn't taking proper care of him. If she had been there, Penny reasoned, there would definitely not have been a man dying on the pavement in Golders Green. She had absolutely never seen such a thing in Golders Green. It was typical Aloo.

'Anyway Danny, apart from things like *that*, I hope you're having a lovely time with Grandad Aloo. Don't forget you can still see any of your friends. Call Sam and Adam and Ammi and see if they're free. And you can call me at the hotel any time.' Finishing her conversation by repeating the words hug and kiss many more times, she asked to have another few moments with Jack.

'Aloo, I wonder if I could ask you. A big favour. If you could please do something for us,' she said, glancing nervously across the room.

Jack's lips tightened with suspicion as he asked Penny what he could do.

She said, 'Do you think you could to try to keep up the appearance that Simon's life is running normally? I know it sounds weird, but… it will help him. Take any work messages very carefully. Answer them, tell people he's away working on a big project. Anything he's invited to, reply to the invitations – tell them he's sorry he can't come. If editors phone up or email him, just stick to the same line. He's busy, he's away, he'll be in touch when he gets back.'

She longed to be able to explain more about Simon's condition, but there never seemed to be a time when she could speak to Aloo without either Danny or Simon listening in. She went on, 'Simon won't be checking his email any more. Ask Danny to show you how the email works. If you could do this, it will be very, very helpful to Simon when he's better. But don't be too specific about when he'll be back.'

Jack sensed that things were worse than he knew.

* * *

In his constant struggle to stay up as late as possible, Danny was enjoying some advantages while his grandfather looked after him. Jack could not remember when children were normally sent to bed and didn't think it mattered. Besides, he often fell into a doze while watching television in the evening and, with occasional jerks of movement, mumblings or intermittent snores, sometimes remained asleep or half-asleep until almost midnight. All the while, Danny would stay up. In any case, Jack did not like 'sending' anyone, or telling people what to do, or playing the grown-up. He had a mischievous sense – he knew it was an illusion – that he was on the kids' side in their longing for endless freedom.

When he finally did tell him it was bedtime, it never occurred to Jack to supervise the boy or go into his room. He had taken little interest in the bringing-up of his own child, and as a child himself had been almost entirely ignored by adults from the age of six until he left home ten years later. Dutifully, Danny would trudge upstairs alone, put on his baggy pale blue pyjamas and clean his teeth just as if Penny were there. Then he would go back down and say good night. 'Good night, lad,' Jack might say, or 'Night night, sleep well.' The two would hug and kiss each other's cheek.

'Night night, Grandad Aloo,' Danny would say sweetly, gently, almost sadly, because he missed his mother painfully at that moment. Back upstairs he would leave his bedside light on and read, but as soon as he heard Jack making his own way to bed, the light would be switched off and Danny would fall asleep within minutes.

Tonight, both of them needed more comfort than that. It had been a difficult day. True, they had had a good time at Kenwood and on the Heath, Danny joining another boy to kick the ball around, and then sitting at the café with big slices of cake and ice cream. Jack's left knee continued to hurt, though, and his thoughts continually made their way back to an unknown human being lying strangely crumpled on the pavement. Whenever they spoke, their conversation gradually made its way back to that subject. On returning home, there had been something disturbing, too, about the phone call with Penny.

They ate dinner in tired, thoughtful silence. Jack did not fall asleep in front of the television. They played a game of chess, which Danny quickly won. Jack held up the Times crossword and a pencil and peered through his reading glasses at the first few clues. Nothing struck him. He ran his eye over the other clues. The cryptic phrases, which normally his mind delighted in prising apart, tonight remained frustratingly opaque. At about nine-thirty, Jack asked Danny what he thought about having an early night. Danny nodded, saying he'd like to go to bed. They went upstairs together, Jack thinking it was sad for the boy to go alone in this unhappy mood.

Stepping into Danny's room, Jack stood helplessly, overwhelmed by the sight. On the shelves and on the floor, tumbling piles of boardgames and comics, books and toys, curious half-finished sand art creations, paints, large sheets of paper daubed with colour, teddy bears, toy guns, and all over the floor pieces of Meccano, Lego, jigsaws, plastic railway tracks winding like spilt spaghetti. His wardrobe doors swung open, revealing clothes not hanging from the rails but lying in heaps. An amazing, all-embracing chaos was taking every item into its arms. On the walls, posters of jet fighter planes contrasted with others of kittens, football heroes and trains.

'Oh my God,' he said at last.

Almost stepping on a small ball, he bent down to pick it up, thinking it might be a glass marble. It was an old chocolate Malteser.

He pointed at some bizarre plastic objects arranged in the middle of the floor. 'What's that?'

'That's my micro-machines. It's like, a war going on.'

'You're not kidding. Mummy really should get someone to tidy up or help her do the cleaning,' he said.

Danny thought for a moment. 'But we do have someone. Dina. Dina comes on Mondays and cleans everything and puts everything away. Didn't Mummy tell you?'

Jack turned with raised bushy eyebrows. 'No, I don't think so. Does Dina do your room?'

'Ye-ees,' Danny replied uncertainly.

'So this balagan, this, this, this,' he gestured, 'All this… happened *in less than one week*?'

'All what?' said Danny, throwing his head back and pouting defiantly.

Jack grimaced. He would ask Penny about Dina. Danny

quickly changed into his pyjamas and disappeared into the bathroom, returning within one minute.

'Have you really cleaned your teeth and washed your face?' Jack queried. 'You were too quick. Show me your hands.'

Danny reluctantly held up grimy, unwashed hands, the nails long and black. 'I did clean my teeth,' he protested.

Jack sent the boy back to the bathroom to wash properly. 'Well,' he said at last. 'Good night, Danny.'

Time for a final worried question: 'Do you think that man had children?'

'Are you still concerned about him? I expect he's better by now.'

'No he isn't,' Danny retorted, 'He's probably dead. He was probably dead when you kissed him. Can you catch death, by kissing?'

'No, that's not possible. Though you could catch a disease, I suppose, which might kill you. Well, you're right, we really don't know if he's alive or dead, do we? And in a way, it doesn't matter. People die, everyone dies, and we can't keep worrying forever about everybody in the world. We have done everything we can to help him, so we did the right thing. Let's not worry about it any more. We have to just carry on being as happy as we can.'

Danny accepted this philosophy and kissed his grandfather's cheek.

'Big hug,' he said.

'Big hug,' Jack agreed. He pulled the duvet up to cover the boy's shoulders. 'Good night, Danny.'

'Good night, Marvelstein.'

Jack put out the bedside light and went downstairs. There he sat at the dining table, wrote a cheque for the parking fine, and put it in an envelope ready to post. Then, with a sheet of paper in front of him, he set to work to check if 130307 was a prime number. Finding at last that indeed it was, he shook his head in bewilderment. 'How can you explain that?' he asked aloud.

He repeated and savoured Danny's pleasing description: '"A number that's like a long poem." And on the back of a packet of coffee, too.'

4

The sun was making interesting patterns of reddish light through my curtains. I wondered how many days Aloo has been looking after me. Or if it has always been this way. I lay in bed watching the patterns and heard Aloo coughing and loudly clearing his throat. He always clears his throat exactly five times. The sound could be annoying. Daddy would definitely find it annoying. But if Daddy was here, Aloo wouldn't be, so – it doesn't matter. I could be annoyed by it too, but I'm not. Aloo gets up very early, about six, even though he hasn't got any work. Later, he goes to the bathroom, cleans his teeth and coughs and clears his throat.

When Daddy is here he gets up early, too, and goes into his work room. He says it's because he has so much to do. Most of the patterns the sun was making were regular polygons, so I tried to find any where the number of sides was a prime number. Heptagons were the nicest. Most, though, were octagons, which made me think of 'organic oats'. Not only because of the Os and As, but they are about the same shape, too, only more organic than oats.

I do miss Mummy and Daddy, but Mummy speaks to me on the phone, and I can phone her whenever I want. If we felt like it, I s'pose we could be on the phone the whole time and never hang up. I can't phone Daddy, he's too ill. I wonder what can be wrong with Daddy. He always says getting ill is a luxury that freelances can't afford. I wonder how much he's paying to be ill.

Anyway it's much more fun being with Aloo than being with *them*. He just messes around all the time, making jokes and giggling. I asked Aloo, is this how you spend your time when you're not with me? He said, no, he likes studying, going to lectures and concerts, helping a charity, walking in the Forest, reading philosophy, doing difficult puzzles and listening to Beethoven. How boring! Staying here must be a brilliant holiday for him!

At breakfast, Aloo – already smartly dressed with his tie done up – had coffee and toast while I ate some organic oats, and counted the number of times the word "organic" appeared on the carton. I called out the numbers to Aloo, while he just sat thinking and ignoring me. 'Fourteen! Fifteen! Sixteen! Seventeen! Eighteen! That's it. It says "organic" eighteen times. Do you think,' I asked, 'somebody decided the most important thing to say about these oats was "organic"?'

I thought he wasn't listening, but he said, 'That's certain. It *is* the most important thing. Do you think these oats would sell just as well if the word "organic" was written just once, in small letters that no one could see?'

So I suggested maybe in that case – first point – they should use the word organic even more times; and – second point – they could sell even more by leaving off the word "oats" altogether.

You can imagine, can't you, a packet that just has "organic" on it, without saying what it was, and people would buy it. Mummy would, for example.

Aloo said the car mechanic would be coming later, but first he wanted to go to the library, and would I like to walk there with him? Definitely I would. He said, let's try to have a nice day today, with no arguments, car breakdowns, parking tickets or saving people's lives. But it's never quite like that with Aloo.

Hanging around with Aloo is so weird. He gets *involved* in everything. At the library, some big boys – they were rough teenagers wearing hooded tops with the hoods up – were making a lot of noise. Actually, it's often noisy in the library, but these boys were laughing and talking loudly and even throwing the library's newspapers at each other for a joke. I think some people were quite scared of them. Grandad Aloo went to the man at the counter and said, 'Can't you ask them to behave?'

The young man at the counter was tall and thin. Everything about him was long and thin, like spaghetti. He had long, straight black hair and a long, thin, girly face with a long, thin nose. He turned his face aside in a funny way and said, 'No, I'm sorry, I can't do that. The library is for everyone. We don't have a rule of silence any more, you know. And anyway, I'm sorry, sir, I don't have that sort of authority.'

Grandad Aloo has a certain look sometimes. You suddenly see how strong he is. He looks like a big block of wood. The front of his lips press together in a sort of angry little smile and his eyes go a tiny bit narrower as if he knows a secret. That's how he was at that moment.

'Oh, don't you?' he said. And he just walked up to these four noisy boys and said 'Get out!' He pointed at the door. It became terribly quiet. Everyone was watching, and I think some people thought Grandad Aloo had gone too far, and some people were scared and thought the boys would hit him.

The boys stared at him without a word. One of them said, 'Fuck off!' and one of the others giggled at that. There was an incredible silence. Aloo just stood quite still and glared, then repeated in a very serious, angry voice, 'Go on! I said get out!' And then I started to think maybe he was going to hit *them*. Because how could he make them leave if they said no? Then a peculiar thing happened. The boys just went out. They sneered at Grandad Aloo, and threw down their newspapers and shouted as they were leaving. One shouted (I'll just whisper it) 'Fucking cunt.'

It didn't seem to bother Aloo much. It was as though he hadn't heard. His face became normal again, and he just went back to reading his copy of The Times, as if nothing had happened. Some of the other people were looking at him. I think a lot of them blamed *him* for the rude words, because if he hadn't interfered, they wouldn't have been shouted. But it seemed as if the only person in the whole library who didn't care what had happened was Aloo himself. Because I know him a bit, I could tell that he really *didn't* care. Then a man came over and shook his hand, and said, 'Well done, sir.' Aloo looked surprised and shook his hand with a friendly expression, but without saying anything. And a lady smiled and nodded.

Mummy and Daddy have told me a million times not to speak to strangers (it isn't really a million; if they told me ten times a day, it would take about 137 years to say it a million times), but Grandad Aloo sets a very bad example. He is always speaking to strangers, getting into arguments, chatting to everyone. I've noticed that Aloo always starts talking to people without even saying 'hello.' Another thing I noticed, when people ask how he is, he just says 'yes' and chuckles.

When we left the library, we started walking home again. We stopped at Golani's for a bagel, and straight away Aloo interrupted someone's conversation about where's the best place to go on holiday, and they found out they were second cousins three times removed or something, and were laughing and shaking hands like crazy. Then as we walked along eating our bagels, we passed a shop where the lady shopkeeper was standing by the door. So he just said to her, 'Everything all right? How's business? Good? Or not so good?' Instead of being surprised at his rudeness, she began to tell him exactly how business was doing. He stopped walking and they had a good long chat, while I wandered around in the shop looking at all the weird stuff – it was a place where ladies go to get their nails done, but there weren't any at that moment.

As we passed the bus stop, he saw a black lady on crutches. Instead of walking past, like any normal person, he stopped beside her and asked, 'What happened to *you*?'

She looked quite suspicious at first. 'I fell down,' she said. She started to tell him how it had happened, but the bus came. When it reached the stop, Aloo went to the front of the queue and got on the bus and said, 'I'm sorry, this lady needs help.' And he got right on the bus with her, and told some people that they had to stand up so that she could sit down, and then he laughed and said, 'Be more careful in future!' and pushed his way off the bus again. She laughed as well and called out, 'God bless you!'

Honestly, it's embarrassing to be with him.

Then in another shop, he told someone in a queue not to push in, when really, it was nothing to do with him. It wasn't even his own queue – it was at another till. Someone did say, it's none of your business, but Aloo answered, 'Everything that happens in this world is everyone's business.'

* * *

Jack sat in an armchair and flicked through yesterday's newspaper as he waited for Yoav, the Israeli car mechanic. He sat upright, unable to relax. At every moment, his mind returned to the man he had helped yesterday. Was he dead or alive, conscious or unconscious? On this fresh, sunlit morning, was he lying in a hospital bed or in the mortuary? He mused about the strange intimacy of their lips touching. Again and again he saw in his mind the butterfly, cut across and bleeding.

He stood abruptly, paced up and down, paused by the bookshelves, glancing at the titles without reading them. He picked up a photo of Simon, Penny and Danny, taken somewhere under blue skies with low mountains behind, studied it and put it back on the shelf. The mood of melancholy that Jack often felt when on his own, with nothing to do, began to creep over him. Now he went to stand by the open window, peering into the street. Danny dashed about in the front garden, 'playing football', as he called it – just kicking a ball around, or doing tricks like bouncing the ball on his knees.

He watched the unrestrained exuberance of the boy and occasionally glanced at a clock on the bookshelves. He noticed that it was a cheap plastic alarm clock, quite unsuitable for a living room. He longed to throw it away and buy a better one.

Danny gave a running commentary on himself as he played. 'Back to Bergkamp' – as the ball bounced off the fence – 'and he shoots' – kicking it furiously into the hedge, shaking a dozen flying insects out of the foliage – 'and that was so nearly the best goal of the match!'

A large white van drew up outside the house and tooted twice cheerfully, the words Overnight Motor Repairs across the side, repeated beneath in smaller Hebrew letters, with a mobile phone number. A handsome, swarthy man, muscular under a tight black tee-shirt, and with very short tight black curls, sprang out of the driver's door. 'Danny!' he yelled at once, clapping with pleasure on seeing the boy.

Jack stepped outside to meet him and explain about the car. 'Yoav,' the mechanic cheerfully announced, wiping a greasy hand on a greasy cloth and proffering the little finger for a token handshake.

'How do you do?' Jack said, uncertain whether to link little fingers, or shake the finger with his hand. He decided on the second course.

'I'm doing good,' Yoav replied earnestly. It took Jack a moment to hear this, not as a declaration of philanthropy or noble humanitarianism, but as an everyday Americanism.

'Hey, Yo, look at this – I can balance a football on my foot for forty-nine seconds,' Danny immediately declared, and promptly tried to do so, while Yoav counted. The ball fell off Danny's foot after just twenty-seven seconds, to Yoav's good-humoured derision.

The Israeli took the ball and began to bounce it. 'And you can do this?' he asked, increasing the speed of the bouncing until the ball became barely visible. Jack and Danny watched, enchanted.

Danny admitted he could not bounce a ball that fast. 'You should write to the Guinness Book of Records,' he suggested quite seriously. 'Where did you learn?'

Yoav shrugged nonchalantly. 'Oh, at the kibbutz. When I was your age.' He pronounced it kibootz. To Jack he added, 'Please sir, would you mind to open the bonnet?'

Jack struggled to understand the hybrid accent. He explained what problems the car was giving.

Yoav listened attentively. Jack sat in the car while the mechanic peered under the bonnet and called instructions – 'Start the motor!' – the 'r's rolling now like a lion purring. 'Give gas!' – 'More!' – 'Less!' – then a big wave of the hand – '*Maspik*![2] Enough, enough, enough! Stop, stop, stop, stop!'

Jack watched uncomprehendingly as the mechanic worked. 'Which kibbutz was it?' he asked. He and Miri had had friends who made aliyah years ago, gone to live on a small kibbutz in the Galilee, in northern Israel. Perhaps it was the same one. It

2 enough (Hebrew)

somehow intrigued and excited him that this man was Israeli.

'You don't know it,' answered Yoav, offhand, head beneath the bonnet of the car.

'What makes you think I don't know it?'

'A small one, in the north of the country,' came the reply.

'Why shouldn't I know it?'

Yoav emerged to challenge him. 'You know Kibbutz Yad Laszlo?'

Jack shook his head.

'So, you *don't* know,' concluded Yoav with a condescending glance.

'I didn't say I knew it,' Jack pointed out, 'I asked *why you think* I don't know it.'

Yoav acknowledged this pedantry with an amiable, respectful nod, and turned back to Danny. 'So what team you support now, Danielle? Still Arsenal? Yes? You are joking? Now I support Man U., best English team. I like to be in the winning side. You prefer to be in the *losing* side. Come on, be winner!'

'I don't change just because my team's not doing so well,' Danny retorted indignantly. 'I'm loyal. Anyway, we'll show you who's a winner, next time Arsenal play Man U.'

'Ach! Put it in a sock!' laughed Yoav dismissively. His mobile phone rang. '*Ken*?'[3] he shouted into it, at once breaking into high-speed, high-volume Hebrew. Jack wanted to put his hand over his ears, or over the phone, but drew back. Yoav seemed unaffected by his glares.

Jack worried what the neighbours were thinking of all this shouting. Yoav yelled a few more words in Hebrew, ending in English with, 'I'm with customer, I'll call you back.' And, without a pause, turning to Danny, 'What have you done to Mummy and Daddy's car, little shovav,[4] eh? Eh? Eh?'

3 yes (Hebrew)
4 rascal (Hebrew)

The manner was high-spirited and boyish, the language a thick, guttural sing-song, the 'r' rolled French-style.

'How come Danny knows you so well – do you do such a lot of work on this car?' Jack asked.

Yoav grinned. 'Who can forget Little Danny the Football Professor?'

Danny pulled an awful face at this strange compliment, and kicked the ball away to continue his solitary 'football match'.

Yoav returned under the bonnet.

It pleased Jack to see a working class Jew, a Jew with dirt under his fingernails. It reminded him of his own father, a tailor who knew hardly a word of English and laboured all day and half the night at a workbench under a bare electric bulb. Here, today, an English Jew wouldn't touch such work. In Israel, he reflected, it was just as the early Zionists had dreamed: car mechanics, street sweepers, fruit pickers, even the prostitutes are Jews. No, come to think of it, Jack realised, maybe in today's Israel, as in Britain, Europe and America, the new ideal is to find foreign workers to fill all those roles.

Casually, but itching with curiosity, he asked Yoav why he had come to live in London.

Yoav emerged again, wiping his hands thoughtfully. He looked down, as if staring gloomily at something on the pavement. 'My wife. My wife was kibbutz volunteer from England. I was soldier on leave. We fall in love and marry. She want to live in England. Next, I am not in the army, I am not in the kibbutz. I am in Stanmore with two English children. In Israel, she love me. In England, she hate me. We divorce. I don't go home, I can't go, because of my kids. I am *allowed*,' he spat the word out bitterly, 'oh yes, I am *allowed* to see my kids two days a week. Worst of all, they don't *want* to see me. Because I do not speak English. And they do not speak Ivrit – not wife, not kids. She marry again. An accountant. Now they are all English Jews, nice Stanmore family. What am I? A nudnik who fix cars. They are ashamed for me.'

'Of course you speak English – very well.'

Yoav sneered at the remark. 'I speak Ivrit, I speak Aravit. Anglit I don't speak.'

'That's a silly thing to say. One day your children will be proud to have an Israeli father. You are a sabra, I suppose?'

'A sabra? What else? Of course! Third generation *b'Aretz*.[5] My grandparents make aliyah from Hungary before Nazi invasion.' Yoav seemed suddenly bored, or angered, by the topic, but he laughed aloud, 'At the end I am here! Poor grandparents, eh?'

Jack shook his head non-committally. 'They escaped; you are alive. Maybe that's enough, who knows? Maybe it will serve a purpose, you being in England. We have yet to see. Nu, what's wrong with the car?'

'I think distributor cup.' For that is what he said.

'What?'

'Distributor cup,' Yoav repeated.

'Never heard of it. Can you fix it?'

Yoav grimaced. 'But there is many problem here. I tell Simon already – matter of time.'

'Should they be repaired now? Or can it wait a bit longer?'

Yoav raised his eyebrows, like a shrug. 'It's as broad as it is wide,' he said. 'You leave it now you must do it by later. But we can make the car to go, and forget the future.'

'Forget the future!' Jack echoed. No wonder Simon enjoyed talking to Yoav! Jack decided to leave the car's deeper problems for Penny and Simon to deal with another day. 'And? Your grandparents joined the kibbutz?' he asked.

Yoav moved suddenly from the car to his van, opening its sliding side door to reveal a whole workshop of tools and

5 "in the Land [of Israel]" (Hebrew)

equipment inside. He stood by the open door, looking inside, frowning, searching for some tool. 'No, they don't join,' he answered with indignation. 'They start new. They are haverim of Zionist group in Hungary – they pioneer the kibbutz.'

Jack tagged along behind. 'My God!' he exclaimed, peering inside the van. Dozens of metal implements were arranged neatly on racks. 'Some of this must be worth a lot of money!'

Yoav agreed.

'Where do you keep it at night? Aren't you worried someone will break into the van?'

Yoav reassured him that at night it was all under lock and key. 'The big problem,' he added, 'is not the night. In the day anyone can come and take something. Maybe thief, maybe anti-Jewish. With knife. Or gun.'

Jack pricked up his ears at this and asked intently, 'What, have you had trouble? From antisemites?'

Yoav shook his head. 'Antisemites? Anti-Jewish? No, never no trouble – not yet. I think English don't know Israelis are Jewish.'

'From thieves, then?'

'No, no trouble. I am ready, that's all. Always ready. Like in the army. Plenty of Mosslemi in London! I must be careful. Londonistan like Arafatistan!'

'Oh, come come! We must not talk like that. Or *think* like that,' Jack warned. 'You think all Muslims are our enemies? Not at all. They are ordinary, decent citizens, like us. People who want a peaceful happy life.' He wondered if he really believed this. It must be so, surely?

'Yes!' Yoav readily agreed, almost shouting. 'Yes! b'emet! *You* talk to *me* about this? I know more than you. Many Mosslemi don't want the jihad, they don't like war. They must be careful. Keep it secret. They must don't *never* let their friends or family or wife or children know. They must to keep very very very quiet, step carefully in case someone find out – that they want to live in peace with Israel. Because that is not allowed for Mosslemi! Watch out what they say. Look who listens. Never relax. Because their jihadi brothers will kill *them*, too, if they find out.'

'And the jihadis hate Israel, especially, don't they, rather than Jews?'

'Of course!' Yoav exclaimed with a big laugh. '*Everyone* hate Israel! *And* Jews! Even the one who don't want jihad – he hate Jews. You know,' he leaned forward as if sharing a secret, 'when people ask, Where you come from, sometimes I say Russia, Hungary, Turkey, anything better than Israel!' Suddenly he let out another great roar of laughter. 'I don't say it, but my advice for all of them – make friend with Jewish. Who fight the Jews can never win. Suppose they win? What does it mean, win? What, they think Jews will go away? Even maybe the whole world help the Arabs to exterminate Israel – they think it will end the story? Jews will come always and always for their land. Why not make friend with the Jews, be happy with us, and better off? But it's impossible, they can never stop hating us. Hating Israel is a drug for the world. They are addict.'

Jack shook his head. He felt nervous about this intemperate style of conversation, these wild opinions. 'I don't know, I don't know. Not everyone is so full of hate, I think. I believe in good people everywhere.' Instantly Yoav responded with a 'Pah!' and a dismissive wave of the hand. 'You are dreamer, John Lennon.'

'Nu, tell me a little bit about your kibbutz,' Jack asked. 'I'm curious. Obviously it was secular. Did you do anything religious at all?'

Yoav shook his head emphatically. 'No, no, no, no, no. We are *secular*,' he said proudly, pronouncing it sekoolar. 'I am four generations sekoolar. My father's father, and his father before him, sekoolar. In Hungary, they sekoolar. On the kibbutz, before Pesach we pile high with bread and put in the freezer.[6] Why be ashamed? Why hide a light under a bissel?[7] We are sekoolar.'

'Well, I agree with you. Of course I do. And now? Do you still eat bread at Pesach? Do you fast at Yom Kippur? Do you do Friday night?' Jack wondered why he was asking such things. Such personal questions! How did he get into this situation? It was years since he had talked so much about being Jewish – if he ever had. That's what you get from an Israeli car mechanic. It was true, as Penny had said, it was totally different from having an English car mechanic. Just how much serious talk could you have with an English mechanic? Or any Englishman, for that matter? But did Yoav think Simon was… or wasn't… Jewish? Simon liked to practise his Hebrew, which must mean he's Jewish as far as Yoav is concerned. Though if he practised his French, would people assume he was French?

'What's to do on Friday night?' Yoav responded irritably. 'When you live alone? You want I should sing kiddush all by myself? Huh?'

'I'm not saying you should make kiddush. I'm not saying anything. But listen, I live alone too,' said Jack, 'and my wife is dead, so don't get so sorry for yourself. But even when she was alive, and when the kids were at home, we did nothing on Friday night. I still do nothing. We ate bread at Pesach and we didn't fast at Yom Kippur. So don't be so defensive. I'm just curious, that's all.'

'OK, Mr Curious – I tell you the truth. When we lived together, my wife light the candles on Friday night. I can't stop her. What can I do, blow the match? We watch television, the kids and me, and she light candles. What harm is it to light couple of candles? But eat matzah all through Pesach? Fast on Yom

6 during the week of Pesach – Passover – bread is forbidden
7 Yoav has mixed up 'bushel' with *bissel* – a little bit (Yiddish)

Kippur? Why? What for? I don't have to prove I am Jewish. I speak Hebrew, I have Israeli passport. I wore the uniform of the Israeli Army, I was in combat. I fight for the Land. You want I must *pray* as well, to prove I am a Jew? Praying is nothing, just words, just pretending. You beat your chest on Yom Kippur, but it is not real, you mean nothing. Going in battle – that mean something. That is real.'

'What did you do in the army? Where were you?'

'Duvdevan. I was *katsin*… I was officer.' Yoav tightened his face inscrutably. 'I was *tzva keva*.' [8]

Jack shook his head. 'Sorry, I've never heard of it. But what did you do? Where were you?'

'Special operations. In Judaea, in Gaza.'

'*Kol hakavod*.[9] I should thank you.' And Jack nodded as if there could be no more to say. But barely a moment later he turned again, jabbing a finger towards the mechanic. 'You think people pray just to prove they are Jewish? What about because they believe in God, eh? What about because they think it is *right* to atone for our human failings? Eh?'

Yoav put his hands on his hips and looked almost angrily at Jack. 'Atone mean kapparah? What rubbish! How can you ask, when you are same like me? But your problem, you think it's *important* to be Jewish. But it's not *important* – it's just what you are.'

'No!' Jack protested indignantly. 'Absolutely not! I never said *I* was Jewish, did I? Did I say I was Jewish? I should be Jewish all of a sudden? You said *you* were Jewish. I said nothing. I was only asking about *you*.'

'What? You are Scottish maybe? Or Chinese? Funny, you

---

8 Sayeret Duvdevan = elite Israeli army unit of fluent-Arabic paratroops engaged in special undercover operations in Arab communities; katsin= an army officer; tzva keva= literally, permanent army, ie. professional soldier (Hebrew)

9 "all honour to you" (Hebrew)

look Jewish. And yes, you think it's important – that's why you keep asking questions,' Yoav disputed. 'But the world is nothing! Life are short. Here today and gone!' – he clicked his fingers dramatically – 'Nothing important! Everything fall in the sun and be… kaput. Jews too.' He slapped his oily hands together in finality. 'You think Jews are special? They're not.'

Jack bit his lip and shrugged. It would be pointless to argue. Anyway, he agreed with Yoav. Instead, he pointed at individual tools around the van, asking what they were for and what they had cost, at each answer softly blowing an impressed whistle. He pointed at a short metal bar attached to another by a length of sturdy chain. 'And that? What is that for?'

Yoav laughed hard and held it up. 'That one I make for our friend the thief and the anti-Jewish. Let them try, eh?' And he gripped one length of bar, swirling the other rapidly around on the end of its chain. 'I don't mind! I never met one of them – the bastards that scare my grandparents in Hungary. I want to meet some of these bastards. I want to give them what it is for, yes? One day.'

Jack raised an outspread hand and pulled his head back warily, 'OK, OK. Calm down.'

Danny played and the mechanic worked. Jack phoned the Royal Free Hospital. Eventually, he was put through to a woman in Emergency Admissions, with an Australian accent as wide and flat as the beach at Surfers' Paradise. No, Jack told her, he didn't have the patient's surname, but knew when he had been brought in, and his first name was Gavin. The Australian was cagey about giving information. It's confidential? she explained. We can't even discuss the patient? Are you family? A friend?

No, he admitted, I'm just a person who helped him, and called the ambulance. 'I'm concerned about him.'

He heard her call out, hand covering the receiver, 'Someone wants to know about the guy in resuss?'

He didn't catch the reply, but she said to him. 'No, I'm really sorry? I can only give information about this patient to his family? Anyway, apparently it was a woman who called the ambulance?'

That's right, it was, he remembered. The woman in the bank. 'Yes, I asked her to call while I was trying to give him mouth-to-mouth on the pavement. He's still a patient, then,' Jack said. 'So he's still alive?'

'I can't tell you,' she insisted, but her tone had softened.

'Will he be all right? That's all I really want to know.'

'It was very good of you to help?' she said. 'Don't worry. He'll be fine.'

'Was it a heart attack, or a stroke maybe?' he asked.

'No. A hypoglycemic attack? He's diabetic? Too little sugar?'

He was surprised that diabetes could cause such a collapse, but said only, 'Maybe I could send him a card.'

Her tone became suddenly cool again, brisk and dismissive. Clearly she felt he now was going too far in his concern. 'Actually, we don't know the name? We're trying to trace his identity?'

Of course, she was right, Jack realised. Sending a card would be a step too far. He must put the incident behind him.

Jack paused to tell Yoav he was going to stroll to the park. As he left, he could not resist asking, 'And your kids – what about them? What are they? Israeli? Or English?'

In reply the mechanic simply held his head as it were bursting. '*Lo ichpat li!*[10] English! Jewish! Israeli! Who cares? Please – no more questions! Please to stop! Mr Silver, I want

---

10 I don't care (Hebrew)

to work. Mr Silver, I want to mend your car. Mr Silver, I beg you, put it in a sock. Please to stop talking. Leave me at peace. Anyway, how should I know what they are? They are all strangers to me. My children are galut[11] Jews. Mr Silver, if you will please to go away. This car will be ready in the time you will come back from the park. If you want to stand here and talk, it will *never* be ready.'

Jack grinned wry agreement, delighted to be addressed in this way. He gestured to Danny to come for a walk with him, and the boy zig-zagged across the pavement making the sound of… a fighter jet? A racing car? Only he knew. The two of them swung their arms as they strolled down the street, Jack making slow progress as his knees hurt, and Danny explaining that they were pretending to be cloned soldiers.

'Cloned soldiers?' Jack repeated.

'Cloning humans is clever,' the boy observed, 'because then you can just make as many soldiers as you need, if you have a war. They'll all be big and strong.'

Good point, thought Jack. Cloning! That's the answer for Israel. More citizens, more soldiers, more workers, more prostitutes – and all hatched from kosher Jewish mothers. 'They'll do it one day,' he grimaced, 'in every country in the world. Can you imagine? China, Iran, Syria… cloned armies on the march.' He saw it vividly in his mind, millions of identical men marching, uniformed, tall, muscular, with blank faces.

The cloned will get rid of the un-cloned.

* * *

Kandersteg was looking its best, the meadows pale green and flower-sprinkled under fresh skies, the rocky escarpments washed and bright. Simon had been given a spacious top-floor

11 diaspora (Hebrew)

corner bedroom facing the mountains on one side and the pretty village church, with stream flowing beside, on the other. Sunlight filled the room, heightening the colours of antique woods, a fine oriental rug on the polished floor, and a huge bed swathed in clean, soft, down-filled white cotton.

Penny was sitting in one of the chairs, beside the bed. Simon sat in the other, facing out of the window. She felt pained to spend time with him in such a place, and yet be unable to enjoy it. She must get him out of here, get some proper advice, get some exercise, get to grips with the situation. She must decide what to do and longed to talk it over with someone. Absurdly, the person she most wanted to discuss it with was Simon himself. She wanted, terribly, to consult him, as she usually would. She wanted to ask, 'Simon, shall we just go home now? Or do you want to go somewhere else where we can relax, just the two of us? Or do you think you need help, like medication? Or are you going to be all right in a few days?'

Having to decide on her own, she supposed the right thing was to travel home the quickest way, whatever the expense. She didn't know how to travel with him. He was unresponsive, wouldn't cooperate, couldn't be trusted to do the simplest thing. He needed to see a doctor, for sure. What actually was wrong with him? Was it mental, physical… emotional, spiritual? Was this a nothing, a blip, an episode that would quickly pass and be forgotten? Or was this serious, a major crack-up, and would he have to be hospitalised? A ghastly idea chilled her – was he dangerous? Or, might he try to commit suicide? She glanced at him, sitting quietly frowning by the window, staring blankly at the mountains, deep in thought. Her heart was wrenched with anxiety and love. She covered her face with her hands, and held back sudden tears.

She thought about friends she could phone. Her great friends. But how great are friends, really? It would be better if such 'friends' didn't know anything was wrong. She tried to imagine talking to them – *Hi, how are you?* – and it just wouldn't work.

'Hi Penny, how are things?' they'd say.

'Well… fine, I suppose,' she'd say. 'I'm in Switzerland with Simon.'

'Lucky thing! But you sound… Is everything OK?'

She would hold back from telling them everything. She couldn't say Simon had refused to eat, that he cried for no reason and couldn't talk. It would damage him forever in their eyes, even when he got back to normal, if he ever did. Better if this episode could pass and be forgotten and never be known about by friends and colleagues. She would describe it as 'exhaustion'. In her mind she asked what they thought she should do with him, how to help him. Because she hadn't been frank about what had happened, their advice was not going to be much use. 'He needs a holiday!' she heard them say, laughing because it seemed as if he was always on holiday anyway. At the same time, it was obvious that people would guess 'exhaustion' covered something deeper than just feeling tired.

It would be even worse with good friends like Louise: she wouldn't be able to deceive her. People only get on well with you if nothing's wrong. If you have a little problem, they can show concern. It can be a nice little topic for a cosy, girly chat. As soon as you have a big problem, they want to distance themselves from it. That's reasonable – problems are catching. What about her mother? She tried it in her mind – 'Mummy, what shall I do about Simon?' No, that wouldn't work either; her mother was hopeless at such things, especially now she was losing her grip on reality. As for her father, no one could discuss anything with him. Besides, parents always regard their children's partners with suspicion, even after years of marriage. To hear that one of them had gone crazy would merely confirm their doubts.

Who else was there? She had left her address book at home. Most of her friends' numbers were programmed into her mobile phone. In Simon's luggage she found his own little travelling address book, which listed a few editors and useful contacts, and members of his family. While Simon sat in dark daydreams in the armchair, she lay on the bed and allowed her thoughts to drift through the pages of her forgotten address book, and across a mental map of Europe, searching for friends. She found memories of people she had known in the past, places she had visited with Simon. Slipping to the edges of an afternoon doze, she imagined going to her parents' house, ringing the bell and asking them for advice. Vividly she pictured the door opening and walking through it, into her childhood home.

There Mummy and Daddy would hug her, and she them. She saw herself as a little girl, and her parents young again. The house was comfortable and well-padded with rugs and soft furnishings, brocade, and heavy drapes. In the hall, kitsch, sentimental prints hung in ornate gilded frames. A chandelier twinkled and scattered coloured refractions. She ran up the stairs to her bedroom. Although everyone loved her, all was not well, and she shut the door to think and be on her own. But there was a gentle knock on the door and a quiet voice. 'It's Auntie Hilda. Can I come in?' How she was soothed to hear that friendly voice.

Penny woke up, feeling groggy. She hated sleeping during the day. She needed a cup of tea. Simon seemed not to have moved at all. He still gazed grimly towards the mountains without seeing them. How long had she slept? She rummaged for her mobile to see the time, but it wasn't within reach. Yes, what a good idea – Auntie Hilda! She would phone her. Damn! She couldn't – she had forgotten her address book.

Penny told the hotel that Simon would like to keep the room an extra week if possible, and said she would of course happily pay for the whole two weeks, since it was obvious that he had not been working and had not written anything. It would be a huge sum. No, the kindly German owner had insisted, Simon had helped them so much in the past – the hotel had featured in a cross-country skiing piece he wrote – and they were sure he would be hard at work again in the future when the crisis had passed. Penny 'explained' that Simon was grieving for his mother, who had recently died. It was a ridiculous lie that could be quickly found out, but she had not been able to come up with anything better. She dressed as normal, ate meals as normal, ordering the simplest, plainest dishes and feeling irritated by the hotel's holiday mood. She had no desire to enjoy its renowned cuisine, or try Swiss wines, or linger over coffee and pastries.

If Penny was at the end of her tether, Simon was far beyond the end of his. The tether had snapped. He joined her on the bed, where he lay face down, a large, soft pillow over his head. He had abandoned any attempt at grown-up dignity. It was a ghastly, abominable, extraordinary sight. Always, until now, Simon had personified the intelligent, informed adult. He possessed a charming, ironic, disdainful scepticism. His face hinted at a rigorous intellect and strength of mind which intrigued and attracted her. Tender, considerate, yet he gave an impression of rigidity and firmness. With brisk short hair and clean, sharp features, thoughtful, penetrating eyes behind glinting metal-framed glasses as thin as a pencil line, he looked, someone had once said, like 'Lenin in love'. From his father he had inherited a robust, constantly questioning intellect; from his mother, a ceaseless energy. From both, inner fire and independence of mind. More highly educated than either of them, he was also more taciturn. When going about his work, he was resolutely professional.

Penny felt deeply happy to know this man, without his masks, hearing his secret certainties and uncertainties and complaints and desires. He could be irritating, yet she regarded it as a privilege. She always cautiously and sensibly answered his many requests for advice. Especially, he wanted help understanding how things were done between people, what they would think about this or that detail of dress or speech, what should be said, what he should project to this one and that one, as if he had been brought up in a different world where there were no people. Lean, tense and strong, Simon's slender body perfectly matched his temperament. She loved him with a passion.

Penny reached to put a hand on him.

'Dear Simon,' she said very softly. 'Tell me what happened.'

He did not reply.

'What do you feel? Are you angry? In pain about something? I'll do everything I can to help you. Can you talk to me? It will probably help to talk.'

Now she heard his voice, quiet and muffled: 'Shut up. Leave me alone.'

It was such an unusual response from him that she nearly smiled.

She tried quite a different approach: 'Are you aware that you have stopped functioning normally? Can you explain why? It would help me to know – I have to try and keep life going for myself and Danny.'

He sat up angrily, throwing off the pillow. 'Danny, Danny, Danny! Stop trying to use Danny to blackmail me.' He held the sides of his head.

She gasped with something like shock and grasped his hand. She felt almost that it could hardly be Simon who had said those words.

'Look at me, Simon,' she implored him. 'I haven't come to make things worse for you. If mentioning Danny was the wrong thing, please, why don't *you* do the talking? Tell me when this thing started.'

Now he sobbed, which tore at her. Very occasionally he had been moved to tears – perhaps more often since his mother died – and in the past Penny had been able to comfort him. This was different, a wild, uncontrolled sobbing, like grief. 'Anyway,' he said at last, softly, 'I can't talk. It hurts my face.'

It was true. When he spoke, his heart raced, the muscles around his cheeks seized up. His teeth could hardly be prised apart. His breathing became too shallow to form words. Sweat prickled his forehead.

Penny lay down on the bed beside him and put an arm over him. 'Let's talk very, very slowly and quietly. We'll take our time. We'll stop whenever you want. Whisper it to me – through clenched teeth if you like. When did this start?'

But Simon had closed his eyes and was far away, walking, walking, walking alone in cool air under a dark sky, in forests, in streets, beside water, he knew not where. And Penny was scared, wondering where Simon had gone, and when and whether he would return.

But he would return. Already, at the back of his mind, the mood was softening. Penny's presence in the room, for hours at a time, brought speech closer to him. And later, after dark, when she suggested a walk around the hotel grounds, though panic rose in him at the thought, slowly he nodded.

* * *

The red light was flashing. Danny showed Jack how to operate the answering machine. Straight away, they heard Penny's voice and Danny became attentive and motionless. Jack hoped her message would not disturb the boy and was uncertain how to protect him as they stood there, quietly listening. However, she seemed to have had a similar thought.

The voice was bright and good-humoured. 'Hello, Danny

and Aloo,' she began, 'You must have gone out somewhere. I've seen Simon, and he's not very well, but he'll be all right after a while. I'm going to stay here for a bit and look after him. Aloo, remember we talked about keeping Simon's working life running normally? Checking his email? Well, could you look in his diary for me? It's in his room. Can you let me know what's in it for the next week or so? And I need something for myself, from my address book. Well, I'll speak to you about that when you call. And Danny, I hope you're having a lovely time with Grandad Aloo. Don't forget you can make arrangements to see any of your friends. If you want to ask me anything or talk to me, call me at the hotel.'

The other messages were of just the type she had mentioned. One about an invitation already sent and no answer received – could he come. Another, a hassled young woman asking Simon to call about editorial for the next issue. The third, a supercilious male voice asking Simon Silver to call the travel desk at The Times. There seemed to be a suggestion that he would obviously call at once.

Jotting them down, Jack was surprised how many messages Simon received. That was not all. Soft, feminine American tones said she would call again – it was about next week's discussion on Secular Judaism. She was sure Simon would have much to contribute. Now followed the young man at The Times again, rather peeved this time, asking if Simon could call *this afternoon* if possible. There was still more: a warm, masculine voice spoke about Simon being behind schedule, a woman invited him to join a trip to Italy. The machine clicked and whirred and finally uttered an unlikely American voice, 'End of final message'.

'Does Daddy always get so many messages?' Jack asked.

'Oh, yes,' said Danny. 'He just deletes most of them. He gets lots of letters, too. But I think he throws most of them away too without really reading them.'

'I must give your Mummy a call. But first let's go and check Daddy's diary and his email, shall we?'

Watching as Jack scrolled through Simon's inbox, Danny said, 'I thought old people weren't any good with computers.'

'Don't know much about me, do you, boychick?'

'OK, tell me something I didn't know about you.'

Jack chuckled. 'Well, it looks as though maybe you didn't know that I was one of the world's top computer experts. But computers were very different in those days. They were huge. And they didn't use words, only numbers. And only two numbers – zero and one. And there were only a few in the world. I'll tell you more about it in a few years time when you've got your maths 'A' level.'

'It's funny,' Danny mused, 'a person's life is hidden inside them and can't be seen from outside.'

* * *

Didn't you always say I was nosy? I've pored over the pages of his diary; I've been reading his letters, the faxes and emails he's sent, and the replies. Yesterday evening after Danny was in bed, I spent hours on it, opening files on his computer, looking at his internet history, sorting through his papers.

I know it's wrong to pry, Miri. But we need to find out what happened to our little boy, don't we? I hardly remember what he was like – I didn't pay much attention. I was as busy working then, as he is now. I think I remember a nice, bright, cheerful little lad. Had a fringe, didn't he, and a dimple in one cheek? I can picture little Simon in his grey flannel short trousers, with a graze or two on his knees, a bruise on a shin, and that smile, his raggedy hair and dazzling, intelligent eyes. A good boy, he was, enthusiastic and eager, quick. Or was that my little brother? Or am I thinking of Daniel? I don't really remember him, Miri. I think everyone had high hopes for Simon. He was bright. But they have high hopes for all kids, don't they? All parents think their kids are bright. Today, there's something wrong with our little boy. Seriously wrong. Why is that?

This much I can tell you: Simon meets a lot of people, writes a lot of articles, goes to a lot of events, sends a lot of emails. But what is wrong with him – that I can't tell you. And what on earth is Secular Judaism? What is he getting mixed up in? He goes to meetings and lectures on Secular Judaism and Jewish Socialism – why?

Miri, I'm sorry, but I hardly know who Simon is. He's just a man, any man. A stranger. Maybe, as his mother, you feel differently towards him. He's still your baby, after all. But you know, I realised that I never saw Simon's office before, his work room. Not just this one in their new house, but in their old place either, I never once saw his place of work. Funny – that's when your child really has grown up and left you, isn't it? They have rooms and spaces and places in their life that you never see or know about.

Simon's room is small, cramped, full of paper, brochures, work in progress, with shelves covering two walls loaded with books and files. On another wall, scores of pieces of paper pinned or taped up: notes, lists, of names, numbers, articles, dates, addresses, computer file numbers, some with colour coding.

I haven't a clue what's the matter with him. Penny asked me to think back, try to throw some light on what's happened. I do remember that when he was Danny's age, he'd play truant, and be brought back to school by a policeman. He never liked being cooped up, did he? He didn't like sitting in class with the others. He wanted to go his own way. He was always an outsider.

Forty years later, the emails he receives are full of polite, friendly rejection.

He makes suggestions for articles. Winetasting in Cyprus? A walk in the Amazon jungle? The quiet side of Ibiza? Time-warp hippy hideaways? A heritage centre in the New Forest? Beaujolais at Nouveau time? Kids' Paris? Routes to the Med? Christmas Markets within a three hour drive of Calais? The Great Lakes? Motor-homing in Australia? Gambling Casinos on the Indian Reservations? A jazz festival in Italy? The murals of Derry? Still no. He just churns out ideas like tickertape in the hope that something will grab someone's attention.

It's hard to know if they were answered. Most don't seem to have had replies. Maybe he doesn't keep them. Sifting back through the Inbox, though, there is a steady flow of messages all saying thanks, but no thanks. The reply is that they did it already. The answer is they asked someone else to write it. He wonders if they know about the amazing, unforgettable this or that. The answer is, it's not for them.

Perhaps Simon doesn't mind, perhaps it's just normal in his line, but I'd feel a bit cut up at sending out scores of faxes and emails and receiving so few replies. Then one says *Yes, I want that*, and all of a sudden there's a spurious urgency. Not only do they want it, but they wanted it last week.

From this he makes a living? Yes – and somehow, he does make a living. I see that the document he's been working on most recently is an article called Under the Redwood Tree, about walking in California. You'd enjoy it. And it appears that he's also writing a guidebook to Burgundy. It's hard to see when he works on Eurotravel magazine. I see there's a Eurotravel editorial meeting every month or so. For a travel writer, he's not away as much as I thought. The last trip was last month, when he spent three days in Burgundy. In May, he was in California.

That must be when he walked under the redwood trees. Penny and Danny went with him on that one. It looks a good life, for them at least. Apart from the deadlines and rejections, I almost envy him.

So what's wrong?

On the shelves, a dozen display folders bulge with cuttings dating back nearly twenty years. For years, we kept all his cuttings, didn't we, proud parents! Since you died, Miri, he's even more productive, and I don't bother with the cuttings. I admit it: I don't kvell like you over his success. Of course, I'm glad he's done well. But what with the TV programmes as well, I'm getting quite used to having a famous son.

This week, I see he's written something about Constable Country in the Observer, and Cycling in Normandy in the Standard. Two articles in one week is also not bad! Does anyone read them? I never do. But then, I'm not interested in Constable, and I'm not about to go cycling in Normandy, or anywhere else.

So I sit in the garden wondering what to make of Simon's breakdown. The obvious thing is that he must be suffering from overwork. People do work much harder nowadays. And what he does is worrying. After each job, you just have to hope there will be another. Yet – work doesn't really explain it. Other people also work hard and have plenty to worry about. Look at me! But did I have a breakdown?

What I'd really like to do is go there now, to that hotel in Switzerland, and see him for myself. But I'd have to take Danny. And that, of course, is precisely why I'm here and can't go there: Penny doesn't want Danny to see Simon. She doesn't want him to know what has happened to Simon. But can it be so bad?

While I'm pondering, Danny dashes into the garden to join me. He looks truly and perfectly boyish, with his khaki shorts, his tee-shirt and tanned, skinny limbs, and tousled hair in urgent need of a trim, and a smile of unalloyed joy, just like Simon at the same age. Yes, I think I do remember, after all.

'You look glum, Grandad,' he says. 'Are you glum because Daddy is ill? Don't be glum. I've tried being glum, and it doesn't work.'

5

He looked uncertainly into a crowded Piccadilly. Jack hadn't been here for years. At first he walked the wrong way, towards Hyde Park, before realising his mistake and turning round. The balmy freshness of the early morning was now altogether gone, replaced by heavy summer heat. The sun blazed, buses and taxis edged forward slowly, pumping exhaust. The warmth and dirt gave the static air a physical presence; he felt it brush his face, rather pleasantly. Alongside Piccadilly, in Green Park, office workers lay or sat in hundreds, enjoying a sunbathing lunch break, girls immodestly sprawled or cross legged, some stripped to the flimsiest of underwear, unaware – or aware – of the men stationed just a yard in front or behind. Suit jackets were folded, shirts unbuttoned to the waist, polished shoes removed. The men pretended to eat a sandwich or read a newspaper while they gazed intently.

Jack tried to straighten his tie. Sunbathing he did not understand. A goyish activity if ever there was one. Where did it get you? And stripping off – why? He regarded it as exhibitionism, plain and simple: a perversion. On the other hand, he knew that as a younger man he too would have enjoyed a close look at some of these underdressed shiksas. Even now he wouldn't mind.

For the moment he had other concerns: he himself was overdressed, for the weather and for the occasion. He had not brought a suit to London, and hadn't been expecting to need one. He was not wearing his corduroy cap today, but a sports jacket really wasn't appropriate either, he knew. Maybe he'd be excused on the grounds of being an old buffer.

Penny had told him to do this, but he remained full of doubt. Reading Simon's diary entries aloud on the phone, he had blandly informed her, 'First of all, the Travel Trade News Summertime Lunch at Le Meridien, this Friday.' He didn't mention that he already knew what was in Simon's diary.

'Oh my God,' she said, 'he really should go to that. He's promised he would. It's important.'

'Are you sure it matters all that much?' Jack had said. 'Can't he just say something has come up?'

'I really don't know,' she said, 'I'm just not sure what to do.'

In the end, she considered this a 'must do' engagement and they agreed Jack would attend on Simon's behalf. Penny would make the arrangements with the PRs – the press relations people who organised the event.

An instinct told Jack it wasn't the right approach.

'No, no, it's not unusual,' she reassured him. 'Sometimes an invite is addressed to a publication rather than an individual.'

'An invite?' Jack queried. 'You mean an invitation?'

'Yes. Or it's to the editor, but editors are always sending someone else along instead. The invite sometimes actually says you can send someone else, a deputy. Simon told me there was one travel editor who sent his car mechanic on a foreign trip in exchange for a free service. Mind you, he said that was going too far.'

'But in Simon's case,' Jack said uncertainly, 'surely it's him they want to see?'

'Ye-es, that's true – but the trouble is,' Penny replied, 'he needs to be on the list of people who attended the lunch. You might think Simon's doing well, but he says you have to stay close to "the power and the purse strings", as he calls it. The editors have power, the travel trade hold the purse strings. At least if you go,' she said, 'they'll be reminded of him, and he'll be on the list of people who attended. But don't, whatever you do, don't tell them there is anything wrong with him. Tell people he had to dash off unexpectedly to a meeting in Switzerland. It will only enhance his image. The fact that you're his father might work, too. It's the sort of unconventional gesture Simon is expected to make sometimes. So long as you do the job properly, no one will mind.'

'What is the job, exactly?'

'Oh, you know – eat, drink and shmooze. But don't, absolutely don't, get drunk, though I know you're not likely to, Aloo! Be polite, shake hands with the Minister of Tourism – yes, he'll be there. Give people Simon's cards and say Simon's name about ten times to everyone. For goodness sake, though, please don't let on that he's not well. Say you're Simon Silver's father; it will interest them.' He could hear she was trying to sound cheerful.

'What do you mean by "cards"? Business cards?'

'Yes, there's a whole stack of them by the front door. And in his working room. Don't you remember? You noticed them when you arrived at the house. Simon Silver, travel writer and editor. This is a big, smart do, prestigious. It's an annual thing, always at the end of July, no expense spared. It's important, because it's one of the few things that travel editors go to en masse, and where only the best of the freelances are invited. And it's the only event of its kind during the summer.'

'Anyone in particular I should speak to?'

'Editors and travel editors. They're perfectly ghastly, most of them, but freelances have to stay on the right side of these people. Part of Simon's job is being on good terms with them and putting himself about. Especially say hello to Ernest Bully from the Mail-on-Sunday. Give Simon's regards to Sally Forth from the Standard and Anita Pilbert-Oroquin from the Observer. Do you want to make a note of those names? Some of them are very young, just children really, and they don't really know Simon. They're the new generation, and he's the old.'

'Simon is old already?' Jack shot back, 'What does that make me?'

'Aloo, you're beyond old – you're retired. A senior citizen. You're the grey dollar. But Simon's old enough that he must work even harder to stay in the same place. Basically, look at the lapel badges and if you've heard of the publication, say hello from Simon. Please, Jack, don't discuss Simon's health or his state of mind, or anything like that. Oh, yes, I think he said he was hoping to meet someone from a new TV travel programme, Paradise.'

'But there's something more than a lunch? There's a presentation, speeches?'

Penny laughed, a little falsely. 'Basically, it *is* just about lunch. And shmoozing. Oh, and Aloo,' she added, 'have you had the car done yet?'

He told her he had. 'It was the distributor cup.'

'Distributor *cap*, I think, isn't it?' she corrected him.

'Cup, cap – what do I know? I'm only telling you what your chap told me.'

When she put the phone down, Penny could not remember if she had explained clearly enough that Jack should act with dignity and restraint, not get drunk, and not let on that Simon has some kind of problem. Still, he would be sure to do the right thing, she told herself anxiously. And damn – she had forgotten to ask him to look up Auntie Hilda's number.

Arriving at the hotel, he stepped suddenly into a cool, opulent world. He marvelled that Simon was used to such places as part of his work, while he – Dr Jack Silver – had only ever been inside a hotel like this on the rarest of simchas and celebrations. Their big anniversaries, special birthdays, long-ago weddings and barmitzvahs. He imagined Miri on his arm, shapely and stylish in a nice dress, the years restored to them; he was just fifty again. No – forty, thirty years old, and Miri in her twenties. He turned to her with a grin. 'What do you think, eh, darling? Nice place for a cup of tea?' he said under his breath, almost seeing her lovely smile once more. He glanced around with her, admiring the polished woodwork, the uniformed staff.

A pretty girl, her face, her hair and smile as radiant and uplifting as sunshine, helped him fix a badge with the name Simon Silver onto his lapel. After the first glass of champagne, handed to him by another pretty girl just as soon as he had signed in, Jack quickly realised he was thoroughly enjoying himself. He rarely drank champagne, even at simchas – it wouldn't even cross his mind to do so. Walking with his golden, frivolous drink into a vast stuccoed room with huge glittering chandeliers, he looked around at the crowd and once again marvelled that his son should be accustomed to such things.

Everyone else was so much younger than himself. It often struck him. Here, the oldest among them were not much more than his son's age, forty-seven. And it was true that others were not dressed like him, but not as he had imagined: several of the men weren't even wearing jackets, and some didn't even have ties. Open-necked, short-sleeved shirts seemed acceptable, perhaps only because of the weather. Many had casual shoes that he wouldn't wear to do the gardening (not that he would ever do any gardening). There was a convivial, relaxed atmosphere, but English-style, with hardly a Jew in sight.

Again Jack experienced a wave of pride and disbelief that his own son should be so completely, so successfully assimilated. Some people standing close by greeted each other loudly and, when he turned to look, one of them noticed his badge.

'Any relation to the other Simon Silver?' she asked, puzzled. It was a dumpy, forty-something woman encased tightly in a good linen suit. She had tired eyes, lanky hair and coarse skin.

Jack made as if to look with surprise at his lapel badge – hers said Marion Papier, Travel Editor, The Guardian. He introduced himself amiably, admitting that his name was Silver but not Simon.

'Maybe it should say Jack Silver, Father,' he suggested, and she looked surprised and amused. 'You're really his father? He sent his father?'

'Of course. Why not?'

'Were you a journalist, too? Or are you still, I should say?' She looked him over, focusing on his reading glasses, hanging on a cord around his neck. She glanced at his pale, watery eyes, the eyes of an elderly man.

Jack shrugged, as if to say, *Who's a journalist?* And he explained, as he had been told to by Penny, that the real Simon was at an editorial meeting in Switzerland. He could see that Marion Papier did not think that justified sending a relative. Jack wondered if Penny had made a blunder. Perhaps his presence here would be damaging to Simon.

Another woman in the group, short, well padded, nicely turned out, beautifully coiffed, held out her hand. 'I use Simon, he's one of my regulars.' It made his son sound like a gigolo. He peered at the name on her bosom: Ruth Fine, Jewish Chronicle. Their eyes met for an instant as each acknowledged the Jewishness of the other in this goyish gathering. 'Nice to meet you.'

A man in a dark, well-cut suit had moved to the door, and

began greeting some of the arrivals by name, shaking their hands warmly. Perhaps he was the host. Suddenly he stepped in their direction and greeted Marion almost too fondly with a kiss on the cheek. It was easy to see that his apparent joy was underlain by certain calculations that Jack knew nothing about.

Jack found himself among a large group swapping anecdotes. Journalists' misdemeanours, someone had slept with someone on a recent press trip to Florida. Jack felt awkward, thinking that just as such things cannot be discussed in front of children, so too it is wrong to mention them in front of old people. But he was saved as one tall, thoughtful man changed the mood with a tale about his trip to a Maasai village. Jack could not remember who or what the Maasai were, but – for Simon's sake – restrained himself from asking. He found the alcohol going to his head and vowed to continue only with fizzy water, but his champagne was immediately topped up, and he did not resist.

Soon, rosy-cheeked, gesticulating and becoming a little too loud, Jack found himself doing most of the talking, as the group clustered round to trade jokes, tall stories and gossip. A wine waiter came by with a bottle of champagne. Jack held out his glass and said to the man, 'Why do you keep going away and coming back again? Just stand there, with that bottle. That's right.'

At lunch, people were seated at named places around large circular tables richly laden with glasses, silverware and thick white napery. At each place was a small gift, which, Jack noticed, some of the journalists pushed aside without interest, while others eagerly tore open the wrapping. It was a transparent spherical paperweight engraved with the words Travel Trade News. He offered it to the well-spoken young woman on his right.

'Such a nice gift,' he said. 'Would you like two?'

She held his arm lightly. 'Where do they find such things! Are they made specially for us? In Third World sweatshops?' She chuckled conspiratorially, as if that were an amusing thought, and craned to peer at his name on the place setting. He seemed… not shabbily dressed, far from it, but… artlessly, inappropriately, with his tweed jacket, as if he thought he was going out for a walk on a blustery autumn afternoon rather than to a lunchtime celebration in high summer. And he was too old to be here, surely old enough to have retired long ago – was he a gatecrasher, perhaps? Or some eccentric, world-famous writer? An ex grandee editor? To her surprise, the name read Simon Silver.

'You're not Simon Silver!' she protested amiably. 'Did you swap places with him?'

Again Jack explained. They exchanged business cards, he pointing out that he must be Simon Silver because it said so on his card. The young lady's name was Larissa Lunt, and she was editor of a new weekly television programme on eco-tourism, or 'green travel', called Paradise. The name rang a chord in his mind, but he did not know why.

'I think I've heard of it. I'm not sure,' Jack confessed. 'Is the name ironic? Or naïve?'

'Naïve? Moi?' She looked at him with amused caution. 'What do you mean?'

'Paradise Lost or Paradise Found?' he replied quickly, glancing sharply into her eyes. 'Or just a travel show with a twist of green?'

Taken aback, she said, 'Both lost and found, I suppose. It's a little bit ironic,' and she wondered if they could use him on the programme in some way. This old man wasn't the duffer he looked. 'We try to deal seriously with places, mentioning what life is like there, what people do for a living, the impact of tourism and so on, while still using white beaches, blue seas and colourful locals.'

'Oh, I see,' he nodded. 'Prick consciences, while still encouraging tourism?'

She bit her lip and smiled. No, they could never use such a truculent, argumentative voice. Her neighbour on the other side caught her attention, and she turned away.

For the first time Jack noticed the serious-looking, rather overweight but attractive woman on his left.

'Cathy Pincher,' he read, from the name card in front of her. 'What do you do, Cathy?'

She took out a business card and handed it to him. He offered her one of Simon's in exchange, but she waved it away. 'It's OK, I don't need a card. I'm a freelance writer, like Simon. I'm quite often sat near him at do's like this, because we're both vegetarians. I see he doesn't get that from you.'

Jack opened his eyes wide. 'I didn't know Simon was a vegetarian. Are you sure?'

'Quite certain!' Cathy exclaimed. 'I've travelled on many press trips with your son, and he won't eat the meat. I've met his wife, too, your daughter-in-law – what's her name? Ginny, Jenny?'

'Polly, isn't it? Or was it Penny?' he replied uncertainly.

'Penny, yes. Silver penny – how could I forget such a name! She's a vegetarian too. Nice lady. Simon's an interesting guy. Very guarded. But nice. And a very hard worker. He's good, too. A real artist. In fact, it's my ambition to be as good as him. Or at least,' she laughed, 'to get as much work as him.'

'That's your ambition? To be like Simon?' Jack felt mildly flattered. 'Of course I'm much too old to have any ambition myself. I'm so old I can't even remember if I realised my ambitions. Though I suppose without any ambition at all, one dies. At my age, ambition can mean only the desire to see tomorrow. I haven't read any of Simon's work. Is he really so good? Travel writing doesn't interest me. I'm a mathematician.'

She chuckled merrily at this outpouring, with its final confession. 'I wouldn't say that too loudly here. They might throw you out. But I'm not sure about your theory that it's just the desire to live that keeps people alive. Some people wake up in the morning and find they are still alive, and perhaps wish they weren't.'

'True.' He thought of the Holocaust.

A curious dessert was being served, a black ice cream which according to the menu should be called pepper glacé. One or two people said it didn't work, and was a mistake. Jack took a spoonful then pushed his aside. Cathy, too, after a single spoonful, left her pepper glacé untouched. 'I don't mind it being black,' she said. 'But I prefer my ice cream sweet at least.' She glanced at him. 'So don't mathematicians go on holiday?'

There seemed something almost coquettish about her manner. He could not help responding to it, which made him feel amusing and attractive, and at the same time, absurd. He suspected that he was being a silly old fool whose drink had gone to his head. 'I didn't say that. Mathematicians also dream. But you said Simon is an artist. Presumably the best travel writing is also a science? Doesn't it deal in facts?'

A man at some distant table was tapping the side of his glass with a spoon. A good-humoured silence gradually fell as he stood waiting to address the gathering.

Jack turned and whispered to young Larissa on his right. 'Who's this chap?' He wanted a break from Cathy Pincher's appealing flirtatiousness.

She said it was the French Minister of Tourism. 'Because the French are sponsoring the lunch this year, look' – and she pointed at gold-embossed words on the menu. Clearly accustomed to giving such speeches, the minister thanked 'members of the British press'. Jack's mind wandered as figures, facts and more figures were intoned and soothed him almost to sleep – market, the UK, leading position, over 60 million arrivals.

Leaning pleasantly towards him, so close that he felt her breast resting against his arm, Larissa hissed into his ear. 'They massage the figures, you know. You know, to enlarge them.' She giggled. He had not touched a woman's breast since Miri died.

The minister finished by commenting on the excellent meal. Had the food been that good? Jack could not remember. He felt people were clapping the man's Frenchness. He picked up a gold-embossed menu to remind himself what he had eaten. Terrine de poissons à la crême de ciboulette. Fish terrine! Yes, very nice. Aiguillette de boeuf au gros sel. That must have been the beef, he supposed. Brie de Meaux – of course, that was squidgy cheese. The Minister of Tourism sat down to general applause.

Plates of petits fours were brought to each table, coffee was served. Holding her cup, the woman on his left, Cathy, politely asked him, 'What exactly is this editorial meeting that Simon must attend in Switzerland?'

'Do you know,' he answered, 'I have absolutely no idea.'

'You really don't know much about your son, do you?' she chided him, as though wondering whether he might be an impostor. 'You don't know he's a vegetarian, or the name of his wife, or what he's doing in Switzerland. Are you really his father?'

'I know that he earns his living, pays his bills, and cares for his family. What else is there to know about a son?'

She raised her eyebrows. 'Is that all there is, then?'

With a shake of the head, Jack made a wry, melancholy expression. 'Yes, that's all. Our trouble is, we think there's more to life. We think we are something greater than… than bugs in the garden.'

Cathy raised a bemused eyebrow at the way the conversation was going. This old man could give any subject a too-philosophical turn. 'Oh, but we are, surely,' she said. 'What about art, for example?'

'Yes, yes, it's true, isn't it? You're right. We are something more than worms.' Jack reconsidered. 'Art raises us above the animals.'

'And love?' she wondered aloud. 'No,' she replied to herself, 'love dies. But art goes on forever. Jesus, I've never talked like this at a press lunch before. Shall we talk about the travel industry? No, of course not, you're a mathematician, aren't you? Shall we talk about numbers?'

'Yes, people do die,' Jack nodded. 'But I don't hold that against them. Some of my best friends are dead. So you are an artist?'

'No, no. I'm the sort of ignoramus who only "knows what she likes."'

'Yes, and?' he asked.

'I know nothing – but music must be the most human of all things, isn't it?'

'No,' he said. 'Birds have music. Whales have music. Who knows, maybe even the worms in the garden make music. They also make love. But art they don't have.' He noticed that many people were standing up and leaving. 'Is it time to go?'

'Yes. It's past three o'clock.' Abruptly, she stood up herself, feeling that she must end this ridiculous discussion. 'Well, give my regards to Simon. When will he be back?'

'Oh, we don't know,' Jack replied carelessly, getting up from his chair. 'When he's well enough.'

Cathy frowned. 'Why, what's wrong with him? You said he was at an editorial meeting.'

Larissa also chipped in. 'Did I hear you say Simon is unwell?'

'No, no,' Jack said anxiously. 'He's perfectly all right, I was thinking of someone else.' He beamed and held out his hand. 'Lovely to meet you. Don't forget your balls – your paperweights, I mean.' The two women laughed together.

Jack walked to the lift with Cathy Pincher. As they left, they were each given a small paper carrier containing a press pack and another gift. They didn't look inside. 'How old are you?' she asked. 'You don't seem old enough to be Simon's father.'

'I'm eighty.' Even to him it sounded impressively ancient.

She looked him up and down. 'You're very fit,' she commented. 'What's the secret?'

'Interesting idea, that,' he replied. 'The idea of a secret. Secret knowledge. The secret of youth, of health, of happiness. The secret of life, of the universe. The secret which we common folk do not have. Where does this idea of a secret come from, do you suppose? The Greek myths? Christianity? Or is it simply part of the human condition?'

Cathy grimaced painfully at this too-weighty response to her light-hearted remark. As the lift doors closed behind them, she looked puzzled. 'Just tell me again – is there something the matter with Simon? Why are you being so cagey?'

'I'm not being cagey at all. I'm insisting that he's perfectly well, aren't I? But I literally don't know. I think it's happiness, not health, that's the problem.' As he heard the words slip out, he could have bitten his tongue.

'Has the great Simon Silver got problems? Tell me it isn't true,' Cathy said with a subdued note of glee. 'He's the freelance role model. It can't be money – he's doing better than any of us. Is everything OK between him and Penny?'

Jack looked troubled. 'Of course it is! What a thing to ask! I don't think he has anything wrong at all. He just fancied a bit of a break, I suspect.'

Cathy listened thoughtfully. The lift doors opened and they walked out into the hotel's quiet, opulent foyer. Suddenly Jack realised he was quite drunk. 'Is it a stress thing?' she asked. 'Overwork?'

He shrugged. 'Maybe.' He felt miserable and angry with himself. He had been under strict orders not to mention that there was anything the matter with Simon, and here he was discussing it openly.

As they left the air-conditioned chill of the hotel, a warm, heavy humidity enveloped them. It felt stormy; Jack glanced at the sky. The sun was vanishing behind banks of shifting haze. They stood on the noisy Piccadilly pavement as weary tourists pushed past them. 'Shame about Simon,' Cathy said. She looked sympathetically at Jack: 'If it's a stress thing, I know a really fantastic therapist.' She smiled and held out her hand, 'Very nice to meet you. Give my love to Simon, I hope he's feeling better soon. Remember me to Penny.'

Jack walked glumly in the direction of the station. The effort of pushing along on the overcrowded pavement was irritating. He turned into Green Park and sat on a deck chair. Away from the press reception and the falsely festive atmosphere – after all, they weren't actually celebrating anything – he realised he was exhausted, and longed to be his real self again, Dr Jack Silver, rather than Simon Silver. The park had cleared a lot. The sunbathing office girls and their secret admirers had mostly gone. He slowly put on his reading glasses and looked in the carrier bag. The press pack was a folder about tourism trends to different parts of the globe, and details of the travel industry's projections for next year. The gift was a neat wooden box containing a small bottle of armagnac – Jack had never heard of it, but guessed that it must be something like cognac – and a tin of pâté de foie gras. Giant drops of rain began to fall and he made his way out of the park. He gave the gift to a beggar at the station entrance.

On the train back to Golders Green, he looked around wearily, reading the ads and studying the other passengers. There were black people, Indians or Pakistanis, East Europeans. Was he the only English person in the whole carriage? He looked them over more carefully and decided that he was indeed the only Englishman. Then he recalled that he himself was not exactly English. He fell asleep, but did not dream that his day was about to get a great deal worse.

* * *

It's been a *brilliant* day, nice from the start. As soon as I woke up, my skin felt nice because of the weather. Aloo had to go somewhere for Daddy, and he asked me what I would like to do today. I said I really wanted to see my friend Josh Shinberg. I didn't tell Aloo that Mummy doesn't like Josh or his family. She says they have more money than sense. They've actually got quite a lot of both – you must have quite a lot of sense to make so much money, if you think about it – *and* Josh has got the latest version of Space Warrior.

It's so fun at his house. They don't care what videos and DVDs he watches. He watches 12s, 15s, even 18s. He's got his very own DVD player and TV in his room! He's allowed to watch *anything*. Some of the things he watches are totally gross, or crazy. I actually don't even like to see some of the things he watches. After a couple of hours of Space Warrior, his mum said maybe we shouldn't stay indoors all day on a lovely day like this? She made us go out. Well, not exactly made us, because Josh doesn't have to do anything if he doesn't want to. They even let him have days off school if he just says he doesn't feel like going. His dad says school never did *him* any good. But she asked us if we wanted to go out, and made it seem like we would be stupid to say no, so we said yes. But it was OK: they have a fantastic pool and a basketball thing.

I said I didn't want to swim. Actually, I would have loved a swim. I said it because I didn't want to borrow anyone else's swimming trunks and didn't want to swim in my underpants, so I just said I didn't feel like swimming. We played basketball, then football, and the au pair gave us lunch of pasta. We watched the cartoon channel while we had lunch. Then it started to rain hard, with thunder, and we played Space Warrior again and had ice cream. It was like being on holiday somewhere. Josh lives like that all the time.

Then it turned out I was staying for dinner, and going to have a sleep-over with Josh! Brilliant! Mummy just would *never* let me have a sleep-over with Josh! But there was definitely something wrong with Aloo, and I guessed that's why I'm sleeping over. They put him on the phone to me, and he said he was all right, but you could just tell.

'Are you *really* all right, Grandad?' I asked. Something in his voice made me want to give him a big hug.

'I fell over and hurt myself,' he said. 'Someone helped me, and I'm having a cup of tea with them now.'

That really sounded strange. Falling over is not something you see grown-ups do much, but Aloo is very old. 'Where? How did it happen?' I asked. 'Did you slip on something? Did you get a bruise?' I told him I got three huge bruises on my leg playing football with Josh today.

Aloo said he'd like to see my bruises, but that his own bruises were nothing, and anyway, they could not be shown in mixed company. I suppose that means mixed grown-ups and children. He said would tell me all about it tomorrow, and I could spend the night. Then he said I'd have to borrow anything I needed – which I don't like doing, especially something like pyjamas, though that isn't as bad as swimming trunks. But he said Josh's mum had new things I could have, or would just get me anything I wanted, which was true. She just sent the au pair to Brent Cross to buy me some pyjamas, swimming trunks and a toothbrush.

At Josh's, normally everything like cooking is done by their au pair. But for dinner today, Josh's mum helped the au pair lay the table, very nicely, and did some weird things. One thing was she put two loaves of challah on the table and covered them with a cloth. I laughed when I saw it. Actually I've seen this before – it's something Jewish people do sometimes, I think, except that we would never do anything silly like that.

Another thing was, even though there were several of us, she put just one mug on the table, a silver mug without a handle next to the wine.

I said, 'That's a nice cup,' and Josh's mum said it had belonged to her grandparents in Lithuania.

'Did they only have one?' I asked, and she looked at me kind of strange and said yes.

She put candles in two silver candlesticks on the table, too, like in posh restaurants sometimes.

When it was time for dinner, Josh's dad showed up in a smart, very dark suit, and a big gold ring. Josh doesn't see his dad much because he goes out to work before Josh is up in the morning, and comes back sometimes after bedtime. With my dad, it's different. I see him a lot. Well, I don't see him at all when he's away, but when he's not away, he works at home. And he never really minds being interrupted.

Josh's dad gave me a kappel – that's what Daddy calls it, but Josh's dad called it a kipper – the little round thing that Orthodox men have on their heads. I couldn't stop grinning when I put it on. I did try very hard to stop grinning. I have worn them before, at Jewish people's houses sometimes. It always makes me feel, like, what's going on? Are we pretending to be Orthodox? Josh's sister Mel was there. She's fourteen. But

Josh's older brother wasn't there. He was out.

There was a whole spooky moment when Josh's mum lit the candles and mumbled something in a foreign language. It made me think of someone casting a spell. I didn't know what was going on, so I asked Josh what language it was. He whispered, 'Hebrew, silly.'

I said, 'What, does she speak Hebrew, then?' but he put his finger over his mouth to shush me.

Then Josh's dad poured some wine in the silver mug thing, and lifted it and now he said something in Hebrew as well. While he was saying it, Josh's mum's mobile rang and she said 'Where are you, Nathan? Yeah, we're making kiddish. Like, it's Friday night, remember?' – her voice was a bit sarcastic – 'Yeah, well, tonight we are. Come home and eat with us.' When Josh's dad had finished, he handed round the silver thing of wine, like some sort of special ceremony, and everyone had a sip *including the children*. While they were passing it round, Josh's dad took a call on his mobile, and he was still talking when suddenly Josh uncovered the challah loaves and said something quickly in Hebrew. I thought – uh? I didn't know this whole family spoke Hebrew. Are they Israelis, or something? I looked at Josh, like, 'What's happening?' but he ignored me and broke pieces off the bread, and sprinkled salt on them, and gave a piece to everyone. I was thinking – wow, this is, like, I don't know what, just weird.

Everyone sang a song, and I was the only one who didn't know the words. Even Josh knew this song, even though it just wasn't the kind of music he normally likes *at all*. I thought – where did everyone learn this song? I never even heard it before, not on the radio or anywhere. We kept the kappels – the little round bits of cloth – on our heads the whole time. It was like being in the school play.

Only then did we start eating. As soon as we'd started,

Josh's brother Nathan came in and pulled up a chair and sat at the table and joined in eating but not saying much. He's seventeen. Josh's mum asked him something, and from his answer it sounded like he plays in a pop group. After a while he just left the table again, and went upstairs. We could hear him playing his electric guitar. Everyone tried to chat, but it was a bit uncomfortable. Josh's mum and dad laughed a lot. His mum has a way of laughing that's very loud and a bit like shouting: Ah! Ah! Ah! Ah! Josh's sister got bored, so she went away as well, and we could hear her watching TV in the other room. She came back for pudding. It was a lokshen pudding – we have it at home sometimes, sort of like a hot cake made of spaghetti – with ice cream. Yummy. Josh's sister had loads of it. She was just going away again when Josh's mum said, 'Stay with us and bentsh, Mel. You know how to bentsh better than we do.'

Mel opened her mouth and looked as if she truly couldn't believe this request. 'Bentsh?' she said. 'We never bentsh.'

'Of course we do,' said her mum. 'Please Mel…?'

Mel complained, 'Aw! I hate bentshing. It's stupid. Anyway, I wanna watch Naked Gun.'

I kept very quiet, as I had no idea what they were talking about. 'Ach! Let her go,' said Josh's dad. And he started to sing again, kind of like a chant, in a foreign language, which I'm thinking 'is this Hebrew?', reading from a little book. Then I noticed we all had copies of the book and everyone was trying to join in – except me! Hey, even Josh! And I couldn't even find the place, 'cos it *was* in a foreign language. Even the letters were different from English. It *was* Hebrew – I recognised it from the words painted on Yoav's van. But then I noticed that they couldn't find the place either. Josh's dad glanced at Josh's mum with a jokey, worried expression, and she just shrugged as if, 'Don't worry about it.' The others stopped joining in, and after a while Josh's dad decided to stop too – 'Well, that's enough of that,' he laughed. But he turned Josh's mum, 'That was good, wasn't it, Lorrae? Fun. We should do it more often. It's good for the kids.'

Josh and me went back to the computer. 'What was all *that* about – the Hebrew and stuff?' I asked him. But Josh told me they did it *especially* for me. They thought because I was having a sleepover on Friday night, my parents and grandad would like it.

'Why Friday night?' I asked.

Josh seemed surprised. 'You know – like, Shabbat?' His voice sounded like, everyone knows that. I didn't want to seem stupid so I just nodded and said, 'Oh, yeah,' like I knew what he was talking about.

'So your family don't do Friday night?'

I was scared of making a total idiot of myself. 'What do you mean, like, "do" Friday night?' I said, and I'm thinking, how come I'm the only one that doesn't know what's going on? Is it because he's allowed to watch adult movies that Josh knows all this stuff?

Josh said, 'You know, like, *do* – you know, all the Jewish stuff on Shabbat, you know, candles an' stuff, you know what I mean? Jesus – you are *Jewish*, aren't you?'

This was getting worrying, because I didn't know what Shabbat was, but I said, 'Oh, we don't care about anything Jewish.' I hoped Josh would move onto another subject. There have been more and more things like this happening lately.

'Nah, nor do we,' said Josh, attacking the forces from another galaxy. 'We eat bacon and eggs for breakfast every Sunday morning. It's nice.'

I was confused by this, because I am sure Daddy really did say Jews don't eat bacon. I hope Daddy isn't wrong – I wouldn't like that.

* * *

I know you'll say I was shikker, and maybe I was. But I'm sure what happened next was nothing to do with the wine. I think it was just luck – bad luck. While I dozed on the train, there has been a downpour. When I get back to Golders Green, the rain has already stopped. The air has cooled; the wet pavements reflect bright white. Things look washed clean. There's still a lovely sharp smell in the air, the smell of rain on a hot day – what is it, damp dust? My nap has refreshed me as well, though those champagne bubbles still pop around in my brain. I'm just not used to it, Miri – never was!

I crossed the road slowly and thought I was heading for the supermarket car park where I had left Penny's car. You get to the car park down a little lane off the main road. Strangely, I take a wrong turn; it only takes a second to realise I've gone wrong. But I'm sort of assuming this little street must run parallel to the other one, and surely it will take me into the car park.

It gets awfully slummy and narrow. It's not really a street at all, just a mews or service road. I'm passing crumbling old workshops and rows of putrid, overflowing bins at the backs of shops and restaurant kitchens. There are a couple of parked cars – I suppose they've found a way of dodging the Golders Green parking regulations – but no one is driving. It's eerily quiet and deserted. The noise of Golders Green is audible but sounds far away. There's no pavement, so I walk in the roadway, which becomes pitted and cracked. The tarmac has broken away in places, showing cobbles underneath, and potholes are filled with rainwater.

I pass abandoned buildings with broken windows, one of them with a burnt-out car outside, and I'm thinking – is this really Golders Green? What part of Golders Green is this? I decide to take a look round the next corner. If it doesn't lead into the car park, I'll turn back.

I reach the corner and peek around. And I stop dead. It takes a few seconds to understand what I'm looking at. This is what I can see:

A few paces in front of me, jammed between a brick wall and a big metal garbage container, there's an elderly hasid, being roughed up by four thugs. They're quite smart, with check shirts and casual trousers, but they have shaved heads and vicious faces. The hasid is bent forward awkwardly, and one of them is pulling off his kippah and whacking him around the head and shoulders with a piece of wood.

Well, that's how it looks at first. Then it seems more like it's all a game, almost like a dance. It's all happening so fast, I can't keep track. Now the one with the kippah is throwing it on the ground. The movements are fast and furious. One fellow is pulling the Jew's long grey beard, and I suddenly realise that this one is very young, just a little boy, about the same age as Danny. Two of the others are fit young men, with curiously intense, determined expressions. Now I see the fourth one is no young thug at all, but a paunchy, overweight, middle-aged man with a bullet head, not shaved but bald. He looks a hard, brutalised character, but he just stands watching.

In the half-instant that I'm standing there like an idiot, trying to work out exactly what I can see, I'm also trying to rationalise. I tell myself there's a reason for it all. Maybe it's not real? They're making a film? But where are the cameras? And those are real punches, not acting. That's a real piece of wood, isn't it? And a kippah should not be thrown on the ground. Maybe the Jew is some sort of Rachmann-style landlord being set upon by his exploited tenants?

Now the Jew cries out and, by some crazy instinct, I run to help. I'm eighty years old, Miri; I can't run, I can't fight, I can't do anything useful, and I shouldn't be asked to do such things, but I run to help.

Forgive me, Miri. I know what you're thinking – 'Is this what you call looking after Danny? Getting into fights and brawls?' But I was just trying to do the right thing. A Jew calls out for help, what should I do – turn and run the other way?

The answer is, yes, that's exactly what I should have done. Instead I find I'm running straight towards the trouble. The hasid is leaning strangely against the rubbish bin, raising one leg across his private parts for protection, and one arm covers his head.

He's saying, 'Please! Please! Please let me go, I must get home to my family.' His diction is very poor, he has some kind of accent.

The young men roar with laughter at this.

At first the thugs don't even notice me. They don't seem aware of me at all. It's the child who sees me first, and he simply stands open-jawed in amazement as I approach. In any case, I'm not much bigger than him. Up close, the other ruffians seem to be all muscle and movement, with bodies more like metal than flesh. 'Stop! Stop!' I yell, 'What are you doing? Stop!' I rush straight up to the frummer and push at the biggest of the young louts, the one with the piece of wood, but he's as unstoppable as a rogue elephant.

Puzzled, he turns to me and now seems to forget the hasid, who crumples against the rubbish bin, breathless. Only now does the Jew see me. '*Du is a yid?*'[12] he cries out desperately. 'Stop, stop – don't try to fight them. They are madmen, madmen.'

He didn't have to tell me. I wasn't planning to try fighting these muscular young brutes. I put my arm around the hasid and try to help him into an upright position. I say to him, 'We're getting out of here,' and repeat it louder for the benefit of the thugs, 'We're getting out of here.' Yet he doesn't move, instead pulling back, afraid of the thugs, and even, it seems, afraid of me.

---

12 "Are you a Jew?" (Yiddish)

Their beefy middle-aged companion looks me over with a smile of disbelief. 'Are you a yid?' he says coolly.

'Don't fight!' the hasid shouts again in my ear.

How right he is! My reaction had been so stupid. I have been thinking this over every minute since – if I had really wanted to help, instead of running towards the fight, I should have run to fetch the police.

In a sudden movement, the man flicks his bald head forward as if to hit me with it – but it is just a jest, a piece of mockery to test my cowardice. I flinch and duck, failing the test and hating myself for it. I feel inwardly like cringing and begging him not to hurt me, but somehow – you know, it's a streak of something pigheaded in me, Miri, you've seen it a thousand times – I stand up perfectly straight and shout, 'You'd better stop this before you do something stupid and get into trouble.'

Funny, it's not working. They look at me as a cat may look at a mouse it has cornered. Without a word, without a flicker of expression, with one very pure, quick, relaxed movement, the big man whips his left palm flat onto my cheek, and his right fist hits me on the space between my upper lip and my nose. It really hurts. I haven't experienced pain like it for years.

'Scared?' the big man asks.

'Should I be?'

'You will be,' he answers.

It's interesting, pain. I know it's there, yet what I feel is not pain but fear. Yes, he's right; I'm trying not to show anything, but I am scared. At this moment, I am most of all concerned about damage to my nose and the last two of my teeth. While I'm worrying about that, suddenly someone has given me a terrible kick in the kishkes. I'm breathless and feel sick. Like my little sister Pearl with her asthma attacks, when she arched her body backwards and threw open her delicate little jaw, I am struggling to take in some air. The piece of wood is swinging through the air. I try to dodge it, and it lands on my bad knee with a sickening sound. A searing agony passes through my whole body.

Immediately I am wondering how bad the shame will be if I should shit myself, and whether I'd rather just die, and a flicker of a thought passes across my mind, that in the larger scheme of things it doesn't matter what happens to me. It doesn't matter if you live, or if you die, or how you die, or who you are. We are all going to be buried and forgotten. But then, that's exactly why life *does* matter. The futility of life is reason enough to enjoy it to the full. I was born, I am still here, and being kicked to death is not a proper way to leave. And suddenly I understand that I can't talk my way out of this. These people are beyond reason, indeed like animals.

Like a huge bellows my lungs have drawn in the air they want, and to the frummer I shout with all my might, for some crazy reason resorting to the mameloshn, '*Gey! Makhn pleyte!*'[13] My voice is so loud, it startles me. And at last he makes a move, grabbing his battered kippah and running as fast as he can, tsitsis, peyess and long beard flying behind. The boy laughs with thin lips at the comical sight, then turns back to me.

You know, it's a very physical thing, intense fear. It's not an emotional state. In dreams you flee in panic, awake sweating. But now I'm not aware of any emotion at all, nor any sweat, though there's a banging in my chest that seems to rocket round my head. My belly is cramped, my chest feels like it's in a straitjacket, my balls are tightening, and I'm struggling to keep control of my bowels, which seem to be about to empty themselves. Somehow I feel I can hold my bowels in, but not my bladder. So when the four line up to break my bones, the greatest fear at that moment is only that I will wee in my trousers.

---

13 "Go! Make a run for it!" (Yiddish)

Now not just one, but the whole gang are striking me with wooden sticks like clubs – boy, they are heavy, they are hard, and solid. Much more solid than human flesh.

Yet at the same instant I find myself understanding the wonderful, uncluttered simplicity of violence. The unrestrained freedom of it! Freedom from the namby-pamby constraints of civilisation, the seat belt of morality. The appeal of fascism becomes very clear. To dispense with debate and indecision! My face stings and I taste blood trickling into my mouth, I don't know whether from my lip or my nose. Foolishly, I stand my ground and once more try to reason with my attackers, 'You know you are assaulting an 80-year-old man? Can that be right? How is that going to look in court? Do you feel good about that? Do you ever think about right and wrong? Think about it now. What is it you want?' It comes out as a series of gasps, and I know it all adds up to something pathetic.

The older man grins rather sweetly, genuinely amused. It's disarming, his mischievous little smile. You could imagine him as a ladies' man, a lovable rascal. 'Oh shut up! Quite the intellectual, ent ya? Fuckin' right and wrong. I'll tell ya what feels right, what feels good. Puttin' yids in their fuckin' place. We beat yids,' he says brightly. 'We cut yids. If we get lucky, sometimes we can kill a yid.' The others are also smiling pleasantly at this discourse.

While he talks, there is respite. I gather my breath and answer back. 'Whatever you're after, you won't get away with it,' I say defiantly, but I catch a quaver of desperation in my voice, and I'm sure they hear it too.

'Oh, we do always get away with it, jewboy. Always. Don't we?' he turns to the other two men, who laugh. The boy guffaws loudly.

'Not this time,' I repeat. 'Anyway, the whole place is probably being filmed on CCTV.'

Now he smiles with grim amusement at my chutzpah. 'What, this place? Wanna bet?' He pushes me to the wall. Its unyielding brick presses against my back. 'Eighty, are ya? Eighty!' he laughs. 'It's about time you was dead and buried, mate. Don't worry, you soon will be.'

I try to keep my voice calm. 'Anyway, aren't you a bit out of date? I thought it was blacks and Asians that people like you hate now,' I say to him. 'Hating yids sounds like something out of the Ark. I haven't been called a jewboy these last twenty years. You haven't moved with the –' but he stops me with small, nonchalant slap from the back of his hand. 'Shut up, jewboy' he says, no longer smiling. 'We hate the whole stinkin' lot a ya. Yids worse'n blacks. Scum.'

'Is 'e a yid, though, Dad? Is 'e one?' asks the boy. ''E's got no beard nor nuffink. No skowcap.'

'Yeah, 'e's one awright,' the older man tells him. 'Jus' look at 'im. Listen to 'im. He's forgot to put on his 'at, ent 'e?' To the others he says, 'Cheeky little sod, too, en 'e? Let's do this bloke.' He means me. 'Let's take 'im apart. Finks we won't get away wiv it, eh? Let's show 'im what we get away wiv.'

The first to jump in, gleefully, is the little boy. He punches my face and knees me in the testicles, with every blow yelling 'Yid!' Thanks to my trousers, and his being a little shorter than me, he doesn't get a full hit on my testicles, but still it's frightening. Luckily, my balls seem to have become less sensitive as I got older. The other three stand smiling, and egg him on, 'Go on mate!' The boy slaps me hard on the side of the head – 'Filthy little yid!' – and then – 'Die, yid!' – and with each strike, shouts 'Die, yid!' in his child's unbroken voice. Unable to see clearly, I seem to hear a chorus of Yid! Yid! Yid! pounding in my ears, echoing through a lifetime that I'm afraid is about to end. Yid! Yid! Yid!

At last I remember to call out, and start to yell 'Help!' but the little word just echoes absurdly around the walls of the empty buildings in this deserted alley. My cries have a melodramatic, laughable ring to them. I feel now that I should hit back – but instead I struggle idiotically with the rights and wrongs of the situation. Should I hit a child? Will it help? Will the men become even angrier? What have I got to lose? It flashes into my mind that setting a little boy against an old man has the making of a good goyish backstreet sport, like cockfights and dogfights.

I remember that at his age I used to be a good boxer. We Jewish boys were expected to be ready to defend ourselves on the streets of London against just such little thugs as this. Lots of Jewish families wanted their boys to learn boxing. Imagining myself eleven years old again, I raise my fists as I was taught to do, left guarding my face, right ready to punch.

Of course, in those days I had my gloves. I have hardly ever fought without them. I stand up and dance on my feet as I was taught to do. Surely I have some punch left in me?

I can almost hear the audience of those days, cheering and encouraging, gathered round the ring at the boxing club. Today I hear laughter, and the mocking comments the opponent's friends would sometimes call out. I give the kid a mighty *klopp in kop*[14] – a right jab, and a left jab to the side – and he steps back howling. I imagine him stumbling back onto the ropes. I think I might have broken his jaw.

But no, he comes straight back at me, screaming with rage. Again I am ready, and give him a body punch, a hard blow to the guts that sends him reeling. For one moment I am back at the boys' club, it's an under-12s prize fight between Yid and Goy, and I just hope my old Tateh is watching this, because there's a big prize – life. If I lose, I will die.

I hear the boy roar with anger, and he comes charging once more with fists and boots. I hear the crowd – but it is just the

---

14 bash on the head (Yiddish)

three men laughing at my efforts, and I glance around. They are standing relaxed, hands on their hips, smiling at me with scornful amusement. I lash out with another punch, but miss my target. My strength is going – I feel exhausted. I am weak and old now, and my bad knee feels like it will give way. The boy whacks my face and I think my cheekbone may shatter. Another blow on the stomach knocks the breath right out of me. I bend forward to protect my guts. I think the crowd are calling out now, maybe booing, or cheering. One of the young men, placing one big, powerful hand on my head, simply pushes me down, folding me in half like a piece of cardboard. I struggle to stand up, but he is too strong for me. He says, 'Won't get away with it, eh?'

A further push makes my legs buckle and brings my face to the ground, where – leaning his weight onto the back of my head – he presses it hard into the dirt. I don't have to tell you, I kept my eyes and mouth tightly closed to stop dirt getting in. My knee is killing me. Then just as effortlessly he is pulling me up again. I feel his hand slip into my inside pocket and, in a single easy movement, remove my wallet. 'Gi's ya fuckin' jewmoney, then.'

Suddenly there is a metallic shine to one side. The other young man is holding a knife. 'Can I cut 'im now?' he asks, as if he has been waiting patiently. 'Eh, Mick?' Now I really think I may soil my pants. Glancing around in the hope of any escape route, I notice with surprise that I can hear voices approaching. Maybe someone has heard my shouts.

The young man with my wallet swings a big fist towards my face, I dodge it but it catches my neck. That's very painful. It makes me feel almost faint, yet I find I'm still alive and still looking around in the hope of getting away.

The older man nods dismissively, 'Yeah, go on. Quick, quick, come on, someone comin''. Do it. Come on, Kev, use the blade on 'im. Get a move on. If Gash was 'ere, 'e'd be in shreds by now.' Now my fear is on another level. Still it's somehow more physical than emotional. My genitals feel extremely cold and I think I must have wet myself. Thoughts race through my mind – of injury, of pain, of mutilation. I visualise my flesh hanging in tatters, my face slashed and bleeding. I wonder about scars. I wondered about us, Miri, about our life together. Forgive me, but I think – it's better that she's not alive. I even start to imagine that none of it is happening. It's as though if I ignore it, all this will go away.

Once more I see myself as a child, an innocent little boy, afraid of the English kids. I remember sitting shiva for my dear father. I see as a single shining pearl the whole eternal struggle which is each life running into the next, the furtive, fugitive continuation from one day to the next. Above all, I feel a need to survive just to spite these fools. So I find the strength to get out from under the big hand, and lash out again at the thug's face. What have I got to lose? My fist makes contact with his face, grazing my knuckles on his teeth, he shouts out with pain, and I feel immense relief that I have finally struck back at one of the adults. He starts yelling furiously.

The older man laughs. 'Got you there, Kev! Got spirit, en't 'e?'

The knife lashes out suddenly but I dodge it. It nicks my chin and blood starts running. A man comes running around the corner. I see it's only another old chap who won't be any use in a fight. He calls out, 'Police!' I don't quite understand, because he doesn't look like a policeman. He has a huge, booming voice and a strong foreign accent. I see he's holding up some ID and shouting, 'Stop! Police!'

With amazing speed, the men and the boy run away. They get into a car up the lane and it starts to move off rapidly. Through an open window the bald man leans back and calls out to me, in a tone almost amiable, 'That was fun, wasn't it? See ya soon, jewboy. We know where ya live.' A chorus of laughter fills the car as it drives quickly away.

'Get their number,' I shout, feebly running after the car as if, now that they were leaving, I want to pretend that I could tackle the thugs. I try to notice something memorable about it, but what do I know about cars? It's a hatchback, ordinary looking, slightly battered, a pale blue-ish colour. My eyes swim, blurring the figures on the licence plate. I'm just hoping I'll remember them. I notice a pattern – it's 50, 50, 50, I tell myself.

The newcomer, my saviour, quickly said a jumble of things, but I was too tired to know what's going on. He pressed his handkerchief on the cut chin. 'Are you a policeman?' I asked, and I heard him say, 'The police are on their way.' I didn't like him to think I felt physically defeated by the attack. I told him, rather pathetically, 'They have got my wallet.' I felt faint and grabbed onto him for support. My arms and legs were trembling, my bad knee was throbbing and wanted to give way and I discovered aches and pains all over. I think I may even have rested my head on his shoulder before slipping down onto the ground. I had to sit and rest. I felt very weak, and was ashamed of that, but I didn't think anything was broken. There was blood on my hands and shirt, but most of it came from one tiny cut on my chin. I closed my eyes and heard his voice, 'Oh my God – are you all right? I'm calling an ambulance.'

I said, 'No, no, I'm OK, I'm fine. No ambulance.'

'You must, you must – you are hurt.'

I opened my eyes and insisted. 'No, I can't. I don't have time to waste on all that. My grandson is expecting me. I have to go and collect him. Let's just see how I am. If I need a doctor, I'll call one. I'll be OK.'

'You can't go anywhere like this. I'll take you home.'

He kneeled beside me on the ground and held my arm kindly. In gasps I tried to tell him, they had pieces of wood, a knife, wanted to kill me, called me a yid, they were hitting me all over. He nodded sadly.

I still thought he must be some kind of official, or maybe a community support officer, but no, he insisted he wasn't.

'Look, you dropped this,' he said, and reached towards a mobile phone lying half hidden by the garbage bin. Perhaps it belonged to the frummer. Maybe he had been trying to call the police. I put it in my pocket, thinking that if I survived, I would try to return it.

He lifted me and straightened my jacket like a wife. He was a solid, strong, capable man, almost as old as me, I'd guess, but in better shape, with a loud, deep voice and a rather intense, kindly air. Just at that moment a police car lazily turned the corner, blue light flashing incongruously. Inside, two uniformed young Englishmen with clipped, light brown hair and sardonic expressions gazed at the two old Jews.

6

Jack sat still and silent on the back seat of Villy's little car, like a bird in shock, as they drove through wide, tree-lined backstreets. There were painful places all over his body. The left knee was hot and swollen. He struggled to remain rational against a torrent of thoughts, images, memories, fantasies, the faces and fists of his assailants, their shouts, the terrifying movement of a shining knife, words he should have said, things he should have done, would have done. The whole incident was being redrawn and redrawn again, retold in a vivid kaleidoscope of 'should have' and 'what if' alternatives: he saw himself phoning the police, heard the conversation he would have had with them, yet also saw himself with a weapon that he could deftly use, or that bravely he disarmed his attackers, or heard his voice uttering such devastating remarks, or such insightful comments, that their minds were opened to their folly.

With eyes closed he saw the blue lights flashing, heard the siren, the jabbering radio voices and the yelling, as the police arrived in good time, rushing across the dirty alleyway to stop the fight and grab the men. He was half aware that his body ached, his back, his face, his legs, his knees especially. Beneath all, an angry defiance simmered, a desire for revenge. Yet he breathed gulping sighs of relief. His ordeal was over, for the time being at least. He was still alive. He was not even badly hurt. He had returned to the present day. He wished his wife would be at home to comfort him. At this moment, though, he knew with sad clarity that Miri was dead and, wherever he went, he would be alone in the world. Yet not completely alone – this good stranger had come to his aid and seemed for the moment to have taken him under his wing.

Of his rescuer, he saw only the man's neatly clipped grey hair and shaved neck. As they turned a corner, Jack looked out at people walking innocently on wet pavements, some hurrying, each intent on his or her own business, and he wondered about the point of it all, the nature of a happy life.

Suddenly the head and shoulders in the driver's seat jerked round to face him. The man introduced himself – *Wilhelm Bernhardt, please you may call me Villy* – and with a tired nod Jack responded, 'Jack Silver'. Villy said what surprised him was that the attackers were white. We are all expecting such things from Muslims, of course. But we expect them to kill rather than just beat people up. Because global jihad is about mass murder, about waging a war. On the other hand, Muslims are constantly being incited to kill Jews, so maybe a few will actually do it. And we know Jews have always been attacked by white hooligans. But the truth is, there have been so many attacks on Jews by blacks lately, he went on. Jack did not reply, only half listening.

'You read it in the JC, I'm sure,' Villy said, 'about that young rabbi. It was only a few weeks ago, in Stamford Hill – the one who was badly hurt by a gang of black teenagers. I think it said there were fifteen of them, no? Fifteen young idiots against one good, scholarly man.'

Catching the questioning glance in the rear view mirror, Jack just nodded, unsure what Villy was talking about. He never saw the Jewish Chronicle any more. Even if he did, it wouldn't occur to him to buy it. He was nothing to do with that world any more.

'What was that card you showed?' Jack asked wheezily. 'I thought you must be a policeman.'

'No, that's only my senior citizen's travel pass. Those thugs obviously thought it was something else. In the newspapers – I don't mean the JC – the *other* newspapers – of course they don't mention if a gang is black. They think, why mention it? Maybe it would stir up hatred against black gangs! They are afraid it might be against the law even to mention it! Maybe it *is* against the law. It is against the law now even to say that a man is black? It wouldn't surprise me. Eh?'

Again Jack merely nodded, giving the slightest murmur of agreement. He did not know if Villy was right or wrong. He could see the disadvantage of mentioning skin colour. Anything which might increase hostility between races had to be avoided. Villy's point seemed to be that a problem could not be dealt with if people were not prepared to hear unwelcome facts.

'Such people don't discuss – just kick and punch,' Villy added. 'It happened to a neighbour of mine.'

'Oh, believe me, it was no different with these white fellows,' Jack said tiredly. 'Beyond reason.' But he was puzzled by Villy's comments. 'Nu, what have shvartzers got against yids, all of a sudden?'

Villy gave a snort of amusement at Jack's turn of phrase. 'Who knows? All the usual. I tell you this, people don't need a reason to hate us. How are you feeling now? Don't you want to go to the hospital?'

'No, no. But there's usually some reason or other, isn't there? We are too rich, or too poor, you know. We are communists, or capitalists. We killed Jesus – do you remember doing that? We murder those innocent Palestinian terrorists. And we've taken over the world. God knows what else.' He could hear that his voice was weak, but the last thing he wanted was to sit waiting in Accident and Emergency at some hospital. 'Do shvartzers care about such things? Maybe it's about Israel – do you think maybe they see it as a kind of black versus white conflict? Maybe with Palestinians playing the part of blacks? But no, you're right, the reasons come *after* the hatred – they are excuses.'

'Maybe, maybe, maybe. I shouldn't have mentioned it. Just rest now, we'll soon be home.'

'I thought they saw Jews as an inspiration, freeing themselves from slavery, reaching the promised land? Or maybe they blame Jews for slavery?'

'Who knows what they think, such people? Maybe they are just morons. Mindless thugs. Look, it would be better not to discuss it now. Don't get agitated. Just be calm, just rest quietly.'

'What should I care?' said Jack, 'Where I live, there are no shvartzers and no yids. It's a little corner of old England.'

'Really! I didn't know such places still existed.'

'It all comes down to having someone to blame – who better than the Jews? Not that I even think of myself as Jewish any more.'

'You don't?' asked Villy in surprise. 'Let's discuss it later. Don't talk now. Rest.'

'And in a crazy way I'm telling myself those guys got the wrong man – because *I'm* not a Jew, am I?'

Villy raised his eyes to heaven, thinking that the poor fellow he had rescued was raving, or in shock. 'Yes, if I may say so, that *is* crazy. It makes no sense at all. You are a Jew, they wanted to pick on a Jew. Q.E.D. End of story.'

Jack closed his eyes again and let the sense of movement take over. It was like being in a taxi, or a plane, in which one abandons all sense of control over one's journey, and just leaves it to the driver. Villy's comment rang in his head – 'people don't need a reason to hate us.' But Jack kept asking himself, 'Why pick on me?' He struggled to understand how he found himself in this position. He opened his eyes and watched red-brick buildings passing. Quite suddenly, the car came to a stop. They were in a street of gardens and semi-detached houses. It took Jack a moment to realise that he had been brought to Villy's house. He had assumed, stupidly (as he now told himself), that he would be taken home to Simon and Penny's.

Taking one arm very tenderly in his strong hand, Villy eased Jack from the car, his booming voice calling 'Ilse, Ilse, where are you? A visitor is here' even while he was still opening the front door.

He sat Jack on a sofa in the living room and said, 'A nice cup of tea? I'll put the kettle on.'

'Oh please, yes,' Jack replied. He tried to keep his leg straight to ease the pain in his knee. 'But you know,' he added anxiously, as the thought came back to him, 'I can't stay too long. I have to collect my grandson. I'm supposed to be looking after him for a few days, and – '

'Don't worry,' Villy said. 'All that we can sort out. Anyway, he's having a good time, and to be collected is the last thing he wants.'

Left alone, Jack waited in silence, looking round at the modest room, wallpapered in a dull brown pattern, some artless pictures hanging, a big television, a pile of magazines on a coffee table. The carpet and the fabric of the armchairs were well worn, as in so many elderly people's houses, thought Jack, as they debate whether it's worthwhile replacing it for just the few remaining years. Along one wall, long wooden shelves bowed under the weight of heavy books, in German, English and Hebrew, ranging across Jewish scholarship to biographies, travel, history, many leather bound, many clearly very old.

There was a rich odour of food cooking. He could hear the couple talking in German.

'Oh my God! What on earth happened to you, darling!' cried Ilse to Jack, almost running into the room. She was a slender, frail old lady, yet vivacious, radiant with life and energy. Like Villy, she spoke with a strong accent: 'Wait!' and she went for a cloth and some antiseptic to wipe the blood and dirt from his face. As she tended to him with deft movements, she offered him more and more things – 'Look at you! You must have a good wash, upstairs! I will give you a towel. And you need a clean shirt!' When Villy brought in china cups and a teapot on a tray, the two again broke into German, which Jack could not follow. In an instant they returned to English for his benefit. 'Finally came the police,' Villy was saying.

'I suppose it must have been the frummer who called them,' said Jack.

Villy was puzzled. 'The frummer? A hasid was shouting about some shlegers beating a man in the lane. That's why I came running so. But how did you know this? You, when you were so far down that alleyway, you couldn't hear him?'

Delving back into the sequence of events, Jack explained everything that had happened. They listened in amazement. Villy responded, 'Jack, you are a mensh. You have done a great mitzvah today. You saved another man, and took his trouble upon yourself.'

'I don't think it's actually a mitzvah, is it,' asked Jack wryly, 'to take someone's troubles on yourself? It's just rather foolish. And what about you, Villy? You did exactly the same, running up with nothing but a bus pass to protect you!' He reached to grasp Villy's hand. 'I can't thank you enough.'

Ilse castigated Villy for his rash courage, beaming with admiration as she did so. Villy protested, shaking his head.

'But of course,' Jack said, 'the frummer couldn't have

called the police! This is his phone, isn't it?' He reached into his pocket for the mobile phone Villy had picked up.

Villy held out a hand for the mobile. It was sleek and stylish. He opened it, turned it over and studied it, pressing buttons and peering at the bright screen, puzzled.

'It *was* a great mitzvah, darling,' affirmed Ilse. 'And what more can we do to help you, darling?' she pleaded, as if longing to put right all the wrongs of the world.

Jack sipped his tea. 'You're doing it.'

'Anything you need? Something to eat?'

Jack shook his head, but said, 'A glass of water? I'm sorry to be a nuisance. May I ask, do you have some painkillers? Paracetamol? Or Nurofen?'

Ilse jumped up.

Villy closed the mobile and handed it back to Jack. 'Actually, this is a very nice phone. It's really, you know, the cutting edge. It doesn't belong to a hasid, I think. The names in the address book, the list of contacts… no, it can't be his. Just look at their names. If you are dishonest, you can use it yourself. It looks as if it can even take photos, too. And a man like the hasid I saw,' he said, 'does not have a mobile phone at all.'

'Take photos! This must be the very latest thing!'

'But if you are honest, you must give it to the police. This might be evidence. If not, then because it is lost property, no?'

Ilse brought Jack his Nurofen and asked very tenderly if he was in severe pain. He insisted that he felt all right. He laughed that he would have a fine collection of bruises. She urged again that he go to the bathroom to wash and tidy himself. 'I've got some very good ointment for bruises,' she said, 'take it to the bathroom with you. Rub it well into all the places that hurt. And wait – I'll give you one of Villy's best, cleanest, whitest, newest shirts to put on.'

Jack agreed he would accept all these things as soon as he'd finished his tea.

'And the police, did they help?' she asked.

Villy nodded and raised his eyebrows, in a doubtful, ironic Yes, but what he said was simply, 'They said it wasn't a racist incident.'

'The first one,' Jack corrected him. 'The second one said it might be.'

'No, Jack,' Villy retorted, 'in the end, they decided it was not.'

'Not!' responded Ilse in mock amazement, as if she had known all along. 'Of course, you told them what had happened?'

'Because I am not "visibly a Jew", is how the policeman put it. I am not identifiable as a Jew. Well, I was very pleased to hear that, anyway! I was afraid maybe I do look a bit Jewish. But also, because they took my wallet,' Jack answered. '*My* wallet – do I look like a millionaire? Bursting with jewmoney, as they called it. Luckily, in my wallet I don't keep very much. I have a few pounds in my pocket. So, you see, because they took my wallet, it was, after all, not a racist incident. Ach! They made their report, that's all they want. Nothing to worry about. Anyway,' he shrugged, 'so it's a racist incident? So what? What difference does that make?'

'Huh! Only a robbery in broad daylight. Just stealing some money. Not worth caring about at all,' repeated Villy with bitterness.

'No, no, to be fair. They made a record, at least. And they want a statement from me,' Jack admitted. 'I suppose I'll have to go to the police station sometime. What worries me more is the credit cards.'

'Credit cards! Telephone now!' Villy burst out loudly, jumping to his feet. 'Telephone the banks straight away! Those... those... *bastards* – excuse me – might be stealing your money at this very minute!'

'No, no,' Ilse said calmly, 'don't worry. They can't use the cards without your PIN, can they?'

'Oh yes!' retorted Villy. 'On the internet!'

Ilse replied vaguely, with mild indignation, 'That wretched internet again!' She knew nothing at all about the world wide web, except that it was a morass of evil deceits, malicious mutating viruses and an unsupervised playground for the vilest perverts.

Jack grimaced. 'I don't know the bank's phone number. And what's even worse – the business cards with my son's address. The thugs will go there to find me again.'

'No, Jack, I really don't think they will do that. Why bother? That would be asking for trouble. They aren't so interested in you, only in any Jew. And of course, they are interested in the money. Here, let's phone the bank at once and cancel your cards. You don't know what bank it is? Let's phone all of them. No, there is an organisation, I have a number.' As Jack followed him to a phone in the hall he realised that he was indeed in pain. It was hard to walk, one leg shooting fire up his back with every step. His bad knee, especially, hurt with each step.

Jack realised that he was using those precious moments when Friday afternoon moves towards evening. Because of him, he thought with a panic remembered from long ago, Shabbat candle-lighting and dinner might be delayed. When he was a child, Shabbat reigned like a tyranny, Master of Friday, indeed ruling the whole week, controlling his parent's lives. Sunset on Friday, hidden as it was behind thick grey English clouds, itself had nothing to do with Shabbat, which was brought in by the Jewish Chronicle's published 'times for candle lighting'. To delay it was unthinkable, it would bring unimaginable disorder and chaos.

Villy helped Jack up the stairs and showed him into the bathroom. He locked the door and breathed a deep sigh. There on the wall was a large mirror, and turning to look at it, Jack had another shock: the face was hardly his own. Swollen and blue in places, with a livid red mark on the chin, the reflection looked back at him with the sorrow of ages in its eyes. He watched the thin lips move as he muttered sadly, 'Miri, you see what they did to me?'

He returned downstairs to Ilse's cries that he looked smart enough to go to a barmitzvah. 'Look, Shabbes is coming in soon. Stay with us this evening,' she pleaded. 'Bring the boy here, too, why not? We have a spare bedroom.'

But Jack didn't like that. He didn't care for Shabbes, and nor did he want Danny to see his face or hear what had happened. Nevertheless, he didn't want to be at home on his own either, and it would be a relief to be indulged in this way by these two kind, capable, open-hearted people.

He said he thought he would be fine to go home after dinner, and asked if he could phone his grandson. In the hall, he rummaged in his pockets for the number. Villy helped him look it up and left Jack alone to dial. 'Lorrae?'

Lorrae Shinberg said it would be a pleasure to have Danny for Friday night dinner. She put the boy on the line for a few minutes.

'Are you *really* all right, Grandad?' he asked.

'I fell over and hurt myself,' Jack told him. 'In Golders Green. Yeah, yeah, I slipped on something. I'll tell you about it tomorrow. Have a lovely time, Danny.' Why worry the boy? He hung up and returned to Villy and Ilse.

As they sat together in the living room, Villy talked happily with Jack about mathematics and numbers, which, it turned out, was a love they shared. Villy jumped up from time to time to take down a book from the shelves and find a page that contributed to their discussion. Jack relaxed and felt a real liking for his saviour.

Ilse called out that Villy should prepare the table, and soon Villy and Ilse Bernhadt's dining table – exactly like that of the Shinberg family where Danny was staying with his friend Josh – had been laid with fine dinner plates and glasses on a white cloth. Unlike the Shinberg's, here all was calm and harmony. Beside two of the plates, kippot were neatly folded. A white silk cloth, embroidered with white lettering, covered two loaves of challah and a silver kiddush cup was in place on a silver tray. On a polished sideboard alongside, in twin silver candlesticks two white Shabbat candles stood silently ready to be lit.

The very sight imparted a feeling of serenity, order and contentment. Villy and Ilse imagined it as a balm to Jack's soul after his experiences. Yet for Jack, the ritually adorned table evoked only repugnant memories of childhood, awakened his contempt for religion, dislike of tradition, perhaps even a loathing for its complacent certainties. Naturally he would do and say nothing – if he could help it – to offend his good hosts or spoil their Shabbat peace.

Of course, this calm and happy home was nothing like that of his childhood. There, ceaseless bickering and rows, bitterness, shouting and squalor were the background against which the ancient, repetitive rituals were thoughtlessly performed, reaffirmations of belief and trust in a God whom he knew – surely everyone knew – was nothing but an idea in the minds of men. And it's so that we can keep all this that we endure a ceaseless persecution? And because we do this, and supposedly believe in this, the world mocks us and hates us? And because we do this, and declare that we are Jews, the other boys jeer at us and throw stones? And yet we absolutely insist on doing this? To please an imaginary God? Then for pity's sake, if indeed it's only for this that we are being persecuted, let's just stop doing it! Let's forget this medieval nonsense and get on with being civilised rational human beings, a part *of* the world instead of apart *from* it, he yelled inwardly – only ever inwardly, until he left home – at every Shabbat table, at every family gathering.

Yet tonight, as the hour approached to light the candles and gather around the table, even Jack came somewhat awkwardly under the spell of Villy and Ilse's expectant, quietly joyful mood. When Villy put on his kippah, Jack did the same, feeling a little ridiculous in his own eyes. Ilse lit the candles, covered her eyes and recited the blessing that inaugurates Shabbat. Villy said 'Amen', and Jack, startled and embarrassed, realised he should follow suit, and uttered the unfamiliar word, 'Amen.' When Jack and Ilse kindly wished him, and each other, 'Shabbat shalom,' he responded with a difficult smile, finding the whole ceremony absurd and contrived.

To Jack's further surprise, Villy and Ilse began to sing 'Shalom aleichem', Villy's operatic baritone confidently filling the room with music. To his even greater puzzlement, he discovered that he remembered the words, not sung since childhood, and sang them again together with his hosts.

Villy turned to Ilse and, instead of reciting as usual the psalm of devotion – 'A good wife, who can find? Her worth is far above rubies' – he simply kissed her hand without a word. With a simple nod, she showed her understanding that the omission was for Jack's sake, his own wife, sorely missed as they now knew, having died of cancer not so long ago. Villy filled the silver beaker with wine and held it as he sang the ancient Hebrew blessing for Shabbat, and again Jack found himself saying 'Amen.' It sent shivers of repulsion and fascination down his spine.

Villy led the way as the three of them went now to pour a cup of water over their hands, reciting the blessing for the commandment to rinse the hands, and once more Jack was astonished that he remembered the words, hiding in his mind since childhood. Silently the three of them filed back to the table, where Villy gestured questioningly to Jack whether he would like to say the blessing for bread over the two challah loaves. For an instant of panic Jack felt that he should not do this, that it was surely forbidden, a blasphemy, for one such as himself to utter any kind of benediction at all, but he uncovered the loaves and falteringly recited the Hebrew words, breaking off a piece for each person, correctly sprinkling it with salt before handing the bread to Villy and Ilse. The gesture was strangely satisfying.

As they sat down to eat the meal, Jack told them with a mischievous grin that he had not said a blessing of any kind for half a century.

Villy and Ilse were intrigued to know why, and Jack admitted frankly, 'You know, I just don't believe. I'm not a religious man.'

'Not even a three-times-a-year Jew,[15] darling?' Ilse asked, smiling and without criticism.

'Not even that,' Jack confessed.

Ilse laughed with twinkling eyes, 'Aha! So we have a real apikoros!' She said it almost with affection, serving her husband and her guest.

Jack said he hoped he had not upset or offended them, but the provocative edge in his tone made it clear that he would be perfectly happy to argue his corner. 'Yes,' he acknowledged. 'Actually I am an apikoros – especially if the word comes from those Jews who agreed with Epikuros. I think the Epicurean ideal was absolutely correct. A good life, a simple life, a rational life, devoted to the essential pleasures, without any religion or superstition.'

Passing the dishes around the table, Villy and Ilse were

15 i.e. one who ignores synagogue except on the three most pious dates: Rosh Hashanah, Kol Nidrei (Yom Kippur eve) and Yom Kippur

thrilled with the unexpected comments, which few would dare to make at their Shabbat table. 'How marvellous, darling!' clapped Ilse. 'But Epicurus really was not such a bad chap, was he? I think if you want to play devil's advocate, you should choose someone more terrible. A Caesar or a Czar or a Kaiser or someone.'

'While we are on the subject of Epicurus, what about a glass of wine, Jack?' said Villy, producing a bottle.

Jack rarely drank at all and, especially after his champagne lunch, preferred to refuse. He did not want to be ungracious, but the doubt showed on his face.

'I should think it's just what you need, darling,' said Ilse.

Jack agreed to 'a small glass,' his fingers indicating a tiny measure. Villy poured as Jack said, 'You know, poor old Epicurus has been terribly slandered. He was not what we call an epicurean. He did not believe in drunkenness or overeating.'

The three glasses were raised and touched together, as Villy and Ilse said 'L'haim!' Jack belatedly followed suit. 'Wishing you a speedy recovery,' added Ilse.

Villy observed, with a raised eyebrow, that somehow he could not quite imagine Jack enjoying Epicurus' ideal life of simple pleasure, withdrawn from the world. 'Ah, you see! I have read my Greek philosophers! Oh yes.' And he even pushed back his chair and began to look for Epicurus on the shelves until he was sternly called back to the table by his wife. 'I find them rather lacking. In the wider moral sphere – by what laws should a society live? What gives law legitimacy? That sort of thing.'

'Not at all,' retorted Jack. 'Epicurus had the most sensible things to say. About liberty and justice and society. I agree with *all* his ideas. Without exception. He defined justice very simply, as neither to harm nor be harmed. Isn't that marvellous? Concise and correct.'

'Why, he sounds almost like a good Jew, darling!' agreed Ilse. 'We could convert him!' she laughed prettily with glee.

'A good human being, let's say,' responded Jack.

'Why shouldn't a Jew agree with such things?' Villy asked.

'And yet remain Jewish?' Jack asked. 'How can he, if he does not believe?'

'What does it matter what a Jew believes? Only so long as he observes the mitzvot, of course. Judaism requires action, not belief. But the great pity of it is,' Villy said, 'that a Jew who abandons his yiddishkeit, because he does not believe, well, he has nothing left. Nothing at all. Nothing to teach his children. About who and what they are. He is truly a lost soul. Of course, he is still a Jew, but he denies it. And all because he does not believe? Who cares about that?'

Now it was clear that Villy was addressing his remarks directly at Jack, and had remembered Jack's comment in the car – that he was not Jewish any more. Jack drew back from making some scathing retort, right on the tip of his tongue, about Jewish culture. He wanted to remain amiable. Instead he responded pleasantly, 'Isn't it enough for a child born and brought up in England just to learn about being English?'

Villy looked at him questioningly, and shook his head as if Jack were a pathetic imbecile. 'Who's English, Jack?' asked Villy, his loud voice becoming louder with each sentence. 'Is that you? You are English? And I? No, of course, only English people are English. Even a Scotsman can't pass for English, let alone a Jew. My family, and Ilse's, may their memory be for a blessing, thought they were Austrian! What a mistake that turned out to be. Don't your family come from Poland, or Russia maybe? Does that make them Polish? Of course not. Did you arrive on these shores as Poles – or as Jews? Of course as Jews. And long may you remain here as a Jew, in good health. And by turning your back on that, what is left to teach your children? But let's not argue.'

'Villy, my son and his family *are* English!' Jack replied. 'They live here, they work here, they speak the language. Look, they even celebrate Christmas. They don't have a scrap of yiddishkeit between them.'

'Then, excuse me,' Villy continued loudly to Jack, 'you have made a big mistake. Did I say Jews shouldn't live and work and speak the language? Not Christmas maybe, but of course, we play our part in this country. This country took us in and gave us a new home, a safe home. But to think that, inside, we have English souls? No, you are wrong.'

Ilse tutted him. 'It's you who's arguing, Villy! For goodness sake, leave our guest in peace!'

'Can't my child become English? Is that such a bad thing to be? You're right about Poland and Russia, anyway,' Jack chuckled. 'The bad old good old days. In *der heim.* Maybe that's why there are so many jokes about them.'

Villy was suddenly good humoured again. 'Yes, you know of course, that after Tsar Alexander II was assassinated, a Russian official ordered all the leading rabbis to come and be questioned. "Do *you* know who was behind this crime?" he asked them. "No, but whoever it was," one rabbi replied, "I believe the government should blame the Jews and chimneysweeps." The official was puzzled. "Why chimneysweeps?" "Nu," answered the rabbi, "why the Jews?"'

They smiled together at the old joke. Villy drew several more such black tales from a huge store, and had the knack of telling them with perfect timing. After a while, Jack and Ilse could not stop laughing, and for a bleak instant Jack realised he was happily distracted from thinking about the events of the afternoon.

At length Jack felt exhausted and said he must go home. He wondered rather fearfully how he would get there. As a religious Jew, albeit not Orthodox, Villy would certainly not want to drive him. For that matter, he wouldn't even want his phone used on Shabbat to call a taxi. Jack did not fancy walking in the street. It was a long way, he was tired and in pain, and it seemed there were antisemitic thugs around: fascists and leftists, Muslims and Christians, blacks and whites. Who could you feel safe with? He had heard that even the Japanese hate Jews. But for crying out loud, why should he worry – after all, he didn't look Jewish, didn't sound Jewish (for so Dr Jack Silver mistakenly believed of himself). Perhaps he could figure out how to use the mobile phone in his pocket to call a taxi.

'Going to shul tomorrow?' he asked conversationally.

'Of course, darling,' Ilse said. 'Why not join us? Of course you must stay the night here; we have a comfortable spare bedroom and everything you need.'

Jack tried to consider whether or not to spend the night. Villy and Ilse had already done too much for him. They had been so kind and solicitous that he felt embarrassed. He couldn't ever reciprocate. He wasn't badly enough hurt for an overnight stay – there wasn't much wrong with him at all. While struggling with these thoughts, he asked, 'What shul do you belong to?'

'New Golders Green, darling,' she replied. 'It's a lovely community.'

'Masorti,'[16] added Villy.

'Villy is president of the shul,' Ilse said. Villy frowned deeply at this and gestured with irritation to ignore the remark.

Jack nodded politely. 'Masorti, I've heard about them. They're interesting.'

'So you will come? Really, Jack, you definitely shouldn't be on your own tonight. You are shaken up. Maybe you don't even realise it yet. Experiences like you had, they are much more upsetting than you think.'

---

16 literally 'traditional', one of the Jewish denominations, also called Conservative

Jack decided what to do. He insisted he must make his way home and return to the secular realities of life. Saying nothing about driving on Shabbat, Villy offered to take him in the car. Ilse touched Villy's arm with admiration, 'That is a mitzvah, darling.'

At the door of Simon and Penny's house, Jack took Villy's hand, 'Villy – I really can never thank you enough. I think you actually did save my life. It's really impossible to thank you. Can we keep in touch?'

'Jack, what are you talking about!' he retorted, his powerful voice almost indignant. 'Of course we will keep in touch! In fact, come and see us tomorrow. Or any time you like. You think I am kidding? Not at all. Ilse and I must be told how you are feeling, and if your grandson will be home all right, and so, to make sure all is good again.'

His hand gripped Jack's vigorously. 'Here – write my name also, and my number,' he suddenly exclaimed. 'Write it down, why not – it's for the saving of life. It could be important. If there is any trouble so, call me. Straight away. *Straight* away!'

With a sick feeling Jack remembered Simon's business cards, in his stolen wallet. His attackers might arrive at the house at any time. And the car, of course! He – and Villy – had forgotten about the car, still parked in Golders Green. His heart sank as he realised he could not walk well enough to go and get it, and anyway, he wasn't sure he would dare return to that place, even assuming he could find it again. He carried on smiling. 'Thank you so much,' he said, 'and thanks to Ilse, and thank you for getting me home safely, and on Shabbat too.'

Villy said, 'Look, I wish you'd stop thanking me, Jack.' He turned back to his car and called back, 'Good Shabbes.'

'Shabbat shalom,' said Jack.

As soon as the door shut behind him, Jack was overwhelmed with pain, terror and shock. Shoulders, knees, neck, everywhere was aching. The sense of solitude was crushing, as if loneliness was something tangible, encircling him. He raised his hands onto his high, bald forehead and pressed the palms there in despair, standing silently in the empty hallway. As if it could become so simply by wishing, he pictured himself lying peacefully in bed in his own home. He wanted to delve deeply into a restful oblivion in which none of this had happened, to lie beneath an ocean, and find emptiness. Then he again remembered the car.

He needed to sit, and so slumped down onto the steps of the staircase. He straightened his left leg to ease the swollen knee. It was quiet in the house. 'Oy, Miri, am I *af tsores*.' He stared blankly around at the pale walls of Simon and Penny's hallway, noticed his son's framed certificates on the wall. I am the father of a child who is alive in this world, he thought. I made another generation, I took a step forward, carried the light of humanity, and went a few paces further into the endless darkness. He had worked, and loved, and done his duty for his family. Now even his child had a child. Soon he too would have children. And so it continues. People die and are forgotten. I've done enough already, he thought. My turn is over, my time is up. All the same, it's not for us to decide. We don't leave the world, so much as we are taken from it. Who knew what more might happen in a life?

'It's nothing, Miri,' he said aloud at last. 'A Jew is attacked by some thugs. So what's new?'

He must pull himself together. He stood and made his way along the hallway. His hard leather heels knocked against the polished wooden floors, ringing out in the silence of the house. The neighbours, he thought, might hear. The neighbours are not Jewish, of course, in this street. If they were Jewish, he could wake them if he wanted, even go next door and ask for help, even in the middle of the night.

The thought troubled him. But, if they were Jewish, would *they* be able to call on *me*? he asked himself frankly. Wouldn't I say, *What's Jewish got to do with it?* I must think about this. Not now. But you can't have your cake and eat it – saying I'm not Jewish, but I'm Jewish enough to call on Jewish neighbours for help. Anyway, why worry about it now, it's academic. The neighbours are not Jewish and that's an end of it. He must calm his mind, be quiet inside.

In the sitting room, he turned on the light nervously, half expecting to see his assailants waiting for him in the dark. At first he made for the piano, but did not sit down. He touched the keys and played a few notes. Turning away, he paced up and down the room anxiously, then dropped himself into an armchair. For many minutes he sat gazing at nothing, absorbed in directionless thought, a tight-lipped defiance in his face and eyes. He wondered anxiously how to protect Danny.

'After all, worse things have happened,' he said, and grinned bitterly. 'Knock, knock, who's there? Hello it's us again. In smart uniforms, arriving at the door. Stepping inside.'

Yes, of course, much worse things have happened. Hiding from thugs who are inside your own house. Which might be happening to him, soon. If they decide to have a bit more fun. Anyway, much worse things do happen everywhere, all the time, and not just to Jews. But the answer is law, an orderly society. Then all will be protected, and equal.

'Justice, justice, you shall pursue,' he said, repeating his favourite teaching of the Torah. He saw himself, younger than Danny, hearing these lovely words for the first time in the hated cheder where he had had to learn the sacred texts. It was high summer, and the sun was shining outside, its brightness just discernible through windows opaque with dirt. The melamed – he wasn't a proper teacher – was just as filthy, wretchedly shabby, perhaps mad, shuffling between the rows of desks, whacking boys on the head. Jack couldn't remember that there had been any summer holidays when he was a child. 'Justice, justice, you shall pursue,' he repeated, 'that you may thrive, and occupy the land the Lord is giving you.' He remembered sitting at his desk with other boys. Those lines came in Dvarim.[17] Straight away after that comes the paragraph commanding that 'You shall not set up a sacred post, or erect a stone pillar, for such the Lord detests.' He remembered that even as a small boy he had asked himself, if Moses received that information at Sinai, as we have been told, why did he immediately erect twelve stone pillars, as it says he did in Shmot?[18] But even to ask such a question, asking any question at all, was regarded as a blasphemy. There were no questions, only facts, certainties, words, words, words, words to be memorised, wallpapering the whole mind, covering all the cracks. But among them were the gems, the secrets of Judaism, which led the way to human happiness: Community. Law. Justice.

Law, and an orderly society. Maybe the answer is education. An intelligent, aware population. That, he realised, was an impossibility. Some of the best educated people hate Jews. So a liberal, tolerant society? He grimaced at the thought. In his mind he saw ranks of pale, thin-lipped English men and women saying 'we're not antisemitic', the readers and writers of the Guardian and the Independent, sympathising with suicide attackers, calling for boycotts and spreading hatred of Israel. He laughed bitterly. 'Oh no, it's only Israel and its supporters we hate,' he said, 'not Jews.' The Guardian and the Independent and the BBC are leading us to the next Holocaust. Then they will be able to report on it with horrified condemnations. What about the Jews who take that side, too – Harold Pinter and the rest? Fools! Indulging in a pipe dream of being intellectuals,

17 Deuteronomy
18 Exodus

sophisticates, the good people, artists, sensitives, lovers of peace, empathisers with the weak, lovers of the poor and of ethnic prints and attractive skinny Youth throwing stones for Liberty, disdainful of vulgarians who would mention borders, blood, hatred, jackboots, tanks, tear gas, terror and war in polite company.

'Must a Jew be an exile?' Jack asked himself. He pictured his parents, imagined their hasty departure from Russia. He remembered his own fear in the London streets of his childhood. He thought of the Israeli car mechanic swinging his metal bar, wanting revenge.

But his attackers, he realised, did not bother themselves with sophistry. Their hatred was of another kind, a pure and simple loathing, a nausea, a visceral disgust at everything Jewish. He suspected many of the liberal, tolerant people felt the same, and the entire Muslim world, from Morocco to Indonesia, he was sure, boiled with salivating murderous violence towards the Jewish people.

He should take his shoes off, go upstairs and get into bed. Outside, from the next street, he heard the goyish world celebrating its weekend. Drunkenness, shouting, guffaws.

He must not himself be unjust. There were some humane, well-intentioned people out there. Maybe. Just a few. Certainly not all goyim were louts. The people next door were probably not out carousing and menacing others in the streets. Probably they were watching television or even asleep in bed. And some Jews, too, certainly could be… well, no, not louts, or menacing to anyone, but they could be frightfully annoying. Something he didn't like about Jews was the way they wouldn't mind their own business. How many times had he noticed Jews start talking, uninvited, to total strangers? Why did they do that? And at the drop of a hat they would turn everything into a major production, into a performance, drawing attention to themselves! The other day at the café, a woman – so Jewish! – thought one of the tables was rather dirty and needed a wipe down. So that was the very table she chose to sit at, and she starting insisting loudly that the staff stop what they were doing to clean the table. How annoying Jews could be – talking loudly, slamming car doors, so full of themselves, bursting with ego. Not drunk, of course, God forbid! Of course, if that was the limit of their sins, then they weren't so bad. He snorted with derision at himself, at his circuitous, intersecting trains of thought, going nowhere. All these rambling ideas and theories! What nonsense! He should try to be calm. He was tired and should sleep! He had been assaulted in the street by violent fools, that was all. And again speaking aloud, he said to himself: 'You idiot. Just go to the police and make a statement. Then go to a doctor and get patched up. Then get on with your life.'

He rose from the chair and made for the stairs. Reaching them, he suddenly turned back towards the kitchen. There he opened the freezer and took out a bag of frozen vegetables. He pressed it against his left knee. 'Oh, God! That's good!' He turned back towards the stairs. As he turned off the light he feared that the lights had shown the house was occupied. They might be sitting outside right now, watching from their car, waiting for the lights to go out.

It was all very well, thinking about getting on with his life, but how could Danny, or Simon and Penny for that matter, continue to live safely in this house if those thugs were likely to come here?

Upstairs, he did not turn on any other lights. Reaching the bedroom, he walked in the darkness to the window, barely moving the curtain as he peeked out onto the dark street. There was no one outside. The sound of distant voices was clearer now. Perhaps someone was having a party. That's not a crime. People can have parties. But when they leave, drunk and full of laughter in the small hours, where might their sense of fun lead?

He removed his jacket and his tie, sat to untie his shoes, and realised that he could not undress and lie defenceless in bed. He pictured himself without shoes, unable to run. He had better keep them on. He wondered if his behaviour, his fear, was irrational.

'And Miri,' he said, 'I am worried. I am scared.'

'It's just the shock,' he heard her familiar tones. 'You're shaken up. If you can't sleep, don't sit fretting – maybe you can go and make your statement now. Maybe you can see a doctor now.'

But he knew he was only talking to himself, and the suggestions were as irrational as all his other thoughts. He would lean back on the bed, but stay in his clothes, just in case.

Suddenly he jumped in shock – the phone was ringing. Sitting up, he realised that he had slept. There was light shining through the curtains. It was daytime.

7

Penny took Simon by the hand. Together they walked slowly along the carpeted corridor to the hotel's old-fashioned lift, the doors a concertina of criss-crossed metal. Something about the lift alarmed him, so they strolled slowly, still hand in hand, down the wide staircase to the homely reception area, and through to the gardens. Outside, the bright light and refreshing air seemed to Penny as near perfect as a day can be. She felt sure that it must lift anyone's spirits.

Yet it did not seem to affect him either way. Simon had become indifferent to the weather. Penny consoled herself, though. He had improved a great deal in the last couple of days. He was gradually re-engaging with the world. She felt sure this had to do with sex. Penny believed not only in the benefit of a warm human embrace, and of loving, and of knowing that one is loved, but it was her view also that the body and mind of the male animal need sex as birds need to fly or fish to swim. What that need was exactly, what a man meant by 'sex', what desires and dreams and impulses it encompassed, she would not be able to describe. She knew, though, what it meant in practice, at least for her husband.

In fact it was true. After the earthquake that had shattered Simon's mind, two or three things remained standing. First to emerge from the gloom was his desire to find a solution to his problem. After the days of madness came a silent oblivion, and then the glimmer of a thought – amounting to little more than Descartes' proposition, 'I think therefore I am.' In the darkness, this grew and germinated. It emerged into the light as 'I am, therefore I will be. And I cannot stay like this.'

Secondly came art. At first too deeply buried in the rubble to notice, Simon now longed to touch again the creative source, the small bright light of inspiration that he considered the best thing about humanity and about himself. When he tried to think, he wondered how best to express those thoughts. When he overheard some music, a band playing outside, the flicker of joy he felt brought forth a torrent of tears. He seemed to watch the sound with his mind's eye, the changing notes drawing orderly lines of colour on the black canvas of his mood. A calm, intricate harmony was imposed on his mind.

And then there was sex. One small place at the back of his troubled mind still remained hard at work, and nor did it give a damn about the turmoil within the rest of his thoughts. As the days passed during which he had not had sex, it began to stir with its usual impatience, inserting images before his eyes, and insisting that he think about them… the flick of a skirt, the smooth curve, the shape of women, chambermaids in his room and in the corridor, smiling young women returning together from the pool, a clinging summer dress. At first the dark inner tide swallowed up all such images and ideas, or washed them away. But Penny's arrival made this robust corner of the brain even more active. Her thick mass of hair, the mahogany-coloured eyes hiding all emotion, even her nose, the line of the eyebrows thrilled and tempted him. His eye grasped eagerly even at the sight of her bra strap, which had something about it of ribbon tied around a gift. He longed to unwrap it. When at last she took his hand beneath the bedcovers, and laid it on her, and when with caressing fingertips she reached for him, she indeed found that very part of Simon that most wanted a speedy return to happiness and normality.

Simon knew what it was to have difficulty. He had sometimes experienced moments of failure on those evenings when he was too tired, too drunk, or preoccupied with work, or in the wrong state of mind. At first, pessimistic, he lay unresponsive, anxiously struggling with himself. Part of him gave warning that he should keep his distance. If he did not fight the desire, he risked being connected, for a moment, to another person and to the shallow illusion of pleasure. His privations and denials and hungers were the rock on which he stood alone. Penny persisted, slowly and gently stroking, and he felt her soft cheek against his, and her breath on his face, and thoughtlessly he ran a hand over the curve of her hip and began to respond. And as he had feared, he allowed himself pleasure, agreed to succumb to it and abandon himself, and there was indeed a weakness in it, and he gave way and took delight in it. Holding him, Penny adored his lean body as he gripped and pushed. Orgasm was a fire that consumed all his troubled thoughts and left his mind scorched clean.

Afterwards as he lay against her under the sheets, she could imagine all was well again. And when he opened his eyes after that period of rest, sometimes he whispered to her a little of the strange horror in which he had been drowning, his distress and anxieties. But she did not want to share those horrible, gory pictures of blood and mutilation and death. Even though, as he explained, there was no pain, no sound, in his nightmare. He was merely wallowing in blood and fear. This problem was too big for her.

She led him to a bench at the back of the hotel. To one side, the tennis courts were empty. In front, the mountains rose into the blue sky.

Penny wanted to make her phone calls without fear of interruption from Simon. She said, 'I need to go to the bathroom. Do you think you'll be OK here?'

He nodded slightly. 'If no one speaks to me, I'll be all right.'

She tried to use her mobile, but the signal was bad. She couldn't wander away somewhere in case Simon needed her. She rushed back to the room to use the phone there, and was still breathless when Jack answered.

'Hello, Aloo,' she said brightly, 'Good *morning*. It's a lovely day here in Kandersteg. You don't mind me calling so early? I'm just wondering what happened yesterday, and also, I'd very much like to say hello to Danny.'

Jack wondered how on earth she knew about yesterday. It was painful to walk, painful to stand, painful to sit. He pulled the curtain aside and looked out. The street was empty. It was a nice day.

'Don't worry about it. I'm OK now. I'm fine.' He didn't want to talk. He wanted to get off the phone.

She laughed. 'It wasn't that bad, was it, surely?'

'No, it was nothing. Nothing at all. I'm really all right.' There was no point in telling her.

'What's wrong, Aloo? Is something wrong? You don't sound "all right."' All the good humour was gone. It was important that he remain well and in good spirits to care for Danny properly. She felt a moment of nausea at the folly of allowing Aloo to care for her child. She should have tried to make other arrangements. But there had been no time.

He paused uncertainly, drawing into himself like one of those tender creatures with its carapace – a snail, a tortoise, or the quicker, cannier crab, sidestepping danger. His instinct was to say as little as possible about the assault, the attack, the fight, whatever it was. Mentioning it drew attention to himself, something he was determined not to discuss. Besides, the incident had been humiliating. He did not want to talk about it and, narrow-eyed, was resolved to follow that intuition. 'You're asking me about yesterday?' he said cautiously.

'Yes, did something happen at the lunch?'

The lunch! Jack had forgotten the lunch. Had that been yesterday too? The thought struck him – not for the first time – that life becomes longer when many things crowd into a single day. Time expands like a stomach to absorb all the events available. Unless, of course, you *forget* what has happened to you – then, as memories are lost, so the sum of your life contracts. A person's life is what's inside their own head. It's nothing to do with how much time has been measured by clocks, or what other people know about you. You are as large, or as small, as your own mind.

Now it was Jack's voice that sounded falsely bright. 'Is that what you're asking me about? The lunch? Ha-ha-ha! Of course nothing went wrong! I spoke to a lot of people. How's Simon now?'

He was pleased with himself for thinking to ask after Simon, as normal people would.

Penny could not place where her misgivings were coming from. Something *was* certainly wrong. What had Aloo done that he felt he shouldn't have done? But it was Danny she wanted to speak to. She couldn't spend too long on Aloo. She didn't know how long Simon would sit outside the hotel on a bench. He seemed to have recovered to some extent. He had taken to quietly saying a few words about his feelings, revealing a small tip of ice that emerged above the freezing darkness of his mood. All the more reason to be quick and get back to him.

'I think Simon's a bit better. Look, before I forget, could you open the drawer of the cabinet where the phone is, find my address book, and tell me Auntie Hilda's number.'

'Hilda. Hilda. Have I met Hilda? That's your mum's sister, isn't it?' He found the address book and read out the number.

'And Aloo, just tell me quickly before I talk to Danny, who did you speak to yesterday? Can you remember any of their names?'

He threw his thoughts back to the lunch, which seemed so irrelevant now and so long ago. It would be easiest to say he didn't remember.

'I think one of them was called Clarissa or Melissa. And there was someone called Cathy. Cathy Pincher. Those were the people I sat with.' – Penny inhaled sharply with anxiety as he continued – 'What I do remember was a lot of champagne and some ghastly black pepper ice cream.'

'Was it supposed to be black pepper – I mean, was that its flavour?' She didn't have time to let him wander, but it was only fair to make some conversational response.

'That's right.'

'It's a shame you sat with Cathy Pincher. She's absolutely poisonous, always scheming, trying to do people down. I hope you didn't talk to her about Simon. Did she ask about him? Did anyone ask?'

Better not to say. Against Penny's specific instructions, he had told people about Simon's problems. He had particularly told Cathy Pincher. He was a fool, Jack told himself. Of course, Penny was right, he should have kept his trap shut. It really must have been the champagne. That was the cause of all his troubles. The main thing, Jack told himself, was not to let Penny or Simon know anything was wrong.

'I don't really remember. Maybe one or two.'

Aloo was being too vague. Something was up. 'Can I talk to Danny now?' she asked.

'Listen – Danny's not here, he spent the night with a friend.' He knew it was normal now for kids to spend the night at each other's houses.

'Good, that's good. Who was it?'

'Danny.'

Really the man was impossible. 'No Jack, I'm asking, who's the friend?'

'A boy called Josh.'

'Not that Josh Shinberg!' She held back from becoming annoyed. She must remember Aloo was doing them a huge favour. 'Aloo, that's not good. I did actually write down on my list that he was definitely not to visit Josh Shinberg. I *specifically* wrote that. I wrote he could stay with Alex or Sam or Adam or Ammi, but definitely *not* Josh Shinberg.'

Jack shook his head in fatigue and despair. This really was too much on top of everything else. 'Did you? I'm sorry. I haven't looked carefully at the list.'

'They really are the most awful people. And Josh is a terribly bad influence on Danny. If you can't look after him yourself, could you take him to another friend?'

'I'll get him home today, don't worry. Trouble is, the car…'

'Oh God. What is it this time? Tell me. No, don't – I haven't got time. I must get back to Simon. By the way, we're coming home soon.'

'Oh! What day, what time?'

'I don't know. I'll call you later,' Penny said. She struggled to control her temper. 'All right, just quickly – what's the matter with the car now? New problems?'

'Nothing, nothing, the car's fine.'

She hurried back to Simon, who still sat immobile on the bench, facing past the tennis courts to the hills. A couple of girls were playing tennis in spruce white tops and short skirts. She wondered what kind of people they were, to bring tennis gear with them on holiday.

'I feel like I'm wearing blinkers,' he said quietly.

Her eyes prickled and her throat tightened. She could have

wept with delight. It was the first time he had said anything really intelligible about his state of mind.

'It's sort of dark. Even in the sunlight,' he continued slowly. 'And I can't really… focus on things. And what it is,' – but now he was speaking as much to himself as to Penny – 'is that what I see in my mind, is as real to me as what's outside in the world.'

'Like hallucinations?'

'Yeah.'

'That sounds bad,' she ventured cautiously.

He nodded.

'How did it start?'

'Ages ago, I think. Ages and ages and ages. Then suddenly it just sort of burst out, like all the animals in the zoo escaping from their cages.'

'What triggered that? Did anything happen to release… them, it?'

'My jaw hurts when I talk,' he said. 'It might be about… all the worries and hassles. All this work. And money problems, and the questions, questions, buzzing around all the time. I feel as if my head's inside a bloody wasps' nest.'

She placed her hand on his, but he moved his hand away.

'Questions what about?'

But he felt she could not possibly understand. 'It's not just that,' he said. 'All of a sudden everything terrifies me. And all the questions without answers are driving me crazy. I just want everything to come to a stop.'

'It's all a state of mind, Simon. Like a great big bad mood.'

'You don't understand. You don't want to know.'

She remained silent, fearful of angering him with the wrong reply. He continued, 'Now the creatures won't go back down into their cellar. They'll never go back. They're inside the house. Flesh eaters. '

'What did you mean by "questions"?'

'About my father, my son, and you. I dunno. It's like I'm not part of this family.'

'Darling, you are everything to this family. We are three together, one father, one mother, one child. Being a family needs all three of us.'

'A trinity? Three in one?' he said. 'The holy family?'

She smiled a little, happy that he could again be ironic. 'I think we are something a bit less churchy.'

'A Jewish holy family,' he murmured. 'Or an unholy, half-Jewish trinity.'

She bit her lip. How had this silly little matter of being Jewish become so important to him?

'I watched a programme,' he murmured, 'I don't know when. I saw a programme on TV. It was about Auschwitz, about the death camps, the liberation of Auschwitz. They showed film footage. Taken at the time.'

She could not understand. Why was he so very upset about it this time? They had already seen such programmes. Quite a while ago, she realised, on the anniversary of the liberation of the camps, they had watched a whole season of programmes about the Holocaust. Anyway she had seen similar film many times – who hadn't? She knew already. Gigantic heaps of emaciated dead bodies. Gaping dead eyes, faces hollow with starvation. Everyone knew. She thought about it nearly every day, one way or another.

'I first saw stuff like that at Yad Vashem. This was more real. A movie taken by a soldier walking around. And I thought – '

She waited.

'– how many of them, I was thinking, how many of these – these, among them my own blood relatives, naked great-aunts and uncles and second, fourth or fifth cousins, flung on one another like broken dolls, rag dolls with their stuffing leaking out, like junk chucked into a skip – how many of *these* had a Jewish father, but not a Jewish mother, and were not even considered Jews? But now they are all part of the Six Million? And *honoured* for that. Hitler's Jews were everyone with even one Jewish grandparent, so millions died who were a quarter, a half Jewish. But no one questions the Jewish identity of a Jew murdered in the Holocaust.'

'Is that what's bothering you?' Surely this couldn't have led to Simon's complete mental collapse.

'So you see, it's simple really. If I had been murdered in the Holocaust, I would be Jewish. But alive, I am not Jewish.'

The words 'broken dolls' reminded her sharply of her dream. Later in the day, when Simon was sleeping – for he spent much of these exquisite summer afternoons asleep on the bed – Penny made another phone call to England. She desperately wanted to talk to someone who was on her side, someone who loved her and could advise her wisely.

'Auntie Hilda, do you remember that broken doll you had repaired for me, when I was little?'

'Yes darling,' came the sweet, high-pitched voice from far away. 'What was her name? Was it Loppy?'

'That's right!' said Penny happily. 'What a memory you have! How old was I? About six? I loved Loppy so much, do you remember? And you made it all better.'

'Yes, I remember.'

'Well, now I have another broken doll, and I don't know how to get it mended. And I wonder if you know what I should do.'

'Darling, tell me what has happened. Is it Simon?'

* * *

After the phone conversation with Penny, it was all Jack

could do to slump back in the bedroom chair. He covered his face with both hands. He could not say what, if anything, he was thinking. At this moment, no particular thought troubled him, no identifiable anguish. There was only a dark universe of fatigue and loneliness and physical discomfort. He held his left knee with both hands and for a moment rubbed it gently with his fingertips. He leaned back and gazed blankly at the wall, half seeing on it a silent black-and-white film of his life, perhaps lingering at times on certain moments. But he noticed that a part of his mind looked at him as if from across the room, and he realised that the watcher was the real him, observing his plight and his discomforts with a philosophical air.

Suddenly he started to speak in his deep gravel voice, but halted. 'Oh God! Why did I come here, Miri?' was all he could say. He returned to melancholy silence. Yet he was not really in despair. The mind has many facets, and the part of Dr Jack Silver that could watch him from across the room would eventually find a black humour in every situation. So now, perversely, he found his self-pity amusing, and even smiled grimly at his own misery. He began to think about the events of yesterday. A new day does cast a different light. It didn't seem feasible, after all, that his tormentors would drive here especially to attack him. That was the stuff of nightmares, not reality. It's likely, too, that having taken from his wallet anything of value, they would simply have thrown it out of the car window as they drove away. He remembered trying to see their car number through hazy eyes, and recalled that it had made him think 50-50-50. What did that mean? He could not remember, and now yet another part of his mind set about unravelling that little problem.

At length he stood up, mustering his determination to continue with life. He winced as a sharp pain shot through his bad knee, but he limped to the bathroom. Turning to the mirror, he was shocked by his face. It was worse than before. 'That's a heck of a shiner you've got there, buddy,' he told himself, gingerly feeling a purple bruise around his eye socket. 'That's a lulu.' He would have a quick wash, put on more of the pain-killing ointment, have breakfast, go by cab to collect Danny and on from there to collect the car. He tightened his lips at the thought of going back to that place. But he would not be intimidated. He would then try to see a doctor, get checked over. And time would pass, he would feel better about life, and eventually his bruises would fade. After the doctor's, he would go to the police station to make his statement.

No, what was the point of that? At the thought of the police he had to struggle with the despondency that could so easily return. He remembered the two naïve young police constables debating whether he had been the victim of a racial incident, while Villy helped him and they did nothing. All Englishmen in uniform gave him the same feeling, that they know nothing, nothing of history, nothing of the world, nothing of life, that they are proud of ignorance and suspicious of knowledge. He pictured the bland indifference of an older officer in the police station taking his statement. No, he would not simply go and make a statement. He had a different idea.

He took up the strange mobile phone in his hand, a curiously beautiful, enigmatic *objet trouvé*, like some Oriental enamelwork, perfectly black, inlaid with glass and silver. He knew, of course, that it was a tool, not an artwork, and that the enamel was not enamel, the glass not glass and the silver not silver. Its beauty lay partly in the mysterious unknowable newness of the materials of which it was made.

If it did not belong to the hasid, then it must surely have been dropped by one of the thugs. He tried to flip the phone open, but could not see how to do it. He grinned wryly. What an old duffer! He could not even work out how to open the thing. Yet Villy had done it so easily! Jack tried and tried again, turning it over and studying it from every angle. Was the cover locked in some way? He began to wonder if this strange object really was a phone. A shiny black rectangle of hard plastic, with a large black screen on one side and some smaller screens on the other, it had no dial, no handset, no speakers, not even a keypad. Jack put on his reading glasses to study it more closely. On the narrow edges were black buttons marked with symbols that he recognised or whose meaning he could work out – fast forward, fast back, headphones, a camera, and another with a picture of a phone.

The tiny picture of a phone did look exactly like a proper telephone, of the type which no longer existed – a big solid dial phone, with a big handset resting on top, like the one that had stood for years on the telephone table in front halls all over the land. Of course, he thought, this object wasn't really a telephone at all: it was a digital radio receiver and broadcaster. That was why it could do so many things. Indeed, there were many more things that a tiny digital receiver could be made to do, and he wondered why they weren't. At once he began to think about the possibilities, and how they could be achieved. But that wasn't helping at the moment. He laughed aloud, mocking himself, and said to Miri, 'Here I'm trying to work out how to use a mobile phone to pay bills and parking fines and turn on the central heating, but I can't even open the ruddy thing.'

Yet it was true that Villy had opened it, looked at it, gone into the address book and come to the conclusion that it was unlikely to belong to a hasid. Jack tried to force his fingernail into a slender gap between the front and back of the phone, but nothing budged. He tried pressing the buttons on the side – perhaps it would open automatically. No. Anyway, he didn't want to accidentally turn the thing on, in case it rang, and he wouldn't know how to answer it. He put it back in his pocket.

* * *

'I think you must be Prince Scrapeknees,' giggled Danny in the car.

'Who does that make you?' retorted Jack.

'I don't know. Maybe the one who's the king's right hand exchequerman.'

They pulled up outside the house. 'Hey, I found something interesting,' Jack said brightly even before he had opened the front door. 'Come on, I'll show you.'

He handed Danny the mobile phone as soon as they were inside.

Danny looked at it eagerly. 'Wow! Nice one! You *found* it? Are you going to keep it?'

'No, of course not! What an idea! I want to give it back to the owner. I suppose if they don't want it, then I'll think about keeping it.'

Danny frowned. 'So you know whose it is, then?'

'No,' said Jack. 'But I can learn that from the phone itself, can't I?'

Danny nodded with interest. 'Mm, maybe. Have you tried? Have you made a call with it?'

'No – that would be like stealing. Phone calls cost money, after all, and I wouldn't be paying. Anyway, I don't know how to use it. I don't even know how to open it. Do you know?'

'Poor Grandad Aloo!' Danny jumped up and down with amazement and glee, sliding the phone cover open and closed repeatedly to make his point. 'You don't even know how to open a mobile phone! It's *so* simple!'

Jack slapped his forehead with an open palm, flinching slightly as his hand touched a bruise. 'Hey! What an idiot! I didn't think of sliding it!'

'Where did you find it?' Danny asked.

'Ah, yes. I think it was… in the park.'

'Don't you even know where you found it?'

'Yes, yes. It was in the park. Lying on the grass.'

'Well, when was that?' Danny's bright, inquisitive face turned towards him, the intelligent eyes searching. 'Did you go for a walk in the park after falling over in Golders Green?'

Jack felt a prickle of sweat. He really must get his story together. 'No, obviously not,' he agreed. 'It was before that. So… yesterday morning.'

'How could it be? Yesterday morning you were in a big hurry to get ready and go out to this lunch of Daddy's. You took me to Josh's and went straight to the tube station. You were late, so I don't think you went to the park on the way. There's something wrong with you today,' said Danny very seriously, eyeing him with scepticism.

'Well, that's probably because I'm aching all over. How would you like to have bruises like this?' He was thinking he should have said in the street, not the park.

Danny once again paused to marvel at Jack's bruised face, as he had done when Jack came to collect him from Josh Shinberg's this morning. He contemplated it with childish lack of sympathy, impressed especially by the purple patch forming under Jack's right eye.

'You got all that just from falling over! Did you land on your face or something?'

'Well, I suppose I did.'

'When you fall over, don't you hold out your hands? Like this?' He opened his palms. 'There's no point in asking you. Nothing you say today makes sense.'

Jack urged the boy to look at the phone. 'OK, I don't make sense. That's your opinion. So tell me something about this phone.'

Again Danny shot him a quizzical glance. 'If you aren't going to keep it, why are you so interested? You could just give it to a lost property office or the police or something.'

'No, I want to see if I can return it myself – it's a challenge. Like a puzzle.'

Danny nodded. He understood the idea of a puzzle. 'A challenge for me, not you. You've already given up. You know, this is a really great phone,' he said, suddenly an expert on the subject. 'One of the best.' He pressed a button and with a tinkling sound of music the phone lit up brightly like some small alien creature waking and wanting to play. 'It does everything. Look, you can take pictures. Can I look at their pictures?'

Jack had not fully understood that the photographs would be stored inside the phone. So it's like a photo album, he thought. He said, 'That might be prying, mightn't it? Well, show me how, and I'll look.'

But Danny had already opened a picture. 'Hey! Wow! Look!'

'Let me see,' said Jack, but Danny was staring at the screen in amazement.

'This is like something on television. Aloo, look at this.' Jack noticed that in his excitement the boy had dropped the 'Grandad' and addressed him just as everyone else in the family always had. He leaned over Danny's shoulder and on the little screen they saw a picture of people fighting. 'This really happened,' commented Danny, 'and it's really, really bad.'

'I don't like that,' Jack said. 'No, don't look at it, Danny. Save the battery. How can we find out whose it is?'

'Wait. I'm looking in Own Numbers. There's a number here.' He read it out.

'Very good – excellent,' Jack said. 'It might be this phone, or it might not be. Either way, that's useful.' He wrote the number down. 'Tell me some more.'

'Just looking in Messages, but there's nothing there. No texts waiting to be read, no texts stored. Nothing in the Inbox.

That's a bit funny. I'll check Calls. Mm... Received Calls. I can see the numbers that have been calling – there's a number that has been trying to call lots of times, another mobile. Let's look again at Contacts in a minute and see if it's there.'

'What else can you see?'

'I'm looking at Dialled Calls... well, it's hard to say, but the number that has called a lot, this phone has called them a lot too.' He kept pressing keys rapidly. 'Yes, it's there, it's in Contacts. There are lots and lots of contacts. Hard to know who they all are, really. I could try texting one of them.'

'That's an idea. Just text the one that has been trying to call a lot. Danny, can we recharge the battery?'

Danny offered to have it recharged by a friend whose parents' phone was the same make.

But Jack didn't want the precious piece of evidence to go out of his hands. For the moment they would simply try to conserve the battery. 'Send a text, ask if they can see whose phone the message is coming from – know what I mean?'

'OK. So what do you want it to say? "I found this phone." Oh no – predictive text!' Danny said.

'What's that?' Jack asked

Danny carried on, half talking to himself, 'Oh – this is awful. Now, how do you do a space? I can't even write the word Phone – as soon as you type P-H-O it changes to Photo.'

'Is that predictive text?'

Danny ignored him. 'Oh no, I've got to go back... I wonder if I can turn off the predictive text.' He fiddled with the keys, staring intently at the screen. 'I can't work out how. OK, what shall I... um, I found this phone in the ...' He yelled with exasperation. 'If I type T-H it's fine, then I put an E and it turns into the word There. That's predictive text, see?'

Jack waited while Danny typed. At last the boy showed him a text message ready to send.

He read *Hi found this phone in park whos is it tmb*

'Quite literate for a text message, isn't it?' he said. 'What does T-M-B mean?'

'Text me back.' Danny was biting his lip. 'Aloo, I've been thinking. After you fell over, you said, someone helped you and drove you to his house. How did he get you to his car? 'Cos I mean, where was he parked? There's nowhere to park around there, Mummy is always saying.'

Jack grimaced and wondered what answer to give. 'He wasn't parked far away at all. And, I've just remembered,' he said, 'I found this phone in the street as he was helping me to his car. You're right, it wasn't in the park at all. Can you change it to "street"? Or just delete "in the park"?'

'You're really weird today,' said Danny suspiciously. 'I think you got a head injury. You need a brain scan. OK, I've changed it. So you didn't go the park?'

Jack nodded. 'No, that's right. Good. Click Send.'

Immediately a message appeared on the screen. *Error. Attempting to send.* It was repeated endlessly. Danny could not cancel it. He simply switched the mobile off.

They stared at it for a moment, rather hopelessly. Danny pressed a button. The mobile returned to life and again played its tinkling tune as the screen lit up cheerfully.

'All right,' Jack suggested, 'let's use the ordinary telephone, and try calling that number, the "own number" we wrote down, and see if the mobile rings. Can you do it? I don't want to – I'm not feeling so good; I've got a bit of a headache coming.' He was afraid the number might not be the mobile, it might be answered, and that the person at the other end would recognise his voice.

The two of them went into the hall, to the phone that stood there on a polished table. Jack tapped 1-4-1 so his call could not be traced. Danny looked up questioningly, and Jack nodded that he should dial the number.

The boy did as he was asked, listened intently, then held out the receiver.

This number is not receiving calls.

Jack hung up. 'OK, they've reported it missing. And that's why you can't use it to send a text. So let's just note down all the numbers in Contacts and call them on this phone. Or you can call them for me, because of this headache. All you have to do is give them the number of the mobile and ask if they know whose it is. We'll start with the one that phoned lots of times.'

'No,' protested Danny. 'That's a silly idea. There are so many of them. It'll take too long. It could take hours. Most of them won't recognise the mobile number. And suppose one of them does? Then what? What do you expect *them* to do about it? Look, Grandad Aloo, why do you care so much about it anyway? Can I stop doing this now? You're acting like I've been arrested and you're some cop questioning me.'

Jack forced a smile. It was true, he wanted some information and believed Danny could help him to get it. He shrugged. 'All right, let's leave it now.'

Jack went into the kitchen to make himself a cup of tea. He wondered if Simon and Penny had a cleaner, and if so, on what day she would come. The place was becoming a tip. Hadn't Danny mentioned something about the cleaner? He had a vague recollection. He took his cup and leaned back in an armchair in the sitting room, apparently studying the ceiling but in fact lost in thought. Exhausted after a night spent sitting in a chair, he almost fell asleep, but anxious thoughts kept returning him to wakefulness.

Meanwhile Danny sneaked another look at the photos stored on the phone.

'What!' With a yell he ran into the sitting room, holding the screen towards Jack. 'Who is this in this picture? Who is that man, the one who's being kicked?'

Without any doubt, it was Jack himself. He realised he had

not drunk his tea, and now it was cold.

* * *

I think I'm starting to get it. The phone belongs to the people who gave Grandad Aloo all the bruises. He wants to find out who they were. That's OK. I'm going to help him.

I went up to Aloo and asked him, 'All right, I can see that these men hit you. But did you really fall over, did you find the mobile phone, did someone take you to their house and look after you? Which bits really happened?'

And he told me what had really happened. There was still quite a lot I didn't understand. Like, why did they pick on him – were they enemies? And why didn't he just run away – I would have. And why didn't he get the police to come and arrest them? And, well, why – I dunno, just why, why, why.

His answer made it even more confusing. 'Well. It's all about being Jewish, isn't it, boychick?'

I think it's only a few days since he said he wasn't Jewish. Now he's saying he is. He said, it's just part of life for Jews. Because there are always people who don't like Jews. Always have been, always will be. I wanted him to explain a bit more, because I'm not quite sure what Jews are, except that Mummy and Daddy have said that we are Jewish. Is Jewish the same as being Jews?

But when I asked Aloo if Jews and being Jewish is the same thing, he made a funny face. He said, 'I wonder. Maybe I could apply to be a non-Jew but Jew*ish*. Instead of a non-Jewish Jew. But who would I apply to? The government? Only it's not them who decides how Jewish you are.'

'Who decides?'

'No one decides. Rabbis think they decide, but most Jews are not interested in what rabbis decide. Anyway, I wish I could just forget about this blasted Jewish nonsense. Don't let's talk about it any more.'

It was just getting worse and worse, because I didn't know what rabbis were either. 'Being Jewish,' I said, 'it's complicated, isn't it?'

'You bet,' he nodded, without a smile.

I told him about the weird singing and stuff at Josh Shinberg's, when I didn't know the words, and how Josh had said that was because of being Jewish, too.

He just went, *Mm*. Then he said, 'Their car number made me think 50-50-50, but now I can't remember why.'

I knew he wasn't talking about Josh Shinberg. He meant the people who had beaten him up. 'Is it three different ways of writing 50?' I asked.

Aloo nodded. 'Yes, I think it was. Not sure.'

'Well, are there three ways of writing 50?' I suggested. 'Something like 50 squared, square root of 50, and 50.'

'Yes, yes,' Grandad nodded. 'Of course. Obviously. Lots and lots of ways. Think about it. Five times ten, two times twenty five, square root of twenty-five hundred. Or seven squared plus one. Infinite ways.' He sounded impatient or a bit annoyed. 'But you can't make a car number plate out of things like that. Don't forget a car number plate is more letters than numbers.'

'Can't you use letters to write numbers?' I said. 'Did Romans do that?'

'That's right, they did. Letter I for 1, V for 5. Jews do it, too. Alef for 1, bet for 2, gimmel for 3.'

'So do you know the Jewish alphabet, Grandad?'

'Yes, yes, of course. It's called Hebrew, not Jewish. But this car number wasn't written in Hebrew.'

'In Roman, then. What's the Roman for fifty?'

'I think it was L. And it's not called Roman, it's Latin.'

'Was there an L in it?'

Grandad nodded. 'In "Latin"? Of course. It's the first letter.'

'No, silly! Does the number 50 have an L in it, if it's written in Roman?'

'Yes, yes, I think so. It *was* something like that.'

I wondered if it could be XXV, with a 2 in front – like twice twenty-five, but he said he didn't think so. 'It would have taken too long to work out. I only saw it for a second. Well, never mind.' I could see he was thinking, trying to remember. He wasn't as talkative as usual. 'A good start. Let's mull it over.'

I was pleased to have helped. I went to the bookshelves and took down a dictionary, and read out what was written under "L": 'A Roman numeral, 50.'

He smiled and patted my cheek. 'Very good. Good boy. Want to have another look at the mobile phone now?'

Holding their phone, I had a bit of a scary feeling about those men. Because I kind of realised that Aloo was scared too. That's what his problem was today. But we looked at the Contacts again. One of the numbers was called "Dad"; Aloo was very interested in that one. He asked me to read all the numbers out, and he wrote some of them down.

'Right,' he said. 'Let's give it a rest now. Think about something else.'

'Like what?' I couldn't think about anything else. It was like being in the middle of a game of chess and someone suddenly asks you if you'd like to do something else. Obviously not.

'Well, what about something to eat? What have you had today? Would you like some cheese on toast?'

'I'm OK. I had some challah and honey and some orange juice.'

'Josh's parents,' Aloo asked me, 'did they go to shul?'

What is all this "shul" thing? I just told Aloo they didn't. Which must be right, because Josh and me got up and had breakfast that the au pair made, and Josh's mum and dad were still in bed, and then Aloo came to collect me, so unless "going to shul" means lying in bed, then the answer must be no, they didn't.

'Tell you what,' Aloo said, 'would you like to visit another friend later?'

'All right. But what about our phone puzzle?'

'Who would you like to visit?'

I said I'd like to visit Alex. It's nice at his house – they're more like us. Mummy and Alex's mum are good friends. They go to Brent Cross together, and sometimes go to see a film together. And they belong to a reading group where women talk about books they've read. Alex doesn't go to the same school as me. I've known him since before we went to school, because his mum and my mum were already friends. And I thought, if we could tell Mummy I'd been visiting Alex, she'd be glad, and she wouldn't find out I'd stayed over at Josh's as well.

'Where does he live?' Aloo asked, but I didn't know. He found the address on a list Mummy had written out for him.

'Do one more thing for me,' he said. 'Phone the one that says "Dad". I'll listen on the other phone in the kitchen. Just say, "I found this mobile in the street near Sainsbury's," and he's in the address book as "Dad"; say you'd like to return it to the owner and ask if he knows whose it is. Is that all OK? Can you remember all that? If you have any problems, just say you've got to ask your mum, and hang up.'

'I don't know.' It was a lot to remember.

'Well, let's just try and see what happens.'

He pressed 141, and I dialled the number while he went into the kitchen. He listened on the other phone and watched me through the door.

I heard the phone ringing. I'd never really spoken to anyone like this before.

It was answered, and a man said, 'Yeah?' He sounded rude

and angry. He didn't say hello. Just *yeah*.

It was really frightening.

But I sort of thought, I must just do what Aloo has asked me to do, so I said, 'I found a mobile phone in the street, yeah?'

The voice went sort of 'Yee-ah,' very slowly. So I carried on, 'And I'd like to give it back to whoever's it is. And so... well, I looked in the address book. I hope that was all right. And your number is there, and it says "Dad" so I thought you would know whose it is.'

I'd reached the end of what Aloo asked, and it didn't seem to be enough. I think the man thought so too.

He said, 'Who is this?'

I said, 'Well, you don't know me, I'm just like, well, I've found this phone and I thought, I'd better return it to the owner, yeah?'

'Are you a kid or what?' the voice asked.

'I s'pose so. I'm ten.'

'What's your name?'

'I'm not allowed to tell anyone my name. Any strangers.'

'OK, mate,' the voice said. 'Fair enough. That's my son's phone, that is, my little boy's. He lost it. He'd really like to get it back, right? Tell ya what, mate, where are ya – I'll come and collect it, all right?'

'I'm in Golders Green, but I think I must, like, ask my mum what to do? I'll get her to call you.'

'Nah, you don't need to ask anyone. Look, I could meet ya in the street – you say where – and you could just give it to me and that's that. Where do you hang around? In Golders Green? What about outside the tube station, mate?'

'All right, but I still have to ask my mum.'

'OK then, mate. That's a good idea. Is she there? You can ask her now.'

I looked towards the kitchen. Aloo was waving at me to

come to him. He whispered in my ear, 'Say you'll leave it at Sainsbury's customer services. Tomorrow morning around twelve. Or before twelve, because you can't go after twelve. If he's there, you'll give it to him. If he's not, you'll just leave it at the service counter. Don't worry, you won't really go and meet him – but just tell him you will.'

So I went back to the hall phone and told the man.

'Don't forget, will ya?' he said. 'Tomorrow, a'right?'

I thought from his voice that the man felt suspicious.

And I put down the phone. I was gasping and sweating and shaking. Aloo gave me a big hug and a piece of chocolate, and I felt pretty much OK, and kind of proud. He said, yes, he was Prince Scrapeknees – and I was definitely Marvelstein.

8

Jack reproached himself. He shouldn't have said Sunday morning. That didn't leave much time to think things through. Before taking another step, he needed to consider everything carefully. He was fairly happy with the location – inside a Sainsbury's supermarket there would be plenty of other people. What happens if he's not ready by then? He daren't call any of the numbers himself. They might recognise his voice. More than that, they would just know it was a Jewish voice.

Danny phoned Alex and invited himself over. He gathered up some computer games and CDs and Jack took him in the car. It was quite a long drive. Along the way, Jack saw Jewish families walking and remembered that it was Shabbat. As he drove along East End Road, the Jewish neighbourhoods were left behind. They reached a traffic jam in a hectic area where cars edged forward into a busy roundabout. Jack had to pull over to put on his reading glasses and study the A to Z.

Danny's friend Alex lived in a comfortable residential street just off Muswell Hill, at the bottom of the hill. Something about the curve and steepness of the roads reminded Jack of something, somewhere. Fleetingly he saw himself as a young man, black-haired, slim and fit, laughing with friends and girlfriends. It was an old memory and he couldn't place it, but he knew there had been a time in his life when these street names were familiar to him. Had there been some kind of dance place around here, where he had come at the weekends, to dance with shiksas and have fun? Was that around here? And then he saw it, the Odeon cinema, its splendid white 'people's palace' façade, the great curved front still the same as all those years ago. Of course! He used to come here to go to the flics.

Alex's mother, a woman in her forties with nicely cut brown hair, in well-fitting jeans and a cotton shirt, and a pleasure to behold, gasped with shock as she opened the door for them.

'My God, what happened? Have you had an accident?'

Jack grinned. He stuck to his story. 'Ha! No, it's nothing. I fell on some steps.' Danny glanced up at him quizzically before running inside with Alex, whose mother had noticed the glance. She invited Jack to come in for a coffee. Perhaps according to the rules of politeness he was expected to refuse, but she led him along the hallway into a comfortable sitting room. There she reminded him of her name, Louise. He looked around in satisfaction. A piano and paintings, shelves laden with books, an English rose with a slightly posh accent, and an air of comfort and culture. And not one person in the family, thought Jack, had a Jewish bone in their body. This was the gentle, Gentile world he had longed to join. It made his heart sing to think of his own grandson growing up with such friends, in such circles.

Alex's mother, he learned with delight, was a historian, just completing a biography of Mary Queen of Scots, and the father a pensions lawyer who had risen by sheer brainpower from rough West Midlands back lanes to a distinguished firm in the City of London.

Louise seemed as interested to talk to him as he to her. 'Did you really get those bruises falling on steps? You look as if you've been in a fight.'

'A fight!' He pretended amusement. 'Do I look like that sort of chap? No, I slipped and hurt myself. That's all.'

'Must have been quite a fall, by the look of it. What on earth happened?'

'Yes, well, I fell and... well, that's it, I fell. On the, on the,' he was unsure what to say, something that couldn't be checked, something that's nothing to worry about, 'on the stairs. The stairs in... the stairs at the tube station. At Golders Green station.' He hoped she would not grill him as Danny had done.

'What stairs?' She tried to picture this accident.

Beads of sweat broke out on his forehead. Surely there were stairs at Golders Green station? 'Well, the stairs from the platform, I think,' he said doubtfully. 'Aren't there some stairs there, that you come down before leaving the station? Anyway, I'm fine now, I've forgotten all about it.'

'Goodness, I'm sure you haven't! Those bruises look terrible. They must be very painful. How many steps did you fall down? How did it happen? Did you slip on something?'

'I don't know, not too many. It's nothing. Look, I'm all right now.'

'But the station staff. They must have called an ambulance.'

'No, no. They did nothing. They didn't notice. A man helped me. A passenger. He took me home and looked after me. He and his wife.'

Louise looked at him with puzzlement. 'What, a complete stranger took you home and cared for you? That was jolly nice of him! But why did he do that? I mean, it's kind, but rather unusual, isn't it? He could simply have phoned for an ambulance. Was Danny with you?'

Jack squirmed. 'No, no. I was coming back from a lunch when it happened. I had left Danny with a friend. Anyway, why worry about it? I'm perfectly all right.'

'Presumably Simon and Penny know all about it? Haven't they called a doctor out to you? Are you staying with them?'

It was clear that Louise knew nothing of Simon's present problems. 'No, they're in Switzerland,' Jack replied. 'Look, it's nothing. I don't want to spoil their trip.'

'But look at you! You need help. Are you really looking after Danny on your own? Are you well enough to do that?' Again the deeply puzzled frown. 'Is there anything we can do?'

'Well, yes, there may be. Can I take you up on that?'

'Just say the word. We could take Danny for a day or two, if you like. You should stay at home and rest.'

'That's very kind of you.'

She nodded encouragingly, eyebrows furrowed with concern. 'But I still – I mean, shouldn't you have told Penny and Simon what happened? They'd want to know.'

'No, no, no. I don't want them to come back home for my sake. I'm not hurt.'

'Oh, I'm sure they wouldn't mind. You know, Simon's told us all about you. I'm sure he'd do anything for you. I've often wanted to meet you,' she admitted charmingly.

Jack grimaced, flattered. 'What can he have said? What's to tell? What a bad father I was? My wife used to say I should at least try to remember my son's name, even if I couldn't remember his birthday.'

She laughed sweetly. 'Well, he's talked about your background. Struggling immigrant family. That sort of thing.' The tinkling laugh artfully dispelled the gravity of the words. 'Very interesting. Poor Simon is frightfully confused about it, isn't he? About, you know, Jewish heritage, that sort of thing.'

Jack tutted involuntarily. He didn't want to hear that blasted J-word again. He couldn't seem to get away from it today, what with Danny and now this unexpected interrogation. And all his troubles yesterday stemmed from that one dreadful J.

He shook his head and shrugged, 'What's to be confused? We've never cared anything about any of that. I think we're all perfectly English, aren't we? What about Penny? Maybe it's her who's confused, not him.'

Louise smiled. 'Oh, no. Penny couldn't care less about it. Honestly, I don't think she's mentioned being Jewish even once. No, no, of course you're right. It's not something to get confused about. Actually, I'm a little tiny bit Jewish myself.' She laughed shyly at the idea. 'It's true! Yes, it was… my great-grandmother. Let me get this right. My mother's grandmother on *her* mother's side it was. All the mothers. She was Jewish. She converted to Christianity. God knows why!' Again the pleasing laughter. 'Or presumably He does! So that makes me, mm, what is it? Is it a sixteenth Jewish?'

Jack corrected her, 'One eighth. But in Judaism – I expect you know this – you are actually one hundred percent Jewish, because it comes down the female line. It's a very simple rule. If your mother is Jewish, then you are Jewish.'

Louise demurred. 'No, I *don't* think so, thanks! My mother wouldn't have liked that. She was an Anglican, very devout indeed. And of course, we grew up in the Church. I'm the daughter of a Home Counties parson, for goodness sake. How could I suddenly be Jewish? I still go to church. Well, sometimes.' She thought she might have offended him and said emphatically, 'Nothing against anyone else's beliefs, you know, it's just I'm happy to be a Christian! I'm sure you're right about the female line – you know more about it than I do – but that's one of those strange quirks.'

'No, no,' Jack assured her, nodding and pointing his finger towards her. 'Law is law. You are as Jewish as anyone can be. As Jewish as the Chief Rabbi. The Chief Rabbi of Israel, even. All Jews are equally Jewish. There are no half Jews. There are no proportions or fractions or half-measures in Judaism. And no legal technicalities. Anyone without a Jewish mother is out. It looks like you're in. Hundred per cent. You see, it's all about the mother.'

She smiled pleasantly, tolerantly, flicked back her hair. 'And may I refuse this honour, sir?'

'Nope.'

'Well, I'm sorry, but what I feel is "No thanks."' She half laughed. 'Anyway, it would mean being Jewish is nothing. Which would be nonsense. And *nothing to do with faith?* So anyone at all could be Jewish – you know, one-thousandth part Jewish but it was down the female line. That could be true of anybody. And even if no one knew, not even them. That would be… well, you find the right word, but it would be a pointless rule.'

'Except it's not a rule, it's the law. Oh, I agree with you. It's quite mad. It's not *my* idea.'

'And that would make Alex Jewish too, wouldn't it? Which he isn't, is he?'

Jack nodded. 'Oh, yeah. Yep. Poor kid – don't tell him, he doesn't have to know.' Now he was smiling mischievously, so she wondered if it had all been a joke. A Jewish joke.

'Anyway, Danny is welcome to stay, but tomorrow is tricky. Do you want to pick Danny up about lunchtime tomorrow?' she said awkwardly. 'Like early lunchtime. I'll give him something, but then we have to go out. He's welcome to come back again on Sunday, if that would help.'

There was no right turn out of Alex's street, so Jack couldn't go back the way he had come. He turned left and looked for a chance to do a U-turn, or perhaps go round the block. The traffic was heavy, crawling past parked cars, and he felt anxious about either stopping or turning. The side roads were all No Entry. He quickly became lost as the flow of traffic moved him forward. A street called Tottenham Lane sounded a chord, or a discord, deep within him. How far away was Tottenham? His knee and shoulder were hurting, and he wished he had rubbed on another dose of the pain-killing cream, which had been so wonderfully effective.

He pulled in quickly at a bus stop, and again put on his reading glasses to study the pages of the A to Z. He was on the same page as South Tottenham, where he had lived when he was Danny's age.

He never liked the past and normally would not try to return to it, or even be reminded of it. A pilgrimage was anathema to him. Yet yesterday's events had set him on a strange path. So much in London, and in all the world, had changed during his life. Yet some things remained the same. For example, himself. He turned to the index, finger running down the Ks, turned back to the page and found the right square. Inside it, his very own street. He held its name in his mind, like a stone clutched in the hand, and did not know what to think.

A single grid square on the map contained all his young life. For years it had marked his small boundaries. He gazed sadly at the little street shown in white, with the wide High Road at one end and, at the other end, the maze of small terraced streets he had known so well, walking with brothers to the Talmud Torah at Egerton Road Synagogue. Until – it must have been just before his barmitzvah – he stepped outside the square and joined the kids on the bus going to the Jews' Free School near Spitalfields. Now one of the big boys, he ventured into the whole dirty goyish world, belonging to pale, slovenly, evil-faced beings. What had seemed a long journey at first became routine, a daily monotony marked by a straight stretch, a junction, a turning, the market, and into the Jewish world again as they pulled up at the school gate.

Jack took off his reading glasses and pulled out of the bus stop. His drive took him along increasingly grimy streets of terraced houses. He sat in queues of traffic at Turnpike Lane and in West Green Road, with windows open, looking out at the crowds, listening to them as they passed. Almost all came from other parts of the world, many were black, others a sallow white, with foreign features, foreign moustaches, foreign clothes. Most were in Islamic robes, the men in white, the women in black. Groups of young black men strolled easily, arms swinging, as the crowd parted for them. Occasionally he glimpsed the pinched, depressed paleness of an English working class face passing among the others, lost and downcast. A slight, dark man with a loose cloth wound around his head stood at a traffic-choked street corner and inhaled from an asthma inhaler. Jack shifted his position in the car, he was aching all over, bruises throbbing, his knees warning of a mutiny if he did not give them a rest soon. The neighbourhood was vile, a hell of multiculturalism in which nobody felt at home. A human mish-mash. And in the midst of it, three bright little black children being walked to their violin lesson, carrying their cases, led by an elderly black lady, the very picture of well-dressed propriety.

The idea popped into his mind that like matter and anti-matter in the universe, the collapse of Empire created a sort of black hole into which cultures and peoples were endlessly sucked, to be crushed and disappear. It would go on until the black hole itself – in other words Britain – vanished into its own void. At last the cars began to move slowly forward, and he marvelled at the teeming social chaos through which he passed at little faster than walking speed, crowds milling around an Indian Cash and Carry, a shop called East European Continental Foods, a Turkish supermarket, three halal butchers next to each other, Beirut Gate Lebanese Food Centre, and an enterprising store front marked Internet Money Transfer and English School. For an instant his mind fled from the scene, and the traffic noise dimmed to nothing as he imagined the bare earth, stripped of paving and all that had been thrown down here, the tranquillity of earlier centuries, fields worked by English labourers under

English skies, while his own family toiled in Russian shtetls and prayed for a return to Jerusalem.

He followed a sign to South Tottenham and reached the High Road. The road was wide enough for other traffic to pass, so he crept along, full of anticipation as he looked for his turning. And there on the left, the name of his old street jumped out at him, Kilbroney Avenue, attached to the brickwork of a corner house. A strange meaningless word, yet it glowed with dark meaning for him. This was the very place, for years the centre of his universe. He turned there, and suddenly all was quiet. Immediately came peace, a deep tranquillity. It was the utter calm of Shabbat. There were no cars moving, few people walking. To his surprise parking was allowed here; there were no restrictions and plenty of parking spaces. He stopped in the first space and turned off the engine. So! Here he was at last in Kilbroney Avenue again. Why had he made the effort to come here? What on earth did he think he could find? His childhood? Why would he ever want to find that again? A street is just a street. Surely his Kilbroney was just a memory, no longer a real place. Yet there was joy in being here. He stepped out of the car and, tight-lipped, grinned with pleasure. Slowly and painfully he walked along the pavement to his old home, often pausing to rest with one hand on a garden wall.

These were small semi-detached houses, much smaller than he remembered, with net curtains and tidy front yards, well kept despite a certain squalor, in a civilised street with a few trees, and on nearly every house, a large mezuzah. He took a few more steps and paused again. A poignant delight, to be among the yidden, away from the insanity of the last hour, the madness of the world.

A frum couple approached in their Shabbat clothes. Jack thought they must be Gerer hasidim. The man, tall and bearded, wore a tallit that trailed down to his knees, knickerbockers tucked into black socks and, poised on his head, a huge shtreimel like a fur-covered cake tin. The slender young woman beside him had a clean, rosy face, a plain black hat, a long white coat and shoes like black plimsolls. They glanced at him as they passed, instinctively recoiling for the briefest moment as they saw the bruises.

With an inner tremor of emotion, he reached the house and simply stood outside, looking at his front door. In there he used to go. The door would swing open and there everybody was. Even now he recalled the steamy cooking smells and the enervating disagreements and noise and annoying disorder of his too-crowded home. The old place looked amazingly unchanged, though it was smaller than he remembered. How could you get a dozen people into such a house? A corner of the net curtain on an upstairs window abruptly flicked up and a small, solemn face framed with peyot peered at him intently. Jack did not want to attract attention. He crossed the road and looked from the other side.

He murmured, 'That was me. Did you see me, Miri? At the window? In that same room a whole lifetime ago. Except of course for the peyess. No, that wasn't me, or anyone I remember. Not with peyess.' And silently he continued, lips moving like someone in prayer, Here was I too a little one, a child in all innocence of what life would deal out, the good and the bad that was to come. I used to come out of this same door, and walk along here with my sisters or my brothers, sometimes holding hands. Where did we go together? Shopping? To friends? Apart from Talmud Torah, that miserable Talmud Torah, and the cheder, did I ever go to shul? Yes, for friends' barmitzvahs, when we all reached that age. And at the start of the school year, for the High Holidays, then did we dress up and slick our hair and, spick and span, all emerge from the house as one to join the little streams of others: Jews, all Jews, all my friends and neighbours, joining the great sea of Jews surging along the goyish pavements to our Jewish palace, the majestic synagogue in Egerton Road.

He tried to see how the area had changed. It used to be much less frum, and much more Jewish. There was no one else here in those days. Only idealists went to Palestine then. Now, everyone has friends and family in Israel. The Holocaust has destroyed the world of our ever-present *heim*, that muddy poverty-stricken place in the memory and in the mind, which was both the warm heart of our traditions and the slavery from which our generation had fled across the parted waters.

'Aloo!' A low voice startled him, little more than a whisper in the ear. It was his mother's voice, or just a strange and gentle breeze passing, a movement of air on his face, or it was an echo returning after a lifetime. Her voice was not sweet and kind. It was peremptory, imperious and sharp. Her face was held tilted slightly back, the better to look down her nose at her domain and at all the world around.

'Aloo!' he heard his older brothers say loudly, young men with black hair and black suits, young men with an air of mischief and savage good humour. 'Aloo!' cried his dark-eyed sisters in wheedling tones, with sly smiles, older ones trying hard to be pretty and grown-up with hairdos and ill-fitting shoes and cheap dresses, younger ones playfully nasty, trying to stop him doing his homework, giggling, sneaking, and his parents, his aunts and uncles, everyone slovenly, faces open and loud, overflowing with laughter and amiability, or roaring their anger and flaring ill-temper, but in repose always tight-lipped, bitter, thoughtful, determined.

'Aloo! Bubeleh!' In this house he crawled on the lino floor, in this house he was the lauded, besuited bashful barmitzvah boy and toast of the community, in this house he discovered in himself the insistent, insalubrious desires of manhood and their seedy gratification. 'Aloo! Where are you? What are you doing?'

Here too, when the piano at last arrived, he sat and played it to the jeering admiration of his family, and in this house, where no one ever read anything more than a newspaper, he discovered that everything in the world had already been explored and illuminated, all had been written about in English words, and so he read everything and worked and studied to be free. And as he pored over library books and school books, the air around him was bright with knowledge coming into focus, and sharply fragrant with food being prepared, and secretive with the hissing, whispered schemes of brothers and their friends, or loud with shrieks of pleasure or anger and never-ending complaints and extravagant endearments.

Jack jolted from his reverie as a front door opened, not of his own house but the one next door, and a frummer stepped out. With him came a small boy, peyot flowing from beneath a handsome kippah, and a small girl, neat and quiet. The man himself had a long black beard that trailed onto his chest, and he was tightly wrapped in a bekishe like a long dressing gown. He wore polished black leather boots, and on his head too was perched a fur cake-tin. The boots, Jack thought, identified him as a Skverer hasid. He looked towards Jack, and raised his chin questioningly. 'Nu?'

Jack bristled at the impudence. 'Gut shabbes,' he responded in argumentative tone. 'I'm just looking. You don't mind?'

'What are you looking?' The frummer spoke as thickly as if he had a flannel in his mouth.

'Is it a crime to look?'

'It might be,' the frummer pointed out. 'It depends.'

Jack shrugged. 'I'm looking at where I lived. When I was a little boy. You heard of family Zilberman?'

'Maybe. There are lots of Zilbermans. Where you lived?' came the sceptical retort.

Jack pointed at the house. 'My family home. Family Zilberman.'

'You are Zilberman?'

'Avrom Zilberman,' said Jack.

'Papa,' said the boy impatiently.

The frummer nodded, looked him up and down with pursed lips. 'It must have been a long time ago. Family Silkin have lived here since forty years.'

Jack nodded. 'It was a long time ago.'

'So why look? You are hoping the past is still there? What's to see?'

Again Jack nodded in pensive agreement. 'Nothing. You're right. There's nothing to see. Nothing at all. I see nothing of myself here any more. Gornisht.'

'Papa,' the boy repeated his cry.

The man shrugged dismissively. 'So enjoy looking at nothing.' With a perfunctory 'G'Shabbes,' he turned and walked briskly away, clasping the hand of a child on each side.

'Shabbat shalom,' Jack answered. And he trailed them with his eyes, remembering. On the same pavement, and along all these streets, even hand-in-hand with an older brother, he had walked always afraid, looking this way and that, as they made their way to cheder, to friends' houses, always wary of the sneering, mean-eyed yok kids who came here in search of trouble.

More than once, he was set upon by the horrible, coarse, snot-nosed beings, progeny of the malicious Gentile hordes who surrounded them like a threatening sea. He would square up and raise his fists, his assailants backing off with taunts. Once, some more serious older boys surrounded him and battered him with fists and boots till he fell onto the pavement and crawled away, blood streaked, their guffaws sounding in his ears. No, some things do not change. No one went to the cops afterwards. What's the point? Anyway, we must expect it.

This is what he had wanted to find again. Lost in thought, at last he returned to that endless fear, and he felt it still. In the end, he had lived in the house with only the two youngest girls, and then he too left, conscripted into the army, where even in the midst of the war his comrades mocked that Hitler was right about one thing – the yids. And when the Nazi war was over, he returned every few weeks as they gathered together once again and talk about family and health and business and property. Came the day when he brought his fiancée to meet them all. He wanted to say, you see, even a shiksa can be a shayneh maidel. By then the old man was confined to his bed, and would call out irascibly in Yiddish, sometimes forgetting the names of his brood of a dozen fully-grown English speakers. Mameh and Tateh accepted Mary with tight-lipped politeness, could not say Mary, called her Miri, and did not reproach him for his choice, merely condemning him with disappointed smiles.

One Sunday as they all sat together, cups of tea in hand, someone made a remark about marrying-out. Aloo's temper flared and he vowed to keep away from this family of foreigners. Yet soon afterwards he and Miri had to make another visit, when the whole mishpohah greeted their non-Jewish grandson Simon with a more convincing display of joy. They were perhaps even happier to learn the sad news that Miri could not have any more.

Miri, so bright, so lovely, those clever eyes, that happy smile of youth, and just as keen as he was to escape the squalor of her childhood and climb up and up into a comfortable, solid detached house with good furniture and a charwoman who came in to do all the washing and cleaning. And no mezuzah at the door, oh, that had been his dream. Just to be English through and through. Like Miri, like Simon. His son had completed the job, become what he longed to be himself, English and educated.

Jack made his way back towards the car. He took a rest, leaning against a wall. 'Miri,' he muttered aloud, 'you have no idea. I never told you. How horrible it all was. The Jewish life. I started at Talmud Torah – cheder – when I was only four years old. Everyone did – all the boys, that is. About six hundred boys used to go to our cheder. There were more than a hundred in my class. Just picture it, Miri. It was crowded, sweaty, barbaric. We had to keep quiet – three hours every evening and two hours on Sunday morning. Can you believe it? No one would inflict it on a four-year-old now. The teachers were brutes. They used to hit me on the side of my head. Some of them weren't even teachers. They were tailors, cabinet-makers, same as our dads. Ignoramuses.'

As a group of Orthodox boys approached, Jack realised he was talking to himself. Embarrassed, he stopped. They fell silent as they passed, giving him suspicious glances. All had long peyot around pale faces and wore white shirts, black kippot and black suits. Soon came a group of girls, perhaps their sisters, chatting quietly and giggling. Every one of them had an identical dark blue skirt well below the knee, sensible shoes and hair neatly brushed back in a pony tail.

He watched the two groups with something like fellow feeling and something like a pain in his heart as they reached the end of Kilbroney Avenue and turned into the High Road.

He felt utter contempt for frummers, couldn't stand them, the way they did things, the uniformity of mind as of dress, the mindless routine, repetition, monotony, the gabbled daily prayers, the phoney learning, the ignorance, the prissy shallowness, the nauseating dullness, the cooked-up nonsense of the Mishnah, the absurd circular logic of the sages, the impossible beliefs. Ach! The time for believing the impossible was past.

He wasn't too keen on secular Jews either, their constant shmoozing about business and holidays, each vying to be the most in the know about deals and contacts and how much to pay gardeners and cleaners and au pairs and caterers and dressmakers and how to save a quid on a car or a computer or a kitchen worktop or a three-piece suite.

Ever since he had been the age of these very children, he had distrusted 'belief' and had revelled in real knowledge, the challenges of intellect, the demands and integrity of hard study, learning and honest debate. Despite setting up his own software-writing business – and later selling it at a handsome profit – Jack had a gentlemanly distaste for any talk of money, trade or commerce.

Yet now a horrible fear rose through him as he thought of those nicely brought up Jewish children walking there, in that busy street where all around them swirled the madness, the viciousness, the stupidity of the goyim, violent Jew-hating Muslims, muscular, bullet-headed East Europeans and demented English thugs full of insanity and slavering hatreds. He wished he knew how to protect these young frummers and their goodness.

He wondered if Jewish boys were still taught boxing to defend themselves.

Jack sat in the car and bowed his head. He was dead beat and all washed up. But suddenly the urge was strong in him to flee this place, leave the past behind, to forget it all. He started the engine and drove away quickly without saying his last goodbye to Kilbroney Avenue.

An hour later, Jack arrived at Simon and Penny's empty house, shut the front door and sat on the stairs. He frowned with concentration, like a man playing chess. He wanted a cup of coffee, walked into the kitchen and put on the kettle. After some moments, he turned off the kettle before it had boiled and went into the sitting room. He didn't want a cup of coffee after all. He wanted something, but he didn't know what. He sat down and ran a hand over his face, fingering the bruised swellings. He went back to the hall and moved around some scraps of paper on the small table there, finding a number he had jotted down a few days before. After a moment's thought, he picked up the telephone receiver and made a call. He heard the blunt Hebrew voice answer.

'Yoav?' Jack said. 'Shabbat shalom.'

'Who's this?'

'You've forgotten me already. This is Dr Silver, Jack Silver, Simon's father.'

'Gut shabbes, Mr Curious – no, I don't forget you. More trouble with the car?'

'Not at all. I want to ask you something.'

'Ask.'

'It's private.'

There was a slight pause before the car mechanic's voice responded. 'Don't worry, there's no one here.'

'No girlfriends?' Jack quipped.

'No girlfriends, bad luck for me. Is that what you want? You look for girlfriends?'

'No. Something more serious. Are you doing anything? Busy?'

'On Shabbat?' The Israeli's voice was full of mock indignation.

'You mean you don't work on Shabbat? You said you were secular.'

'Nu-oo-oo! Don't start again already. Yes, I work on Shabbat. You think I can afford to rest on the seventh day?'

Jack cleared his throat. He must try to stop fooling around. 'I have a problem, it's very serious, and it's not about the car.'

Yoav's voice, suddenly drained of humour, sounded flat and urgent. He said simply, 'Tell me.'

'Remember you wanted to meet some anti-Jewish thugs?'

* * *

Penny had thought she was reading, leaning back comfortably in the armchair by the window. Now she felt she had probably been asleep. She had been startled into wakefulness; at first she did not know by what, and for an instant remained at ease. The book rested on her lap and the sun shone through half drawn curtains, making a soothing light in the room. Small white clouds cast a fleeting pattern of shade from time to time. Only then did she notice her phone ringing, and took it quickly from the chair to the bathroom, quietly closing the door. She did not want to wake Simon, who lay stretched out on the silky eiderdown, breathing shallowly. Even in sleep, a troubled, unhappy, angry expression remained on his face.

'Hi Louise,' she answered softly into the phone. 'It's so lovely to hear from you.' And it was; like being in London before all this happened. Involuntarily, she sighed as if exhausted. 'Yeah, I'm good. Good-ish. Well, maybe not so good. I'm in Switzerland, by the way – I'm not at home.'

'Yes, I know. Just you and Simon, that's nice. It's nice to get away together sometimes. Of course, you and Simon do get away more than most.'

'Perk of the job.'

'Lucky things. Well, I've met your father-in-law at last. He came round to drop Danny off, and he told me you were going for lots of lovely walks and lounging around the pool at some gorgeous mountain resort in La Suisse. Well, actually he didn't say all that, but I filled in the gaps myself. Sounds like it was a sudden decision. You didn't mention you were going anywhere. It's a holiday, then?'

'Yeah, well, it *was* sudden. Maybe a holiday, I don't know. Simon asked me if I'd come out here. He was feeling depressed. How are you?'

'We're all OK. What do you mean, depressed? Simon? You don't usually fly out to join him just because he's feeling a bit in need of… what's the word… wifely companionship? You know what men get up to if you leave them on their own.'

Penny snorted with amusement. 'Not after just one week, surely?' In fact, she *didn't* know. She imagined Simon happily spending the evening alone, writing up his notes, watching a good film on television, reading a book. He had always liked solitude. Did he watch porn on TV? Almost certainly. They had never had occasion to discuss it. Did he sleep with other women? Almost certainly not. He was an intense man, stirred by ideas, and a lover of good things, yet not passionate. And he was loyal by nature, and faithful.

'Not every time, no,' she said. 'Just this time. It's not far. Truly it isn't. It takes hardly any longer than driving over to your place. What d'you think of Simon's dad?'

'Interesting man. He just came round and dumped Danny on me for a sleepover. Well, that's not fair – I suppose I did offer – sort of. It's not a problem. Glad to have him. It's nice for Alex. They're in Alex's room right now.'

'That's sweet of you, Louise. I called Jack, but I can't get any sense out of him at all. Does he seem all right? Is he coping with Danny? Obviously not.'

'You don't know then? When he came over here, he was limping terribly, and covered in terrible cuts and bruises. According to Danny, he had been beaten up by some *gang*, in the street or something.'

'*What*?' She paused to take it in, to picture the scene. 'You mean, like mugged? He was mugged? Is it true? This happened to Jack and he didn't tell us? He's *limping*?'

'But what was *so* weird was that he didn't even tell me about it. When I asked how he got all the bruises, he cooked up some ridiculous story about falling down stairs. He flatly denied being assaulted. I thought he must've told *you*, at least.'

'Oh God! That's Jack all over. You never know where you are with him.'

'He should have told you. I'm sure you would want to know something like that.'

'But maybe he did fall down some stairs? Who says he was mugged?'

'Danny told me. He had wheedled it out of him somehow.'

Penny pressed her hand against her forehead. 'Well, you're right. He should have told me.' But if Jack had been attacked in the street, she was certainly not going to criticise him. 'Did they take anything?'

'According to Danny, it was more of an antisemitic thing.'

'You are *kidding*. What does Danny know about *that* – does he even know the word?' But Penny listened, horrified, as Louise repeated Danny's account, and said at last, 'I hope Jack went to the police. It's hard to believe. I'd better talk to him.'

'Yes, I do think he should go to the police. Except, they can't do anything, can they?'

'Can't or won't. But you still have to go to them.'

'When I asked how you are, Penny, why did you say you are not-so-good, or only good-ish?'

'Is that what I said? No, I'm OK. It's just that Simon is… I dunno. He's very busy. He's tired. Sorry Louise, I'd better go now. We're coming home in a few days, a couple of days. Maybe Wednesday. I'll call you then. Thank you so much for having Danny.'

She returned to her chair and picked up the book that rested there. She tried to find her place. She could not remember seeing any of these words, these sentences. Turning back through the pages, she could not remember having read any of them. Simon continued to sleep restlessly. Distant voices somewhere outside enhanced the tranquil stillness.

* * *

Darling Miri, I know you won't approve, so we won't discuss it. You know, and every woman knows, that men do things and keep them secret. Don't ask me why. It's just a fact. Am I right? From the lowest to the highest, from the noblest dustman to the meanest government minister, men are driven to do things that they must keep secret. Little things that they think don't matter. Women have secrets and share them with friends – or desperately want to. Men don't blab, and they don't blub. They just do what they do and keep shtum about it afterwards. Yes, even in this day and age. They don't have a desire to tell, because what they have done is shameful. And men have discovered that shame goes away if you ignore it. Yes, it does. But this time, my secret is not about money and of course, it's not about sex. Sex? Are you kidding? That, I *would* have to keep quiet. But about this particular secret, I know you wouldn't approve. I wouldn't be able to tell you anything. So maybe it's better that you are not here. Please forgive me for saying that.

9

Jack peered into the mirror and touched the purple marks on his face gingerly. They looked worse today, if anything. He washed and shaved carefully and rubbed ointment into his bruises. He dressed neatly, sat on the bed to give a shine to his shoes with a soft cloth, and put on a jacket and tie as usual. Downstairs, he turned on Radio 4 and listened inattentively to the Sunday programme. An interviewer's irritating, petulant voice pestered someone. He moved the dial to Radio 3. Rousing choral music, Christian music, extraordinarily beautiful, filled the kitchen as he made coffee and toast. His thoughts were on his plans for the morning.

After inspecting himself again in the mirror and looking around to make sure everything was in order, he put on his corduroy cap and left the house, slamming the front door behind him.

Outside, in the fresh morning air, he knew he had now started on something slightly insane. It was not too late to draw back if he wanted to be sane again. What was sane, what was sensible? To do nothing, to acquiesce as the police do nothing, to lie back and be walked on by louts, to allow injustice to prevail? He drove to Sainsbury's car park, parked neatly and walked slowly across the tarmac to the shop entrance, where he had to wait with other customers for the shutters to be raised, because on Sundays the shop did not open until eleven. He had wanted to be here well before any of Mick's gang, but now he wondered if being one hour early was enough.

Suddenly he felt acutely the difference between thinking of doing something and actually doing it. This really was crazy. He was sickeningly vulnerable. If one of those thugs arrived now and saw him standing here, what might happen? Jack looked around in fear. No reason why they should be. But you never knew. As the customers shuffled inside, he looked at his watch. Exactly eleven o'clock. He had always admired punctuality.

Sainsbury's was as busy on a Sunday morning as at any other time. All kinds of people streamed in and out. Just inside the wide entrance, two members of staff were on hand at the Customer Service desk to deal with problems and questions. As these were few, the pair also sold cigarettes, newspapers and lottery tickets.

Jack passed the Customer Service desk and placed himself behind the rack of newspapers. He realised that his knees were trembling. It made him think of the expression 'weak at the knees'. In his case though, he told himself, it wasn't caused by emotion, just weak knees. Probably he should sit, but there was nowhere. Customers walked in and out of the shop, and he asked himself what he would do if no one turned up. He had been counting on them wanting to see who returned the phone, and to get hold of it as soon as possible. But someone might not come for hours. Maybe even days. What then?

He grew tired of gazing towards the Customer Service desk. He leafed through the News of the World, looking for the kind of stories that had made him laugh in the old days. Sex Romp Vicar in Palace Mercy Dash. But he put the paper down, discovering he was not in a laughing mood after all. And he needed to pay attention – suppose someone came while he was reading? He decided to change position and limped over to the fruit and vegetables. From here he could see both Customer Services and the store entrance. He picked up some oranges and put them down again. Probably he should hold a shopping basket, in order not to arouse suspicion. He'd prefer to sit than stand. Perhaps he ought to be within earshot of the service desk, in case someone came and asked very quietly for the mobile. This knee! Killing him. He strolled among the vegetables. Walking was no better than standing. He would go to the hospital later. He could sit there and rest – for hours – waiting to be seen. Where could he sit now? It was becoming urgent to sit. There were some plastic chairs near the check-outs. He looked at them longingly. He leaned heavily against a stand of organic potatoes. He returned to the rack of newspapers.

His reverie was broken by a raw, working-class voice asking if someone had left a mobile. It was a female voice, as sharp as a splash of vinegar on a portion of chips, harsh with the sound of the London street, of metal, beer and broken glass, of run-down concrete and brick; a modern old-fashioned Cockney voice, rough, unapologetic, strongly accented, spit-in-your-eye defiant, confident, surly, pig-ignorant (Jack was sure that such a voice could not even tell you the name of the Prime Minister). He loved the voice and was terrified of it.

'You sure?' The tone rang with insolence. You sho-wah? Shapely, zaftig, a very pale-skinned woman in her thirties. She wore a tight, thin pink tracksuit with a clear view of the underwear beneath. A clinging, hooded top stretched over a buxom Page Three chest. A handful of flesh bulged nakedly above pink jogging pants. And pink high-heeled shoes, shining patent leather. She carried a small carrier bag of groceries and had emerged unnoticed from among the other shoppers. Her face was round and plump, almost featureless except for dark make-up, and her blonde hair tied back so tightly that it looked painful.

The pretty, quietly spoken Hindu girl at the counter was quite sure: No one had left a mobile phone at the Customer Service desk. Her movements were graceful and demure.

The Cockney in pink approached the newspaper stand, lips pursed irritably, as if to look at the headlines and pass the time. From behind a stack of tomatoes, he watched her warily, heart beating hard.

'I didn't think of that, Miri,' he murmured under his breath. 'A woman. Not what I expected.'

'It's OK,' he heard Miri's voice whisper in his ear. 'They sent a woman because they thought they'd be meeting a child. It makes no difference.'

A few minutes after twelve, the woman took out her own mobile phone and made a call. 'Mick? Iss me. No one ain't dropped off no phone. I noo they wasn't goin to. Tell ya what, mate. It's a big con. No one's gonna drop off nuffin. You bin done, mate. 'Ow do I know what kind of con it is? Might be the police, like a set-up, innit? It's a feelin I got. Just a feelin. A feelin. Doncha know what a fuckin feelin is? Like when you know someone's lookin at ya. You sent me 'ere on a fool's fuckin errand, that's what ya fuckin done, mate. Orright, orright. Ar stay 'ere till arpast twelve.'

She suddenly peered around, taking Jack and the tomatoes into a sweep of the whole area. 'No, I don't see no one. I reckon the kid's chickened aht. If it's a kid. Tell ya what, mate, maybe 'e wants to keep the phone after all. What? There ain't no kid 'ere. Kid, or yid? What old yid? Don't make me laugh. There's old yids all over the fuckin shop.'

It was true, there were old men in every direction. It seemed that the call had ended. She stared impatiently at the service desk.

Suddenly she made for the exit. Jack noted disapprovingly that she had not kept her promise to wait until half-past twelve.

Outside, she did not turn towards the car park. He had been expecting to follow her in the car. Nothing was going as he had expected. He told himself what he already knew from long experience – you can plan what you will do yourself, but not what others will do.

Jack stood on the pavement outside Sainsbury's and watched as she walked away. She turned in front of Golders Green station and started up North End Road. He followed on the other side of the road. For a moment she halted, stood looking at a row of taxis for hire, then walked on. She came to rest at a bus stop.

What was he to do? Wait at the stop with her? Go back and get the car and lose her in the meantime?

He turned and hurried back for the car, limping, breathless, teeth gritted from the pain. It struck him as comical. A bitter, wry smile came to his lips. Into his mind came school sports days at Simon's primary school – three-legged races, and races in which the children had to hop, maybe carrying an egg in a spoon, or run backwards. All sorts of madcap, made-up games that he did not remember from his own schooldays. Like getting an old man with a bad knee to run for his car. He heard the jeering crowd, the laughter of his attackers, mocking voices from the sideline. And certainly he was hobbling with pathetic vigour, as if he really hoped to win this race.

The queue had gone when he returned. 'And the bus stop was bare,' Jack said aloud. He stopped the car and wondered if he was going crazy. He tried to remember what sane people do. Yes, he should go back home and sit down with a newspaper until it was time to pick up Danny.

Danny! What time was it? For one moment fear swept through him. But no, he had not forgotten to pick up Danny.

There was plenty of time.

He stepped out to check the bus number and its route. Back in the car, he put his foot down and soon caught up, tailing the bus as it progressed slowly, stopping and starting all the way through Hampstead, then creeping down Haverstock Hill towards Chalk Farm (though by now Jack did not know where he was), studying the passengers as each one stepped down onto the pavement. She was not among them.

Until, yes, as several passengers burst from the folding doors, there she was. Pink and shapely, as before. She no long carried the carrier bag, but was eating a doughnut. Jack's heart pounded. He watched as she walked away down Pond Street. Now what? He sat in the car. He turned the corner and followed from a distance, pulling in to let traffic pass.

Behind a row of leafy trees, a single building rose all along one side of the street, concrete and glass, with a dark driveway beneath a red sign: Accident & Emergency. He wanted to drive in and ask a doctor, a nurse, anyone, to take a look at him. Jack made a mental note to remember the place. As soon as this was all over, if he survived, he would come back here and get this leg seen to. His plump, pink quarry ambled past the hospital. At the bottom of the street, a big flower stall filled the pavement with sprays of colour. Trees stood all around a crossroads and a pretty little square with an ornate fountain. Now Pink paused outside a supermarket, Marks & Spencer Simply Food. But she did not go in. Instead she made a right turn there.

No Entry – he could not follow. At least, not in the car. But there was nowhere to park. He passed the turning and looked for a way to follow her. His sense of direction had never been good. *I must be mad*, he thought. *What am I doing here?* He eventually took a right turn at random, a hopeful left turn, another uncertain right, becoming exasperated, angry with himself. I must get out of this, go home, he thought. And there she was, walking towards him. He drove straight past and stopped on a yellow line, watching in the mirror.

On the other side of the road, a council estate stretched out in long parallel lines of five storey red-brick blocks. No vehicles allowed. She turned into a walkway between two blocks and disappeared from view.

He sat in the car and wondered what to do next. He would follow.

But by the time Jack reached the walkway, she had gone. Anxiously, he took a few steps along the narrow concrete path edged with graffiti-scrawled brick. He came to an open space, overlooked by narrow balconies. Here a few people came and went, many Muslim women shrouded in cotton, speaking quietly together, black men laughing throatily, chatting white women, one lean young man helping a frail old woman, black and white children playing together. A few white, crew-cut kids sat on a wall together, talking with tight little mouths. In every face Jack saw his attackers. A chill of terror crawled over his skin. He forced himself to keep walking forward.

His fear was that he stood out horribly, like a lamb in a lion's cage. And as Moshe Dayan had said, if the lion is going to lie down with the lamb, that's fine, but I'd prefer to be the lion. Instead he was an old man. A man limping. A man marked and bruised from a thrashing. A white man. A weak man. A middle class man. A man in a jacket and tie and neatly pressed trousers. A brainy-looking guy among those who hate brainy people. A man carrying a wallet ripe for picking. Above all, a Jew. A very Jewish-looking, smartly dressed old Jew, limping and helpless in this place where Jews did not belong. No matter whether they considered themselves Jewish or not. Grimly he continued to walk forward, half aware that the atmosphere was good-humoured and no one had remarked on him at all, but at every moment expecting to attract hostile attention.

Worse was the sense that he might be seen by one of his attackers, who at that moment might be gazing down at him from one of the balconies. They would kill him. And if they did? So what? What did it matter? Who would care? Would he care? Suddenly he remembered Danny and glanced at his watch in panic – God! He ought to be collecting Danny from his friend's house. And he didn't even know how to get there from here. If he had one of those damned mobile phones, he could give a call and say he was going to be late. Except he didn't know the number. For that matter, he couldn't remember her name – the mother. He turned back, limping as quickly as he could, glad to have a reason to flee. Even before reaching the car, he spotted the bright yellow sticker. A parking ticket was fixed to the windscreen.

He ripped it off and, breathless and exhausted, dropped into the driving seat. He tore open the ticket and, after putting on his reading glasses, saw handwritten the name of the street where it had been issued. Southampton Road, NW5.

He picked up the A to Z of London, lying on the passenger seat, still open at the South Tottenham pages from yesterday's pilgrimage to Kilbroney Avenue. He turned back a page: Muswell Hill. He could visualise the street where he had left Danny, the fine red-brick houses. What was it called? Keeping his finger in the page, he found Southampton Road in the index. He studied the page. The hospital, he remembered, was the famous Royal Free (he really must make time to go there). Map-reading had never been his forte. He flicked to and fro, tracing the roads with his finger, reading their names out loud. None sounded familiar. Uncertain, he started the engine and moved forward. He would find it somehow.

* * *

I got in the back seat and Aloo drove away. Alex's mum was incredibly fed up that Aloo hadn't come for me earlier. Right up to the second when he rang the doorbell, she kept tutting and looking at the clock. I thought she was getting really, really cross. When he arrived, it was already teatime. But she was *so* smiley-friendly, and when Aloo asked, *Am I late?* – as if it was only a minute instead of hours and hours – she said it didn't matter at all.

'Where to, guv?' Aloo said, like a taxi driver. I could see him looking at me in the mirror, but I looked out of the window. I felt a bit cross with him too. Anyway, I thought it would be weird to look into a reflection of eyes as if they were real eyes.

But I was curious. 'So what happened?' I asked.

Aloo turned and faced me. He was frowning, question-mark style.

'Well, it's Sunday,' I said. 'Isn't it?'

'Nu?'

'Did they come for the phone?'

'I didn't think you'd remember about that. Well, the answer is, yes and no. It's not as simple as I thought.' Then he told me a long story about some vegetables. And a woman in pink.

It wasn't part of the story when he said, 'And what am I doing, discussing this with a ten-year-old?'

I didn't think it was a suitable subject for discussion either. But Aloo wasn't really asking a question. It was more like he was talking to himself, or no one.

Again I could see him gazing at me in the mirror.

'It was right next to the hospital,' he said. Then, mumbling to himself, 'This leg. It's hurting more and more.'

I said, 'Let's go there now. To the hospital. I don't want to go home.' He smiled at me in the mirror.

He drove very, very slowly. When Daddy drives around in London, it's like being in a rally or something, a race, where you have to get to the front of every queue and accelerate through traffic lights and dash round corners with wheels squealing. All the other cars, Daddy treats like they have been put there just for him to pass. Daddy hates wasting time.

But Aloo! He is always wasting time. He doesn't care when anything is done. And when he set off to the hospital, it took so long it was like being on holiday somewhere.

When we go abroad with Daddy, it's never a holiday. Daddy is always working. But when he drives in foreign places, he goes more slowly, and you never know when he might suddenly decide to make a detour. It's what he calls 'research'. He'll say, 'Oh, that village up there must be – ' or, 'I'm just to going have a look at that church.'

That's how it was with Aloo. Most of the time he was just following a bus, which he said would know the way. When it stopped, he stopped.

'But Grandad Aloo, aren't you going to the hospital?' I asked him, when at last I saw Whitestone Pond. 'It's down there.' I pointed down East Heath Road to the Royal Free Hospital, which I could see from the car window. He said, 'No, this is the way. The bus goes there. I know what I'm doing. I know this way.'

We went through Hampstead and down the hill. It took ages. Then, when we finally reached the hospital, he didn't stop.

'I'll show you the place,' he said. 'The place where the woman went. The woman who came for the phone. The pink woman.'

I knew all along that he would do that. I knew he wanted to show me the place. He carried on round the block and parked.

He turned off the engine and for a few seconds we just sat there. 'That's the estate. Where she went.' He pointed at some long rows of council flats in neat red and white lines. I saw him glance in the mirror at me, but I looked away, out of the window. I wasn't quite sure what we were doing.

'Now what?' I said.

He shrugged. 'OK, let's go.'

'To the hospital?'

'I suppose so.'

Then I kind of changed my mind. I knew what he wanted. 'No, let's wait. Maybe we'll see her. Or someone.'

'OK.'

So we waited for a bit. Aloo turned on the radio. It was set to Capital Gold. 'What's this racket?' he said. He kept pressing the buttons until it arrived at Radio Four. It was people talking. After a while, Aloo said, 'It's Pick of the Week.'

When that finished, he said it was The Archers.

I said, 'You're not supposed to have the radio on if the engine isn't running. Mummy told me. It makes the battery go flat.'

'Yes, that's true,' he said. He turned off the radio and we sat in silence.

'OK, maybe we should just go,' I said. 'We haven't seen anything.'

'Yeah,' he agreed.

As he pulled out of the parking space, I saw the car number.

'Hey, on the other side. Over there. Fifty fifty fifty.'

Aloo was staring around, trying to see what I was pointing at. Then he saw the parked car. He looked at it for a moment, nodding his head quickly over and over and over again. 'Hohma!'

'Am I right?'

'Yes. That's their car.' He read the number aloud. 'L252 FFT. Such a clever boy,' he said. He laughed merrily. 'You were right about the Latin, too.'

'What do we do now?' I asked. 'Carry on waiting?'

Aloo looked scared. But he laughed again, or pretended to.

'L, two times twenty-five, fif-fif-tee. Very good, very good. What other ways could it have been done? It could have said 225, of course.'

I looked to see if he had heard me. 'What should we do, Grandad?' I repeated, 'Just wait?'

'What, until they come out? We've already waited ages. They might never come out.'

'Do you, like, think they're dead, or they've sold the car and gone to live in another country, and will never come back to this car again? No. I expect they are in one of the flats. I think we should wait all day and all night if we have to.'

'Suppose they came out,' Aloo said. 'Suppose there was a fight. Suppose we were in danger. How would I protect you? What would your mother think of me for putting you in danger?'

'I'd protect *you*. I'd fight them for you.'

When I said that Aloo pulled such a funny face. 'What about teatime?' he frowned. 'We missed teatime.'

'I'm not hungry yet. I had a big lunch.'

'You know what?' he said, 'I forgot to have lunch! I didn't have anything!'

'OK, let's wait here till you're hungry.'

'I do feel peckish. Sure you couldn't eat something? What's your favourite meal?'

This was quite an easy question, because I have thought a lot about this subject. 'Pizza Margherita and Sprite followed by vanilla ice cream and chocolate sauce,' I said.

That's when I noticed a man walking from the flats towards the 50 car. He had a shaved head. Aloo became very still, and I thought he had stopped breathing. But he whispered, 'That's Kev. The one with the knife. The one who did this.' He touched the big plaster on his chin.

I said, 'If he goes somewhere in the car, shall we follow?'

Aloo sat and thought about it. 'Maybe. Yes. But we'll have to be very, very careful.' Aloo was making a weird expression, with his lips tightly pressed together and his tongue stuck into his cheek.

Kev didn't go anywhere. He opened the boot and took out two boxes, one on top of the other, then a third, until there were four boxes in his arms. Shutting the boot awkwardly, he began walking back to the flats, carrying the boxes with both hands, straining to look round them, since he could not see over the top.

'Looks like cases of beer,' said Aloo. 'Blimey – he's strong!'

I opened the car door. Aloo hissed, 'Hey, what are you doing? Close it!'

'But he doesn't know *me*, Grandad Aloo. It's you he mustn't see.' And I ran away into the estate, watching Kev from a distance. I didn't take any notice of the other boys hanging around, and they didn't take any notice of me. Kev went to a door, which had a sign on it: Flats 14 to 25. He didn't take the lift, even though he was carrying all those boxes. He went up the stairs, so I guessed he wasn't going far, unless the lift was broken.

The door slammed behind him and I peeked through the glass. Lift on the left, stairs on the right. Flats 14, 15 and 16 on the ground floor. Flat 14 by the lift. Flat 16 at the bottom of the stairs. So three flats on each floor, door numbers going round to the right – that's called clockwise. Windows of Flat 16 facing this way. Must be the same on each floor. I ran over to the other side of the block, so I could try and see which flat he went to. Straight away you could see that the flat on the first floor had a balcony, with a whole row of England flags on it. There were quite a few people inside, making a bit of noise. Then I saw Kev again. He came onto the balcony with two other men. I didn't want anyone to notice me so I just ran back to the car and jumped in. Jack started the engine and we drove off.

I was breathless and could hardly speak. 'Flat 19,' I said.

* * *

At the Pizza Express in Golders Green, they sat down comfortably and looked through the menu, even though Danny already knew what he would be having. 'By the way,' he asked, 'When they say fruits of the forest, what forest is it?'

'Do me a favour,' replied Jack.

The waitress, pretty, honey blonde and friendly, wore a short tight black skirt and winked at Danny with a smile. He grinned back as he ordered Pizza Margherita and Sprite.

'Where are you from?' Jack asked her.

'Croatia,' she replied.

'That's interesting! How did you end up here?'

Impassive, she answered, 'It would take a long time to explain.'

Jack persisted, 'Why? What happened?'

'I can't talk about it now. My parents were murdered.'

Jack bit his lip and nodded sadly, ashamed of his inquisitiveness. 'I'm sorry to hear that.' He reflected that the Croats had supported the Nazis. But perhaps she was a Serb. Peering at the menu, he asked her for a Pizza Reine and another Sprite.

She calmly wrote it down and thanked him.

Jack's eyes followed as she walked away. 'I'm a fool,' he said. 'One stupid little question can revive a whole nightmare.'

Danny asked, 'What's a Pizza Rain? Sounds like a whole lot of pizzas arriving all at once.'

Jack shrugged. 'Reine means "queen" in French. It's just a pizza. Queen of the Pizzas, maybe?' He picked up the menu again and read aloud. 'It has ham, olives, mushrooms, cheese, tomato…'

There was a startled intake of breath and an almost tangible silence from Danny's side of the table. Amazed and horrified, Danny simply opened his mouth without words. Jack looked at him expectantly. The boy was literally dumbfounded; what had upset him? At last Danny managed to say, 'But Grandad Aloo, that's treif!'

'*Treif*?' Jack protested with a puzzled grin. 'What's going on here? What do you know about treif? This is Pizza Express – it's all treif. The whole place is treif from top to bottom.'

Danny looked so hurt that Jack nearly called the girl back to cancel his order. The boy sat small and unhappy, wishing his mother and father were with him instead. His father had explained to him about things being 'OK for Jews to eat', which was called kosher, or 'Not OK', which was called treif.

His mother had said it's not all that important. All the same, his father had told him, it's kind of nice to try to stick to things that are OK for Jews to eat. They would know how to continue the argument. He didn't know what Grandad meant by the whole place is treif. How can a *place* be treif, if it means you shouldn't eat it?

'After all,' explained Jack tenderly, 'we aren't frum. Are we?'

Danny was annoyed at not knowing these unfamiliar words. He was not sure what it meant to be frum.

'It's silly to say "we aren't frum so we can eat treif,"' he said angrily.

'No it isn't…' Jack protested.

'…or,' Danny added, 'as silly as saying "Let's stop being Jews."'

Now Jack was speechless. Here was the proof of his failure: this bright, lovely grandson. Jack had made every effort to free his son Simon from such folly, free him from the burden of religion and dark superstition. He and Miri had brought up

Simon without being Jewish, or non-Jewish for that matter, and gave him the ability to rise above such divides, to throw off faith and live in the real, true, commonsense world. Now here was Simon's son, his own grandson, telling him not to eat a pizza because it was against Biblical law.

'Jewish? I should be Jewish?' Jack retorted with a flare of anger, quickly held down. 'Who says we're Jewish?' he exclaimed in despair. 'Oy yoy yoy yoy! I have failed. I wanted to be English and have an English grandson.'

Danny looked unhappy.

Jack didn't want to make Danny unhappy. He should not have suggested Danny had failed him. It was a terrible thing to have said. He could hear Miri reprimanding him and reminding him that he was dealing, after all, with a ten-year-old child.

'But Grandad Aloo,' the boy said, pouting, 'I *am* English – aren't I? But would you have been sad to have a French grandson, or an American? Or is it only *Jewish* grandsons you don't like? Anyway, does a person have choice whether to be English? Can a person choose to be Jewish or not?'

Jack raised his eyes to heaven. The boy was definitely bright. How was he going to answer this? No, he thought, but at least they can choose what pizza to eat. But he mustn't go against the boy's own parents. He said no more, and rested his hand kindly on Danny's. He said, 'Don't let's get broygus with each other. You don't make me sad, Danny. I'm sorry I said that. I'm sorry. Let's just love each other and be happy again. You are a good boy, I'm not sad with you at all – it was silly of me to say that. I'm very proud of you.'

Danny fingered the green stem of a strange plant with a single white flower, standing on the table in an elegant blue vase. Jack touched it too, just to see if the plant was real. It was. Danny nodded and smiled miserably. 'Yes, let's stop arguing,' he said. 'I don't like it.'

Maybe, Jack wondered, Danny had got all this from his mother? But Penny seemed such a down-to-earth, thoroughly intelligent girl.

But for Simon to invoke Jewish law would certainly be ridiculous, since Jewish law held that Simon wasn't Jewish. As he had explained to someone yesterday – Jewish mother, Jewish; no Jewish mother, not Jewish. Had they all forgotten that once upon a time, long, long ago, Miri had been thoroughly English?

Penny, though, might have given the boy these stupid ideas. She had a Jewish mother but her father, Morrie Eisenberg, despite the name, wasn't Jewish. (Because *his* father had married-out, of course. *What was it with all these Jewish fellers marrying shiksas?*, Jack asked himself in exasperation. *They just made life confusing.*) They were a lovely couple, in a small way of business, admittedly dim, but kind, and full of life. That Jewish mother of hers made Penny completely kosher. Not that Penny's mother had ever done a Jewish thing in her life. She had never belonged to a shul, couldn't marry in shul, obviously, since she was marrying out. No way would she even step inside a shul – not on Yom Kippur or on any other day. Probably hadn't been to shul since her batmitzvah – if she had had one. Probably hadn't heard of most of the festivals. And wouldn't recognise a lokshen pudding if it slapped her face. A yiddishe mame she wasn't; still, she was a Jewish mother.

Given her background, it seemed unlikely that Penny had been filling Danny's head with such Jewish ideas. Jack held back from pointing out to Danny that Simon wasn't Jewish. The boy might not be aware of it and would be even more upset.

Danny knew he would not be able to debate with a grown-up. He half laughed as he tried to have the last word, 'Anyway, Grandad, why pretend? You look Jewish, you talk Jewish. You just *are* Jewish and that's that.'

'So I don't have the same choice of pizza toppings as everyone else?' Jack enquired innocently. He was annoyed with himself for not letting it drop – and with a child, too.

Danny thought for barely an instant. 'You do have the choice. It's called a menu. It's like someone gave you a menu of good and bad things to do. You have to choose.'

No, there was really no doubt the kid was bright. It was frightening – wondering how to rebut the argument of a ten-year-old. He said, 'Is this what Daddy has told you?'

'Yes it is, Grandad Aloo.'

'What else Jewish do you do, apart from eating kosher?'

'What else is there?'

'Well,' Jack said. For example, do you light candles on Friday night? Do you go to shul? I saw you didn't have a mezuzah on the door.'

'No,' Danny replied sulkily, 'It's not fair, just because I don't know what shul is, or mizizum or whatever you said, and I never heard about any candles or anything. But Daddy says we should remember we are Jewish. Hey – candles on Friday night! That must've been what they were doing at Josh Shinberg's.'

Jack shrugged and shook his head. You can't interfere with how people bring up their children. 'Well, it's only a pizza,' he said. 'So, I'll order a different one.' He was deeply disappointed: the boy had got religion from Simon, not Penny.

'No, Grandad Aloo,' Danny struggled to make grown-up sense. 'It's *not* only a pizza. S'pose one of the pizza toppings was delicious little bits of human beings. Then what?'

Jack laughed. His heart truly went out to the boy, pluckily answering back. Not slices of human being perhaps. But slices of pig, why not? He held back from saying it – the discussion was upsetting the child.

'You remember when I said I changed my name because I want to leave the past behind?' he asked gently.

Danny looked at him fiercely and didn't answer.

'Well,' Jack said quietly, 'being Jewish was one of the things I wanted to leave in the past.'

'Well, you can't.' Danny exclaimed. 'A person has things about them that they can never change.' He tightened his mouth, trying to control his frustration, tears suddenly not far away. 'Anyway,' he added, 'it's a bit stupid to choose the name Jack Silver, 'cos that's a Jewish name too, isn't it?' On this, he was fairly certain of his ground. English people, he had noticed, were never called after anything precious like gold, silver, pearls or rubies. Maybe that's why jewellery was called *jew*ellery, he wondered.

Again Jack shrugged. 'Not as Jewish as Avram Zilberman,' he replied tenderly. 'At least silver is an English word. People might think I had changed my name from Da Silva – that's Portuguese, not Jewish.' Who knew, but the kid was right. He'd been trying to forget it for 50 years. Actually, 'Silver' had not been the best choice – something like Green or Black or Brown or White might have been better. He hadn't known. The waitress arrived with their pizzas, and Jack leaned over, put his arm around Danny, kissed the top of his head and said, 'Tell you what, I'll take the ham off my pizza.'

'All right.'

'Danny, whose house do you most like for a sleepover?'

'Definitely Josh Shinberg's. But I went there on Friday.'

'Maybe you can go there again.'

'Let's have a hug,' said Danny, getting out of his seat to embrace his grandfather. His nose touched Jack's glasses, leaving an oily smudge. 'Whoops! I've dodded your glasses. That proves I love you.'

When they returned home, the red light on the answering machine was flashing. 'Might be Mummy!' cried Danny eagerly. They pressed the button and heard an unfamiliar man's voice.

'Jack? Hello, Jack. It's Sunday afternoon. I hope you are feeling a bit better now. And I hope you went to the doctor, and to the police also. This is Villy – Wilhelm Bernhardt, from yesterday night. Please do give us a call and let us know how you are getting on. And, if you are free, come over sometime this evening? Bring the little boy too if you want. Did I say, this is Villy. Love from Ilse, also.'

Jack did not know how to respond. He had been neither to the hospital, nor to the police. He picked up the phone and dialled.

He hissed to Danny, 'What's Josh's mum's name? Remind me.'

'Hello, Lorrae? It's Jack Silver here, Danny's grandad. I wonder if you can help me with something?'

'Of course. What is it?'

'I have to go out very early tomorrow, Lorrae, and… well, I'm wondering if you could have Danny for me again tonight, just for the night. I'll be back tomorrow afternoon.'

Danny's eyes opened wide at the deception.

'No problem,' said Lorrae Shinberg. 'Drop him off anytime. If we're not in, there will be someone here. It'll be nice for Josh. You don't have to rush back. If you're stuck or anything, just leave him here. He can even bring another friend over. Just invite anyone. The au pair can keep an eye on them when we're out.'

Jack told Danny to run off and give him some privacy. He dialled another number.

'Hello, Mr Curious.'

'Those people we were talking about. I think I've got them for you.'

10

Kev pushed the door open with his foot. Inside, laughter and good humour. Mick held court in an armchair in the corner, his senile bull terrier half-snoozing on the floor beside him. All the lads milled around. Mick's favourite rude-boy punk and ska music from the Seventies blared out of big old hi-fi speakers. On the walls, posters of gigs Mick has been to over the years. A big feller called Scally has got his shirt off so he can flash his new tattoos – and his muscles, which are bloody huge. Some of the guys saw Kev coming in and ribbed him, 'Where ya fuckin bin, ya cunt? Look at that, 'e's drunk 'alf of it 'is fuckin self!' But when Scally turned and saw the fresh supplies coming through the door, he cheerfully yelled 'Top geezer!' and stepped over to lend a hand, taking the cases of booze from Kev's aching arms. Scally had a strong East Anglian accent that made him sound like a country bumpkin, but in a half-mocking way he liked to use what he thought was London slang. He was apt to be told, when the others couldn't follow what he was saying, to 'Talk fuckin English!' But Scally took everything in good part.

Because, for the rest, all were Londoners born and bred, rough council estates ingrained in their souls. All dressed in neat casual gear, lightweight black or white track pants with three stripes, white casual shirts and black and white leather trainers, some guys a bit slicker in smart cotton trousers and nice black and white check short-sleeved shirts and smart shoes, bristle-short haircuts or glistening just-shaved heads. It's good to hang around with a bunch of people like yourself. There's a nice feeling of being fit, smart, one of a crew, on top of things. Kev gave out the beers, or hands grabbed to help themselves. Jokes all round about the fight after yesterday's match, seems like everyone also has a comment or two to make about the game, trying to be clever, and because *we won* both the match and the fight, the mood is good.

Now Scally's gone over to hand Mick a beer and he stays standing there, joshing Mick and another bloke, called Gash, and Kev joins them.

Kev laughs, 'We had a brilliant fuckin ruck on the way back 'ome.' He grins broadly. 'Bumped into a few cunts near the station. Fuckin losers. Smart fuckin alecs. They was just wanderin about like a load of wankers, lost their way. Ha! Ha! Ha! We give 'em such a scare. Don't get me wrong – they was game all right – they stood up. But they'll make fuckin sure to get a map next time they play away.'

The others roared with laughter.

'Been a while, innit? Where ya bin? Been 'avin fun?'

'Tell ya what, mate. I 'ad a fuckin laugh when I went to see me brief. His office is over in, like, Kensin'ton – he's got these, like, Albanian or Polish builders workin there. I went over with me cousin and 'is little boy. I saw the brief, and after, we tried to nick a load of the builders' gear. Just to wind 'em up. Tools an' that. They was up a fuckin scaffold, an' we was down below chuckin all their gear in the back a me cousin's van. Ya shoulda seen 'em come down the ladders. Such a funny sight. Summink in a film. They put their fists up, all old-fashion like, so funny. We got into a bit of a stomp, big brawl, bruised ribs all round, brilliant. The brief come flyin out of 'is office, and he's like,

"Now now chaps, what's going on here, give 'em their stuff back or I won't handle your case." I dint want that, so I give the Albanians their bleedin stuff back – never wanted it anyway – and said sorry, 'cos he's a good brief, even if 'e is a foreigner – he's an I-tie or summink. At least he's not a yid.'

'Ha! Ha! Talk a yids. We got one fuckin good yid Friday,' Mick answers from his chair, 'Dint we, Kev? Went out on a little Jew jaunt. Just four of us, and Shell's little kid, Bailey – he put up a good show, an' all. This filthy old geezer we cornered, what a hammerin we give 'im. I 'ad to wash me 'ands after, dint want to catch nuffink.'

'Ha! Ha! Ha!'

'Then, ya never believe it, this other yid come runnin up, and he's like, "Shtop! Shtop! Please to shtop!" Wasn' 'e, Kev, eh?' Kev laughed out loud as he nodded assent to Mick's account. 'So we give 'im what for, an' all! The pair of 'em!'

'Ha! Ha!'

'A brace of yids. A good day out. Fuckin lost me phone though.'

'Shit. Prolly nicked it while you was smackin 'im,' throws in Gash. 'Can't trust 'em, can ya? I bet he was like, "Oy oy oy, here's a little summink for nuffink my boy, gotta pick a pocket or two. It's an ill wind what blows no good." Prolly used it to call a fucki' ambulance. Manna from heaven!'

'Ha! Ha! Ha!'

'Funny thing was though, mate,' retorted Mick, 'It wasn't 'im what found it. Some little posh kid called up, and he's like, "Oh, I say, hello, excuse me, I found it on the floor. Like, shall I get Jeeves to return it to you?"'

'Really? Ay, ay! I woont trust that, mate. No way. Sounds dodgy. Dodge-y.'

'Yeah, it's what Shell said. Said she had a feelin.'

Kev said, 'Shell had a feelin, did she? Mm. Ar give 'er a

feelin. No comment! Ha! Ha! Christ! I'm gettin a hard on.'

'Shut the fuck up, mate. Or I'll cut your balls off and feed them to the pigeons.'

Kev missed the unamused tone and carried on. 'Good thing Shell ain't 'ere or she'd do it herself. Prolly do it wiv 'er bare 'ands. Which sounds quite nice, dunnit? Mm. I could fancy that. Especially if she'd forget about feedin the pigeons. Ha! Ha! Nah, sorry mate, only kiddin. No offence, like.'

The others laughed uncertainly but stopped abruptly when they saw Mick's expression. 'Shut the fuck up about Shell, mate,' he said. 'I'm serious, son. That's no way to talk about your own fuckin sister. At least, not in front of me, or yer mates. For cryin out loud, 'ave some decency. And you about to be wed! It's no way to talk, is it?'

Kev apologised, and good humour was restored at once. To show his forgiveness, Mick reached out with one long muscular arm and whacked Kev in the belly. Both laughed. 'Be a good boy,' Mick said with his tight grin, 'and change the music for me, will ya? You know what I like.' Kev changed to a Madness album.

Later, music went off and Mick clinked two bottles together in a call for silence. 'Right then,' he said. 'Down to business.' That was the reason for this little family gathering. Mick and the boys liked to get together to plan a bit of mayhem. This time though, the mayhem would be in Budapest, in Hungary, where the whole gang – they preferred to call it the firm – were going for Kev's stag weekend in August.

An almighty piss-up, a tour of lap-dancing bars, a paintball battle, tank driving and a session in a shooting gallery were on the itinerary. While Kev remained in ignorance of these treats planned for him there, it was decided to give him a free hand in deciding what sort of trouble to cause.

Budapest was considered a brilliantly inspired choice.

Budget flights and modestly priced hotel rooms had been booked, and best of all, Budapest had the biggest Jewish community in Eastern Europe. When Mick told them the main Jewish centre was in a part of town called Pest, there was an uproar of hilarity. It was all too beautiful! Kev's idea: a Pogrom Party in Pest before his big day.

Business done, the party resumed, but finished fairly early. By midnight, most of the lads had made their way out into the night to go back to their homes. Kev, Scally and Gash stayed at Mick's, sitting around talking until one or two o'clock, then crashing on the floor or in the spare beds.

It was about six-thirty in the morning when the doorbell rang. The bull terrier twitched and snored. Unanswered, the bell rang again, until Mick called out from his bed, 'Who the fuck is that? Get it, one of you, will ya?'

Kev pressed the answerphone and peered at the screen. 'Bloke with a parcel,' he called back, and pressed the buzzer to unlock the door into the hall downstairs. He shuffled to the front door of the flat.

* * *

Jack, already dressed in jacket and flannels, with neatly polished shoes, was peering out of the upstairs window before five. He hoped to see Yoav's white van coming up the little street, although they had not arranged to meet until six. When two men appeared on a roaring motorbike and stopped outside, he experienced instead a wave of fear: perhaps it was his attackers. The pillion passenger removed his helmet, and Jack saw that it was Yoav. He was carrying a package of some kind, a long roll on a shoulder strap.

Puzzled, Jack watched from the window as the driver took off his helmet and the two men said a few words to each other.

Both wore black leather jackets. This was a change of plan, and Jack felt uneasy. He went down to open the door.

'*Boker tov*,'[19] he said, with a questioning glance at Yoav.

The mechanic made no introductions. He said glumly, 'Maybe they are not there this morning. This is like an eagle in a haystack.'

'A needle. A needle, not an eagle.' Jack grinned at the mistake.

Yoav shrugged as if it made no difference.

'You don't even know what that means,' Jack said. 'Do you?'

'A haystack?' Yoav shrugged again, 'I know. Dead grass. So what? Mr Silver, this not the time for an English lesson.'

'Oh, never mind.'

In the meantime, Yoav's companion had said not a word. Jack turned to him. 'Hello, are you with Yoav? What's your name?'

The man merely nodded, as Yoav answered for him, 'He is my Krav Maga[20] partner. His name Ehud. He want to help you,' he explained, adding unnecessarily, 'We use his motorbike,' rolling the R in the back of his throat as if it were a motorbike engine itself.

'What's Krav Maga?' Jack took a closer look at Yoav's companion. He was broad and tall, powerfully built, with shaved head. Though he wore all the outward signs of toughness, even brutality, he had an enigmatic air of gentleness. Jack imagined him as a great success with the ladies. He looked like one of those fit young security men who accompany Israeli politicians.

'I will explain you, not now,' Yoav said.

In an effort to get a response, Jack again said, 'Good

---

19 Good morning (Hebrew)

20 'Contact fighting' (Hebrew), a system of hand-to-hand combat developed for the Israeli army by Hungarian-born immigrant Imi Lichtenfeld

morning, Ehud.' The man glanced into his eyes and nodded with something like a secret smile.

'I think you will not find these men. Not like this,' said Yoav.

'Yes I will,' Jack retorted, yet immediately he shrugged as if to say, what the hell. 'Maybe you're right. Maybe like this, I won't,' he admitted. 'If this doesn't work, we can try something else.'

'*If* you will find, we will help,' replied Yoav, with a deeply sceptical emphasis on the 'if'.

Ehud caught Yoav's eye.

'Let's go. I drive your car, Ehud follow.'

Again Jack wanted to take the meandering bus route through Hampstead. But Yoav drove fast up West Heath Road and down East Heath Road. To Jack's surprise, the whole journey took barely five minutes. When they reached the flats, his chest was pounding painfully. He was full of doubt. Yoav freewheeled beside the building, looking for Flat 19. He stopped outside the nearest entrance, but Ehud pulled up alongside and pointed to a better parking place, out of view.

Nervously, Jack pursed his lips. 'I've been thinking,' he told Yoav. 'I only saw one of the men here, and it was last night. I think you're right: he might not be there any more, and even if he is, we might not find the others. They might not come for days. If ever.'

'So, better, wait and see. Today we decide we are here, we look, if not tomorrow, and day after OK. Turn and turn about.'

Jack barely understood this little speech, but nodded thoughtfully. 'You're much too busy to spend time on this, Yoav.' He glanced again at his watch. 'It's still early. Maybe this is a bad idea. Shall I just wait in the car? Yes, I think I will. I'll just wait in the car.'

Yoav said. 'And what will you do if you see them?'

Jack nodded. He had been asking himself the same thing. He was confused and afraid.

Now Ehud leaned against the car window and spoke, quietly, in Hebrew, to Yoav.

Jack looked on quizzically.

'He says,' Yoav explained, 'that you must not wait alone. He sit with you, and I take a look round. Very important, they must don't see you here.' He went to reconnoitre.

Sitting with Jack in the car, the taciturn Ehud scanned the surroundings expressionlessly. Jack, mouth dry, sat with thoughts racing. He placed a hand on Ehud's arm: 'Suppose the woman is there, and children?'

Ehud said, 'We can deal with that. They won't be hurt.'

Surprised, Jack said, 'Suppose they have a vicious dog?' He had a great fear of goyim with dogs.

'They have a vicious dog, sure,' Ehud replied quietly. Jack was amazed that his English was better than Yoav's. He had not said anything in English at all until now. 'We always assume there is a dog. And a gun. Then, if there's no dog, or no gun, you are lucky.'

Jack wondered what he meant by 'always'.

Yoav returned and spoke to Ehud in Hebrew. In English he said to Jack, 'There is locked door for this building. We can maybe go in, we don't know. You must to come with us. When we go inside, you can tell us who is who is. There is balcony, not too high for them to jump down to run away. We must stop that.'

Ehud got out of the car and walked around to open Jack's door, like a chauffeur.

From his pack, Yoav produced surgical gloves. The two Israelis put them on.

Now Yoav held up an aerosol spray questioningly. Ehud looked a little doubtful, but nodded. To Jack he said, 'Don't worry. It's just pepper spray. In case they are many.' He took the can and put it in a pocket.

Yoav showed him protective glasses and tooth-shields, but to these Ehud shook his head dismissively. He had a slight grin.

Yoav said, 'Very important, Jack. When we inside, don't use names. Never say our names. Ehud name *alef*, me you call *bet*, your name *gimmel*.[21] It's OK?' He slung his pack over one shoulder and the three of them turned into the flats, Jack limping, and stood outside the door that gave access to flats 14 to 25. It was indeed locked.

Jack said nervously, 'You could press a few bells and see if someone opens the door for you.' He almost giggled in his nervousness.

Ehud and Yoav remained relaxed and seemed to be thinking. Jack wondered if they were thinking about what he had said. He wished he were at home in bed and had never started this. It seemed to have got completely out of his control. His mouth was dry.

Now Jack suggested, 'Or – you could just ring number 19 and tell them you have a parcel. They would open the door for you.'

Yoav said, 'Maybe, yes.' To Ehud he added, 'Break it? Or too noisy?'

Ehud pressed the door lightly with his fingers for a moment.

Now Yoav opened his strange bag and produced a crowbar.

Suddenly a woman could be seen inside the hallway. She was a Muslim, wrapped in thin black cloth. She came to the door, opened it for them without a glance and stepped out, silently shuffling away. Yoav and Ehud grinned broadly at each other. Yoav still held the crowbar in his hand. He put it back into the bag.

---

21 alef, bet, gimmel – first three letters of the Hebrew alphabet

Each taking an arm, the two helped Jack up a few concrete stairs laid with cheap pale mosaic. The air was cool and dank, with a hint of disinfectant. At the first landing, Jack saw with terror a featureless wooden door with the number 19 screwed onto it, a letterbox that would not close, and a grubby doormat outside.

Ehud and Jack stood together on the far side of the door, the big Israeli seeming nearly twice the height of the little Russian Jew he sheltered.

Yoav glanced at Ehud and quickly slipped back downstairs. He opened the door of the building and – holding the door open – pressed the doorbell of flat 19 for several seconds.

No reply. On a third press, the answerphone crackled. 'Yeah?'

'Fedex delivery. Need a sign for,' Yoav said. He held up his pack to the camera.

The buzzer sounded to release the outer door lock. Yoav stepped quickly up the stairs. As he reached the first landing, the door of flat 19 was already opening. Kev was standing inside waiting for the delivery. 'Oh my God,' Jack said in fear, 'That's him, the guy with the knife.'

Hearing Jack's voice, Kev looked outside curiously. Ehud at once grabbed Kev's throat with one hand and banged his head hard against the wall a couple of times. He took Kev's arm and pulled it almost from its socket. Tightening his hold on Kev's windpipe and lifting him off his feet, Ehud pushed him into the flat, followed by Yoav, who was urging Jack with the words, 'Come on, Mr Gimmel, we need you to help us.' As he came in, Yoav locked the door behind him and took the key.

Ehud walked Kev backwards along the corridor, still grasping his windpipe tightly, like a can of beer. His other hand held one of Kev's wrists, pressing hard in the space between the wristbone and the palm. Kev was in excruciating pain, his one free hand pulling in panic to loosen the grip on his neck. The corridor opened out to become a front lounge. There Scally, massive and bare-chested and wearing only underpants, jumped up from sleep and stood in the centre of the room. Somewhere in the flat, the dog barked wheezily a couple of times – 'Af! Af!'

'What the fuck? Who are ya?' Scally was open-mouthed with surprise.

Yoav was smiling. He pulled a skullcap from his leather jacket and put it on. 'We are the Jews,' he said. Ehud said nothing, quickly took stock of the space, its entrances and exits, and squeezed Kev's windpipe hard. To one side, metal-framed french windows, probably not locked, gave access to the balcony. There were no other windows. Beyond the lounge, another corridor led to rooms with closed doors.

'Jesus Christ.' Scally remained motionless, then yelled 'Oi – Mick, Gash, where are ya? Get in here quick.'

Mick was already running like a bull into the room, half dressed but wearing boots, yelling 'Wassup?' and at once taking a swing at Yoav, but his fist went wide of its mark. 'Fuck – three of 'em. Who are they? Shit. Go on Scally, do summink, for fuck's sake. Gash, get in here. Come on Scall, get to work, do yer stuff.'

Scally stepped forward to confront Ehud. 'Let 'im go, you cunt,' he said, meaning, release Kev's throat. Ehud seemed indifferent to everything done or said around him, like a man meditating. Kev was clearly in agony, in serious trouble and, as Ehud further tightened the grip on his windpipe, seemed about to expire.

Using his fingertips alone, Ehud caused Kev to squirm with pain before dropping him limp onto the floor and moving quickly towards Scally, who thrust two massive fists towards

Ehud like solid steel pistons. Calmly, Ehud grabbed Scally's right hand and pulled him sidewards, rapidly poking his fingers into Scally's eye. The big man yelped and stumbled backwards, hands over his face. He howled, 'Come on, Mick – you do summink for a change – I thought you liked bashin yids. Now's your fuckin chance.'

Yoav spoke to Jack, 'Which one ask if you scared?'

Now excited and exhilarated as well as nervous, Jack indignantly pointed at Mick.

'Oi, I remember you!' Mick cried out. 'Fuck me – 'ave you come back for more?'

'No, I've come to get my wallet and hear you say sorry.'

Mick smirked at this, but looked puzzled. 'Are you blokes yids? 'Ow did you find the place?'

Yoav nodded. 'Are you scared?'

'No mate, but *you* should be,' Mick replied. He turned his head, yelling 'Get in 'ere, Gash, hurry up, will ya? What's the matter wiv ya Scally, you ain't turned chicken?' Again the dog could be heard, 'Af! Af! Af!'

Yoav laughed. 'Good answer. If you don't scared, you will be.'

'Talk fuckin English,' sneered Mick.

Yoav said, 'In a minute, I teach you to speak Hebrew.'

Ehud spoke sharply to Yoav –

[22]חייל חדל ברבורים. תרחיק אותם מהמרפסת.

Kev lay motionless, gasping like a fish lying on the deck. Across the room, Mick aimed an artless right kick and a big left fist at Yoav, who grabbed the foot, raised it high in the air and brought him crashing to the floor as Gash entered the room holding a knife. Gash was fully dressed in a smart, short-sleeved black shirt, black trousers, heavy black leather shoes and black sunglasses.

---

22 Ehud to Yoav: *'Stop bullshitting, soldier. Just keep them away from the balcony.'* (Hebrew)

Jack stood well back and watched in horror. He had been given Yoav's pack to hold and pressed himself with it hard against a wall, out of the way. He struggled with conflicting irrationalities, one urging him to prevent Ehud and Yoav hurting these people, another rejoicing at the hurt being inflicted. The sight of the shining metal brought back all his fear. 'Look out!' he cried, 'Chap here's got a knife.' Gash seemed taken aback to find Mick lying on the floor. He paused to consider the situation. He pulled off his sunglasses and put them in his shirt pocket. 'Hey!' exclaimed Jack, 'I know you!'

'Fuck off,' Gash shot back, looking at Jack with disgust.

'You're diabetic, aren't you?'

Gash was puzzled. 'Jesus! Do I know you? Are you a doctor?'

'He was in the gang who attack you?' said Yoav.

'No, before that.'

Gash and Jack turned to look as Mick retched with pain and his big body writhed across the floor. 'I'll get you,' he gasped.

Ehud said calmly, 'Didn't I say there would be a dog and a knife?'

'No, you said there would be a dog and a gun,' Jack answered.

'Oh yes, and there is always a knife. The gun I already know about – it's us that have the gun,' Ehud replied.

While keeping his gaze on Gash, Yoav suddenly stamped one foot onto Mick's neck, bringing his whole weight onto it, in effect briefly standing on Mick's throat. He swung the other foot to land a kick squarely on Mick's testicles.

It was clear to Jack that the two Israelis were not so much fighting as methodically causing injury with the minimum of fuss. He had seen men fighting before, men in bloodlust, desperate to cause damage, unmindful of any harm to themselves. It was never like this. Ehud and Yoav were calm, unflustered, and had not yet even been struck, let alone hurt. Mick roared like an injured bear, his whole body thrashing about in agony.

Yoav's hand shot out to push down Gash's forearm, then suddenly he was holding the arm, rapidly twisting it like someone cranking a handle. It made Gash spin round as if he were dancing rock 'n' roll with the Israeli. Yoav was relaxed, smiling slightly. 'So, tough boy, you like knife? Me too. We play knife together, you and me. No problem. I skin you like apple.'

With his free hand, Gash lashed out useless punches. After a glance at Scally, who shook his head and backed off, Ehud stepped over to Gash, jabbed an elbow into his solar plexus and grabbed his face as if squeezing a wet sponge, forcing liquids out, pushing it backwards while Yoav continued to twist the arm. Gash struggled to speak, and as Ehud released his grip the frightened voice yelled, 'Please! You'll break it – stop! It's breakin!' His hand weakly opened and let the knife fall. Yoav said, 'Yes, you right. It will break. In a few more seconds,' at which tears came from Gash's eyes. 'No, hold up mate – don't do that. That's not fair. You cunts!' he screamed, 'Two against one is easy, ain't it! We're gonna burn you alive. No, please.' He gasped with a sudden shock and pain.

'Burn us alive,' Yoav repeated.

From the floor, Mick shouted out, 'Go on Scally, why don't you take them?'

Scally was now sitting quietly on the floor, holding one painful eye and watching with the other. 'No, mate. You're the boss. You love to bash a yid – now you get on with it for once. Let's see how you get on with a yid who can fight back.'

'Get dressed, there's a good chap,' Jack said to Scally. 'You can't stay like that all day. It's not decent.' Scally pulled on a pair of black trousers.

Ehud had picked up the knife and bent down to prod Mick's

eye socket with it, close to the eye. He did not draw blood, yet Mick squealed urgently, 'No, mate, please. Don't do that. You woont take a man's eyes out, would ya? Fair do's. I know I'm beat. You win. What more do you want from me?'

Jack flinched and turned away, revolted. He did not want to witness a man being deliberately blinded. He regretted causing this to happen.

'This is not a game, with winners and prizes and return matches. Lie perfectly still,' Ehud replied, 'and remain silent. Or next time it goes straight in. Do you think I don't mean it?'

'Now, Mr Gash,' said Yoav. 'I decide not to break your arm. I injure the muscles instead. It will hurt very badly, but you are tough boy. I want you to be very quiet. If you not quiet, I must to injure the other arm too. Don't worry, not very serious. Good as new in no time. A few months.'

'Yes, I remember!' exclaimed Jack to Gash excitedly. 'I do know you! So, you got yourself some new sunglasses. Gavin, isn't it?' Yoav listened with interest. He eased his hold to let Gash reply.

'You don't know me. 'Ow do you know me? No one calls me Gavin. I never saw ya before. I never hurt you – I swear. I wasn't even there.'

'No. Before that. I saved your life,' said Jack.

'No you never – what are you on about?' Gash gasped. 'I tell ya I never seen ya before.'

'In Golders Green. You collapsed on the pavement. You were unconscious. Nobody wanted to help you – they said you were only drunk, but I knew it was serious. I gave you the kiss of life. I kissed you to save your life. I put my lips on yours and breathed my air into your lungs. Then I called an ambulance and they took you to hospital. They told me you might have died. It's great that you recovered. How are you getting on? I'm glad to see you looking so well.'

Scally laughed. 'Fuckin brilliant! He's glad to see ya lookin so well. Gash, are you glad to see *him* lookin so well? Gash, you was *kissed* by an old Jewish guy! Was it nice?'

'Fuckin liar! He's makin it up!' shouted Gash furiously.

'I can prove it,' said Jack. He paused. 'You have a butterfly tattooed below your neck. On your collar bone.'

From his side of the room, Scally called out gleefully, 'Yeah, 'e 'as.' He stood up, strolled over to Gash, held in Yoav's grip, and pulled the black cotton shirt open. 'See?' There was the pretty butterfly, cut across with a scar.

'Jesus, oh Jesus,' Gash cried out. 'I wish I had fuckin died there and then. I would rather be dead than be saved by a fuckin yid.'

'Really?' Scally was incredulous. 'Is that the truth? Rather be dead? Then you must be fuckin stupid. A stupid prick. I've had it with you. You don't know what you're sayin – if it wasn't for this guy, you'd be dead and buried. We would all a bin to your funeral. Your mum and sister woulda cried buckets and said what a lovely boy you were – not. They woulda let your dad out of nick to be there. It didn't happen, though, mate – you ain't dead yet – 'cos this one nice little yid saved your life. You oughta be fuckin grateful. You oughta be sayin Thank you, guv'nor. Let's hear it.'

But Yoav had tired of the conversation and gave a quick twist on the arm. A curious sound was heard, like a rubber band twanging. Gash stifled a long scream of pain.

Scally moved to Jack, stood beside him: 'Why did you save his life? He says he'd rather be dead. OK, why not finish him off? I'll help you. D'ja wanna know summink – I never met a yid before. Except to thump.'

'Really? I should keep it that way – I doubt if many Jews would want to make your acquaintance. But since I'm here, tell me, why do you hate us so much?'

'You know what, mate?' Scally said in his East Anglian accent, 'It ent personal, like. I hate everyfink foreign. 'S only natural. 'S a 'uman instinct to look after yer own. People that don't'll be soon wiped out.'

'Now boys,' announced Yoav, 'we must to circumcise you. Make you into proper Jews like us. Would you like that? Get onto your knees and pull your pants down.' Scally stopped speaking. Apart from Ehud, who ignored his friend's nonsense, everyone present fell into unbreathing terrified silence. Even Jack was afraid of what Yoav might do next. 'First one is poor Mr Kev, if he still alive. Then the little idiot, poor Mr Gavin. Then the big idiot, poor scared Mr Mick. But first, I must punish you for what you do to my grandmother in Budapest. That might hurt a little bit, but you big brave boys, so you not to cry. You remember my grandmother in Budapest?'

From his position on the floor, Mick's powerful voice sounded subdued and strangled. 'Budapest? We ain't even bin there yet! How do you know about that? I don't even know your grandmother.'

'You drove her from her home – burnt the house.'

Mick nervously retorted, 'Honest to God, mate, it weren't me! On my baby's life. I never bin to the place.'

'So what? I blame you. You blame all Jews. You think all Jews the same. I think all anti-Jews the same, blame all anti-Jews for everything what they done. *If* you in Budapest, you burn her house. What's the different?' Yoav was incoherent with emotion.

Jack spoke up, 'I think my friend is saying he has learned something from antisemites, and he has taken on board the principle of collective responsibility. After all, Jews have suffered from it for many, many centuries. Still are. All Jews past and present are seen as a single entity. Well, that's how he sees *you* lot.'

Yoav continued angrily, ‘Mr Gash, you burn us alive? You already try to burn my family alive. You tell my grandmother she kill Jesus! Two thousand year before. Is my grandmother two thousand year old? You agree with that? Yes? Yes? You agree with that? You do? Yes? So, it’s fair enough, I blame *you* for what *they* done to her.’ He was close to shouting.

Ehud spoke quietly, addressing his companion by name –

יואב תרגע וסתום ת'פה אל תהיה אידיוט. מה נעשה איתם עכשיו?

שנקשור אותם או שנפוצץ להם ת'צורה? [23] – Yoav was suddenly subdued, gritting his teeth with rage, his voice calm.

‘What are you fuckin sayin?’ Mick asked.

‘Shut up or eyes out,’ answered Ehud.

‘It’s the blessing before circumcising,’ explained Yoav. ‘Oh, Mick, by the way, where is my friend’s wallet, his money, his cards? Then I teach you to say “Slicha” – it mean “I’m sorry” in Hebrew. Ha! Ha! You will say it before we circumcise you.’

To Ehud: או שרק ניקח אותם למשטרה?

Ehud replied: לא לא. הזקן כבר יקרא למשטרה.

[24] כשהם יגיעו לכאן אנחנו נעלם. תן להם את הזריקה שהבאנו לכלבים.

Jack sat in Mick’s armchair, waiting for the police. He rubbed his knee. Scally squatted on the floor beside him. In the corner, Gash, Mick and Kev lay asleep, arms and legs tied, with tape over their mouths. Yoav and Ehud had left the flat after a warning word to Scally. They were sitting on the motorbike outside, ready to leave if the police showed up.

‘It’s like a pure, perfect hate. You can’t even stand the thought of ’em – yids, Jews. Even the word Jew. Makes you

---

23 Ehud: *‘Yoav. Calm down and shut up. Don’t be an idiot. What do we do with them now?’*

Yoav: *‘Should we tie them up, or just beat the shit out of them?’* (Hebrew)

24 Yoav to Ehud: *‘Or just take them to the police?’*

Ehud to Yoav: *‘No, no. The old man will call the police anyway. When they get here, we’ll vanish. Give these guys the injection we brought for dogs.’* (Hebrew)

see like blackness. Like summink evil, drippin poison. You can't stand the sight of 'em neither, their foreign bodies, their black coats and 'ats, slitherin about in our England, schemin against us,' said Scally. 'It's not us hatin them, mate – it's them hatin us. The weird get-up. The sly faces. A yid is a disease, summink deadly, a virus that wants to eat you up, you and your country. Like – what's that word – gangrene. Stinkin rotten putrid. Sewage. A yid lives by drinkin your blood, suckin the blood out of England.' Scally grimaced to show his revulsion. 'When I think England, I think like, clean and strong, great, proud. Healthy blood in our veins. I love our English flag. I do. Blood red and pure white – just love it. But when I think Jews, ugh, I see a bag of maggots, parasites, disease, fungus, rottenness, cancer.'

Jack listened with unfeigned fascination. 'That's a bit strong. I don't think you are really talking about Jews. It's something else. Something in your mind, something inhuman that you fear. After all, Scally, look at these bruises. This cut. Your mates did that to me. Why? You must be mad. Look at me.'

'I am lookin at ya,' protested Scally, and indeed he was. 'Yeah, you do look rough.'

'All right. So why do this to me? You don't feel like that about everyone who's not English, do you?' replied Jack. 'What about the Scots? Evil poisonous slime? Or is it just blokes like me? Jews?'

Scally sniggered. 'Scots? Nah, not Scots. It's yids we hate. Jews. I tell ya – I admit it's an obsession. If I even see the letter J, it makes me think "Jew". I see that letter J every-fuckin-where.'

Jack nodded. 'Yes, I have that. Exactly the same. If there's a capital J on a page, it leaps out at me – I'm wondering if it says "Jewish". I see that J everywhere. I'm always looking for the J-word. I want to see that word. Actually, I think I really am obsessed.'

'Yeah, if there's summink in the news about yids, or about Israel, we talk about it over and over – like, filthy scum should be exterminated. We can talk about it all day long.'

'Yes, I could read and talk about Jews and Israel all day long – just like you. You and everyone else. Just look at them all, every single day, people lining up to condemn us. It seems that just about everyone wants to exterminate Israel. So-called academics at second-rate British universities, especially. And their so-called students. They don't care about any other thing on this planet. What do you think would happen? Even if you all succeed in destroying Israel? You think Jews will just give up on Israel? But it fascinates me too. I'm always thinking about the constant criticism. The bloody Independent and bloody Guardian and all their self-satisfied, complacent, shallow, pseudo-intellectual readers who think they are on the Left, who think they occupy the moral high ground on every subject under the sun, idiots supporting any mad tyrant who will oppose Israel, hearts bleeding for the poor Arab murderers. If I open a newspaper, straight away I start looking for the anti-Israel article. Ach! Make you sick!'

'Only, even you got to admit, mate, yids have their snouts in the trough. Fingers in every pie. Control everyfink. I mean, *you* might say, good luck to 'em. But they are basically runnin every-fuckin-fing for their own good, innit? Not for England's benefit. True, innit?'

Scally considered it a fact so uncontentious that surely even Jews would not deny it.

'How does that work, then?' Jack affected genuine interest.

'Ya what?'

'Who exactly are these Jews that are running everything? I mean, when do I get a say? I'm not getting my share of the cake. Where do I start? How does it work?'

'Nah, well,' Scally explained. 'it's only a few, innit – the leaders.'

Jack's very eyebrows seemed indignant. 'What leaders? Jews don't have leaders. And if it's only a few, how many? I mean, if it's only a dozen or something, their names must be common knowledge. So who do you mean? The president of Israel? The Chief Rabbi? Some big macher on the Board of Deputies? That's not how it works with Jews, let me assure you. No one is in charge of the Jews. Anyway, I think you'll find it's still English public schoolboys who are running the country. Whitehall. The CBI. Tony Blair's not Jewish is he? He's a devout Christian. How many MPs are Jewish? Think about it, Scally. I mean, it's a democracy, isn't it? If a small group of influential Jews were doing anything improper, against the nation's interests, our MPs would certainly demand an investigation. Think what would be done if it were really true. There would be a Parliamentary committee to look into it. People would be questioned. There would be prosecutions. No, I suppose your answer to that is that all the MPs are Jews, or in the pocket of Jews. Jews are really like the great unknown to you, aren't they? Tell me, Scally. Have Jews taken over the Army or the Royal Family? Or the House of Lords? What *have* they taken over, exactly?'

Scally was overwhelmed by this torrent. He mustered his argument. 'No, it's all secret. Like the Freemasons. They take things over in secret. They've got influence.'

'Make up your mind – is it Freemasons or Jews? Anyway, if it's secret, how do you know so much about it? I mean, even I don't know anything about it, and I'm a Jew. Funny, it's only antisemites that know all about this big secret.'

'Tell ya what they took over – the fuckin media,' Scally retorted. '*That* ent no secret. Everyone knows.'

'You think Rupert Murdoch is Jewish?'

'Is that that Aussie bloke? Well 'e's a fuckin yid for sure. Even if 'e ent, wha'bout the journalists?'

'Oh, do me a favour!' Jack batted away Scally's remarks with a dismissive wave of the hand. 'Funny they're so anti-Israel. Anyway, please tell me, Scally, what would be the point of running everything? Where's the benefit? Besides, when did this start? How long have we been running everything? If we're running everything, why did we allow the Holocaust to happen? Does it go back to the Crusades, the Inquisition? I'm only asking, Scally, because I haven't understood. Explain a little more about it. That's all I'm asking.'

'Oh, fuck off. I'm sick a this. I don't know all that much about it. I ain't read no history books, an' that. Ya made yer fuckin point. But England! That's the best! Even the word – I just love it,' Scally said. 'Ing-gland!'

'Oh, come off it,' retorted Jack. 'People like you – what do you know? You don't know any English history either. I bet you can't name a single great English artist or scientist; you can't even use the English language properly. You probably don't even drink English beer. What do you drink? Lager?'

Scally was outraged. 'I know all about yer fuckin Shakespeare an' that shit. Tell ya what though, mate, I can name all the English footballers ya fuckin want. But don't you get it? England is not about rich, famous people. It's about us. The most common-as-muck people, the English workin man. That's who I fuckin believe in.'

'Good for you, lad. Basically, you are a good old-fashioned nationalist, socialist and racist. In other words, a bloody Nazi. Are you a member of some group? Combat whatever it is?'

'Nah! Course not. That's all bloody politics.' Scally dismissed the idea. 'I ent into that. But ya know what done it for me, mate? What got me fuckin thinkin? It was Gash sayin he'd rather a died than be saved by a yid. How stupid can you get? What a fuckin prick.'

'Well, that shows how strongly he feels about us, doesn't it?

Can you stop saying yids? Call us Jews or Jewish.'

'All the same, mate,' Scally insisted. 'Say what ya like about 'em runnin everyfink, or not, but I reckon these *Jewish*' – he said the word as if it pained him – 'is eatin away at England. It's all take and no give, these rich bloody Jew bastards – innit? Tell ya what, when ya see, like, three or four a these geezers all together in their black 'ats, it looks like a fuckin Mafia convention, dunnit? Pigs rollin in dosh. Where did they get all their money, eh? That's our money, that is. British money. English money.'

'Don't talk such rubbish,' Jack replied angrily. 'A lot of the Jews you bullies pick on are dirt poor. And as for the rich ones, what do you think this country would be without them? They create businesses, work hard, earn money, give to charity, play their part, pay taxes. At least they don't carry knives or rob anyone in the street, like some scum I could mention. Look, it's Monday morning – why aren't *you* at work? England would be better off without you. But what would happen if the Jews all left? Think of it! Jewish business, Jewish initiative, Jewish ideas, Jewish brains, Jewish creativity. Without them, this great country would sink into the North Sea.'

'No, it bloody wouldn't, mate! It was afloat and proud long before the ruddy yids got here. Germany and Japan seem to be doin all right without any yids. Sorry, *Jewish*. But these mates a yours – those what done that,' Scally nodded in the direction of the three bodies in the corner. 'What are they? Are they proper yids? Sorry. We never met any, you know, Jewish like that. Fighters. That's another fing – when it come to a fair fight, turns out we was rubbish. These Jewish geezers a yours made fuckin mincemeat of us. Makes you fuckin think. It made me wonder if the lads only like pickin on yids if they can't fight back.'

'Can you stop saying yids all the time? It's annoying.'

'Sorry. So, like, basically, I don't even know what a yid – I mean a, you know, Jewish – I don't even know what they are, even though I can spot one from a hundred yards.'

'Can you? Yes, so can I!' Jack agreed eagerly. 'If I even see a Jewish fellow walking in a crowd, especially in a place where there are not many Jews, I spot him at once. And he spots me. Just a quick glance, maybe not even that, and you pass – but you think, Jewish. One of us.'

Scally nodded vigorously. 'Yeah. Exactly. I can spot one in a crowd. I got a good eye for a yid. So tell me – might seem stupid – but what exactly is a yid? It's the same like sayin "the Jewish faith", innit? What is that? Yids got their own religion, right?'

'No, it's more like saying "the Jewish people" or "the Jewish nation". We're not a religion. It's not a faith community. True, we've got our own religion – and it's helped us to keep going. But we're very mixed, like the English nation. We're an ancient tribe that survived.'

'Fuck me! An ancient tribe! But what about these horrible smelly guys with the long beards and the, y'know, like hair hangin down round their ears an' that? And can't walk proper, jus' shuffle along all bent over? And, like, white threads hangin, an' all that shit? Whass that all about? You say you're a yid, but you ain't nuffink like that. Why not?'

'Well, those fellows are very religious. I'm not. OK, I'll explain all about it. But look, why on earth can't you stop saying yids? Are you a complete idiot?'

'You *what*? What did you say?' Scally bridled at being called an idiot. In an instant his face had become a mask of rage, teeth gritting together, eyes aflame. 'I ain't no idiot, you cunt. Stop sayin that. Shut the fuck up. Are you sayin I'm stupid?'

Jack's temper flared too, with amused indignation. 'Stupid? Don't make me laugh, you big shmegegge. Of course you're stupid. What kind of moron beats up defenceless elderly people?

Don't give me the old tough guy shtick – you're a mindless dope, an ignorant bully.'

Just as suddenly, Scally was contrite. 'Ya know what? I really am.' He almost laughed at the absurdity. 'Now that I'm talkin to ya, like, I do feel, y'know, *sorry* about all the geezers we picked on. You're right, I 'ave been proper stupid.'

'If you're so sorry, would you like to make it up to us?'

'Yeah. Maybe. By doin what?'

The doorbell rang. Outside, a powerful motorbike engine roared away.

11

Miri – the policemen's faces! Big, uniformed goyim with close-cropped hair. They just stared and stared at the chaps tied up and snoozing in the corner. I explained that a couple of them were in a gang that had assaulted me. I pulled the plaster back and showed them the cut on my chin and pointed at Kev's motionless body. 'That fellow there did this.'

So the one officer eventually gets on his walkie-talkie and says they need an ambulance, and after a good deal of thought the other one says to me, 'No, sir, with all due respect, as far as I can see, it's these men who are the victims of a crime. What's gone on here? What's happened to these men?' He looked me up and down – maybe he noted the beady eye and fine ex-boxer's physique, but more likely saw an old man in a smart sports jacket and pressed flannel trousers, hair neatly trimmed, polished shoes, tie in place, reading glasses around his neck – and said, 'I'm not saying you had anything to do with it, sir.' Then he took a more suspicious look at Scally, a beefy giant of a man nursing a bloodshot black eye. 'What about you? Do you know about this? What's up with them? Are they drugged?'

Scally said, 'They might be. These are my mates. This gent arrived here' – he meant me – 'with two other fellers. I was crashed out on the floor there. The other two fellers done all this in about five seconds flat and left. It was all over in double-quick time – just seconds. One of them done this to me eye.' He pointed at his bad eye. 'I never even got a look at their faces – I dunno 'oo they was.'

'Me neither,' I said. 'I came here to get my wallet and credit cards and money back. These thugs stole them from me a few days ago. They robbed me in the street.'

'Don't mind me saying so, but it was very foolish to come here, sir. You might have been hurt. You might have been the victim of another crime. Or you might have committed a crime yourself. Taking your money back might be regarded as theft. You should have called the police.'

'Yes, well. I didn't. There's no law saying you must call the police. I didn't break in when I arrived. I simply rang the doorbell. Have a look at the door – it hasn't been forced. Only you see, I was afraid to come here on my own. So I asked a pair of sturdy looking fellows if they wouldn't mind coming with me. For a bit of support in case things turned nasty. I really don't know who they were or anything about them. Wouldn't even recognise them again. I met them in a cafe, told them what had happened to me, and they were keen to help. But I do know who *these* blokes are.' I pointed at Mick, Kev and Gavin lying in the corner. 'I've got all their names, pictures of them assaulting me, and witnesses. And this good chap here is ready to give evidence against them.'

'Did you take your money back?'

'Oh, they gave my wallet back very willingly. I only had to ask.'

The officer looked around as if he thought he might be on Candid Camera. 'I think we'd all better go to the police station for a chat.'

'What about the dog?' I asked.

'What dog?'

'They have a vicious bull terrier. I've shut it in the back bedroom.'

'*You* have?'

'Will you make sure it is properly cared for?'

He gave me such a look. It was priceless.

Since I was at a police station anyway, it seemed like the right time to make a statement about last Friday. Then they wanted to know about what happened today. After three hours, they let us go. Scally said he lived in Somers Town, near Kings Cross. I gave him a lift as far as Golders Green tube station. We sat side by side on a brick wall by the station and talked a little more. I think he's coming round to realising Jews are human. We went into Regent Patisserie and I bought him a salmon and cream cheese bygel for the journey, and one for myself.

Apparently they're keeping Mick, Kev and Gavin at the Royal Free Hospital under police guard. Looks like they'll be charging Mick and his gang, and half a dozen other people, with assault, racially aggravated robbery, conspiracy and God knows what else. Scally is giving them all the names and addresses and details of their Jew-bashing activities.

Ach, Miri, all I ever wanted was a quiet life. It's been a long day, and still only lunchtime. Penny's latest message says they're on their way back. Boy oh boy, am I ready to go home! Home to my little bungalow. I'll just stay indoors until they get here! Every time I step outside, something happens. Stay indoors and shluf. I could shluf for a week. A whole week. Of course, I can't do that. A man reaches the age of eighty and still he may not rest.

And this knee! It's not a joke any more. Somehow I hadn't noticed how bad it's getting. Now the pain seems to be in my hip as well. No, don't worry, Miri – it's not so bad at this moment: I took a couple of Nurofen, had a cup of coffee, and I feel I'm back in the land of the living. If you were too, Miri… we could have stayed together. You should be with me now.

* * *

Angry enough to cry, Penny remained cool and efficient. From the floor she picked up a couple of Simon's shirts and placed them neatly on a chair, deliberately holding her mood in check. He lay on the bed, leaning back on a pillow, lost in thought. She was bitter that Simon couldn't or wouldn't help with such tasks, angry that their income was in danger, that their mortgage was in danger, that their holidays were in danger, angry at the thunderbolt of events that had struck her life and thrown it into disarray. She kept reminding herself to feel sorry for him, but always ended up feeling sorry for herself and Danny, and angry with him.

Things looked better after her talk with Auntie Hilda this morning, but that mood was passing. Tomorrow – on Tuesday morning – they would be leaving this lovely hotel, and they had had no pleasure from it at all during their stay. 'Fancy another little walk in the gardens?' she said. Her tone was serious. There was no smile.

Simon reached his hand out to hers. Its physical warmth seemed a kind of electrical current of sympathy that flowed from one to the other. He understood that she was doing everything for him, cared about him, was enduring inconvenience for him. He understood it, but felt indifferent. He pushed aside nightmare visions that threatened to come back into view. Like being in a cinema with locked doors and sound turned up, a horror movie of bodily mutilation had swept over him for a few days, consumed and exhausted him.

In fact, the movie was over now, or rather, the movie probably went on, but he had escaped from the cinema. He found it was now possible to avert his mind, but still, nauseating scenes returned to his thoughts again and again: slashed flesh, red incisions, severed body parts, blood and veins, his own flesh – and hers – that made him shudder and recoil. 'I don't want to talk to anyone,' he said nervously. 'My face hurts when I talk. The muscles seize up.'

Penny nodded. His curious nervous cramp seized the muscles around his jaw and under his cheekbones and refused him contact with other people. 'Then don't talk to them,' she said. 'Just remain silent if anyone speaks. We're leaving tomorrow anyway, so it doesn't matter.'

'Leaving? Where are we going?'

'Darling, we're going home.' She blinked back tears that moistened her eyes.

As they passed through the *gemütlich* entrance hall with its big hearth, unused in the summer warmth, the day's lunch menu was displayed on a stand. Penny longed for them to inspect it together, as they had so often done. Behind the broad, polished woodwork of the reception desk, the hotel's proprietor looked up. He nodded tentatively at Penny. Simon said, 'Guten morgen, Herr Wetzler.'

Pleasantly surprised, but taking a cue from Penny's cautious expression, he kept his reply as brief as it could be. 'Morgen, Herr Tsilver, Frau Tsilver.' He smiled encouragingly.

Simon and Penny pushed open the hotel door into the gardens. Once again, Penny instinctively thought that the bright sunlight could not help but cheer Simon. Yet to him the light was a kind of darkness, its dazzling brilliance casting sharp, opaque beams that narrowed his field of vision. The sunshine seemed menacing. Together, they leaned on a little bridge and stared into the fast-flowing stream beneath. His anxieties eased.

'The air,' he said quietly. 'It's lovely to come out.' He swallowed nervously.

'Yes. You haven't been out much these last two weeks.' Penny regretted her tone, the impersonal cheeriness of a nurse to a patient. She wanted to cut through, to reach her Simon within all this… whatever it was that kept him from her. But she couldn't find the voice for it, or the insight.

'You know, Penny, something weird has happened to me,' he announced, as if she might not have noticed.

'Yes,' she nodded ruefully. 'What is it?'

'Sickening nightmares. After that programme. They… they busted out from behind locked doors, filled my whole brain. Oh, I don't want to talk.'

But after a period of silent walking, he said, 'I'm not sure yet. I need to talk, but I can't talk – talking makes my face hurt. And… it's too horrible. But I would like you to know, to understand. I haven't been able to get it across to you.'

'These hallucinations you were having. Is it still like that?'

'No. Not really.'

'Want to walk a little bit further?'

'With you, yes,' he said.

They passed wooden outbuildings and continued along the path as it began to enter a wood. Simon turned and looked back. Penny too turned to admire the view. There the hotel stood small in the distance, on the edge of the pretty village clustered among green meadows, at the foot of soaring grey mountains, their crests dusted with frost. Simon felt in the scene something worrying, menacing, but he could not pinpoint where the danger lay. Something that stirred in his memory. He put his hand over his eyes.

'Have we really been here two whole weeks, Penny?' he asked.

Gently she reminded him that he had. She had been here with him for most of a week herself.

'I don't remember that. Have I been asleep the whole time? What *has* happened to me, Penny?' he whispered.

'I've no idea.' She pressed her cheek to his, held his hand. 'We're here, we're together and I love you.'

'I am afraid,' he said. 'Scared. Of people. Of talking. Of everything. Of myself. Of insanity.'

'Of me?' asked Penny. She pulled away in order to see his face more clearly, fearful of a reply.

He shook his head. 'No, not *scared* of you.' He looked back at the hotel. 'We came here once before, in the skiing season.'

She nodded and he went on, his voice tired and flat. 'All this where we are now, was covered in snow. It was hidden. Where we have just walked was where we ski'd together.' She said, 'Yes,' and waited for him to go on, wondered what he was leading up to, but apparently that was it – he had no more to say on that subject. After a silence, he asked, 'Will I see these images, feel these things, for ever now?'

'I have no idea, Simon. Our life was good. I hope it will be good again one day. I think you need help. You need to talk to someone, about your feelings. You said you need to talk. Will you talk to a therapist?'

'You are the only person I can talk to. Anyway I can't talk at the moment. My mouth won't work.'

'They say it's good to talk to someone who will just listen, someone who won't be hurt by what they hear.'

Suddenly he was angry. 'Don't keep disagreeing with me!'

She bit her lip and did not respond. He was so touchy, so on edge. 'Simon, with a therapist you'd be able to take your time, say one word at a time if you wanted. There would be no fear, no embarrassment. In any case, tomorrow we are leaving this place.'

'Are we?' That appealed to him. Maybe he could get away from all this.

'Of course. I just told you.' Had Simon really forgotten their travel plans already? Penny led him back towards the hotel.

They sat on a pair of canvas chairs, set out in the shade of a tree, a carpet of clipped lawn all around them. At first, Simon said nothing at all for a long time. Penny had been getting used to that. She drifted into thinking about her situation, about work, Danny, the house and the future.

'I'm not in a good state of mind,' Simon murmured, as if the thought had struck him for the first time. The voice had a ring of normality. Penny looked into his face. She could not read the emotions there.

Nervously, quietly, she said, 'Can you tell me about it?'

He nodded. 'It's fear. Panic. Over nothing.'

She thought for a moment, wary of making the wrong response. 'Can you say what makes you afraid?'

'Fear that… things are sliding away. In every direction, slipping underfoot. Breaking up. Coming apart. This whole life that I… am.'

Penny felt again that she just did not know what to say. What was the correct reply? She could not help him.

She began to speak, but Simon continued: 'It's frightening. The others – you – all of you – you have trust in life, in continuity, in the world. You are sure the next moment. Will safely arrive.'

She nodded. That much, at least, was true. 'And you don't?' she asked.

'I am afraid. Of everything and nothing. There will be a car accident, a flood, a riot. I am on edge, waiting. My nerves… can't take it.'

She wanted to help, searched her mind for gems of wisdom. What clever thing could she say? He was the clever one. She leaned forward and put her hand on his knee. Neither spoke for a few moments.

'I used to think suicide was pointless,' Simon said at last. 'Because you wouldn't be there to appreciate what you had done.'

Penny gritted her teeth and closed her eyes.

'I used to think,' he said again, 'that anything at all would make more sense than suicide.'

She waited.

'Now, I understand it. To place the final full stop, end the final paragraph. I don't want to see what happens next. I want to be like a character in a novel, who simply ceases to exist when you close the book.'

Tears came to Penny's eyes. At first welling around the lower lid. A patch, a line, of moisture on each cheek. She held her hands together in her lap. Suddenly she was sobbing. Not covering her face, but slumping forward, so that her face almost touched her knees as she moaned. Simon looked at her, more puzzled than concerned. At last she sat up and gazed at him with red, wet eyes.

'We never wanted much,' she said. 'We met, we were happy, we had hopes. We have had the simple happiness of ordinary life. I had confidence in you, in your talent. Working. Paying the bills. Bringing up our child. Having fun. Looking to the future. Everyday life is good when you love each other.' She looked at him for understanding and sympathy, but there was none. Her tears had gone, leaving salty traces. She asked sadly, 'Just two weeks ago, everything was still all right. What went wrong?'

He frowned. In truth, he was touched by her misery. 'Well, it was that programme. About the death camps.' And he began to tell her again, 'I saw people – and at first I thought it could be myself and my family. People piled like rags, in naked heaps. That limp bag of bones, dead limbs lying like twigs, is a great Jewish violinist, a modest Jewish shopkeeper or a successful

Jewish manufacturer, a grumbling old curmudgeon or a kind-hearted family man, a brilliant Jewish mathematician, a talented scientist, a poet, a loving Jewish mother with a good soup recipe, a bright Jewish child, everywhere the tortured bodies of good, clever Jewish children. But then what I realised, and so strongly… was that I – am not one of these people. Yes, I could have been in that heap of bodies, because I was a *mischling*,[25] a half-Jew. But all of them would say, no he is not one of ours. *Hoo lo shelanu.*[26] He is no Jew. They too reject the *mischling*.'

'Would they?' Penny shook her head emphatically. 'Last time you said a lot of *them* were *mischlings*. Anyway I'm sure those people cared nothing and thought nothing about such things. They had something else on their minds: they wanted to stay alive and in one piece. When was this programme? You don't mean that series we saw together, ages ago? I don't remember anything since then.'

'No, it was on here, before you arrived. I watched it in my room, on the first evening. I remember now.'

'Why did it make you so afraid?'

'I don't know. But at first it was like a wave of anger. It had a voice-over in German, and I could picture all the Germans watching. It made me think of the Museum of an Extinct Race. But then it was like being two people who are both angry – with each other. Or two half-people, a half-Jew and a half-non-Jew. The whole being less than the sum of the parts. Because I consist only of fragments. Because my world, already cracked from top to bottom, started to crumble and disintegrate as I watched the programme,' said Simon. 'At the end of it, I wished I was dead.'

She listened, and he said, 'But now, it's the opposite. I am not dead, after all, am I? I feel I am going to be rebuilt.

25 Nazi terminology for a person of mixed race (German)
26 He's not one of ours (Hebrew)

I am like, you know when you're driving on a country lane somewhere and the road peters out? At first there is grass growing through the tarmac, but you carry on. It becomes a track. Rocks and potholes that might damage the car. And the way I feel is, it's getting dark and it's raining and I'm lost. Then, wham – something *has* damaged the car. It gives a nasty scrape somewhere underneath, somewhere inside. You grind to a halt. Whoa! Shit! Now what? That's where I am now.'

He leaned back in the canvas chair. His hands moved ceaselessly, the fingertips lightly pressed together, then parted, the palms pressed tight, then the fingers interlocked, then parted, shifting nervously.

'OK, now what?' nodded Penny.

This reminded her of Danny taking his first steps, his little face looking up at her to check she would catch him if he fell.

'At first you wonder what to do. Then you realise your journey can't end there, up a track in the middle of nowhere. You take stock. You think how to get help, if you need to. You collect your thoughts. Question: does the car still go at all? Answer: it does. You give it a push, try to start it in first gear, turn the key and discover that the engine will turn. You are still alive. But you have to decide whether to press on along the lane, risking more damage. Or back out, with difficulty.'

'And? What's it to be?'

'The way I feel, Penny, is like – I am on the wrong track in every sense. And I must find an alternative route, or maybe even, go somewhere completely different.'

Scared of the convoluted metaphor, wondering what all this had to do with Auschwitz, she nodded. 'Just so long as I can come with you. Simon, just don't go on without me.'

'But what I'm talking about – fuck, you don't understand, I'm not explaining properly – is one person's life, my own life. And a life is a journey that can only be made alone. No one comes with you, no one shares your life. They can share your time, and your living space, but they can't *be with* you. Each of us travels alone.'

Penny hoped she would not cry again. 'But that's all I want. Darling Simon, I can't be you, and you can't be me. We are two separate people, leading two separate lives. And we're very different, I know that. But please can I at least share your time and your living space? Companionship, community, is the human life. That is *how* people live – by not being alone. And remember – there is one brand new life on this earth, a new person who is the two of us in one. It's our little Danny, our brave, bright, happy little boy. Please God, let us stay together and give him a good life.'

He did not respond, and she was terribly afraid that she should not have mentioned Danny. Yet somehow the idea of a new person struck him as immeasurably profound.

'In a way,' he whispered, 'I feel – I know I'm contradicting myself – I feel I have no life of my own at all. I am only a son and a father. In my own right, I am nothing. Like in a relay, taking the torch and passing it on.'

'You are someone, you are special to us, to me, and – well, if it's like a relay – you are part of the race, a link in the chain.'

'No – I'm the missing link,' he grinned suddenly at the phrase and for less than a second it was like old times. Then his face returned to a gloomy intensity. 'Because, Dad's Jewish, you're Jewish, Danny's Jewish, but somehow, I'm not. I feel I'm not part of this family.'

'Your mother wasn't Jewish. That didn't bother her.'

'Because she knew exactly what she was – a non-Jewish girl who married a Jewish man. But I don't know what the fuck I am.'

'I know who and what you are. You are my Simon.'

'You know who I am, but I don't. Anyway, I can't talk. My face is hurting.'

'Stop talking. Let's be quiet now. Let's do something nice, something you'll enjoy.'

He thought she meant sex, and he would have enjoyed that. She took him by the hand, stroked his tense, tired jaw, and led him away. But they did not go into the hotel. They walked in silence in the sunshine, in the main street of the village. Penny led the way, anxiously avoiding any stresses – dogs, a child cycling on the pavement, a loud conversation between two large Germans. They arrived at a restaurant table on a terrace.

Looking at the menu, a panic rose in Simon. Sweat broke out on his brow and he was all for leaving at once – he even pushed back his chair, saying 'I can't choose.' Calmly, Penny touched his hand and again the electric sympathy passed into him. 'No choices,' she said, 'no problems. I'll do it.' He sat down again, heart racing.

She ordered for both of them, asking the waiter for rösti – *kein speck, bitte!* No ham! – with fried eggs on top, and a glass each of cool dry white Swiss wine. Simon had been taking pride in ignoring the pleasures of life, but now he discovered a keen appetite for lunch. They ate in silence, but he took Penny's hand and squeezed it. He felt fine now. Yes, he agreed, this was enjoyable.

'It's like a break in the clouds. I see a patch of blue sky.'

'Enough to make a sailor's shirt?' Penny asked. In other words, enough for a change in the weather.

'Maybe. If you can help me. This rösti is delicious.'

At the hotel, as they passed reception hand in hand, the kindly German owner was still standing there. 'Frau Tsilver,' he beckoned to her and asked if Simon had thought of taking Johanniskraut. 'It is herbal remedy, *sehr gut* for this situation,' he assured her, 'very common from Germany.'

'I don't know about it,' admitted Penny, hiding her scepticism.

'Maybe you know Latin? Johanniskraut is Hypericum, I think.'

She led Simon to the hotel bedroom, locked the door and, in a matter-of-fact way, they took off their clothes. Under the covers, Penny held him tight and longed for happiness, and Simon rediscovered that other appetite, simple and strong, running his hands down her back, exploring her, and losing himself and his thoughts inside her brilliant darkness. They said hardly a word, and afterwards, Simon fell into a deep sleep.

* * *

Ilse rushed forward, both hands outstretched. 'Darling! Come in! How perfectly nice to see you both. Jack, Jack, Jack! How are you? Better? Is this Danny? Hello Danny! Are you looking after your zayde, darling? I'm sure you are! Danny, darling, call me Auntie Ilse.' There were warm hugs.

A little overwhelmed, and doubtful about having a new aunt, Danny stepped back nervously, clung onto Jack's jacket. Villy fretted behind Ilse, eager to add his own welcomes.

'I'll be honest with you,' said Jack, 'I'm not feeling so good. This knee – oy! It's bad. My hip, too. Really, I'm getting pains all over. This afternoon, I even have something up in my shoulder blade. And I'm tired. I'm not sleeping so well.'

'And I see you still have the same plaster on your chin. The one I put on for you,' Ilse said. 'That should be changed, you know, darling. You must look after yourself!' She urged them into the lounge as she rushed to the kitchen, calling, 'Give them a drink or something, darling.'

'So the knee is still bad, eh?' Villy asked. 'What did they say at the hospital?' His low, rich voice with its strong Austrian accent, and his way of leaning close, seemed to give even this ordinary question a quality of intimacy.

'He hasn't been yet,' interjected Danny.

This much Jack had confided to Danny, though he had not told the boy how he spent this morning, with Yoav and Ehud, then with Scally at the police station.

Villy looked at Jack sternly: 'Not been! Really? You didn't go? Oh, Jack! Why ever not?'

'I can't be everywhere at once!' protested Jack. 'I've spent the whole day at a police station, making a statement.'

Villy nodded, pleased by that, but said, 'To the hospital on Sunday you might have gone?'

Jack tried to remember Sunday. That was the pink lady day. He and Danny saw Kev. In the evening, there was that awful discussion with Danny over a non-kosher pizza. And it was only yesterday!

He shrugged. 'I don't want to sit for hours at A&E, with all the drunks and madmen. So I didn't go, and here I am.'

'Remember the mitzvah of *shmirat haguf.* You must care for your body – it's a sin, as well as perfectly foolish, not to seek medical help when you need it. Go to a doctor, at least, if you don't want to go to A&E. But I've a good mind to take you there myself after tea.'

'A sin, noch,' retorted Jack dryly. 'Villy, that's kind. But there's no need. I have a car. I can drive there myself.'

'But you won't,' came another aside from Danny. Jack shot him a comical grimace of reproach.

'And by the way,' Jack added, 'the police have arrested someone for the attack. A few thugs.'

Villy clapped joyously and called out the good news to Ilse. Danny looked wide-eyed, uncomprehending. 'But that's not possible, Aloo.'

Jack gestured the boy to be quiet, holding up a warning finger. 'And I have my credit cards back, but that makes no difference because they are all cancelled now.'

Danny tugged Jack's jacket to catch his attention. He shook his head questioningly and silently mouthed 'How?' but Jack again warned him to say nothing.

'But for the peace of mind, Jack! That's marvellous!'

'But Villy, they urgently need you to make a statement too – you are a witness. It's very important. Would you be willing to do that? Do you mind very much? I know it's an inconvenience.'

'To the police station I will go with pleasure, if you will go to the hospital. Or to a doctor, at least.' Villy took Jack by the arm and led him towards the lounge, but halted at the door. 'Jack, I have been looking into prime numbers, and have discovered some marvellous websites about Woodall primes. Would you like to see some of them?'

Jack was genuinely eager.

'As for you, young man,' said Villy, turning to Danny, 'in the sitting room we have a large television with more than sixty channels, and an amazing collection of DVDs, and lots of things for children, because we have grandchildren, you know. Help yourself, watch anything. There's nothing there you shouldn't watch.'

Danny was torn. 'Well, I'd like just to see the television, to see how big it is, but I really want to see the prime number websites.'

'You know about prime numbers?' Villy smiled condescendingly.

Jack laughed. 'He knows plenty. Let him come with us. You'll find out what he knows.'

Danny added, 'Grandad Aloo, how did they discover primes before computers were invented? It must have been *so* difficult!'

'Obviously people had to work them out by hand,' Jack said. 'There were some famous examples. I don't remember them any more. But, for example, a prime with forty-four digits was found by Ferrier in the year 1951, just using a mechanical desk calculator. That's a thing where you turn the handle to make it add and subtract. They don't exist any more.'

'Wow!' Danny was amazed. 'And wasn't the year itself, 1951, a prime number as well?'

The two men laughed with delight.

'Could well be,' Villy nodded.

'Undoubtedly,' agreed Jack. 'If you say so.'

Encouraged, Danny commented, 'But nowadays, with computers, all the Mersenne primes having less than two million digits have been found, and all the Fermat primes up to two billion digits. But even with computers, it's hard to really prove a number is prime, isn't it?'

Villy caught Jack's eye and raised his eyebrows. 'All right, I'm convinced, you know about prime numbers. I think you are on your way to a First in maths, my boy.'

'I don't want to do maths,' answered Danny, 'I'm interested in philosophy. But you know what I'd like?' the boy continued. 'I'd like to live in a place where *everything* is prime. Instead of signs saying No Left Turn you could have signs saying No Multiplication. All the house numbers could be primes. And speed limits could be primes. 31 miles per hour in town, 71 on motorways.'

Villy and Jack were thrilled by the idea. Happily, Villy led the way to his study, where they stepped gingerly over work-in-progress that lay spread on the floor. Papers and books were piled everywhere. Instead of a desk, Villy had a huge sheet of plywood on tressles. Here stood three computer screens, all of them on.

'What a wonderful room, Villy!' Jack cried out.

'Sorry about the mess,' said Villy. 'Normally no one is allowed inside.'

He opened a website devoted to the study of prime numbers, but Jack's eye had been caught by a print-out taped to the wall, listing the date of every Saturday for the next five years. Next to each date, a Hebrew word. He leaned forward for a closer look and recognised them as the names of the *parshot,* the Shabbat readings for that week.

'Ah yes,' Villy explained. 'You see, I teach the children their barmitzvah or batmitzvah portion.'

Jack nodded. Clearly his saviour was a learned man.

'And you, young man,' asked Villy cheerfully, 'do you know yet what your portion will be? Or it's too soon to think about your barmitzvah?'

Jack raised a hand in mild protest. 'No, no. We're not religious. I don't think there is any plan for Danny to be barmitzvah.'

Villy was speechless with shock. 'Not religious! So that's how far it can go, eh? No barmitzvah for a Jewish boy! And you say it's something to do with not being religious? One day you must explain that to me, it sounds most *fascinating*.'

'What is a barmitzvah, anyway?' Danny asked very quietly. He sensed Villy's suppressed anger, he felt the tension between the two men, he had an awareness that it was his own grandfather who was being unreasonable, or at least, at odds with the norm. He had already heard this word, 'barmitzvah', a dozen times, and had some inkling of its importance to his Jewish friends, but had never dared to ask questions for fear that his ignorance was laughable. At his own home it had never been mentioned.

'It's a great simcha, to celebrate when a Jewish boy becomes thirteen,' Villy explained gently. 'A Hebrew reading in synagogue, a little speech, a big party.' Distrustful of any reference to things Jewish, especially after last night's disagreement about the pizza, Danny looked sulkily to his grandfather for confirmation.

'But as you know, Villy,' Jack responded, 'there is no need for any ceremony. Being thirteen years old is barmitzvah in itself.'

'Such a pious comment for an apikoros! Should a boy be deprived of his moment of glory?'

Jack pursed his lips. 'Villy, it's complicated. I haven't told you everything about the family.'

'So what should I know that I don't?'

'There *is* something you don't know – about my wife Miri.'

Villy understood at once. 'In Masorti, we can arrange such things.'

'Can I do it?' Danny asked, eyes slightly lowered. Villy noticed the boy's unhappiness, almost shame.

'That's for Mummy and Daddy to decide,' replied Jack sharply.

'Well, I would be happy to teach you. It would be a pleasure.' Villy beamed warmly, defiantly. 'No need to think about it yet. It only takes a year to prepare, for a clever boy, so you still have two years to persuade them.'

Jack was annoyed. 'My friend,' he said tersely, 'that's kind, but the boy doesn't understand what's involved for the family. Don't do him *nish kein toives*.[27] I'm telling you. We don't want it. The parents don't want it. They don't belong to a community.'

'I want it,' said Danny.

Ilse's voice called, 'Where are you, darling? Bring our guests. There's a cream tea on the table. Or do I have to eat it on my own?'

'So the poor little yiddl is hauled up before a judge – on a false charge, naturally,' said Villy, spooning cream onto a scone.

---

27 (Don't do him) no favours (Yiddish)

'They ask his name, and trembling, he gives his name. They ask what is his occupation. Nervously he says, "Well, your honour, I don't have an occupation, but I am a minyan man, and so, you know, they look after me."

"A minyan man? What is that?" the judge asks him. "Well, your honour, if there are only nine men, they call on me to make it ten." "They call on you – to make nine men into ten?" "That's right, your honour." "What on earth are you talking about?" says the judge sternly, "If nine men call on *me, I* would make it ten."

The little yiddl perks up. Things are not so bad after all. He looks eagerly at the judge. "Also a Jew?"'

Jack smiled. He had heard it before, but never minded hearing a joke again. Villy kept them entertained with one after another, interspersed with jumping from the table to look up something in a book, or show them a newspaper cutting or some family photos. Then, another joke. His timing was perfect.

Jack and Ilse chuckled contentedly, while Danny, who – like the judge in the tale – had never even heard of a minyan, simply tucked in eagerly as Ilse pressed him to take more sandwiches, scones and cake. Awed by the situation, Danny remained polite, saying 'Thank you, Auntie Ilse' as he accepted each new offer. She was delighted.

'They say the only Austrians who can tell a joke are Jewish,' remarked Jack. 'Whoever heard of an Austrian comedian?'

Villy nodded sadly. 'It's not true that Austrians have no sense of humour. I myself was the butt of a famous Austrian joke.'

'What was it?' asked Jack, half-smiling with anticipation.

'It happened when I was a little boy, maybe three years older than Danny.'

Danny looked up and listened intently. Ilse bowed her head.

'We lived in Vienna. I was walking home from school, with my books in my satchel, and my sister walking beside me, when we came to a crowd blocking the pavement. Not of children, but adults. Working people. They surrounded us. We were very frightened. They emptied our satchels, and threw away our books. Everyone shouting that we are Juden. Two men gave us toothbrushes, and said we must use them to clean the pavement. So we got down on our knees and we tried very hard to scrub the pavement with the toothbrushes. There was a roar of voices all around. I remember we had tears streaming down. The people all around jeered and laughed. Some spat at us. Some spit landed on my coat and hung there. But there is something I remember most clearly of all. At one moment I looked up, and saw a woman, nicely dressed, with a small child who was too little to see what was going on. So she lifted up the child onto her arm and pointed at me. She and her child laughed together at the strange sight. Then I had to face down again to keep cleaning, but I will always remember how happy they looked.'

Jack's expression had changed. 'Villy, that is awful.'

'That was the best Austrian joke, but there were some others also very popular at the time.'

'Why did they do that?' asked Danny, 'Why? Just for fun?'

'Because my sister and I were Jewish. These other people were not.'

'Hey, that's like the people who attacked you, Grandad.'

'How did you get to this country?' Jack asked.

Ilse replied. 'Villy and I both came on the Kindertransport. We met in the transit camp and became friends. We remained friends always, and I hope we still are.'

'And, Villy, your sister?'

'Too old for the Kindertransport.'

'And?'

'She went with my parents and brothers.'

Jack stared, asking the next question without words.

'Auschwitz,' was Villy's reply.

Danny began to ask a question, but Jack raised a hand to stop him. 'I will explain later.' To Ilse, he said, 'And you, Ilse, your family?'

'All got out, thank God.'

'Where to?'

'My parents and one brother to England, my other brother to Palestine.'

Villy leaned back in his chair and opened his palms. 'Well, not exactly a subject for a teatime conversation.' He shrugged and half smiled with resignation. 'In every generation …'

Jack nodded. 'Tell me about your children.' He nodded to a colour photo on the book shelves, of a smiling group in formal dress. 'That looks like family. And you have grandchildren, too?'

'Yes,' Ilse smiled. 'We have three fine sons.' She went through their names and where they lived.

'That's nice,' said Jack. 'And the grandchildren?' He had no interest in them, of course, but wanted to move away from the pain of the past.

Ilse's tinkling laugh. 'Seven of them! Lovely, adorable. One of them is very new. Just six weeks old.'

Jack smiled. 'Well, that's wonderful! Mazeltov.'

Villy was smiling too, but more sadly. 'Thank you! All our sons married out, you know.'

'All three of them?' Jack was rather shocked, knowing the pain this must have caused.

'*Ja*. But their wives are charming, lovely girls.'

There was an awkward pause as Jack gathered his thoughts. 'Did… have any of them… converted?'

Villy shook his head. Ilse looked down at her plate.

'So the grandchildren …'

'That's right,' nodded Ilse. 'But what can you do? They are our family, and we love them.'

'But Jack, it seems you did exactly the same thing,' said Villy quietly.

Danny looked around at the grown-up faces, uncomprehending. 'Did what? What did you do, Grandad?'

Ilse spoke to Danny, 'Don't worry yourself, darling. Do you have room for one more little sliver of cake?' Danny nodded. And to the men, 'Now change the subject. Talk about – what is it one mustn't discuss at the table? – talk about politics, religion or sex. No, come to think of it, maybe don't talk about sex just at the moment – there are women and children present!' She laughed merrily, too loud, high-pitched.

Villy nodded, a grin playing around tight lips.

'Me? Sex?' protested Jack. 'What's to talk about? If only!'

'One day in Poland, not so long ago,' announced Villy, 'a Jew was travelling on a train. The only other passenger was a rather ugly looking peasant who kept scowling at him. It came to lunch time, so the Jew took out a snack from his bag and began to eat…'

Jack smiled with anticipation. It was another joke he already knew, in which the Jew makes a couple of kopeks out of a dull-witted antisemite.

12

At last Dr Jack Silver had the long-awaited opportunity to lie in bed and rest. He pictured himself reclining on pillows almost until lunchtime, contented, reading a good book, perhaps with the radio beside him. He could listen to Woman's Hour, to You and Yours. There might be a talk or a concert on Radio Three. Instead, he awoke early as usual, locked himself in the bathroom, shaved, washed thoroughly, rubbed ointment into the painful left knee and hip which had disturbed him several times during the night (the shoulder was not so bad this morning), removed the dirty plaster from his chin and replaced it with a clean one, returned to the bedroom to dress and brush his hair, and stared at himself in the full-length mirror on the wardrobe. He felt that he was looking not at himself but at a complete stranger whom he must learn to love. Nothing like as good-looking as the real him would be. And much, much older. Maybe wiser. Sadder, too.

For all that, Jack promised himself an easy day, at least until three o'clock, when they would set off to collect Simon and Penny from the airport. He studied the sky. Scattered groups of small white clouds could be distant snow-capped mountains. He imagined driving to Golani's to buy a couple of bagels and from there to the park to eat them with Danny. The day spread before him in splendour. He could not walk very well, but happily contemplated reading on a park bench while Danny amused himself.

In the kitchen he made a breakfast of toast and instant coffee (for at last he had bought himself a jar). While the bread toasted and the kettle boiled, he read the titles on Simon and Penny's bookshelves. It was true, as Penny had pointed out, that as well as books on Judaism, there were plenty of other religious works, a whole wall devoted entirely to fiction, shelves filled with history, language, philosophy, travel and other subjects. A book caught his eye. Surprised, he took it from the shelf. It was called simply *Kindertransport*.

He leafed through it as he ate his breakfast, pausing here and there to read a few lines, trying not to get butter on the pages. It was a personal memoir, written in the voice of a child, of escaping from Vienna on the transport. He searched in the index for any mention of cleaning the pavements with toothbrushes, but there was none. Jack read intently. Presumably Villy and Ilse knew about this book. Possibly they had a copy. Perhaps they even knew the author. He finished his breakfast, wiped his hands, and moved to an armchair in the sitting room to continue reading.

The phone interrupted him. He picked it up and heard a woman's voice: 'Simon?'

'No. His father, Jack. I can take a message.' He could hear Danny moving around upstairs. The phone must have woken him.

'Oh! Really? Is that Jack Silver? Hello, Jack. This is Ruth Fine at the Jewish Chronicle. We met the other day. Do you remember? Actually it is you I want to speak to. Or is it too early?'

Jack looked at his watch: just past nine o'clock. Not early at all. The boy should have been up and about for an hour by now.

No doubt he was sleeping off the effects of several late nights at the Shinberg's. 'Sorry, who did you say it was again?'

'Ruth Fine at the Jewish Chronicle?'

Jack was puzzled. 'We met at the lunch, yes?'

'Jack, you remember the assault on you last Friday?'

'You think I might have forgotten it?'

'It happened in the afternoon, in Golders Green, wasn't it?'

'That's right.' He answered cautiously. He assumed she had phoned to express some concern and sympathy. But why? He struggled to pull together the threads that might explain her call. How did she know about the incident? She had told him she often used Simon, so might she have been in touch with him in Switzerland? And Penny's friend also knew what had happened, and had perhaps spoken to Penny about it. But it didn't quite tie together.

'We're doing a piece about Rabbi Shlayfer.'

'Who?'

'Rabbi Naftule Shlayfer?'

'Never heard of him.'

She seemed a little amused by this. 'Really? But Rabbi Shlayfer says you saved his life.'

'What was his name again?'

The quiet and scholarly Rabbi Naftule Shlayfer was born on the 25th day of the month of Tamuz in the year 5686, known as 7 July 1926 in the goyish calendar for that year, in the town of Krzczonómieniec, or Krechonomnetz, in the hill country of western Ukraine.

At the age of fifteen, Naftule inherited from his father, the great Rabbi Yisroel Shlayfer of Krechonomnetz (known as the Risker), the position of Rebbe of the Krechonomnetzer hasidim, a sect small in number, but unrivalled in devotion, fervour and piety. Also distinguished by the particular size, shape and quality of their shtreimel, bekishe, rekelech and zokn, and the extreme tznius of their womenfolk, who do not wear a sheitl but cover cropped hair with a plain, tight tichel, the few Krechonomnetzer hasidim can sometimes be seen hurrying – always hurrying – to their shteibls or to the smaller, more heimishe and most frum of the kosher food stores. The Krechonomnetzers had originated as followers of the Risker's great-great grandfather, the legendary tzaddik, Rabbi Shlomo Tsvi of Pogrpbisht, who travelled to Krechonomnetz and founded there a great yeshiva, in which he died in the year 5554, or 1796, his head dropping down onto the page of Talmud that he was studying with eyes long since blind.

Acclaimed as one of the greatest halachists of the age, in younger days Rabbi Shlomo Tsvi (later popularly known as the Rasper, Rasker or Raster) received questions from communities as far away as America and Eretz Israel. His published responsa showed a phenomenal Torah greatness, compassion, humility and '*ahavas yisroel*', love of his fellow Jews.

To this day, the Krechonomnetzer hasidim relate with wonder that when Rabbi Shlomo Tsvi prayed, a visible light shone from his face, hands and head that caused even the most profane of non-religious Jews to come and listen. In this merit, the Rasper had seven sons, who all became famous tzaddikim, and five daughters all of whom married devout leaders of hasidic communities. So great was the merit that the Rasper's humility and piety bestowed on the hasidim, that his birthday became for the Krechonomnetzers a day of special rejoicing. It was considered especially auspicious that, in our days, Rabbi Naftule Shlayfer should have the same birthday as his illustrious ancestor.

When Naftule was fifteen years old, his father Yisroel was murdered by an anti-Jewish mob. The Shlayfer family fled the Ukraine, travelling secretly from place to place until they arrived in London. Most Krechonomnetzers were murdered during the Second World War, either by the Nazis or by Ukrainian peasants taking advantage of the turmoil, but some survived, scattered in different lands, there establishing new communities faithful to their new Rebbe, the young Naftule. Today, among this anti-Zionist community, although many make aliyah, joining the Krechonomnetzer community in Jerusalem, there is much talk of returning to Krechonomnetz. They say the old synagogue has become a bus station, but nevertheless the hasidic community is gradually being rebuilt.

This year, one week before his birthday, Rabbi Shlayfer and his wife Chaya were driven from Stamford Hill to spend Shabbat as guests of Rabbi Dovid Levinter and his family in Golders Green. The Levinters lived in an opulent mansion in West Heath Drive, and were generous donors to the Krechonomnetzer community. It was understood that Rabbi and Rebbetzin Shlayfer could arrive at any time they wished during Friday afternoon, and could make themselves at home, even though Rabbi and Mrs Levinter would not arrive until six o'clock. Some of Rabbi Levinter's best students had been given the honour of welcoming the Rebbe and his wife and attending to their needs.

Yet after giving their overnight bags to the housekeeper, Rebbetzin Shlayfer decided she wished to wait quietly on her own in the sitting room, reading psalms, while Rabbi Shlayfer decided to stroll in nearby Golders Hill Park to relax and take the air as the week drew towards its close and the peace of Shabbat approached. Two of the students begged for the honour of accompanying him, and it struck them as unseemly that so great a hohem should be walking unaccompanied in a public place. But he said that they were not to trouble themselves, and should not leave off their studies merely to satisfy the whim of an old man.

He had some recollection, from his previous visits, of where the park lay in relation to the house, but by an oversight he was in fact walking in the opposite direction. Certain that all would soon be well, he decided to cut through a little lane that appeared to head the right way. Maybe he would meet some yidden and ask them for directions.

When the venerable rabbi was set upon in the lane by Mick, Kev and the boys, it created quite a stir in the little world of the hasidim. The police were concerned. There was no question that Rabbi Shlayfer was identifiable as Jewish, and, since nothing was stolen, it could not be dismissed as a mere street robbery. Furthermore, Orthodox community leaders – not only hasidim – were alarmed at such a brazen attack on so venerable a personality, and in so Jewish a neighbourhood.

The police could, though, plead lack of evidence, lack of witnesses and lack of suspects. With such excellent pretexts, they need only condemn the attack, declare it a worrying development, urge the Jewish community to be yet more vigilant, express their great concern about racism of all kinds, and close the file.

There was just time before Shabbat came in for one of the Krechonomnetzer Rebbe's more worldly bocherim to contact, at home, the news editors of the Jewish newspapers. By Monday morning, the news desks had been provided with suitable photographs of the modest and retiring rebbe, a mad-looking old man with a huge straggly grey beard. It was a good story, likely to induce fear and outrage in the good citizens of Jewish districts everywhere, and fascination among non-Jews.

Assiduous in gathering information about antisemitic incidents, on Monday afternoon the Jewish Chronicle news desk picked up that a second Jewish man had reported being assaulted at exactly the same time and place as Rabbi Shlayfer.

Could this be the man who, Rabbi Shlayfer claimed, intervened to save him? It was not too difficult to get a name, which at first was only a name and nothing more: Jack Silver. As the paper had a freelance contributor called Simon Silver, it seemed sensible to ask if he happened to know – was he perhaps even related to? – someone of that name. The travel editor remembered meeting his father at a lunch last week. Wasn't his name Jack? Surely that old chap couldn't be the man? But it would be worth asking.

As press day was Wednesday, it was important to have the story written by Tuesday afternoon. So it was that Ruth Fine agreed to meet Jack in the park in an hour and a half, at 10.30am.

A delicious, privileged sense of calm and expectation lay across the rolling grass, undisturbed as yet. The coolness anticipated later warmth, the tranquility anticipated later crowds... but for the moment there were no families with their sticky children and litter on the grass, or flocks of feminine sunbathers, or noisy young men playing radios and ballgames. Danny ran in the distance, lost in some fantasy.

* * *

A park – on a morning like this, Miri, under a sky like this! Heavenly. Warm sun, a light, cool breeze, a few soft cotton balls of white cloud sailing far away in the blue, the grass as clean and fresh as a just-vacuumed green carpet. Glorious! If you were here beside me, dear Miri, everything would be perfect. Except for this damn leg. But maybe you are beside me, in some way. If not, then who am I talking to? Myself? To be honest, I do know you aren't here and aren't anywhere, my dear, and that I *am* just talking to myself. But you'll forgive me for that?

The only consolation for your not being here, I suppose, is that you are in heaven already – where else? So what difference would a park make? And if, after all, there is no heaven except the heaven that human beings can make here on earth, which is what we both know is true, well then, it's me who's in heaven, isn't it Miri? Which is a consolation for you, maybe. Except if heaven is so heavenly, presumably there's no sadness, so consolation is unnecessary? But why waffle on about this, since we both know you are dead and gone, there is no heaven, and I am alone here on earth talking to myself. I'm sorry, dear; I'll shut up now.

But you know, Miri, there's something about the air in London sometimes, out of doors on a summer's morning... the chemistry is just right, perfect proportions of light, temperature, humidity, silence. That silence is peculiar, too: planes and traffic don't seem to disturb it.

After a stroll round the park, pausing to watch the ducks play the fool at the duckpond, at last we made our way to the café. I bought Danny an ice-cream and he sped away again. I sat with a coffee on the terrace outside. At first there were just a few other customers, reading papers, eating croissants, quietly bickering, criticising mutual friends.

Two short, loud Jewish ladies were discussing a third, who had popped away briefly.

'She's always whining,' says the first, *sotto voce.*

'Always complaining,' agrees the other.

'She's got no reason! She's got everything! She hasn't even got anything wrong with her health!'

'She plays bridge in the middle of the week,' confirms the second.

'I can't stand her,' says the first.

The second lowers her voice further and casts an eye over her shoulder. 'Sh! She'll be back in a minute.'

Another short, loud Jewish lady with dyed blonde hair is pushing a baby in a pushchair. She wears a white linen jacket and trousers, and a white tee shirt with a massive bust beneath. How do I know she's Jewish? What else could she be? Scottish? But just to make sure there's no doubt, she wears a huge gold Mogen Dovid around her neck. She's addressing the baby, but talking so everyone can hear, like an actress. The monologue is about a lost shoe or something: Have you noticed how a certain type is keen to draw you into their little private drama? Everything becomes a huge palaver, every trivial thing is a big to-do, and everyone is invited to comment. There's a vast amount of attention-seeking behaviour. They see themselves as centre-stage. This lady is one of those people.

She looks around at everyone with a smile, then lights upon me and starts to explain all about it. What is it that I attract such people? Why tell *me* about the lost shoe of some damn fool baby? Do I care? But she sits at the next table and uses me like a straight man – she's actually telling the whole café, not me at all.

Now her mobile begins cheep-cheeping right next to my ear, like a sparrow attempting to sing Für Elise. She talks as though she's anxious that everyone in the upper circle shouldn't miss a word. 'I'll try to give him some plain pasta, darling. We'll give it a whirl. I already gave him a vienna and some Smash...' I'm the only one who doesn't like overhearing this. The other elderly ladies – all Jewish to a man – are cooing like turtle doves, grinning at the baby and wondering loudly if it was right to give a vienna to such a young child. They glance in my direction to see if I have any views on the subject.

As I turn away to show my indifference to baby shoes and viennas, I notice a frum woman walking past. Obviously she wouldn't use the Park café – it doesn't have a kashrut licence. She, at least, looks quiet, modest and refined. A breath of fresh air among such people! A long denim skirt and a demure, quiet manner. Coming up behind, catching her up on the path, strolls an Orthodox man. He calls out to her. I can't hear the words, I don't know what language they are speaking, and I can't judge from his up-and-down singsong tone whether he is being affectionate, wheedling, complaining, just talking… or maybe all those at once. A little boy runs alongside him, about the same age as Danny, tzitzit flying. The sight of this happy, frum family stirs an almost painful thought, but I can't place it. Like finding an old photo of yourself with other people and not remembering who they are.

In the sky behind, like a theatrical backdrop, hangs a majestic collage of clouds, different shades of white, which appear from nowhere and drift overhead. Another trilling mobile disturbs the scene. To my surprise, it belongs to the frum woman, who thrusts it against her ear and begins speaking very loudly in a staccato Hebrew.

It's half past eleven. The journalist is an hour late. Should I forget about her? No sooner have I decided that I will, than she arrives, together with a photographer.

* * *

In Ward F of the Royal Free Hospital, police officers were taking custody of Mick, Kev and Gash. The three men had recovered consciousness and were immediately arrested. The consultant's report showed that they did not need any treatment, and blood tests had identified a tranquilizer usually used by vets. Protesting their innocence of any crime, they were transferred at high speed in comfortable saloon cars to Holborn Police Station in central London, and there taken downstairs to a cell. Inside it, to their surprise, were many of their old friends.

After an hour, they were taken out one by one and politely

questioned by the custody sergeant, formally charged with racially aggravated assault and robbery, before being put in separate cells.

More than three hours had passed before Mick was brought up. He was still groggy.

'So you're Mr Big, eh?' said the beefy, good-humoured sergeant. 'What's your full name?'

'I ain't sayin nuffin till I get me phone call. I want a s'licitor.'

'Rightie-ho, then,' agreed the sergeant amiably, 'I'll just write down Michael Lewis Stedman? Will that do? Is that your name?'

Mick nodded and gritted his teeth in anger.

'Well, Mick, it looks as though you've been the victim of a serious assault. Who was it put you in hospital?'

'A gang what come in the flat. Oi, I want my phone call; I wanna call my brief.'

'Yes, I met one of this so-called gang. A rather respectable old gentleman in his eighties. Was it him that beat you up?'

'No, it fuckin wasn't. Leave it out.'

'Who was it then? According to your mate John Edwards, it was just a couple of blokes. He says one of them was a little guy, the other one was bigger, and it only took them a few seconds to finish all of you off.'

'John 'oo? Never 'eard of 'im.'

'Normally goes by the name of Scally, apparently. He says the four of you were no match for them. Jews, were they?'

'How do I know? I never said they was Jews. What about my phone call? I wanna call a brief. So, Scally's the fuckin grass.'

'Know many Jews, do you Mick? Some of your best friends Jewish, are they?'

'Yeah, why not? I ain't no racist.'

'Yeah, well, maybe. We've got all these interesting pictures of you and your mates apparently beating people up. And all these people look a little bit Jewish. Know what I mean? Got anything to say about that?'

'You ain't got no pictures of me, mate. I don't believe ya.'

'No? You and your friends seem to like taking a few souvenir snaps on your mobiles.'

Mick faltered, but replied, 'Not me, mate. I ain't even got a mobile.'

'No, not any more you haven't, I know that. We had a good look at your old one, though. Go on then, you can have your phone call. When your solicitor gets here I'll take you up for questioning.'

* * *

Your heart literally feels like it's jumping, like a jogger running on the spot inside you. There are so many people all around, but they don't seem real. We don't know them, don't care about them, wouldn't care if they stopped existing. Do they feel the same about me? Daddy must be better now, because he is coming home. I really really can't wait to see them. There they will be. Except that people keep appearing in an endless stream, and it's never them. Maybe I won't recognise them. Maybe they aren't coming. Daddy is normally first off the plane, first through the doors, same as he does everything else before other people. Something's different today. Maybe his illness is a kind that makes you stop being first?

When I asked Aloo if he would go home now, he said 'How can I? I can hardly walk.' That's good, because I really want him to stay, it's so much more fun with him. Or maybe I can go to his house and help him to walk.

I still don't understand what Aloo did to help the police arrest the men. He told the police what happened, then straight away, the men got arrested. And Aloo knew. How did he know they were arrested? When I asked him, he just said, it's complicated, someone at the police station told him. I wonder if Aloo would lie to me? Yes, he would. All grown-ups are liars, aren't they?

Lots and lots of people have started coming out of the doors. They haven't all come from Switzerland. Some have come from Greece. Some from Budapest. (You can see that. It's written on a screen.) It's interesting to see if you can guess where they have come from. Interesting, but stupid, because you can never tell if your guess was right or wrong, so what's the point? Unless you ask them. Which would be even more stupid, because it doesn't matter *where* they are from. That's the trouble with things being interesting.

Suddenly yes – it *is* Mummy! She runs forward to hug and lift me, and I am buried in her dark hair, feel all her loveliness around me, a warm private world that belongs only to the two of us. Aloo gets a hug too, and a kiss on both cheeks. Daddy just waits his turn. Normally he is the first to run to me and give a big strong hug. Today he smiles, touches my hand gently, and says very quietly, 'Hello, my dear Danny.'

* * *

After Danny's almost delirious joy at seeing his parents, the mood became quiet. Jack led them to the car park, but Penny took the driver's seat. Simon did not want to sit beside her in the front. Danny had the rare pleasure of taking that position and being able to 'see where we are going.' Jack and Simon were in the back together, Simon edgily trying to appear normal.

The adults exchange barely a word. Danny chattered, and Penny kindly responded to all his remarks. After a single glance at his son, Jack thought perhaps he understood the problem. Not its cause, but he recognised a demeanour and an expression that he had seen before during his life. He knew that, suddenly and completely, his son had had enough of playing the game. He saw that Simon's state of mind had little to do with overwork. It was a horse that shies from a jump; the chained dog whimpering to be free; yet somehow too, the desperado with nothing to lose. However, what this meant he knew not. What barrier was Simon afraid to leap? What chain held him back? Simon, he mused, had always been a troubled boy. That was why he had not followed a proper career.

Simon was drifting in mid-stream of a river of thoughts and emotions and had nothing to say. Danny became quiet after a while, sensing unease and tension among the grown-ups. Penny was uncomfortably aware of having to protect Danny. She dreaded, too, anything that might upset Simon. At any moment, Jack might blurt out some unfortunate remark or a too-inquisitive question.

As she merged into fast, heavy traffic on the M4, Jack asked if the weather had been good in Switzerland. Penny felt that even this could be a risky subject with Simon. She said it had.

Nothing more was said for some miles, until Penny turned onto the North Circular Road. Jack wondered aloud if they had ever been to that hotel before. She said they had, but only in winter. Was it a nice hotel? Very, very nice. All four of them noticed that only Penny responded to these questions. Simon wondered if he should try to participate. And indeed, as he made that familiar journey back home from Heathrow, and saw those familiar summer clouds above the familiar vista of red roofed terraced streets and narrow back gardens and small flat-topped commercial blocks devoted to the mean life, he did feel close to his old self. But he remained quiet until they were passing Brent Cross shopping centre. They were almost home. He tried to recall being in Kandersteg that morning, and could not.

Then he said, 'Penny, how did you know to come out to Switzerland?'

Danny and Jack turned in surprise to look at him.

'Herr Wetzler called me,' Penny replied.

Simon pondered this. 'What did he say that made you come?'

Penny anxiously wondered how to reply without disturbing her child's happiness.

Jack found himself saying, 'Didn't you tell me, Penny, that he had had some kind of breakdown?'

Penny winced.

Danny answered, 'Yes, Grandad Aloo, I remember you said Daddy had a breakdown only it wasn't like a car, because nothing was really broken. When our car broke down it couldn't go on and came to a stop. Is that what happened, Daddy? Did you break down?'

Simon felt prickles of sweat all over his scalp, and a racing, dizzy breathlessness. He needed to rest quietly. In absolute silence. He did not reply.

'Well? Did you?' Danny insisted, turning his head to look at Simon.

Penny laid a hand on Danny's shoulder. 'That's enough now, Danny,' she said.

Arriving at the house, Penny struggled to park the car while the others went inside. Only when passing through the front door into the hallway did Simon begin to understand. That he had lost his grip and probably his income. That Penny had abandoned everything to rush out to him. That his elderly father had hurried to London to help.

He saw the answering machine light flashing: there were messages he did not want. He walked into the sitting room, saw the stack of unopened letters and a neat pile of phone messages which Jack had placed there earlier in the day, and which Simon did not want to read or know about. He saw newspapers lying on the sofa full of news he had not heard and did not want to hear. He held his head in despair. He had to look forward. He did not want to drown. He wanted to be… not dead, but someone else. He wanted to live again, afresh, renewed. He must solve his problems and be reborn. What, first of all, was the cause of the trouble? He needed to find out; he needed help, he needed a doctor, a therapist, someone.

When Jack came into the room, Simon noticed his cuts and bruises for the first time.

'Dad, what happened? Did you have an accident?'

'You don't know? I thought everybody knew, by now. I was roughed up by some hooligans.' Jack had forgotten that he had to watch his tongue when speaking to Simon. He dropped down onto the sofa with a sigh.

'*What*? Why?'

'Why d'you think, boychick? For a being an evil capitalist communist Christ-killer and the sole obstacle to Middle East peace.'

'You were… beaten up? For being *Jewish*? You, Dad? That's awful. I didn't know. When did it happen? Are you all right? Did you tell the police? Have you been to a doctor?'

Into Simon's mind come images from the television programme about Auschwitz. Vivid enough that for a moment he cannot see his father sitting in front of him. First that, and now this. Is it a coincidence? Of course not. These are not two events that by chance occurred together. They are two things both happening all the time. The death camps are a constant, always with us, that can never be removed from history. And Jew-hatred is a constant, always with us, all around the world.

'Yes,' he heard Jack's voice, saw him nodding. 'I was beaten up. It was last Friday. I'm not sure if I am all right, especially my bad knee. Yes, I have told the police. But no, I have not been to a doctor.'

Simon shook his head in disbelief. 'How do you know it's about being Jewish?'

Jack smiled wryly. 'Because they told me so. Dirty yid. Evil Jew.'

Simon was horrified. He found himself saying, 'Yes, yes. That's what I want to talk about.' He sat down in an armchair and faced his father intently as if preparing for a serious conversation.

Jack became wary. He remembered exhausting, disagreeable arguments they had had when Simon was a teenager living at home. 'Really? Now? What do you mean, talk about.'

'Why not now? What's now?'

Jack held up a conciliatory hand. 'OK, OK. Talk. But can we bring in the luggage? Can we have a coffee first?'

Simon ignored him. 'Dad, I'm in a total mess: about being Jewish, but not really being Jewish.'

Jack's discomfort brought grimaces to his animated face. This was the sort of conversation he did not like. He shifted in his seat and looked around with furrowed brow and twisted lip, unable to understand. 'Does being Jewish matter so much? It doesn't matter. How can it matter? Look, let's have a coffee and talk later. Talk tomorrow. I think I have to help Penny.'

'No, but Dad,' Simon struggled to explain. 'It matters to *me*. I need to know who I am, what I am.'

Penny stepped into the room but halted and listened. She was afraid Jack would make Simon's condition worse.

Jack was exasperated. 'But it's just imaginary! Identity, nationality, it's all in the mind!'

'Yes, and the mind is quite important, isn't it?' Simon retorted. 'In fact, everything that's human about humanity is all in the mind.'

'No, no, no. Or rather, yes. The mind is like a big marketplace.

The mind is like the internet. Ten per cent good. Ninety per cent trash. And among the rubbish are ideas like race, tribe, nationality. Such things mean nothing at all. Only the intellect matters. Art, music, science. The rest is nonsense.' He looked up at Penny. 'Shall we have a coffee?' She did not respond.

'Dad, didn't you tell me you want Israel to be like Switzerland? What is Switzerland like? Is it anything like Swaziland? Is there any difference between the French and the English? Is there, according to you, even such a thing as being English?'

'OK, OK, I've got the point. I see what you're driving at.' Jack looked up at Penny, his expression pleading for her help in ending the discussion. 'So you are what you are. You're right, people do have an identity. But they don't need to agonise about it. They are born with it. They should try to rise above it.'

'Dad, I watched a film about Auschwitz, and I thought, weird that if I had been murdered in the Holocaust, no one would question my Jewishness.'

'Who's questioning anything? What's to question? What Jewishness? What's the Holocaust got to do with anything? Don't look for reason and logic in the Holocaust. I say, forget about all this Jewish nonsense. It's just words. It's imaginary. Look, Simon, you are what you are. You're thoroughly English. That's what I always wanted you to be. We love you, we're proud of you. You are yourself. We like you that way.'

'Dad, it's just not enough to be yourself. A human being is more than that. Everyone is part of something *bigger* than themselves, a society, a culture. Each person has an inheritance. They need to feel part of that.'

'My dear boy. You are English, as English as they come.'

'With a father whose family came from Russia and speak Yiddish? I don't think so. Anyway, I can't talk any more. My face is hurting.'

Jack shrugged. 'Well, has anyone ever suggested that you are *not* English? Have they? I doubt it.'

Simon repeated, 'My face hurts. I can't talk.'

Penny said, 'Aloo, never mind the coffee. Why don't you pour us all a drink?'

'A drink?' This was not Jack's language at all. 'You mean a sherry?'

To her surprise, Simon had not finished. He spoke quietly and painfully. 'By the way, Dad. All I wanted to say was, will you take me to a synagogue?'

Jack glanced at Penny, whose face remained expressionless as, fascinated, she awaited his response to this unlikely request. He was startled, uneasy. 'I don't think that's such a good idea.'

'Because I'm not Jewish?'

'That could be a reason.'

'So if my own father won't take me, who shall I go with?'

Jack bit his lip. 'OK, I'll take you. With a friend I've made while I've been here.'

They managed to sit around the table together in reasonably good humour for the simplest type of meal. From the kitchen, Danny and Penny brought plates of fresh spaghetti covered with ready-made sauce. There would be a scoop of ice cream to follow.

They were saved from silence by Danny's excited chatter. He asked for some orange juice, then when Penny brought him the carton, he held it up to show the words printed there – Do Not Use If Seal Is Broken. 'So how can you drink this juice?' he cried. 'If you can't break the seal?'

'Of course you can break the seal,' Penny told him. 'That's how you open it.'

'No, but it says, if the seal is broken, you mustn't drink it.'

He worked out the numerical value of all the letters on

the front of the carton, added them up and exclaimed, 'Hey! Incredible luck! It's another prime number!' Jack almost gasped at the announcement. His mouth opened in astonishment. The boy's aptitude approached the eerie, the inhuman. 'That,' said Danny, 'must be why they call it Premium Quality.'

Penny was too distracted to understand, but Jack grinned and shook his head with wonder. He announced blandly that he had enjoyed Danny's company, and enjoyed his stay. It had been uneventful – so he said – but had made a nice relaxing break. For all that, he was looking forward to being back in his own home.

Penny laughed. 'If you call being beaten up uneventful!'

He chuckled. 'Yes, apart from that.'

'By the way, Aloo,' Penny asked, 'did you sleep here Sunday night?'

Jack thought about it. 'Of course.'

'There's a message from Dina. She says she came at eight-thirty yesterday morning, but there was no one here.'

'Dina? Who's Dina?'

Danny spoke up, 'Don't you remember? Mrs Jolly-Jolly the Fairy. I told you she comes on Monday to clean the house.'

'Maybe I went out for a walk.'

'She says she waited for quite a while, then phoned a couple of times later during the day, but there was never any answer. Of course, I'll have to pay her anyway.'

Jack shrugged and said he could not remember as far back as yesterday. He offered to pay, but Penny waved a hand dismissively and said she wouldn't hear of it. 'You weren't here, so you weren't here,' she shrugged. 'But where was Danny?'

Danny shook his head in quick, urgent warning to Jack, but the old man did not notice.

'Let's see, Sunday night… he was with a friend. He had a sleepover somewhere. The mother's name is Lorrae?'

Penny was furious. 'Not Josh Shinberg again! Aloo, I *specifically* asked you not to let him go there any more!' He winced and apologised. She pressed her lips together, blinked back tears of frustration and said no more. The man was impossible.

She offered him more spaghetti.

After the meal, Jack went from the table to the piano. Sighing 'Ay-ay-ay', he began to play.

Simon and Penny lay in their own bed once more. Jack was tucked up in the spare room, and Danny slept contentedly between his sheets, having been kissed good night by both his mother and his father, and of course, by Grandad Aloo. Tomorrow, Penny thought, there would be a lot to do. She set her alarm clock.

13

Even with eyes still closed, she cast her gaze over the fearful landmarks of a new life. Simon's illness (for so she was beginning to name it) was the ominous volcano rising in the middle distance, the centre of everything. Closer at hand, another small mountain to climb, was Aloo's injuries. And across the whole vista beyond, the lack of an income spread as a vast black plateau. Yes, there would certainly be money worries. Penny got out of bed before seven, as if it were an ordinary school day rather than the middle of August. Tying her embroidered silk dressing gown around herself, she left the room without opening the curtains. As she expected, Aloo was already downstairs, reading quietly on the sofa. She noticed the book was *Kindertransport*. An unusual choice for him: he normally steered clear of Jewish subjects.

'Morning,' she said. 'Have you had breakfast?'

He looked up and nodded. 'Good morning. Yes, I've had something, thank you, dear.'

'We'll go to the hospital this morning. How soon can you be ready? Get you looked at. I don't like that knee.'

He said he didn't want to go. There was no need. He wasn't about to spend hours waiting with violent, uncouth drunks.

'A weekday, first thing, is your best bet,' she insisted. 'Take the book with you. It'll help pass the time.'

They drove down East Heath Road to the Royal Free Hospital, just as Yoav had done, Jack surprised once more that it was such a short distance by the direct route. There was nowhere to park nearby, but Jack could not walk far, so despite signs warning that parked vehicles would be clamped, Penny had no alternative but to take him to the entrance of Accident & Emergency and help him inside. It irritated her that only 'Disabled' parking was allowed. Surely everyone being driven to A&E was disabled? She asked a porter where to find a wheelchair. He looked African, tall, slim and black, with delicate features, shook his head without a word. Anxious about the car, she abandoned Jack, leaving him to struggle as best he could, and rushed out. Jack soon persuaded the African to find him a wheelchair, push him into A&E and tell him about his village home in Somalia.

The parking meters on East Heath Road were not working properly: she put in two pounds, but the ticket showed only one pound's worth of time. That wouldn't be enough time to wait with Aloo. She went on foot to find him sitting at A&E. 'Have you been seen? Did you go to the desk?'

There were scores of people ahead of him. It was going to take hours. She decided to leave him there while she took Simon to their own doctor. Back at home, Simon was still in bed, sleeping soundly. She made a few phone calls.

'Jeffrey – I'm back. I'll be wanting a bit more work in the future.'

'I'll see what I can do, Penelope, but I can't promise.'

Penny did some freelance teaching of English as a foreign language at a small college in Golders Green, just filling in gaps when other teachers were away. It had provided useful extra cash, but now, she saw, her English teaching might be all they had to live on. Maybe she could get a more permanent job somewhere. She didn't savour the thought.

Danny was ready for breakfast. 'I love you, Mummy,' the boy declared grandly, perhaps with some other, unspoken message to convey, reaching up to hug her neck. 'I'm sorry about Josh Shinberg. I knew you didn't want me to go. Only I didn't think you would find out.'

Such guileless honesty made her smile sadly. 'God, I just don't know what I am suppose to do. I try so hard to bring you up properly,' she said, mainly to herself, 'but I can't make it go right.'

Simon was referred to an 'emergency' therapist working from the GP's surgery once a week. He had the first session immediately, as it happened to be one of the mornings that the therapist visited the surgery, and she had a cancellation. Simon and the therapist leaned back in low, functional armchairs facing one another in a small, bare consulting room. She was an attractive young woman, and the closed door gave Simon a frisson of sexual intimacy.

She asked if he thought he had a problem. He admitted that all was not well. 'I really don't know what's happening to me, what has happened to me.' Slowly, quietly, he described the cramped jaw muscles and shortness of breath that prevented him from speaking. He told her about his panic attacks, the pounding heart, sweating and anxiety. She listened calmly. At last he mentioned the blood-washed hallucinatory daydreams.

'Will these images ever stop coming? Will they go back in their box? Will everything go back to normal?'

'It would be nice, wouldn't it?' she said. 'But no, probably not completely. I think once the lid has been opened, it never shuts quite so tightly as before. You know what you have seen. This period will pass. The memory will fade. It will matter less and less to you as years go by. But I doubt if things will ever really be quite the same again.'

'In my dreams of oblivion,' he told her, 'there is never any pain. I think of myself being crushed, torn to shreds, bones shattered, blood gushing, but I imagine no agony.'

'It proves you are just fantasising,' she said. 'It shows you don't want death, only happiness.'

'Happiness!' He scorned the idea. 'What's that? A few pleasant moments here and there. A drink, some music, a nice sunny day. Yes, yes. Peace and happiness. Peace and happiness. Escape from problems. Trouble is, when problems are complicated, elusive, and defy solution. When their roots grow in your very soul.'

'Tell me all about them.'

He looked at her in silence. She did not prompt him. At last he said, 'We moved to Golders Green just a little while ago. It made me think more about being Jewish. Every day it was in my thoughts.'

She was puzzled, almost amused. She asked if he was Jewish. *Maybe*, he said. Was he religious? *No, no, not in the slightest*, he told her.

With long pauses to relax his face, eventually he talked freely of his background, his work, his fears, his breakdown, his feeling of not belonging, not being a part of anything, his sense of isolation, of pointlessness, of having no direction. Nodding, she encouraged him to speak, and the very act of talking to a young woman made him feel more alive. He told her about his mother's painful death, which had left him as the only non-Jew in the family.

'This Jewish thing,' he ventured. She listened attentively. 'You see, my father… always impressed on me… be wary of non-Jews. Be careful of them. They are full of hate for us.' He stopped and she waited. 'At the same time, our little secret, I was *not* a Jew. I was one of *them*. Oh, he loved me though. He loved me for that. And his wife too. My mother. She wasn't

Jewish either. Actually *he* was the odd one out! I thought *I* was.'

The therapist waited.

'But I have this weird feeling now,' he said, 'that I don't really exist. My father and my son exist.' He told her how a programme on Auschwitz had plunged him into despair. His mind had erupted like a volcano. He wanted to be among those dead bodies. Then he *would* exist. Even as he said the words, he knew it was insane.

'Can you help me to get better?' he asked.

'No,' she told him bluntly. 'There is no cure for such feelings. The goal is to live with them. Only then might they go away.'

She urged him to take, for a short time, some medication which the doctor could prescribe. He recoiled. 'Let's see how I get on just talking.'

When Penny returned to the hospital in the afternoon, Jack had been moved from A&E into a ward. She walked along shabby corridors that had seen a lot of hard use. Plaster was coming off the walls in places. She remembered when the hospital was new. There had been a local campaign against it, because it blocked a rather beautiful view from the Heath. None of that seemed important any more. Views are soon forgotten. Coloured strips set into the grey lino floors marked the route to different clinics and departments. She took a crowded lift to an upper floor and pushed open the door into the ward. Sunlight streamed into a pale, bright reception area. Nurses in white and blue uniforms moved around. It could almost have been a pleasant scene. Not wanting to waste any time, she walked straight past the desk and into the ward. None of the nurses stopped her.

Beyond the nurses' station were several smaller wards, or rooms, in each of which an assortment of elderly men and women from all around the globe were lying in adjacent beds, nearly touching, some almost unclothed in the heat, their thighs barely covered by trailing, rumpled sheets and stained blankets. She had thought mixed wards were being phased out. Apparently not here. Perhaps because most of the people were elderly, it was felt that sex was no longer important to them. She wondered if that were true – whether it would be true for her. Do old men have lustful thoughts? Surely not about old women. Would it matter? It was seedy. The whole place made her think of slums. With increasing distate, she looked in several of the rooms and finally returned to the desk. 'Which bed is Jack Silver in?' Penny asked. 'I can't see him.'

'He's not here at the moment,' the nurse said. 'He's having some X-rays. You're welcome to wait, but it could be a couple of hours before he gets back.'

There was no point in waiting. She couldn't stay long in any case. She didn't like leaving Danny on his own at home. 'Can I leave a message on his bed?'

'I'll give him a message for you,' said the nurse. Penny thought any message would be lost or forgotten and decided to try to find him. She made her way down to the X-ray department. Sure enough, he was in a wheelchair, clothed only in an undignified and revealing white gown loosely tied at the back.

He did not seem surprised to see her. 'You are not treated like an adult,' he complained, as soon as she came into view. 'Look at this stupid robe. It's intended to humiliate you. You know what I hate? The damn phoney friendliness. Everyone is calling me Jack, as if I were a child. What's wrong with sir? Or at least, Dr Silver? You see why I didn't want to come here?'

She noted his disputatious mood and hoped to avoid being drawn into a row. 'Aloo – think about it. What's the alternative? Have they told you what's wrong?'

'I know already. It's my knee, isn't it?'

'Yes, yes. But what's wrong with your knee?'

'It hurts, right?'

Penny found it difficult to control her irritation. 'Yes, yes, yes. But what exactly has made it so much worse than it was?'

'Could it be because it was whacked with a piece of wood? And kicked? And I fell onto it when I was knocked over? It wouldn't be that, would it?'

She remained calm, struggled to keep her voice sweet and kind. 'Look, Aloo, am I doing my very best for you? Have I tried to look after you? Did I bring you in here? Excuse me, but have I now come all the way back just to see if I can do anything more to help you? Why are you so grumpy with me? Aloo, must you always kvetch even if people are bending over backwards to help you?'

'Shouldn't an old man with damaged ligaments be grumpy? Being in a place like this when I could be reading quietly at home?'

'So is it damaged ligaments?' she asked. 'Did the consultant say that?'

'Of course. You think I made it up?'

'Ligaments – and anything else?'

'How should I know? Am I a doctor? Why do you think I'm having an X-ray?'

She could have screamed. Instead she asked, 'Do you want a cup of tea, Aloo?'

'Thank you. Try and get me a biscuit, will you?'

She ran to the car. There was no penalty notice on the windscreen. Under the parking regulations, it is not allowed to re-start the parking period without first moving the car. She drove onto the stony, unpaved Heath car park, but there was no empty space. She drove up Downshire Hill and back, but there were no spaces. Where could she park? It seemed she might have to forgo the quick walk she longed for. She joined a line of cars creeping up East Heath Road, eventually reaching Whitestone Pond and turning right. At the Bull and Bush pub, she turned into North End and did see a space. She sat with the engine turned off, trying to calm herself. She could have a quiet stroll under the trees on Sandy Heath, or West Heath, or in Golders Hill Park. She decided instead to sit at the park café with a cup of tea. Danny would be all right for a little while more. As she passed through the gate, a wide vista of distant London suburbs on low hills rose far away, beyond the park's statuesque trees and smooth, rolling greensward. She took a turn around the pretty flower garden before returning to find a café table.

As she sipped and meditated, Penny mused that she understood well enough why Aloo would rather be ill at home than cured in hospital. In any case, as he had said, the hospital cannot actually heal damaged bones and ligaments. He would have to do that in his own time and in his own home. She could barely wait for him to leave her in peace. He had done her a great favour, but she could not cope with Jack as well as Simon. She must do her damnedest to make Simon happy, even if it were difficult. She would make a good dinner tonight, try to give Simon a good time. And Jack must return to his own home as soon as possible.

* * *

This evening was the first time for ages we have been all together, just Mummy and Daddy and me. They poured out a drink, and Daddy lifted his glass and said, 'May we be happy.' Mummy said, 'Amen to that.'

I said, 'It's lovely being us again.' Mummy agreed. She had

put on a lovely dark blue dress that Daddy gave her on her birthday, which she doesn't usually wear at home. From each ear hung a small dark blue square on a little silver chain. She looked so beautiful. I like it when she wears an apron on top of nice clothes. The feeling in the house was lovely, with music and the smell of cooking and the three of us. She made a nice pastry, like a quiche, but with onions, tomatoes, feta cheese and olives. Daddy didn't do anything to help, just sat on the sofa listening to the music. But it was nice that he wasn't upstairs, working as usual. Mummy asked Daddy to choose a wine to have with dinner, but he didn't move, so she brought a bottle and showed it to him. 'Would that be a good one?' she asked. He nodded, with a funny little smile. 'Open it,' she said, and he did. I don't think Daddy is ill. Just worried about something.

How worried can a person be? Suppose a person was already as worried as it is possible to be, then they were given even more to worry about. What would happen to the person? That's Daddy. He was nice this evening, but quiet, thinking and worried. He sipped his wine and said the food was delicious.

Mummy asked me who I had seen while she was away, *apart* from the Shinbergs, who she doesn't want to hear about, and what it was like having Aloo look after me. She asked about when we saw a man dying and Aloo saved his life. I said he got a parking ticket for doing that. I told them about our Mobile Raids, where we try to interrupt someone talking on their phone, but they didn't seem to think that was funny at all. Mummy said, if Aloo does that, he's asking for trouble, and one day someone might give him some.

I said, maybe that's why those people attacked him. Maybe he interrupted their phone call. That might explain, somehow, why he had their phone. Mummy was surprised by that. 'Did he have their phone?' She asked me to tell everything about the attack, but I didn't want to. I think Aloo and I have a sort of secret about it. I asked them if they knew Villy and Ilse. They didn't know them at all.

'Did you meet them?' Mummy asked.

'Yes, we went there for tea. Villy tells a lot of jokes. But I don't understand them. He speaks with a foreign accent. He knows all about prime numbers.'

Mummy said Villy sounds like a nice man and they should thank him for what he has done.

'And he says he'll teach me for my barmishlah or barmitzlah, whatever it's called,' I said. 'Because he teaches that. It's part of his job.'

Mummy and Daddy became very quiet. Daddy sighed and lowered his head and gave Mummy a weird look.

'If you don't mind,' I said. Still they just sat there. 'Me having one.'

They didn't seem to know what to say.

'What is it again, that word? Is it barmitzbah?' I asked.

'It's barmitzvah,' Mummy said. 'But do you actually know what a barmitzvah is, darling?'

Of course, I didn't, but I could remember everything Villy had said about it. 'It's a very special occasion,' I said. 'To celebrate when a Jewish boy becomes thirteen. You do a reading in synagogue, make a little speech, and have a big party.'

'Why do you want to do this, when we don't even belong to a synagogue?' Mummy asked.

I didn't really know the right answer to this, and I didn't know that a synagogue is something you belong to; I thought it was a sort of place or a building, but I said, 'Because I'm a Jewish boy, and I will be thirteen.'

Daddy's face became very sad, and he rubbed his cheeks, and his eyes, and his neck. He had a few little prickles of sweat on his head. He looked out of the back window into the garden as if he wished he could be out there. But he said quietly to

Mummy, 'What about a secular barmitzvah, kibbutz style?'

'We can discuss it. There's plenty of time. Danny, it was very kind of Villy to offer that, wasn't it? I think I'd better phone him. And what about Ilse, what's she like?'

I noticed that Mummy gave Daddy a strange look. He was sweating quite a lot, even though it wasn't hot or anything.

Later, when I went to bed, I could hear them talking downstairs. That's one of my favourite things. They were talking about being converted. I'm wondering how a person can be converted into something else. When you have a loft conversion, you turn the loft into a bedroom, but I don't see how you do that to a person, unless you turn their head into something else, like put their heart in their head and their brain in their chest. Or electric current can be converted, like from 110 volts into 220 volts. Maybe it's like that. To make you more powerful. Decimals get converted into fractions. Money gets converted, like from pounds to euros. What about people? Measurements can be converted, like at school when they teach about turning metres into yards, and grams into ounces. Maybe it's like that: the person is exactly the same, but measured differently. When a car is convertible, the roof opens up and instead of just driving along like everyone else, you have the wind in your hair and the sun on your face, feeling free and happy and special.

* * *

'It's a mad idea. He'd be barmitzvah, and his dad won't even be Jewish.'

'Darling, I'm not saying I want him to be barmitzvah. We've never wanted it before. We can certainly say no. But if he wants to, what's the harm? It's not the first time it's ever happened. There are families like that. Plenty of them.'

'Families like what?'

'Where not everyone is Jewish. I mean, halachically.'

'But for crying out loud, I *am* Jewish. Not halachically, OK. So what? If we're not religious, then what do we care about halacha? This whole situation is driving me insane.'

'Please darling. I'm on your side with this. You could convert if it matters that much.'

Simon's eyes opened wide. He shook his head. 'Convert! From what? From Jewish to Jewish? Anyway, how could I? I don't see myself wearing a kippah and tsitsit, or making a blessing every time I eat a sandwich.'

'No, no,' she said. 'That's Orthodox. You'd make a Reform conversion or something. Anyway, you're already steering clear of treif food, and you're already circumcised, so you're most of the way there already.'

'I don't even believe in God! Let alone the mad rules and rituals …'

'Do you think God cares what you believe?' Penny said. 'No one cares what you believe. It's not Jewish to believe in anything. Jews never discuss belief. Judaism is about action, not faith. It's about doing the right thing, not believing the right thing. The only thing Jews believe in is being Jewish.'

Simon listened ruefully, and commented, 'Ruth said, "My people are your people." I can go along with that.'

'And if that involves performing a few ancient rituals,' Penny said, 'observing a few crazy festivals, then so be it. You can convert to being a normal non-believing Jew. Like the rest of us.'

'Unfortunately, you can't,' Simon replied. 'That's not how conversion works. The people who carry out religious conversions are all very religious, believe it or not. Damn them. And the next bit of what Ruth says is, "My God is your God."'

'So lie to them about what you believe,' Penny urged him.

'Lie to them?' Simon was shocked. 'That would be rather hypocritical, wouldn't it? My conversion would be based on a lie. It wouldn't be real.'

'Dear Simon – a conversion is *not* real. Do you think you will be a different person afterwards? You will be exactly the same. There is no such thing as a conversion. It's a sham. A person is real. And a person is a mass, and believes a mass, of confusing, conflicting things. Think of it as telling a lie to become an American citizen. Anyway it's not lying – it's just being insincere. Is that such a crime? Would you be willing to do that? Like, swear an oath of allegiance to a flag, or whatever meshugass they do there?'

Simon listened gloomily. 'Yeah, that's another idea. Maybe I should be in America.'

When Penny came into the bedroom, Simon was already propped against pillows in the bed, daydreaming or thinking. He smiled at her slightly. 'Thank you for trying to make it a nice evening,' he said. His state of mind seemed a little better than before. With reference to nothing, he added, 'And why shouldn't he be barmitzvah? I thought his reason was a good one. I don't want to give him all the same problems as me. Let him be a proper little Jewish boy.'

'I thought the problem was, it's a religion, and we don't want him to have a religion.'

'That's right. Well, I'm confused about that, too. After our discussion. About lies. About converting.'

Penny stood close to the bed so he could watch as she unbuttoned her dress and slipped it off. She wanted him to take an interest in her. She shook her hair and ran her fingers through it, put her hands behind her back to unhook the bra. She bent forward to kiss his head affectionately, her hair enfolding him, her breasts resting on his face. 'Dear Simon,' she said. 'Will everything be all right?'

At that moment, he felt everything was already all right. He reached around her waist, ran his hands over her, tugged at her knickers to pull them down. She took them off and joined him under the duvet, held him close. She wore only her necklace, a slender silver chain.

'Do you feel alone, unloved?' she asked. She pressed herself against him. One hand reached down to fondle him.

'We are each of us alone, aren't we, with our thoughts?'

She felt he might even be joking, parodying his depression. 'Alone with our thoughts, that's true. But physically together. Living together, sharing everything, as you said before, sharing our time. Naked together. We are always alone in our minds, but we can get awfully close in other ways.'

'And in your mind, what would I find if I could see in there?'

'I'm thinking… thinking, let's see… I'm thinking about you. And I'm wondering, wondering… just how close can two people get. Purely physically, of course.'

He smiled. He was grateful for her efforts to amuse him. He looked at her face, dark and Italianate, the eyes holding him with a deep tenderness. At that moment, it seemed to him that something in his mood or his mind had created a warm light around her. He saw in her the staunchest ally, someone who could easily have turned her back on him, but chose instead to stand by him. True, she did not want to hear his worst nightmares, but nor did she want to abandon him to them. Her skin, with the necklace resting on it so delicately, seemed like finest silk, her breasts themselves a kind of exquisite jewellery. She touched and guided him, and he slipped into her and held her, each of them lost in unhurried sensation, and memories of their years of love, and at last, in the immeasurable moments of satisfaction.

* * *

Awake half the night, Miri. Is this any way to treat sick people? Lights blazing all round the clock, porters clattering about, nurses doing humiliating tests without closing the curtains around you, patients calling out and pressing their buzzers while nurses ignore them. Staff calling you 'love' and 'dear' when they couldn't give a damn if you live or die. No one will tell you what's wrong with you, no one knows or cares. Consultants see you for less than one minute, treat you like a speck in a test tube. I buttonholed the fellow who came to the ward with his little team yesterday. He was talking to them about me as if I was a bit of research material. They stared at me like I was a nasty mess on the sitting room carpet.

The patient presented this, the patient complained of that, he had debris behind the knee, patella, meniscus, bruising, age, complications, healing process, this, that and the other.

His manner was so annoying I could stand it no longer. I sat up furiously. 'No, no, no – you listen to me,' I interrupted him. 'Don't talk about patients in the third person in that way. It's extremely demeaning.'

He looked at me with, let's say, a faint hint of amusement as well as surprise, as if I was some sort of performing flea.

I wanted to shout out, *Everyone should be spoken to decently! Treat every patient with humanity, with courtesy and respect.* But I was afraid it would sound pompous, or priggish, or both.

He looked at the chart to check my name, and said, 'Mr Silver – '

'Dr Silver.'

'Dr Silver, if you are unhappy with the way you have been treated…'

'My dear fellow, you miss the point entirely,' I said. 'I am not speaking about myself. What do you know about the people in this ward? Is one of them a war hero? Is one of them a great scholar? Are they loving parents? What suffering have they known in their lives? People come here to be cared for and cured. Instead they are insulted. Because, yes, it's insulting to be spoken about in that way. And all because they are ill. Is that a crime?'

Am I right, Miri? Am I? Should people in hospital be humiliated?

Nurses gathered at the door to listen. Some raised their eyes to heaven as if I was a madman. Perhaps I am. The ward sister bustled forward, 'Come, come, Jack,' she said, 'the doctor is too busy for this!'

The doctor held up a hand to stop her. He said, 'Dr Silver, since you are clearly an intelligent man – '

'Don't patronise me, for God's sake,' I said.

'Well then, Dr Silver, let me come to the point. I'll be very frank. A hospital is about caring for a whole population. If we don't know the patients' names, or anything personal about them, it's because we don't need to know. But I assure you, we do truly care about the patients – perhaps as a whole, rather than as individuals. We're doing our very best for you, and for the next person in this bed, without ever seeing the difference between you.'

'Well, that certainly *is* very frank,' I said.

'You know, sir, we save lives here. We don't bother to learn people's names. We learn what treatment they need.'

'Very good answer,' I admitted. 'But none of us deserves to be humiliated.'

'Fair enough, I'll take that on board,' he nodded. Now the ward sister put her hand on his arm and led him away from me, followed by his little troupe. As they went away, the sister was saying, 'Well, I'm sorry about that.' The woman in the next bed cast a disparaging, expressionless glance in my direction. An old-fashioned look. I started to feel like an idiot. All the same, it *is* humiliating to endure all these discomforts and then be spoken about in that way.

Two of the other nurses, stocky, tough-looking lasses, one black, one white, approached as if they were going to give me a thrashing for speaking out of turn. The black one looked at my chart, saying, 'What's up, then, dear? Not happy? What is it? The food?'

'I didn't say I wasn't happy!' I protested to them. 'I was telling the doctor how nice and how good-looking the nurses are.'

The black nurse laughed throatily. The white one gave me a wry smile. She looked at me as though I were a mischievous child. 'This is a tough job, you know,' she said. 'I bet you wouldn't like it.'

'How do you know I wasn't a nurse?'

'You!' she said. 'I bet you was a professor or summink. You look like a maffs teacher. Was you a nurse?'

It's like being in some sort of lunatic asylum, crazy people shouting and officious staff with the power of life and death. I feel as if I've been banished to the poorhouse of some parsimonious, cash-strapped parish. Three times in the night someone called to be taken to the toilet but was told, *just do it in the bed, we'll clean it up in the morning*. OK, she was probably deranged in some way. I came to that conclusion myself. Mess on the floor, the stink is unbelievable, the filth and squalor, it's nauseating. A tall, lean African man with the body of a runner strolled into the ward and lazily ran a floor-polisher down the centre of the room. When I asked him if he could possibly clean under the bed, where there were rolls of dust, he smiled and nodded amiably. He did not know enough English to understand me. I want to see a brisk no-nonsense Mrs Mopp in here with a bucket of water and a smell of Dettol. I want to see someone as keen as mustard, mopping right up to the corner skirting boards. Miri, I'd rather be dead on the carpet at home than alive in a bed in this place.

People are suffering enough when they come in to the hospital. No one comes here for fun. And do they shower you with sympathy and loving kindness? Do they show you that you are appreciated? Do they make things as easy for you as they possibly can? Do they heck. I should cocoa.

Is it a relief to be in hospital knowing that at last you'll be properly looked after? You know the answer already – you were in and out of hospital for two years, eventually more in and than out, until finally that hospital became your last home – and mine, too, because I haven't had a proper home since you left, Miri.

Some of the nurses are absolute gems, treasures. There are girls working here who deserve a medal. Two medals – one for public service, another for courage. These are the decent human beings. They are considerate and caring. They do talk to you with human love and concern. Perhaps nursing attracts more of them than most professions. They're swimming against the whole ethos of this place. They'll have to change or leave. There's no place for such people in an institution like this. I was to-ing and fro-ing to the nurses' station all night long, trying to get them to help patients whose problems were being ignored. I almost carried one old chap to the toilet all by myself, even though I could hardly walk any better than him. Then I sat by a woman's bed as she wept and told me her troubles. I hardly had a wink of sleep. How could I have done, with all the racket going on?

The last straw is the fleas. When I found fleas in the bed, I decided to leave. But how can you leave, if you can't walk? We're like prisoners here, being experimented on. You are barely allowed to communicate with the rest of the world. It costs the earth to make or receive a phone call. Why? I dressed, put my things in a bag and sat in a chair beside the bed. This morning, I set off to find a public phone. It was so far, I ended up practically crawling there. I waited for the clock to show seven-thirty. I know that's when Penny gets up. On the dot of seven-thirty I dialled.

'Come and get me,' I said, 'I'm discharging myself. I want to go home.'

To her credit, Penny arrived by eight. She had a copy of the Jewish Chronicle in her hand.

'Have you seen this?' She held it up for me to see.

* * *

The JC is a most unusual newspaper. Sold by every newsagent in Britain's Jewish areas, it falls somewhere between a local free-sheet, an international journal and a Monty Python sketch ('Here is the news for parrots: No parrots were involved in an accident on the M1 today'[28]). It has exceptionally well-informed news and features from Israel and the Jewish world, and, hardly less expert, from the Arab world too. It covers with depth and insight the political intrigues of the Middle East and Manchester, Gaza and Golders Green, Lebanon and Hendon. Its stories and pictures of Jewish community members in the news may find figures of worldwide renown rubbing shoulders with personalities little known outside a small neighbourhood, such as Rabbi Naftule Shlayfer.

'Rabbi Shlayfer assaulted in street' was the headline. With a fine portrait of the fabulously hirsute rebbe alongside, the main story detailed his experience on the afternoon of Friday last, when the spiritual leader of the worldwide movement of

28 Monty Python's Flying Circus, episode 20, 1969

Krechonomnetzer hasidim had come from Stamford Hill to Golders Green to spend Shabbat with the somewhat sleeker Rabbi Dovid Levinter, of whom there was also a fine portrait, and whose pious words formed a pull-out quote: 'A great and holy man set upon by ignorant thugs'. The Krechonomnetzers would be celebrating with even more fervour and gratitude than usual the birthday of their rebbe, who would be 77 years old this Friday, the 25th of Tamuz in the Hebrew calendar for this year.

The second story on the front page, on the right hand side, headed 'Mystery rescuer found' was accompanied by a striking picture of Rabbi Shlayfer's 80-year-old saviour, the crop-haired, clean-shaven, unsmiling, tight-lipped Dr Jack Silver, his red cuts and purple bruises looking especially vivid.

Beneath a subheading, 'Seven held after Golders Green attacks', was told Dr Silver's story. How he went to the aid of Rabbi Shlayfer and set out to track down his assailants and bring them to justice, without any help from the police, eventually confronting three of his attackers in a dawn raid at their own home in Kentish Town. The three were hospitalised by Dr Silver and arrested when they regained consciousness. Four further arrests had since taken place, police confirmed.

It is not clear, the story continued, whether Dr Silver acted entirely alone. Neither the police nor Dr Silver were prepared to give any details. A Krechonomnetzer spokesman said it was impossible to fully express their gratitude to Dr Silver, who was invited with all his family to the home of Rabbi Shlayfer for the birthday feast.

No one in the Silver family would ordinarily buy the Jewish Chronicle, unless Simon had an article in it. Nor would Rabbi Shlayfer, for whom it was a secular, trivial, little better than goyish publication.

Arriving at the hospital just as its newsagent's shop was opening, Penny's astonished eye fell upon the image of Jack's stony expression at the top of a stack of JCs beside the door.

She grabbed a copy and stared in dismay. Her mind could barely comprehend the story as she went over and over the words. Is this how Jack spent his time while 'looking after' her little boy?

Jack read it at the hospital bedside. 'Not a bad paper, this,' was his inappropriate response. A grim expression gave nothing away. He flicked through the other pages. 'Good letters. There used to be a good columnist, Chaim Bermant. He must be dead by now. He was old when I was a boy. This new fellow, Professor Alderman, is interesting, isn't he? Look, can we go? I don't want to spend another minute in this dreadful place.'

'Is this why you weren't at home on Monday morning?' she challenged him.

'Let's go home,' he said. 'Don't stay here; you'll catch fleas.'

'The fleas probably came from one of the other patients. It's not the hospital's fault.'

Jack said, 'Did I say it was their fault? It's painful to walk. I'm not sure I can make it. Where's the car?'

A young nurse approached quickly as they made their way out of the ward door. 'You're not leaving, Jack? Has anyone said you can? Does doctor know?'

He put on his reading glasses to read her name badge. 'You can tell him for me, Katie. And thank him sincerely for his humanity and kindness. They're going to send the test results to my GP, aren't they? So, no problem.'

'Shall I get you a wheelchair?' she said.

Jack nodded. 'Please. That's good of you, dear.'

Penny wheeled him quickly along the smooth, lino-floored corridor. Anger filled her with energy. 'I think it was irresponsible. It was very risky. Foolhardy.'

'I didn't know it would be on the front page,' he protested.

Reaching the hospital door, she continued into the pleasant, cool morning air outside. 'I'm sure what you have done is very wonderful, but suppose you had been badly hurt? Well, that's your choice. But what would have happened to Danny?'

'You've no idea the trouble I went to, making sure he was safe and sound while this was going on.'

'My God!' she exclaimed in horror. 'I should have found someone else! I don't know who, but anyone else would have been better.'

'Danny really knew nothing about it. I assure you. What was I supposed to do? The police weren't interested. They would have let these hooligans get away with it.'

'Oh my God. You're making it worse. Don't tell me any more.'

'Anyway,' Jack added, 'he was such a great help in tracking them down. I really couldn't have done it without Danny.'

'*What?*' In her fury, Penny was tempted to run the wheelchair off the kerb and tip him onto the road. Instead, she continued along the pavement. As they reached the car, she said, 'Have we really been invited to Rabbi Shlayfer's home? That would be interesting.'

'No, I haven't heard anything about that,' Jack replied honestly. 'I think it's just a thing hasids say. You'd better take the wheelchair back. Someone else may need it.'

Villy phoned at nine. Penny answered. 'It's not too early?' came the German-sounding voice. Somehow she knew at once who it was. 'Is it Penny, Jack's daughter-in-law? Well hello, hello. And did you see today's Jewish Chronicle?'

'I saw it.'

'We had no idea. He must be mad.'

'Oh, he is, I assure you. Quite mad.'

'He could have been killed!' Villy exclaimed.

'I'm aware of it,' Penny said. 'And he misled me. He deceived me about it.'

Villy chuckled. 'He lied, you mean?'

'That's the word.'

'But what a hero! What a mensh!'

Penny faltered. She had not thought in those terms. 'Up to a point. But he was supposed to be looking after my son.'

'Oh, Danny! We met him. Really a lovely, lovely boy! Very clever. A genius.' Villy said fulsomely.

'Thank you. Oh, and I meant to say, by the way, thank you so much for looking after Jack. He says you saved his life.' She decided not to mention Villy's offer to teach Danny his barmitzvah portion. They were undecided what to do about that.

'Well, you know,' Villy paused as if to allow space for a little modesty. 'But what else could I do?'

'You sound as bad as Jack. That's the sort of thing *he* says.'

'You know, we too had not an inkling,' Villy said. 'We knew nothing about these adventures with the hooligans. I thought he was at home resting in bed, as he should have been. How did he do it? Do you know?'

'You can ask him yourself. I'll get him.'

* * *

As soon as Villy and Ilse arrived, and even while Ilse was still hugging Aloo and laughing and saying all in one breath, 'Darling! How are you? You brave thing! You are a dark horse! No one knew what you were up to, darling! You are very stupid, you know – things could have gone so badly wrong!' – that's when I asked Villy when he could start teaching me for the barmitzvah. Everyone suddenly stopped talking for a moment.

He said, 'Have you asked your mother and father?' They were standing right behind me, so Villy looked at them for an answer.

Mummy said, 'It's very kind of you. There's quite a lot to decide about that. How much does it cost? Anyway, we aren't shul members.'

'No problems, no charge. Why not join our shul? It would be an honour to have you.'

I noticed that Mummy reached out to Daddy's arm and gave it a squeeze, but Villy was already holding out his hand and saying, 'Simon, it's a great pleasure to meet you. I've heard all about you from Jack. Yes, *everything*. And I've read so many of your marvellous articles. So you would need to speak to our rabbi, of course, if you were interested in joining a shul. Jack has explained your situation to me.'

Daddy has been acting a bit strangely lately, which is all because of his worries. It definitely was not normal when he just suddenly said, 'What can I talk to a rabbi about? I don't even believe in God.'

Ilse heard this and laughed in her tinkly way, 'What! Another apikoros! Obviously it runs in families!'

Villy is so nice that he just said, 'Well, so long as you don't tell the rabbi what you do and don't believe, I'm sure everything will be all right. It might be better if you don't tell me, either! But why not come along with us to shul this Shabbat, see what you think of us?'

Mummy seemed slightly alarmed. Daddy looked amazed and confused. 'Thank you.' He turned to Aloo and just said, 'OK, well, that's good. Although, Dad… I'd really like to go with you one day.' Aloo looked funny too. He sort of smiled and nodded and shook his head and shrugged all at the same time, and made a squeaky sound like 'Uh?'

But Daddy was so *very* strange today. Even though we had guests, he went upstairs to lie down on the bed. He shook his head and said to Mummy, 'I can't cope.' But when I ran upstairs to see him, he said, 'I'm all right, just a bit tired.' There was one weird moment, while I left Ilse looking at some flowers in the garden, when I came into the house, and I heard Mummy talking quietly to Villy. 'There is something Jack probably didn't tell you about Simon.' And I couldn't hear what it was exactly, but Villy said, 'He should…' – something, something, something, and I didn't hear what it was Daddy should do. He said, 'It's well known in Austria, but here it's called…' and Mummy said, 'Really! A fellow in Switzerland recommended it to us too.'

Later, I found out Aloo is going home first thing tomorrow. I didn't even know. They didn't tell me. Villy and Ilse said they'd be happy to have me for the day, because one of their grandchildren was coming over, and he's the same age. I'm not sure that will work, because just being the same age is not really enough to be a great friend of someone. For example, a girl in Iran, who can't speak English, supports al-Qaeda and hates Jews, can we be friends because we are the same age? Prob'ly not. But I don't mind giving it a try.

The grown-ups were all talking to Aloo about being at home on his own, and whether he would be all right.

Mummy said she would take Aloo home in the car. 'I'll get you settled in, make sure everything is sorted out with your doctor and the local social services.'

Ilse said, 'You have friends, I hope, darling, who will help you?'

But when he heard that, Aloo said, 'Friends? Of course not. I don't remember what they are. When you are young – in your twenties and thirties – you make a lot of friends. You spend the rest of your life losing friends. Until you haven't got any.'

Everyone laughed, and Ilse said it was a dreadful thing to

say, but you could see she didn't really think it was that bad. Villy said, 'If you belong to a shul, you always have – if not friends – then a community of people, of which you are a part, to whom you belong.'

Aloo answered, 'Oh, but I do have that, Villy.'

Aloo lives in a village in the New Forest. It's called Thornbrook Saint Peter. It's near Christchurch. You must know Christchurch. It's got a famous church, and a river full of little boats. There's a garden centre there as well, and a big supermarket too, but it doesn't sell challah.

Later, Villy and Ilse left, and soon it was bedtime. Mummy and Daddy came in to my room together to kiss me goodnight. Then Aloo tapped on the door and came in. He tucked me in and we had a big hug. I was really sorry he was going.

'We've had a good time, haven't we?' he said. 'We've had adventures. You'll come and see me soon?'

'Grandad Aloo,' I said, 'You never finished the story. What happened to them in the end?'

'Who?' he asked, frowning.

'Lord Sir Gentleman and Miss Ladywoman. Or the King and Queen of Otherland?' I said.

He smiled in his lovely, twinkly way, as if he was bursting with a big joke inside. 'Oh, them!'

'Or Princess Prettybows and Prince Scrapeknees?'

'Don't worry!' Grandad Aloo said. 'It's not a story with an end.' He leaned his craggy face and watery eyes down and kissed my forehead, 'They're still there. In Otherland. Where the speed limit is 31 miles per hour and all numbers are prime numbers.'

14

Dr Jack Silver sat in the favourite armchair where always he had sat. Beside him, bookshelves reached from floor to ceiling and door to window, entirely covering one wall of his modest sitting room. Miri's chair was empty. Jack leaned back and passed his eye over the books. 'Nothing on the Kindertransport, Miri,' he said aloud. Idly he pulled out an amusing study of prime numbers and other curious numbers. 'I'll give this to the boy, one day.' An idea came into his mind. 'Maybe as a barmitzvah present.' He wondered if there was a book about the number 13, and thought of writing it. On a lower shelf, his own son's travel books made a proud display. He took one and opened it at the dedication. 'For my parents, Jack and Miri Silver,' he read aloud. He limped to the french windows and stepped out into the garden. Neatly tended flowerbeds circled an elegant oval of clipped lawn. On the grass stood a white garden table and two white chairs. Jack hobbled awkwardly to a chair. 'But I just don't see myself walking with a stick,' he said.

'If you want to walk, Aloo, use a stick,' he could hear her voice. 'Otherwise, don't walk. Until you're better.'

'You really think it'll get better?'

'No,' she said. 'That's why you'd better get used to a stick.'

Once, this little garden was Miri's great joy. Now a local gardener kept it in good order. Each day, in good or bad weather, she would open the french windows and tempt birds to fly down by throwing out a few breadcrumbs. On every fine day, and sometimes not so fine, she would step outside, wearing an old skirt and cotton blouse and a kitchen apron, to spend an hour or two weeding, tidying, clipping, he knew not what. He had never quite understood. The Miri he understood was the bright, ambitious girl, with intelligent eyes, a good brain and a good figure, who danced with him when they were young, advised him so correctly about his career, and talked with him so calmly and sensibly during the many, many times in life when there were troubles. In good times and bad. None worse than when the scan showed that she had cancer.

He listened to the birdsong. Not far away, a neighbour's lawn mower started up. 'Well, Miri,' he said, 'shall I go and get the paper?'

Despite the aching, hurting places, he felt comfortable. It was a joy to be home, to have a stack of clean shirts to choose from, a different jacket to wear. He went to the car. Straight away there was a new problem. He should have foreseen it. Operating the clutch was painful. He drove slowly to the village shop. Saturday morning gave Thornbrook St Peter a pleasing, animated air. Supported by the walking stick, he made his way inside. The store was arranged as a mini-supermarket, a couple of aisles of shelves and an old-fashioned wide wooden counter at one end. The rich, delighted voice of Mr Smith, the shopkeeper, greeted him kindly. 'Jack! You're back.'

'Hello, Chris,' Jack replied cheerily. 'Yes, back at home at last. Everything all right?'

'Goodness me,' said Mr Smith, 'what have you done to yourself? Your face! And what's the walking stick for? What's happened?'

The other customer in the shop emerged from an aisle to see for himself. He gasped in shock.

'Hello Len!' Jack nodded to him grimly. 'I got mugged. In London.'

'Dear God! Well, you shouldn't go up to London!' said the shopkeeper. 'I never go there.'

'Oh, Jack, what an awful thing to happen!' said customer Len. 'You look terrible! Been to the doc?'

'Oh yes,' Jack told them. 'My daughter-in-law brought me home yesterday. We spent half the day at the doctor's and the other half at Christchurch Hospital. She's sorted me out.'

Len shook his head in disgust. 'What kind of people would do something like that? Did they take anything?'

'Well they did take, you know, my money, credit cards, that sort of thing. But the police got it all back, thank goodness.'

Both men were surprised. 'The police? Did that? You were lucky.'

'Well,' said Len, 'if there's anything we can do... You know that.'

Jack bought a copy of The Times and returned to the car.

'What's with the stick, Jack?' called out a woman from across the little street. She was pushing a pushchair. 'Hurt yourself? Oh, my goodness! I can see you have.' She paused, full of concern.

'It's nothing,' he called back with a wave and a smile. 'I'll be all right.'

Inside the store, the shopkeeper commented that an experience like that could kill a man Jack's age. Better make sure people know to keep an eye on him.

Jack drove the long way back to the house. At its edges, the village touched broad open heath. In the distance, a family of ponies grazed on gorse and grass under a vast dome of blue and white English sky. This had been a favourite walk of theirs, before Miri's illness. Then he had walked it alone. Now he wondered if he would ever walk here again. He thought, Danny is doing a lot of things for the very first time; I, for the very last. He opened the car window and turned off the engine. Small birds darted about, chippering, clicking, quietly sounding their sweet little high-pitched notes.

Not one house in the village had a mezuzah. Jack had checked. Indeed, there wasn't one from here to Christchurch, so far as he knew. Nor had he seen one in all Christchurch, either. At least no one around here would set upon you for being Jewish. Not that they knew.

For Jack confidently believed that they did not know. Jewish or not, the village understood that Jack – small, stocky, outgoing and voluble as he was, and with something foreign in the accent – was not a local New Forest man and that Silver was not a proper English name. Yet they did not think of Silver as a Jewish, or as anything other than Jack's name. And if it happened that some residents of Thornbrook St Peter generally distrusted Jews, the feeling was never mentioned.

That was the thing. He had had to choose: noisy, vulgar Jews or quiet, civilised antisemites. He hated religion, superstition, irrationality, did not like tradition, nor did he want to be part of any proud nation. He belonged, he thought, to those people of all nations who were above such concerns, a people of the mind, a people without a flag or borders.

He had grown up here among the antisemites. And here he lived among them still, in a place as nearly perfect as anywhere on the earth could be.

'That, of course, was how Jews in Germany and Austria must have felt,' he said aloud. Villy's tale came into his mind again, of the bright little boy and his sister, walking home from school in that most civilised of cities, pre-War Vienna. How the sister was too old for the Kindertransport.

He eased himself out of the car and walked a few paces on the rough turf. Far away, the group of ponies moved slowly, heads always bowed to the grass. Already on the masses of brambles, blackberries were ripening that Miri would have picked. There were some calls he had to make. He returned to the car and started the engine.

The phone rested on a polished mahogany cabinet in the hall. Beside it, a small wicker chair with a cushion, chosen by Miri. Sitting there always made him think of her.

'Yoav?'

'*Hello*, Mr Curious! Boker tov!'

'Working on Shabbat again?'

'Don't start! Who is using the phone on Shabbat, uh? What's the matter – car problem?'

'No, no. No car problem. I'm not at Penny and Simon's. I'm back at home now.'

'Yoffi. In the country! So what can I do for you?'

'Yoav, I want to thank you. Very much. For what you did. Last week. I should have said it before.'

'No problem. My pleasure, Mr Silver.'

'The police came and – '

'We saw everything. Don't tell me. We know what happened.'

'And Ehud, I want to thank him too. How can I get in touch with him?'

'Who?'

'Ehud?'

'I don't know no one called Ehud.'

Jack understood. He chuckled. 'Anyway, thank him for me.'

'It was a pleasure for him, too.'

For the second call, Jack had to think a little harder. He paused before tapping the numbers, uncertain what to say if it were answered. Even as the phone was connected he hung up again. What exactly did he hope to achieve? After a little more thought, he pressed Redial.

'Yeah?' came the curt reply.

'Scally?'

A long pause. 'Oozat?'

'It's Jack, Jack Silver. Remember?'

Another moment of silence. 'Right, yeah. Wassup?' The distinctive, rustic East Anglian accent seemed stronger.

'I wanted to say thank you. Thanks, for what you've done, Scally.'

Again a long pause, as if this took some digesting. 'Yeah, well. Not over yet. Gotta go to court, innit? When is that, do you know?'

'Couple of months. Yes, we'll have to go to court. Did the police tell you about it?'

'I made me statement, so why do I 'ave to go to court?'

'You just do, Scall. You won't meet them though. Mick and the rest. You'll only see them in court. They're in custody. If you've got any problems about it, or questions, just give me a call.'

Scally sighed deeply. 'Heavy. Very heavy, what I done.'

'It was the right thing,' Jack said. 'I've been wondering what you're up to. If everything is all right. Where are you?'

'I'm back at home. In Suffolk. Southwold. I can't stay in London now.'

'Seaside place, isn't it? Scally, I've got a tip for you. Don't get in touch with any of your old pals. Don't let them find out where you are.'

'Yeah, I know that already. They'd kill me.'

'Exactly. Are you working?'

'Nah – what can I do?'

'Have you got any qualifications? Have you got GCSEs and all that? Have you got a trade or anything?'

'Nuffink.'

'What does your dad do?'

'Don't make me laugh.'

'Why – what does he do?'

'A bit of duckin' and divin'. This and that. Only I ain't seen him in years. Me mum don't even know where he is. She don't want to. 'E's in and out of nick. 'E's a nutter.'

Jack leaned back in the chair and wondered what to do for the lad. How should a young man like this go forward in life? What was his best route?

'Is there a college near you?'

'Ha! Ha! What – you think I should go to college?'

'Why not?'

'I ent got the brains for it, that's why not.'

'Course you have. You don't have to be Einstein to learn a trade. What kind of work is there around Southwold? Go on the fishing boats. What about farm work? Or you could join the army – they'd teach you a trade. It's a serious profession, and you might be able to fight for your country. It would suit you. You might do very well for yourself. I think you would. Honestly, I do.'

'I dunno, mate. I dunno.'

'Look into it. Do that for me, Scall. Go to the Army's website. I'll tell you something, Scally. All of us who do something useful and try to make the world a better place – believe it or not, we have a much better life.'

'Better than who?' Scally's voice had its familiar note of bitter defiance.

'You,' Jack replied bluntly. 'Look lad, I'll call you in a few days and see how you're getting on.'

The final phone call did not need any thought, but would have to wait until this evening. Villy and Ilse would not answer on Shabbat.

* * *

Among the things Danny did for the first time in his life, that August morning, was step inside a synagogue.

Penny held his hand as they walked into a large high hall where just a few seats were occupied. She had been to a few Reform batmitzvahs, and was wary of being drawn into something 'churchy', something of the sickly, too-welcoming 'Songs of Praise' Anglicanism she remembered from schooldays, the only organised religion she had ever experienced. She had been to a few Orthodox occasions around north London, too, and had found there an impenetrable exoticism and disorder from which she could hardly wait to escape. Frankly, she was dreading her morning in shul. As she entered the hall, she realised once again just how much she thoroughly disliked the piety, worthiness and self-righteousness of religious people, as she perceived them, and was repelled by the very notion of worship.

Simon was filled with joy. Inside the hall, men and women had been separated. He did not wish to be parted from Penny, yet the division fascinated and stirred him. Here he saw great primeval issues brought to the fore. Men were on the right of an aisle, each one cloaked in his capacious prayer shawl, or tallit, which appeared as archaic a garment as could be imagined, a simple piece of fringed white cloth, and each with his head covered, and an open siddur in his hand. Women were on the left, they too holding their open prayerbooks. All, men and women, even the person conducting the service, were facing the same way, yet did not appear to be facing anything at all, other than a curtain. They faced, as Simon already knew, not only towards the Torah scrolls concealed in the ark behind the curtain, but beyond the ark towards the ruined site of the Temple in Jerusalem, upon which now stood the Muslims' Dome of the Rock. Within the synagogue, Simon saw not religion or spirituality, but history and politics, and eagerly stepped inside.

Danny knew nothing of church or synagogue, and stared around in amazement.

For Villy and Ilse, the Shabbat service was as familiar as anything may be, which one loves and experiences every week. Indeed, for Villy, the synagogue was a place to visit daily, as he did for the early morning service. Ilse and Penny sat together on one side of the aisle.

'I didn't realise you had separate seating,' Penny said quietly to Ilse. 'I thought Masorti…'

'Had mixed seating?'

'I thought it was egalitarian.'

'No, well, we are, darling,' Ilse whispered. 'We try to be egalitarian but traditional also. You know, that's Masorti. But each Masorti shul does its own thing. We call women to the Torah. Some don't. Each one does as the community likes best.'

Penny raised her eyebrows. 'How confusing.'

Ilse bridled slightly, but remained pleasant. 'Not at all, darling.'

Faces turned as Villy moved among the men, conducting Simon and Danny to his preferred place close to the ark. President of the synagogue, and a founding member, he was well known. A few watched Simon and Danny as they followed. Perhaps they were relatives of his. Or guests of the community.

Penny took up a siddur and looked inside awkwardly. There was a copy at home on the bookshelves, but she had never opened it. Ilse kindly guided her from page to page. Penny scanned the English translation, dismayed at the archaic sentiments. Simon sat beside Villy, and found that, thanks to his Hebrew classes and his having looked through the book at home, he could follow the service either on the Hebrew page or the English. Little or nothing of this ancient text met with his approval, and intellectually it would not seem capable of much scrutiny, yet he was thrilled by its ceaseless references to the Temple, to sacrifices, to ancient laws and to Jerusalem. I am prepared to say this, he kept telling himself, not because it is true, but because it goes back to our beginnings. We are reading our cosmology, talking about the Jewish dreamtime. Danny fidgeted, needing something to entertain him.

As the prayers and blessings were read, with periodic 'Amens' from the congregation – pronounced Amain or Omain – and getting up and sitting down, more people arrived. When the Shema was said, the first line aloud, the rest in a whisper, Simon and Danny watched as the men wrapped their prayer shawls tightly around, grasping the tassles and touching them to their lips, each person nearly inaudible. And in the silence of the Amidah prayer, each one stood, muttering as they read, or recited from memory, taking three steps back and three forward, and bowing at certain moments. Simon, eager to understand, noticed everything. He longed to ask questions.

As 10 o'clock became 10.30, the numbers in the synagogue increased, members of the community arriving alone or in pairs, or in family groups. Some slipped quietly to their seat. Others came in talking. Some elicited an indignant 'shh'. At times, it seemed that almost everyone was at least murmuring to his or her neighbour. An air of preparation and expectation intensified as men stepped up to open the ark. The time had come for the Torah service. To the singing of a curious tune by the whole gathering – a chaos of robust, indisciplined voices, singing as one – the curtain was drawn back, and the doors of the ark opened wide. Within, the wooden spindles of large decorated scrolls, concealed within coverings of embroidery and silver, rested in place.

One of those standing at the ark reached in and lifted out a scroll, handing it carefully to the leader of the service. Clearly, it was heavy. Simon and Danny watched with interest as he leaned the decorated object against his shoulder and turned towards the now large crowd of Jews.

In loud chanting tone he proclaimed, 'Shema, Yisrael! Adonai Eloheinu! Adonai Ehad!' Simon knew the phrase already, but now his Hebrew allowed him to understand the words, and he was struck by the syntax, the literal meaning, the absence of the verb 'to be': Hear, Israel! Lord – Our God! Lord – One!

Simon wondered how he could be party to such ideas. Throughout the morning he had heard, in Hebrew, of a whole universe run as a medieval state, with King, Lord, Master, Ruler. This was certainly not his politics, nor his understanding of the cosmos. Yet he shivered with recognition, thrilled as the whole nation of Israel is instructed to 'Hear!' Standing, watching, with Danny and Villy on one side of him, and complete strangers on the other, it seemed to him that each congregation of Jews at their Sabbath services around the globe on that day, listening to the unchanging proclamation in untranslated words of prehistory, were joined in some larger congregation, Jews of every time and place, all of that most hated and despised and enduring tribe.

Clad in the grey suit he sometimes wore for press conferences, with black leather shoes wiped over with a handkerchief to bring up the shine, he could almost feel the sand beneath his feet, and the desert sun.

Danny succumbed to the sights and sounds, absorbed the warmth of the men all around him, the relaxed and contented air, the singing. He tugged on Villy's jacket for an explanation. Villy leaned down to whisper, 'Ask me later. I will tell you everything.'

* * *

It was utterly silent. He noticed that no distant cars could be heard, no plane or helicopter crossing north London, not a bird fluttering in its roost nor passer-by in the street. Penny slept soundly in the bed beside him. Like last night, again the darkness of the room was a vivid kaleidoscope of images and emotion and restless, wakeful thoughts. Yet as he stared around the blackness, the shapes of the bed and wardrobes becoming clear, there was no doubt that he could see better in the dark than usual. And in the daytime too, these last two or three days, the sunlight had glinted more sharply, dazzling him sometimes so that he could barely open his eyes. His skin had become more sensitive to the sun, quickly becoming red and burnt. He felt washed in the sun's scorching light, scoured by it, inside and out.

He wondered if it was something to do with the hypericum, or St John's Wort, that he had started to take three nights ago. Sitting at Simon's desk, Penny had searched on the internet for days and called out to him to come and look at websites. He had almost given up using his computer and did not even want to go into his work room. She had typed in 'depression', 'exhaustion', 'nervous breakdown', 'anxiety', and came to the conclusion that, after all, Simon could be much worse. At least he was trying to get better. People with severe depression don't do that, she learned. Simon sometimes seized on little, inconsequential things that he believed would help; he had decided to wear dark, sober colours, and wanted a new pair of black jeans; he insisted now on going for a short walk alone each day; he had unrealistic plans to have the whole house redecorated in a plainer, calmer style. Penny leaned back in Simon's chair, emailed German doctors to ask for advice and sometimes printed pages out for him to read. He would look through them, sceptical but intrigued. Both he and Penny had been persuaded that the remedy was worth a try.

Finally Penny had dropped Simon at a pharmacy, where he found St John's Wort on a shelf of herbal remedies. One packet was decorated with psychedelic pictures of the St John's Wort plant in full flower, the blooms as yellow as a luminous safety jacket. It had ornate, colourful writing, and required three tablets of 300 micrograms to be taken each day. Another was a plain grey box with simple undecorated text requiring that a single 900-microgram tablet be taken daily. It was hard to decide. Since the breakdown, he had come to hate choice of any kind. That familiar dry, sweating panic rose in him, and he grasped the box with the simpler design. It would be easier to remember to take just one tablet a day. That very night he took the first.

Since then, he had been unable to sleep deeply. His mind was in turmoil. Insights and ideas tumbled one over another. He felt that he knew, that he understood, had grasped, but he could not say what. It was as though someone had switched the light on: the sun shone and daylight streamed into his mind. Everything was illuminated. Even in darkness he could see better.

The bedside clock showed ten past two. He slipped from the bed and went to the window, pulled back an edge of curtain. Even at this hour, he saw, the sky contained some light that hinted either at the previous day or the next. Streetlights cast yellow reflections on the empty pavement and parked cars of his neighbours, and suddenly it seemed that all this sleeping world fitted together like a glorious symphony. Each person in his solitude, couples clinging one to another, children mimicking their parents, all walking together through the years, supported by each other, a community of strangers who work for one another and pay their taxes to one another, behave decently to one another, and help the poor and the sick. The great, unchanging, timeless moment of human existence.

Simon opened the bedroom door and, finding he could see without turning on the landing light, went to his work room. A couple of boards creaked. He gently closed the door and pressed the button to start the computer. The fan whirred loudly into life. Strange, the sound was almost inaudible in daytime. Now he was afraid it might disturb the others. He clicked the icon to connect to the internet. The light from the monitor seemed painfully bright. He reduced the brightness, but it was still as dazzling as oncoming headlights.

He searched for 'St Johns Wort' +depression, 'St Johns Wort' +research, 'St Johns Wort' +'side effects', 'St Johns Wort' +light. There was a lot of material, much of it in German, which he read with difficulty. It became clear that the only side effects of hypericum were that it interfered with the efficacy of other drugs and greatly increased sensitivity to light.

He returned to bed and edged close to Penny. He lay awake. It seemed to him that there was a great dichotomy in the human mind, between the great heart-warming illusion that life had a direction and was enjoyable, and the cold truth that it was pointless and difficult. As the dawn light glimmered beneath the curtains and the first birdsong of the new day began, Simon listened for a moment and fell asleep.

* * *

Sentence was pronounced. Mick and the boys were led away, grinning. That was it, the trial was over. Scally left quickly, worried and disappointed. Jack didn't have a chance to speak to him. He would call later. Villy held Jack's arm and helped him down the hall and out into the chilly street. Something in the grey, misty light seemed to enhance the brightness of the leaves that hung doggedly to the branches, yellow and orange and copper brown. Those that had fallen had been heaped along the side of the path. The rowan trees were hung with big bunches of red berries.

The two men said little to each other. Simon and Penny walked slowly behind. Both were lost in thought. Ilse drove around the corner and drew up alongside to pick up Villy, who said, 'Why not come with us, Jack?' His voice sounded strangely flat.

Jack nodded wordlessly. Villy opened the rear door and Jack got in, leaning back exhausted. It reminded him of the first time he had sat in this very seat.

Penny was puzzled. 'Not coming with us, Aloo?' She too sounded tired and depressed.

'We'll take Jack,' said Villy.

Simon leaned in and spoke to his father. 'You were amazing, Dad. Very brave. You have great courage.'

Jack reached out and briefly touched his son's hand. 'It had to be done. You have to try.'

'Where would you like to go, Jack? What would be best for you? Do you want to come back with us for a cup of tea, darling?' Ilse asked.

He said he would.

Ilse drove away from the courthouse, through suburban streets, joining a main road. Jack broke the silence. 'Would anyone prefer to go to Golders Hill Park? Get some air. We can have a tea there. It would be nice to get out.'

Ilse agreed. 'After spending all day in that place. With those people.'

'The funniest moment,' said Jack after a while, 'was when the rebbe came in.'

The other two snorted with laughter.

'The chaos they create. It appeals to me,' he added.

Ilse and Villy shook their heads as one. 'No,' said Villy. 'For me, not. I don't like it.'

'How did he manage to have all those people with him? Why were those yeshiva bochers allowed to stand in the witness box with him? What a sight they made! And the judge couldn't keep them quiet!'

'They were his carers,' Villy said. 'But maybe it didn't help that he was so…' He looked for a word.

'Mad?' suggested Ilse.

'It's amazing,' Jack said, 'that he agreed to give evidence in a goyish court.'

'Maybe he did it for you,' Ilse said.

'It was for the saving of life,' Villy explained.

They remained silent for a time, not wanting to discuss the issue that preoccupied all of them. Eventually Ilse asked, 'And was justice done, darling?'

Still they could not speak about it, and there was no reply.

'All those charges!' Ilse returned to the subject angrily. 'They said it all, yes darling? Racially aggravated grievous blah blah blah, robbery with blah blah, threatening to kill, conspiracy. What else! My God! And still they don't go to prison! What exactly is community service? And how long is 200 hours?'

Jack quietly responded. 'It's nothing at all, because they won't do it. But they do have to wear tags.'

'Tags! They take them off. They can do anything,' Villy said.

'No one ever wanted to investigate this, and no one wants to punish anyone for it,' Jack said wearily. 'My efforts were wasted. What good came of it?'

'But they might not be in such a hurry to beat up Jews any more?' suggested Ilse.

The men made no reply.

At the park café, they sat at an outdoor table, their coats buttoned. Suddenly Jack said, 'May I walk on my own for a few minutes? I need to just… you know.'

'Clear the head?' suggested Villy.

It was falling dark already. He walked slowly. Trees on the broad slope of greensward seemed lit from within by their autumn colours. The cool air and covered sky threatened rain, imminently or later this evening. Yet strangely, in the Golders Hill Park flower garden, roses were still blooming. Jack paused to sniff at one. He wondered if this was the last time he would enjoy the scent of roses this year. Or perhaps ever. Certainly one day soon would be the last time for everything. He dreaded what was coming. Pain, and ceasing to be, were more than he could contemplate. But he wanted to share in Miri's experience. It had always bothered him that he could not share death with her. Whenever he thought such things, he called himself a damn fool, because of course, even if he too were to die of cancer, he still would not have shared it with her. We live together, die alone.

'Well, Miri, what a day!' he said aloud.

He stood silently for a moment, contemplated the grey sky. 'What would you like me to do next?' He seemed to be addressing the heavens.

He took a few steps more and paused. 'Well, so they did get away with it, after all. Mick said they would.'

He walked painfully, leaning on his stick, pausing often. 'This damn leg,' he muttered. He made his way to a bench. In this muggy, damp air, he told himself, he could catch his death.

'This is not what we used to call winter,' he said. 'Maybe in the New Year it will get colder.'

'Well, Miri, did we expect any better? To think that after all my efforts, those hooligans got off more or less scot free.'

He looked up again at the pale monotone of the clouds. A group of pigeons flew in an arc across his field of vision, a lovely sight.

He stood with a sigh and turned to walk slowly back towards the top of the park, and the café.

* * *

The turmoil died away. Simon steered clear of complex, stressful situations. He avoided choice. What remained was a sense of space. There was no pressure. By the time of Eurotravel magazine's next editorial meeting, he felt able to attend so long as he had some reason to leave after one hour. He changed to a different therapist. The first one kept pressing him to say he was angry with his parents.

He stopped contacting editors, never offered them work or ideas. Few of them noticed. His name simply ceased to appear in their pages. Ruth Fine at the Jewish Chronicle gave him more work than before. There was no travelling involved. He had already been to the places he wrote about. He could use the internet to update. Fellow freelance Cathy Pincher scented that there was something wrong and called him to learn more. When he heard her voice, the old tension in the jaw started up and he spoke with difficulty.

'I read about your father in the JC,' she said. 'Did you know, I sat next to him at the TTN lunch last summer? That was weird. He was wearing your name badge. It said Simon Silver.'

Simon frowned and tried to make sense of what she was telling him. 'That really *is* weird. I don't even remember the lunch.'

'You were away, in Switzerland.'

'Was I?'

She said the name Simon Silver hadn't been seen so much lately. If there was any work he was turning down, could he pass it on to her?

'Hardly anyone offers me any work,' he said.

'I hate successful people,' she said. 'I like people with problems.'

* * *

On Sunday, either I go to Villy's house, or he comes to us. He is as nice as nice, just like Aloo, but in a very different way. Villy doesn't skip or jump like Aloo tries to do, even with his bad leg, or pretend to play silly games. He does tell a lot of jokes, but usually I don't understand them. I laugh anyway. Then we read my portion from the Humash. Villy carefully corrects me and tells me how to get the tune right. Then I read my Haftarah. Then I sing all the blessings.

What most people do for their barmitzvah, is they read the Maftir and Haftarah. Villy thinks I should do more; he says it's not difficult and would be a good thing, and there's plenty of time to learn. So I am going to read quite a lot, maybe the whole sedrah. If I don't do all of it, the rabbi will read the rest. It's a nice sounding-language, Hebrew. It makes me think of big cubes of feta cheese, salty and strong and chunky. But after it's over, if I am at Villy's house, we have a little snack. Not feta, but usually a glass of milk and piece of plain cake.

Another thing Hebrew makes me think about is prime letters instead of prime numbers. As Grandad Aloo told me, in Hebrew you make numbers with letters of the alphabet. In a way, groups of letters can't be divided because they make a word, with a sound. When I think how long people have been reading my Torah portion, and all the different people standing in different kinds of places around the world, and in all the different times, that makes me think of prime words as well.

Because even if you tore the Torah into pieces and threw them all away, it sort of would still exist. Anyway, there wouldn't be any point, because lots of people know how to write it exactly as it was before.

Actually, it makes me think that Jewish people are sort of like a country, which, even if you take the country away and try to smash it up and throw its people all over the world and kill millions of them, nothing changes, they still stay the same, and can't be broken up. So Jews are like a prime number. And a prime letter. And a prime word.

When I told Dad, he said, that's why people hate Jews. Everyone wants us to be like them, but we aren't.

Why is that? Villy thinks it's to do with God. Dad said that's not true. He says it's to do with politics and history. Mum says the trouble with Jews is they think things matter. She says she wishes Villy would just stick to teaching me my portion.

When the class is over, Dad often wants to hear my reading too. That's annoying, because by then I have had enough of Hebrew and Torah. But he's really doing it to help with his own studies, not mine. His Hebrew is so good now, he can turn the reading into English without looking in the book. On Saturday morning, I go to shul with Dad, and Mum comes with us sometimes (not very often).

In the shul, we sit with the men, and the women sit on the other side. It makes you feel as if you're not just part of your family, but more like part of the shul. But if Mum comes, I can sit with her, because you can be on either side until your barmitzvah. If Mum doesn't come to shul, when we get home, the table is laid nicely, with a kiddush cup and challah and all that. And she says Shabbat Shalom, like a real Jewish family, and kisses Dad, and says 'How was it?' Usually he says something like, 'It was good. The rabbi spoke well. Of course you have to understand his references to God in a rather different way than he intended.'

Dad and the rabbi are not exactly friends, but Dad visits the rabbi a lot. He has been to our house a couple of times too. He is such a nice man. He would make a good uncle, if you hadn't got any uncles. When he first came here, he was kind of interested in things like – what do we eat. I was glad to hear that Dad was right about treif food. I had a feeling Aloo was wrong about that. You remember, he told me Jews can eat any damn thing they like.

Once, the rabbi was sitting on the sitting room sofa, and Dad was in the armchair, and I listened quietly to find out what grown-up men talk about. I couldn't quite get what it was about. The rabbi said, 'I'm not going to question you about your private beliefs. I'm not going to ask you, Do you believe in God?'

And Dad said, 'That's not a very Jewish question.'

And the rabbi said, 'Well, I'm not asking it. But if you don't, please don't tell me.'

And they laughed, but just like Villy's jokes, I didn't see what was so funny.

Mum says she is glad it all happened. She says it's a shame about Aloo's knee but it was all besheert. She doesn't mind lighting the candles on Friday night. She had trouble starting to say the blessing that goes with it. At first she said she didn't want to, it was ridiculous, and anyway she didn't know the words. Now she does, and it's nice.

15

'Mazeltov! Mazeltov! Mazeltov!' The Silver and Eisenberg families sat in the front rows, closest to the bimah, women on one side of the aisle, men on the other. Naturally, pride of place belonged to the barmitzvah boy himself, but after her months of obsessive, all-consuming preparation, choosing a party venue, designing invitations, booking flowers, finding a caterer, discussing menus, making table plans, at last a spotlight shone on Penny too, as she moved from moment to moment through the great day, on a dazzling high, as if time had slowed, basking in greetings and expressions of love from friends and relations and the members of New Golders Green Synagogue.

For her first outfit of the day, she was wearing a supremely elegant dark blue skirt and jacket she had long coveted, with an exquisite cream shirt and lovely slender blue shoes. She wondered why she had never indulged herself like this before, not even for her own wedding. This waste of money, perhaps because it was to celebrate Danny rather than herself, thrilled and delighted her.

But anxieties remained to keep her on edge. There would be no relaxing until it was all over, the family lunch, the evening party. Sitting beside Penny, her mother, now suffering from mild dementia, neatly dressed in an elaborate pale green suit, stared around vaguely, perhaps remembering to feel proud, a little overawed, amazed, and liable to do or say something embarrassing at any moment. Next came her mother's sister, favourite aunt Hilda, who was now closer to Penny than anyone else in the Eisenberg family. Beyond were sisters, cousins, who had made long journeys to be here.

On the men's side, where from this day forward Danny would be condemned to remain, never again wandering at liberty across to the women, Danny wore a well-chosen new suit, with open-neck shirt, and small white kippah clipped to short hair spiky in the latest pubescent style. He was cloaked in his own brilliant white new tallit. His father sat still and attentive, alert for any mishap or mistake. He too wore a small white kippah and, beneath his tallit, a new suit, black and well-cut, with a grey shirt, his new narrow black-rimmed glasses and hair cut close to the scalp. And at last he was in shul with his father – Aloo on his right hand and Danny on the left – and could witness him in tallit and kippah, and even hear his father's deep, rough voice singing in unison with his own, as it had never done before. Next to Jack sat Penny's father Morris and, further along the row, all the Zilberman and Eisenberg brothers, cousins and uncles. Close by, Villy took his usual seat near the ark. He nodded encouragingly to the boy.

Danny's heart beat hard, and he knew that all the difficult moments for which he had prepared were starting now. The weighty Torah scroll was taken out of the ark, placed into the hands of the leader of the service, who turned and chanted *Shema Israel!* and carried the scroll around the kehilla to the sound of their singing. As the scroll was laid upon the shulhan to be unwrapped, Danny plucked up his courage and stepped from his seat and onto the bimah. Turning to the hundreds of faces, he read out his d'var Torah. He had already read it at yesterday's Friday evening service, but few people other than his family had been there. That was like a practice run. Today, on Shabbat morning, he was conscious that he spoke in front of his community for the first time.

The first to be 'called up' to the Torah must be a Cohen – one of the still-remembered priestly caste – and the second, a Levite, one of those whose ancestral role was to minister to the priests. While Cohen & Levi today may be a law firm, advertising executives or real estate agents, in synagogue their illustrious story is not forgotten. Only after them may ordinary Israelites step up to the sacred scroll.

The Hebrew name of Dr Jack Silver was originally, of course, Avram ben Shimon, being Avram the son of Shimon Zilberman, because his name was in fact neither Jack nor Aloo, but Avram. And Simon, now that he had been 'converted' from a half-Jew into a Jew, had the name Shimon ben Avram, being Simon the son of Avram. By these Hebrew names they were called in turn to the Torah. Jack, leaving the walking stick hanging on his chair, made his way slowly. He waved away willing hands to show that he did not need their help.

On the bimah, the rabbi shook his hand. The blessings Jack had to recite were printed on a card next to the Torah scroll. He was shown where on the scroll Danny had reached, and he touched the place with a corner of his prayer shawl. The scroll was rolled shut while Jack stared uncertainly at the Hebrew blessing: the words meant nothing, the letters were just shapes, the vowel marks had become nothing more than meaningless dots. He had forgotten how to read Hebrew! It would not be a disaster – he knew that in shul, everyone is on your side. If you can't read, someone will say the words for you to repeat. Yet suddenly from his mouth the blessing came forth in the old Yiddish pronunciation and accent of his childhood. He beamed with good-humour and contentment, as if he found the situation slightly comical.

While Danny read from the scroll, the tip of the ornate silver yad running along the line, Jack's eyes darted about. His thoughts flew through the years from one place to another. He had not stood on a bimah since his own barmitzvah, one full lifetime ago. Yet everything struck him as familiar: the melody, the chanted words, the faces of the congregation. Or, it was all so different: the casual mood, the informality of the clothes, no hats, the colours, everywhere colours, even in shul! He looked down at the scroll that Danny's thirteen-year-old voice turned into sound. Its handwritten Hebrew formed solid black columns on the parchment. Within each column, hundreds of words, and within each word, every letter a world in itself, a world of ideas and meaning, subject to the scrutiny of ages.

After one has been called to the Torah, he remains on the bimah until the next to be called has also completed his blessings. So it was arranged – for women could have aliyot at New Golders Green Masorti – that Penny was called up, then Simon, in order that both were on the bimah together as Danny completed his masterful reading.

Penny had practised saying the blessings, and delivered them confidently in a London accent. She knew that the women all around (and maybe most of the men too) would be more interested in her shapely skirt and beautifully cut jacket, and (more in the women's case) admiring her expensive shoes, than in listening to her Hebrew blessings. Simon had learned the blessings too, and re-read them to himself again and again in the minutes before being called up, afraid that there would be some terrible slip, that his mind might become a blank, that something crazy might happen: he would faint, be sick, or be struck dumb. He stepped up, apparently quite at ease, and in clear voice recited the words with perfect Israeli pronunciation.

When the Torah had been wrapped again in its coverings and carried around the synagogue once more to the sound of singing, Danny stood on the bimah alone and still, and read the Haftarah aloud from the Humash. The shul listened in silence to the hypnotic rhythm of his boyish voice. Even Danny's young guests, Jewish and non-Jewish friends sitting in a row together, stopped their jostling, sniggering, smirking and whispering, and remained perfectly quiet. Only when he had completed its final blessings did their wrapped sweets fly through the air to a roar of *sh'koach.*

Danny grinned rather sheepishly with satisfaction. The job was done. The one difficulty that remained was to make a speech tonight. After that, he vowed, he would party and do absolutely nothing else difficult for several months, or maybe years. He grinned across at his friends. He knew by now what a barmitzvah was. He had been to several since joining the shul. This time it was his turn.

This evening, guests would arrive as the band played, his parents would greet them with hugs and kisses, they would bring dozens of gifts. Last night, at home, there had been presents from the family, a marvellous indulgence of lavish generosity. Aloo had handed him a small gift that he unwrapped eagerly, finding the slickest, slimmest, shiniest and most advanced of camera phones.

He had been delighted at the cleverness of it, the secret joke between the pair of them.

'Nice idea, Aloo,' Penny had said, 'but it's setting him up to be mugged.'

This was so true, and so alarming, that they had laughed. Danny knew well enough that people could be attacked and robbed in the street. He and his friends were already scared of muggers, gangs, groups of kids. Coming home from school, he always went to a stop further from the house so that he could walk by a safer route.

Tonight there would be loud music and a big dinner, and all

his friends would have one riotous long table together while the adults sat at elegant round tables, chatting in adult style, then jumping up to make big circles or abandoning themselves to the hopelessly pathetic and ungainly dancing of the older generation. There would be speeches. Dad would give one. And he would give one. And it would all go well. But it didn't matter much if it went well. Everyone was on your side anyway.

All around him, the youngest members of the community scrambled to gather up the sweets for themselves. He looked down from the bimah at his parents, his father transfixed with pride and relief, and his mother's shining joy making glistening tears in her eyelashes. As he stepped down and returned towards his place, to more cries of *sh'koach* and warm smiling nods and hands reaching out to congratulate him, Penny rose and hugged and kissed him. Danny was as tall as her now. Simon grasped his hands and kissed his cheek. Aloo reached out a hand to the boy.

Danny turned to him. 'And did you do that once, Aloo? Read your portion in a shul somewhere?'

'Yes, in Tottenham. I'll take you there, one day.'

'Is Tottenham a place? I thought it was just a football team.'

Danny bent forward so Jack could kiss him on the cheek. 'Tottenham is a football team? Never heard of it. Very well done, Marvelstein.'

Some of the women dashed to say a quick word to Penny and to Danny, and on the men's side, Villy approached to grasp Simon's hand. 'Mazeltov!' He held the hand and did not release it.

'Thank you for teaching him,' Simon said. There would, in any case, be a gift to Villy.

'It was an honour.' He lowered his voice. 'It's a great day

for you, I know. I know what it means to you especially.'

Simon nodded. Villy continued in almost conspiratorial tone, coming close, 'We never talk about it. But how are things now, Simon? You seem well lately. You look well.'

Simon nodded. 'Thank you for asking, for noticing. I am well, I am well.' He shrugged. 'I'm working properly again now; I can deal with people. Everything is fine. But you know my… my depression is… it's never very far away. Always at the back of my mind. But I am happy, too. Very happy with the way things have gone.'

'Good, good. *Ja*. Today, at least,' declared Villy, his voice suddenly loud, 'you certainly should be! Mazeltov!' Their hands parted and Villy turned away to give Jack a warm embrace. The two moved to the end of the row to sit together.

Penny's father, Morris, slipped across into Aloo's place, next to Simon.

'Didn't he do well?' Morris said. 'You can be proud of him.'

Simon shook his head with emotion. 'You know, Morrie, if it hadn't been for Danny suddenly wanting to be barmitzvah, I wouldn't have made this journey.' He rarely spoke with Morris and found himself opening up to him awkwardly, eager to tell him. 'I never knew anything like this would happen – to him, to me, to us. It was never planned.'

'We never expected it. It's a bonus. Tell me,' Morris asked. 'What made you convert?'

'It's like this, Morrie. I used to feel that I was half Jewish and half English. Two halves that didn't add up to a whole anything. Now I feel both fully Jewish and fully English.'

Morris nodded. 'That's nice,' he said clumsily. 'You know, I'm in a similar position to you...'

He was cut short as the atmosphere calmed suddenly. The rabbi had stepped onto the bimah to give his sermon.

After finding in this week's Torah portion something that touched upon the human condition, and something funny, and something relevant to today's world, the rabbi turned to address the barmitzvah boy and his family.

'Danny, they told me you were bright, and you proved it today with your magnificent leyening. It's a joy to see all your family here, your grandparents. I know your other grandmother, Miri, would also have been so happy and proud today. Obviously a skill with words runs in the family, your father Simon being a journalist, and your mother Penny having set up her language school just last year, and we wish her every success with it. And we are so very grateful to Simon, who almost as soon as he joined the shul, redesigned our monthly magazine and has been editing it ever since – a labour of love if ever there was one. And *kol hakavod* to him for regularly taking time out to spend a couple of weeks volunteering in Israel. Danny, you've played your part in this community too, being one of the keenest members of our youth football team. But Danny, I understand that your real love is not words, nor football, but numbers. And, of course, that too is part of our tradition, isn't it? After all, we are instructed to... *multiply*.

'And if you come up here, Danny, we'll say the blessings together.'

The rabbi placed his hands over Danny's head and recited what is known as the 'priestly' blessing: May the Lord bless you and keep you, make his light to shine upon you...

At which Danny, to mark this point in his life, said the Shehehiyanu, addressing God: *Baruch ata adonai, eloheinu melech ha olam, shehehiyanu, ve kimanu, ve higianu l'zman ha ze.*[29]

'Who is he talking to?' Jack hissed to Villy. 'There's no one listening, you know.'

---

29 Hebrew blessing recited on reaching any special time in life

'*We* are, Jack,' whispered Villy. 'We are listening.'

'Blessed are you Lord, our God, king of the world, who has kept us alive, sustained us, and enabled us to reach this moment.'

And the community replied, 'Amen.'

* * *

Simon and Penny and Danny sometimes made the journey down to the New Forest to visit Aloo, more often now that he had so many health problems. Jack rarely travelled far. On Saturdays, he might drive to the Masorti synagogue in Bournemouth, which he had joined after Danny's barmitzvah. 'Not because I am religious,' he was at pains to explain, 'I'm not religious – but I want to connect to the community.' For the rest of the time, a drive in the Forest or around the little village, to the supermarket at Christchurch, these were his outings now. This summer, Simon had a chance to drive him up to London for a little get-together with the family and with Villy and Ilse.

'Leave me at the park for a bit, will you?' he asked. 'Come back in an hour so or.' And they dropped him at the café. It had been raining. The sun shone through breaking cloud. A band played on the bandstand.

He limped across the wet grass with his walking stick. The pain in his leg was not really a pain at all. It was part of being himself, part of his old age, part of the world that both sustains and destroys you. Besides, it did not stop him walking. Indeed, his mood was joyful. 'Miri, at least I lived long enough to discover one thing about myself – that I am a Jew.'

If there were a heaven, and if I died and went to heaven, he thought, this is how it would be. For this indeed is heaven. Gold and green grass, wet with rain, the music of the brass band drifting across the gentle hill, the sun shining warmly from a clean, washed sky, and all the world alive with light and birdsong.

Yet this, if it is heaven, is heaven on Earth, for that is where I am. Paradise is here... it comes in brief moments, instants of happiness, in our own dear world. Suddenly the bandsmen reached the end of a number and stopped playing.

And if there were a God, Jack thought, I would soon be approaching him, and he would ask me the great question. The question that all must answer one day: "Did you make the world a better place?"

But, ripostes Jack in his native Yiddish, don't *all* believe they have tried to make the world a better place?

Even antisemitic thugs? retorts the Lord in the same tongue.

Yes, answers Jack, surely everyone thinks they are following the right path?

Nu, Aloo, says the Lord, you think no one is right or wrong?

Not at all, replies Jack. It's just that people *don't know* they are wrong. But I, for one, am doing my damnedest to make the world a better place. And you, God? Eh? What are *you* doing?

It's not for me to perfect the world – that's your job.

It can't be done, says Jack.

I know it, says the Lord, I just wanted you to try.

Let me ask you something. Is my dear Miri there?

She's here. As you know, Aloo, I exist only in the mind. And so does she. But yes, she's here.

'My dear Miri,' Jack whispered aloud.

'Aloo, I love you' came her familiar voice. He reached a bench and could go no further. He sat and murmured, 'Justice', before falling asleep as the band started up again.

Glossary

af tsores	in trouble (Yiddish)
alef	alef, bet, gimmel – first three letters of the Hebrew alphabet
aliyah (1)	'ascent'(Hebrew);'givenanaliyah'='calledup'insynagogue to say a blessing at the Torah before or after a reading
aliyah (2)	'make aliyah' = ascend, i.e. emigrate to Israel and become a citizen (English and Hebrew)
Anglit	English (Hebrew)
apikoros	heretic or non-believing Jew, insulting (Yiddish)
Aravit	Arabic (Hebrew)
ark	focal point of prayer in synagogue, a ceremonial cupboard housing the Torah scrolls (English)
balagan	chaotic mess (Yiddish and other languages)
b'aretz	"in the Land [of Israel]" (Hebrew)
barmitzvah	traditional religious celebration for a boy on reaching 13 years of age (Hebrew)
batmitzvah	more recent religious celebration for a girl reaching age 12 [Orthodox] or 13 [Reform] (Hebrew)
bekishe	long satin jacket worn on Shabbat by certain hasidim (Yiddish)
b'emet	in truth, really!, really? (Hebrew)
bentsh	chant or sing blessings, especially birkat ha-mazon (which concludes a meal) (Yiddish)
besheert	fate, destiny (Yiddish)
bet	alef, bet, gimmel – first three letters of the Hebrew alphabet
bimah	raised platform from which readings are given in synagogue, literally 'a stage' (Hebrew)
bissel	a little bit (Yiddish)
bocher	young man, yeshiva student. Plural *bocherim* (Yiddish)
boker tov	good morning (Hebrew)
broygus	angry (Yiddish)
bubeleh	darling (Yiddish)
bygels	Yiddish pronunciation of beigels or bagels – a ring-shaped roll traditionally made by boiling the dough (Yiddish)
called (up)	'called up' to the Torah scroll to recite a blessing. *See*: aliyah

challah	special bread, with egg in the dough, for Sabbath; pronounced *halla* (Hebrew), *holla* (Yiddish)
cheder	Jewish religion school for children (Hebrew)
chochem	*see*: hohem
chuppah	*see*: huppah
chutzpah	audacity, effrontery (Yiddish)
d'var Torah	a talk about the week's Torah portion, a sermon (Hebrew)
der heim	the home, meaning Eastern Europe (Yiddish)
Duvdevan	literally 'cherries' – elite undercover Israeli army unit operating inside Arab areas (Hebrew)
Dvarim	Book of Deuteronomy (Hebrew)
Eretz Israel	'Land of Israel' – i.e. Israel (Hebrew)
frum	religiously observant (Yiddish)
frummer	observant Orthodox Jew (Yiddish)
galut	Diaspora (Hebrew)
gey	go (Yiddish)
gimmel	alef, bet, gimmel – first three letters of the Hebrew alphabet
gornisht	nothing (Yiddish)
goy(im)	gentile(s) – i.e. non-Jew(s) (Yiddish)
goyish	non-Jewish, or 'as done by the goyim' (Yiddish)
HaAretz	'The Land', i.e. Israel (Hebrew)
Haftarah	reading from Prophets after the Torah reading, usually incorrectly spelt Haftorah (Hebrew)
haham	*see*: hohem
halacha	literally 'the way' – Jewish law (Hebrew)
halachic	according to halacha (English from Hebrew)
halachist	scholar of Jewish law (English from Hebrew halacha)
hasid	strictly observant Orthodox Jew, disciple of a particular rabbi; often spelt chasid (Hebrew). Plural *hasidim* or *hasids*
haver	plural: *haverim*; member or friend (Hebrew)
heim	home (Yiddish); *see*: der heim
heimishe	homely, unpretentious and traditional (Yiddish)
hegdish	properly *hekdish* – slum, mess (Yiddish)
hohem	usually spelt *chochem*: wise man, great scholar (Yiddish, from haham, Hebrew)
hohma	intelligence, wisdom, cleverness; often spelt *chochma* (Yiddish)
hoo lo shelanu	he's not one of ours (Hebrew)
Humash	the Torah in book form with annotation and commentary; usually spelt *Chumash* (Hebrew)

huppa	canopy, i.e. for a traditional Jewish wedding (Hebrew)
hutzpah	*see*: chutzpah
Ivrit	Hebrew name for the Hebrew language
Judaea	southern part of the 'West Bank' of the River Jordan (Hebrew)
kappel	Jewish skullcap (Yiddish); *see*: kippah
kashrut	Jewish food laws. *Kashrut* (Hebrew) or *kashrus* (Yiddish) is the noun from which *kosher* is the adjective (Hebrew)
katsin	army officer (Hebrew)
kehilla	community, congregation (Hebrew)
ken	yes (Hebrew)
kiddush	benediction over wine to sanctify Shabbat or a festival (Hebrew)
Kindertransport	special trains that brought 9000 unaccompanied Jewish children from Germany and Austria as refugees to England, 1938-39, saving them from the Holocaust (German)
kippah	Jewish skullcap; plural: *kippot* (Hebrew)
kishkes	guts (Yiddish)
klopp in kop	bash on the head (Yiddish)
kol hakavod	"all honour [to you]" (Hebrew)
kopeks	1 rouble=100 kopeks (Russian currency used in Poland 1850-1924)
Krav Maga	"contact fighting" (Hebrew), hand-to-hand combat system developed for the Israeli army
kvell	burst with pride, e.g. over your child's success (Yiddish)
kvetch	grumble, whine, complain (Yiddish)
l'chaim, lehaim	the classic Jewish toast, literally 'To life!' (Hebrew).
leyen(ing)	read(ing); specifically, reading aloud from Torah scroll (mixed Yiddish and English)
lo	no (Hebrew)
lo ichpat li	I don't care (Hebrew)
lobbus	rascal (Anglo-Yiddish)
macher	literally a 'do-er', decision-maker, one who is involved, a 'big cheese' (Yiddish)
Maftir	final lines of the Torah reading, repeated by the person reading the Haftarah (Hebrew)
Magen David	Star of David (Hebrew)
makhn pleyte	run, make haste, make a run for it (Yiddish)
Mameh	Ma, Mum, mother (Yiddish)
mameloshn	mother tongue, i.e. Yiddish (Yiddish)

Masorti	Jewish denomination (also 'Conservative') that accepts Torah as sacred but views it as a human work
maspik	enough (Hebrew)
mazeltov!	congratulations! (Yiddish, from Hebrew *mazal tov*)
mechaye	a joy, delight (Yiddish)
melamed	teacher (Hebrew, Yiddish)
mensh	a fine example of a human being (Yiddish usage)
meshugass	madness (Yiddish)
meshuggeneh	mad, crazy (Yiddish)
mezuzah	small holder on doorpost containing a religious text (Hebrew)
minyan	minimum ten adults (only men in Orthodox communities) required for certain prayers (Hebrew)
minyan man	man who attends prayers to ensure the presence of a minyan
mishpohah	family (Hebrew)
mitzvah	plural: *mitzvot;* Biblical commandment, a good deed (Hebrew)
Mogen Dovid	Star of David (Yiddish, from Hebrew *Magen David*)
naches	pride and satisfaction (Yiddish)
nish, nit	not (Yiddish); nish kein toives– no favours
noch	Yiddish interjection, often ironic – even! yet!
nosh	snack (verb and noun)
nu	Yiddish interjection or question, roughly 'well', 'so', 'and?'
nudnik	a dull pest, a useless nuisance (Yiddish)
Orthodox	Jewish denomination based on principle that Torah was given in its entirety by God to Moses
parsha	plural: *parshot*. The week's portion of the Torah (Hebrew)
Pesach	Passover (Hebrew)
peyess	long, untrimmed locks of hair, growing just in front of the ears, usual for male hasidim (Yiddish, from Hebrew *peyot*)
peyot	*see*: peyess
Reform	Jewish denomination adaptating Jewish law to modern times
rekel(ech)	long wool jacket(s), weekday wear for some hasidim (Yiddish)
sabra	native-born Israeli (Hebrew)
sedrah	plural: *sedrot*; the section of Torah for that week (Hebrew)
sh'koach	*see*: yashar koach.
Shabbat	the Sabbath (Hebrew)

Shabbes	the Sabbath (Yiddish)
shayneh maidel	beautiful girl, with goodness as well as physical beauty (Yiddish)
shehehiyanu	blessing recited on reaching any special moment (Hebrew)
sheitl	wig worn by an observant married woman to avoid showing her own hair in public (Yiddish)
shikker	drunk (Yiddish)
shiksa	non-Jewish girl – insulting (Yiddish)
shiva	initial 7-day deep mourning following death of a family member, usually 'sitting shiva' (Hebrew)
shleger	thug, bully (Yiddish)
shlep	drag, carry, or make a tiring journey (Yiddish)
shluf	sleep (Yiddish)
shmatte	rag (Yiddish)
shmegegge	empty-headed dope, buffoon, fool (Yiddish)
shmirat haguf	taking good care of one's body (Hebrew)
shmooze	chat, talk comfortably (Yiddish)
Shmot	Book of Exodus (Hebrew)
shovav	rascal, bad boy (Hebrew)
shteibl	meeting place for prayer (Yiddish)
shtetl	small town (Yiddish); pre-Holocaust E. European Jewish town
shtick	an act, performance, 'routine' (Yiddish)
shtreimel	wide circular fur hat worn on Shabbat and festivals by married Hasidic men (Yiddish)
shtum	silent (Yiddish)
shul	synagogue (Yiddish)
shulhan	literally, 'table'; synagogue lectern (Hebrew)
shvartzer	black person – disrespectful (Yiddish)
siddur	prayerbook (Hebrew)
simcha	literally 'joy', celebration, eg for barmitzvah, wedding (Hebrew)
streimel	*see*: shtreimel
tallit	prayer shawl with trailing tassles at the four corners (Hebrew)
Talmud Torah	religious primary school (Hebrew)
Tateh	Dad (Yiddish)
tichel	headscarf to cover the hair of a married woman (Yiddish)
Torah	original Jewish scriptures, the 'Five Books of Moses' (Hebrew)

treif	non-kosher (Yiddish)
tsitsis	Yiddish pronunciation of *tsitsit*
tsitsit	trailing threads on tallit or undershirt worn by observant men (Hebrew)
tsores	troubles (Yiddish)
tzaddik	righteous or saintly man (Hebrew); plural: *tzaddikim*
tznius	tznius (Yiddish) or tzeniut (Hebrew) – modesty
tzva keva	standing or permanent army, professional soldiers (Hebrew)
yad	literally 'hand'; pointer used for reading Torah scroll (Hebrew)
yashar koach	'well done', esp. for accomplishments in synagogue (Hebrew)
yeshiva	seminary, school or college for Jewish religious study (Hebrew)
yeshiva bocher	young man studying at yeshiva (Yiddish)
yid(den)	Jew(s) (Yiddish)
yid(s)	Jew(s) – as an abusive racist insult (English from Yiddish)
Yiddish	the language of East European Jews (Yiddish)
yiddishe	(pronounced *yiddisher*) Jewish (Yiddish)
yiddishe mame	(pronounced *yiddisher mama*) Jewish mother (Yiddish)
yiddishkeit	Jewishness, Jewish culture, Jewish knowledge (Yiddish)
yiddl	little Jew (Yiddish)
yoffi	beautiful, great! (Hebrew)
yok	non-Jews, esp. men – insulting (English Jewish backslang)
zaftig	plump and appealing (Yiddish)
zayde	grandad (Yiddish)
zokn	long socks or stockings (Yiddish)

About the Author

Andrew Sanger is a freelance travel journalist who has lived and worked in several countries. He has contributed to a wide range of British national newspapers and magazines, and for ten years edited French Railways' travel magazine. He is the author of about thirty popular guidebooks to France, Ireland, the Canary Islands and Israel. In recent years he has lived in north-west London.

Acknowledgments

Thank you
Claire Buckley, Laurence Phillips, Leslie Reuben,
Ofer Ronen, Rosalind Ross and Stephen Ross
for your help